Weather or Not . . .

The raiders were regrouping. Druyan saw Valadan rearing, striking out with his forefeet. Putting her lips together, she found barely enough air to whistle. But the stallion heard and swung toward her. So did something else, farther away and swifter yet.

An icy gust of wind howled through the gap between the outbuildings. Thatch lifted off the kitchen roof; great, stinging pebbles rode choking dust. Valadan reached Druyan's side, and she scrambled aboard. Two draft horses, used to working as a team, rallied to Valadan's call and galloped at the raiders.

Rain came in sheets, as if lightning had ripped open the belly of the clouds. The wind drove it sideways; thunder cracked; and Druyan squeezed her legs to send Valadan running with the storm.

Kellis yelled something from the roof, yelled three times—and suddenly there seemed to be thirty horses running with her, and they swept through the gate at the raiding party's heels . . .

By Susan Dexter
Published by Ballantine Books:

THE RING OF ALLAIRE

THE WIZARD'S SHADOW

The Warhorse of Esdragon
THE PRINCE OF ILL LUCK
THE WIND-WITCH

THE
WIND-WITCH

Book Two of
The Warhorse of Esdragon

Susan Dexter

A Del Rey® Book
BALLANTINE BOOKS • NEW YORK

A Del Rey® Book
Published by Ballantine Books

Copyright © 1994 by Susan Dexter

All rights reserved under International and Pan-American Copyright Conventions. Published in the United States of America by Ballantine Books, a division of Random House, Inc., New York, and simultaneously in Canada by Random House of Canada Limited, Toronto.

Library of Congress Catalog Card Number: 94-94419

ISBN 0-345-38770-8

Manufactured in the United States of America

First Edition: November 1994

10 9 8 7 6 5 4 3 2 1

This book is for:

Nancy Griffin and the Otter Creek Store of Mercer, Pennsylvania—one of the most consistently inspiring and uplifting retail establishments I have ever had the pleasure of visiting.

Poor, to whom Rook owes her beauty and her courage.

Nikki, Alyssa, and Kristen—hope this makes up for all those times I told you I couldn't come out and play because I had to work on The Book.

Janet Parris—now you owe *me* a book dedication, so get cracking!

Elvira Jane—guinea pig extraordinaire.

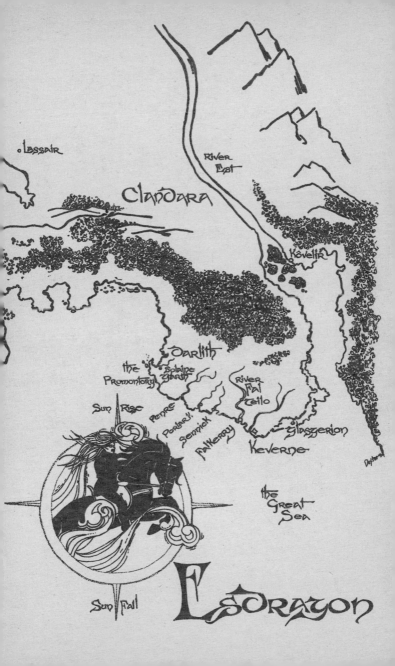

o Lassair

River Est

Clandara

Kavelir

Darlith
the
Promontory
Solaine
Yarith

River
Fal Teilo

Sun Rise

Penre
Pordrul
Sennick
Falkerry
Glaszerion
Keverne

the
Great
Sea

Sun Fall

ESDRAGON

THE WIND-WITCH

Prologue

THE DUCHESS KESSALLIA ruled Esdragon with an iron will all her days, no matter that her slight, white-maned frame seemed the most unlikely of vessels for the power she wielded. Kess was born to what she had, on both sides of her blood, and lived up to it with relish.

Leith of the Isles—her consort—was more concerned with living down his blood heritage, a curse of ill luck. He knew better than to meddle with his wife's governing of Esdragon. Instead, he put his happenchance observations of the Beriana Mountains to practical use and searched Esdragon's becliffed coast for places that resembled them. He found tin and copper—even traces of gold and silver—in quantities worth mining. Kessallia applied her arts to his welfare, and whether she overwhelmed his curse or it naturally faded, in the end the mines prospered and Leith's luck was deemed to be superior to the average man's. Esdragon was well served and made wealthy.

Kessallia would have welcomed a daughter, would have passed on certain teachings that had come to her from her own renowned and sorcerous mother. Perversely, she bore three sons instead, and when those were each in turn wed, 'twas to conventionally minded women unlikely to welcome witch daughters with enthusiasm. Kess kept an eye open for signs of gifts she might nurture, but she generally saw her grandget only as infants—the very time when mag-

1

ical tendencies were faintest. If the witch taint in her blood indeed bred true, Kess could never be certain of it.

Leith was three years his wife's elder, and felt his years sooner, as men are wont to do. His step slowed, beyond the hitch in his gait that he had borne from his birth. In time he began to ail in more serious fashion. The Duchess Kessallia meted out physick and magick with liberal hands, and kept him by her long after Leith himself was more than ready to depart, his every breath become a burden. Autumn turned to winter, with no promise of spring.

Finally Leith schemed to evade his lady for an hour's space, slipped away to Keverne's stables, and stood before the black stallion whose years were nigh a match for the prince's own—years that sat invisibly on the horse, just as his sable coat bore not one single white hair. Valadan's sire was the ageless wind; one man's lifetime had not marked him, and could not. Leith begged his old friend for one last boon—that the horse bear him away, just far enough that he might do his dying in peace, without distressing his beloved Kess.

Sorrowing, Valadan complied, and knelt before the master who could no longer otherwise climb onto his back. He and Leith of the Isles would adventure this last time together. Mist closed around them, and the stallion returned riderless to Keverne.

Kessallia was never to forgive Valadan for helping Leith to leave her. She saw her husband decently mourned, her pale head unbowed by grief, held as high as it had ever been, no matter what fate had decreed. Next day, her eldest son Brioc woke to discover the ducal signet ring round about his finger, and of his mother there was nevermore a trace to be found.

Some said the duchess had thrown herself from Keverne's clifftops into the sea, choosing by such means to rejoin her lifemate. There was no reason to suppose such rumors true—Kessallia's own mother had been mourned sixteen years and yet discovered alive, if the tales were true. But there was no knowing—after long years fact and fancy had mingled, had become impossible to disentangle. The warhorse Valadan, who had kept a watch upon the clifftop, could have told the truth of the lady's disappearance—but none questioned him. Folk no longer believed that the stallion had spoken literally with his late master, no more than they believed him immortal and ageless. That was only foolish fancy, they declared—the Prince of the Isles chose always to ride a black horse, and named each successive steed Valadan, for sentiment. The legends were nothing more than that, suitable to be shared out around a winter fire, forgotten come break of day . . .

Claimed

DRUYAN HAD NEVER stepped foot in Keverne, till her grandsire's funeral assembled her extended family there, and her uncle's unexpected accession to the ducal authority kept them there weeks past the few days they had planned. Lastborn of her father Ronan's eight children by a succession of three wives, she had in fact never been from home before, and as home—Glasgerion—was land that sloped gently toward the sea pastures leagues away, Druyan had never beheld a lofty cliff, either. Pent too many days within stone walls by interminable ceremonies, she seized the chance to escape and explore.

Though her untiny feet were firmly upon the ground, Druyan felt that she walked high in the air, for there were noisy seabirds wheeling all about, and those on her right hand were actually *below* her, flying over the white boiling of the sea. She knew the ground was solid under her sturdy boots—yet she could feel the beat of the waves through it, a curious sensation indeed, like a great heartbeat of the cliff.

The air moved about her like a sea itself, teasing her heavy skirts, tugging and plucking at her foxy hair till it slipped free of its plaits and danced about her. Some of the escaped hair got into her mouth, and Druyan scooped it away, then turned so the wind could scrub her face and banner her hair out behind her. The sea breeze pressed

4

against her like a great salty cat, the plaintive mewing of the gulls its wheedling voice.

Druyan wended her way between tufts of sea pink and mounds of germander, stepped carefully around nests brimming with speckled seabird eggs. When she licked her lips, she tasted salt, wind-carried and misted over her. She studied the hawk soaring in great lazy circles far above, where the air was more settled. She watched the clouds, higher still and moving stately as the turn of the seasons. One foot led the other, and somehow she was half a league from the gateway that had let her out of Keverne, with no shelter in sight if rain came—but for a wonder Esdragon's sky remained mostly blue, as it had been all the morning. All the clouds were fluffy white tufts like scraps of fleece escaping a sheep shearer, none of them threatening to do anything but continue inland.

Her wandering path had curved more than the cliff did, and gull cries and wave crashes were left behind. The breeze was more tentative, sporting some yards above Dru's head, bound on business of its own.

Its freedom was to be envied. Wind obeyed no master, answered to neither parent nor nurse, was constrained by no rule of propriety. It went everywhere and anywhere, just as it chose, saw all that could be seen, roved far and ranged wide. Its persistence had trained the branches of the apricot trees Druyan now strolled beneath, all of them streaming inland away from the sea and its breezes—but the wind was not tied to the trees as those trees were bound to the earth from whence they sprang. Wind was *free*.

A wisp of breeze tickled the leaves, like ghostly fingers brushing green harp strings. Druyan pursed her lips and whistled a counterpoint.

Above, the hawk abruptly tumbled out of its circle, recovering with a frantic wingbeat. Apricot branches clashed and clattered, and tiny unripe fruit pelted the ground like a spatter of rain. A swirl of wind circled roughly about Druyan, whipping her hair, stinging across her eyes, winding her skirt so tightly about her legs that she stumbled. Her lips went slack, her eyes went wide, her whistling instantly ceased.

The wind died.

A coincidence, Druyan thought, and denied her fear, ignored the race of her heart. Her nurse had told her—amid a score of other do-nots—that proper-bred ladies did not whistle. 'Twas unseemly. That long-standing prohibition had naught at all to do with those other tales—unfit for her tender ears to hear—of witch women who could whistle up the wind and unleash it at their pleasure, raising storms and wreaking havoc with the weather for gold or for spite. So the wind had not come to her whistled call. But she did not like, somehow, to test the matter further. The earth was littered with green fruit, her unbound hair was tangled and full of twigs. There was no sense even taking a *chance* that the cautionary tales were somehow true.

Dru looked up, so as not to have to look at the litter of ruined apricots and suffer pangs for something she could not have been guilty of—and saw the horse.

She had heard no hoofbeat, but there he was, black as wet slate and big as life, impossible to have overlooked even if he had been grazing unobserved nearby when she arrived in the orchard. His pricked ears pointed right at her, his nostrils flared wide to take in her scent and thereby identify her.

If she stirred, he would bolt. Druyan's father bred horses; she had come to know them well. No creature was warier of strange situations, none half so ready to flee what it took for danger. But so long as she did not move, this horse would feel safe to observe her, else he would have run already. So they looked at one another, measuring, curious.

There might be other horses pastured nearby—the black was a stallion, Druyan noted. But 'twas unlikely a band of mares would be let run free so close to Keverne. There were fields and gardens and orchards all about, any of which would suffer from free-ranging horses. Perchance the stallion was a stray, escaped from the ducal stables and not yet captured. He might have seized the chance of freedom much as she had herself. She smiled to think of it.

He was well bred. That showed from his high-set tail to his refined head, and at every point between the two. He was deep through the heart and short through the loins. His croup was level, his hindquarters solidly muscled. In front, his shoulders sloped, promising free action under saddle. All his legs were clean as a deer's, the fetlocks unfeathered. He was holding his handsome head very high, to see her better, and he could do that easily, for his neck was long and perfectly set on. When he arched it, 'twas like a black rainbow. His eyes were bright, missing nothing, and his flaring nostrils mimicked wine cups, even to their scarlet insides. His looks promised speed and the ability to sustain it over a distance—the match for anything she had seen in Keverne's stables.

No sensible man bred a horse with the frippary of its tail in mind, but the stallion's was a glory—even held high, its ends brushed the ground like a black rain. His mane flowed down his neck like water, though it was wind-snarled and carried a twig or two. There wasn't a single white hair on him that Druyan could see—each and every one was glossy black, like a crow's wing. There was a powdering of dust on him—yet beneath it, he shone.

What must he see, looking back at her? Nothing harmful, that was sure—he was relaxing visibly, and his alert stance was no longer a certain prelude to flight. A thin girl of fifteen years, done growing upward and despairing already of ever rounding to a womanly figure. Hair even more tangled than his, unable to make up its mind whether to be red or gold, and so a washed-out in-between blend of both hues. And her great shame—her hands. So big, never to be a lady's hands, long-fingered with joints that looked huge as walnuts to her critical eye, when she wasn't hiding them in her skirts. But maybe a horse didn't care, so long as those hands were gentle . . .

She was debating whether she dared chance a step toward him when he took one nearer to her—and another.

And then he was within reach, letting her stroke his neck while he nosed at her skirts. Druyan knew just how to tell him she was a friend—she scratched and rubbed at the hair on the side of his neck, where mares nuzzled their foals and grown horses exchanged nibbles of greeting when they met. When he turned his long head and blew a sudden breath out of his nostrils into her face, she did not startle back, but returned the breath with one of her own, because that was a greeting, also.

Her hands, too coarse for a lady, were ideal for pleasing a horse. He permitted her touch, even sought it, and Druyan revised her guess about other nearby horses. This beast was alone, and lonely, turning to her for the companionship he would have sought from his own kind if any had been about.

All at once, he presented his side to her. He all but shoved her off her feet and she tangled her fingers in his mane just above his withers and held on tight while she recovered her balance. He sidestepped into her again instantly, then lifted his right forehoof to paw the earth.

Only an utter fool would mount a strange horse in a strange place—without so much as a bit of rope to grant control, without saddle or bit or spur. Only such a fool would think the horse *wanted* her to climb aboard, that he was pledging her safety.

He was rolling an eye back at her. It sparkled merrily, daring her to trust him. He pawed again—the hoof farthest from her own feet, Druyan noticed.

Well, he wasn't so *very* tall. At worst she'd slip off, and it wouldn't be such a long drop to the ground. She'd ridden bareback often enough, and knew she could get herself down without risking a hard fall.

His dark eyes were full of little blue and amethyst lights, like the tips of the sea waves when the sun catches them. And sparks of green, pale as sunlit leaves, deep as emeralds. Druyan tightened her grip on the handful of mane. Before she could change her mind, she vaulted onto his back.

With her full skirts hindering her, she nearly didn't gain

her objective. Druyan felt the stallion shift beneath her, as if he'd moved to catch her. That was foolish—at best he was only trying to keep his own balance, which her clumsiness must have disturbed. But she was up, safe, settled securely just behind his withers in a spot that seemed made to hold her.

Now what? Dare she ask him to move out? Was he trained to a rider at all? It seemed to her that he surely must be, but the reality of lacking reins made Druyan tense and anxious all over again. All very well to think she had only to slide off to be safe on the ground again—but she'd still put herself at his unknown mercy, foolishly. If he ran, he could give her a nasty fall . . .

She felt his hindquarters bunch under her. Druyan's mouth opened, probably to scream. But there was no need—after that first dismaying leap, they were going smooth as water flowing over glass. She felt the press of wind about her again. Her hair streamed back. The black mane lapped her hands.

She thought of the wheeling gulls, the effortlessly soaring hawk. A bird in flight must feel just so—the land streaming away, the wind a joyful companion . . .

To be aboard a runaway horse—even with bit and bridle, saddle and stirrup and spur for control—was a terrifying thing. Yet Druyan knew no fear at all. This stallion was running from joy, not fright or anger, and she knew in her heart that he would heed the slightest shift in her weight or her will, that he would turn or halt in an instant, a heartbeat, if she asked him, if she was frightened to continue. He would certainly not harm her, never willingly distress her. He loved to run. It was the heart of him, to run over the land, free as the air.

Druyan loved his running, too, as she had never known she could love anything in her life. She leaned forward into it, her face split by a wide joyful grin as they merged with the wind. She felt as she did in the first moments of a thunderstorm, before the exhilarating forces of wind and lightning grew so intense that enjoyment shifted to dread. She

rode this wind, did not stand buffeted by it. She was part
of it, and it of her, as they swept on and on and ever onward . . .

They might have galloped to the ends of the world;
Druyan wouldn't have known, nor minded. When she felt
the stallion shorten stride and slow, she wanted for a moment to weep—as one wakened from a dream too beautiful
to be true, too precious to bear losing. But her eyes, wind-
dried, could produce not one single tear. And her mouth
was still stretched into a grin.

She shoved a tangle of hair out of her face, instead, and
sat back a trifle, as befit the slower gait. Ahead rose
Keverne's gray towers, growing magically as she neared the
castle, higher and broader. Clever horse, to run in a great
circle and bring her back almost to the very spot where
they'd met. She had never felt him turning at all, the course
had been so subtle.

She must make him walk, Druyan told herself as his
silky canter became a gentle trot. A horse heated by fast
running could not be allowed simply to stop and stand all
lathered with sweat, or even to graze the grass. He could
not even have water till he was cool. He would founder, or
colic, but horses didn't know that. She ran a hand down his
near shoulder, trying to gauge how warm he was, how long
before he'd be at his ease.

She expected his hide to be sweat-soaked, but it felt like
sun-warmed silk beneath her questing palm. His neck
was more of the same, not a hair out of its place, no
damper than the sea air. She was herself perspiring more
heavily than the horse was. Druyan frowned at the puzzle,
seeking a solution.

Perhaps they hadn't run all that far. Or all that fast. His
stride was longer than her fat pony's, maybe she'd been deceived. Maybe he ran so smoothly, it only *felt* fast. In any
case, the strange horse wasn't hot, so there was little sense
persisting in trying to make him walk himself cool. When
the stallion halted of his own accord, she slid down his side

to the ground, then pressed her cheek against his neck, her arms encircling it.

"Where do you belong?" she whispered, envying whomever he'd strayed from. To ride so whenever one wished . . .

Here.

Druyan looked about, startled. She saw no one, and the stallion was gazing steadily at her, his ears pricked, but unalarmed by any intruder. His attention was on her. His eyes were sparkling with those amazing colors again, tiny rubies, emeralds, topazes, swirls of sapphires. She'd never seen such eyes on any creature, certainly never on a horse . . .

I am Valadan.

Valadan? The magic steed Leith of the Isles had adventured upon? How was that possible?

"Druyan!"

The stallion shied away from her, and she stumbled, then caught what balance she could—barely enough. The horse had vanished like smoke in a high wind, leaving only a hoofprint or two to suggest he hadn't been purely a daydream. Druyan was still staring, heartbroken, at the trampled grass when her brother's hand seized her elbow.

"Where've you been?" Robart demanded to know, but gave no space for an answer. "We've been calling you for an hour! The horses were being saddled when they sent *me* out to look—" He jerked the elbow he'd captured. "Come *on!*"

"Mother *said* I could go for a walk!" Druyan protested, trying not to sound guilty. She hadn't meant to be gone so long.

"She thought you were in one of the gardens. Father's set to leave, and if we're all still in our saddles at midnight, we'll hear of nothing else for a week! What are you doing out here?"

Druyan, walking along as rapidly as she could—and a deal faster than was strictly comfortable, since her legs were not quite a match for her brother's—looked back at the fruit trees. "I was only petting a horse." She needn't admit to the ride, if Robart hadn't seen. Plainly, she was in enough trouble without explaining she'd been careening about bareback on a strange horse. There was no sign at all of the black stallion.

"What horse?" Robart asked impatiently, marching her faster still and not looking back.

"A black one. A stray, I think. *Ouch!*" Her toe found a rock among the long grasses.

"Wonderful." Robart swept her on, heedless. "You stray after a stray horse. As if you haven't got one waiting to carry you home this minute. Can't you walk any faster?"

Her imprisoned arm was starting to ache. Her toe still hurt. She was out of breath and had a fiery stitch in her side. By the time Druyan reached Keverne's bailey, where her parents waited testily amid restless horses, offspring of all ages, annoying hounds, and general bedlam, she had quite forgotten the black horse.

The horse had not, however, forgotten *her.*

Druyan took no note, as their procession straggled untidily along the road, raising dust, of the addition to their company, for he kept a long way off the road. One needed to have fixed one's eyes on the exact right spot at the exact right instant, to catch the briefest glimpse of black hide through a tiny gap in the gorse bushes that flanked the track. Dru was far too occupied with keeping herself out of her father's sight to be gazing at the scenery. She rode near the tail of their double file, just ahead of the baggage, but her assigned place did not much ease her task—before her rode her elder sister Tavitha, upon a golden-coated jennet for which Dru's stolid brown pony had a hearty dislike.

The jennet did not much like the pony, either. Threats and counterthreats were exchanged with pinned ears and snaked heads, and Druyan had all she could do to keep back out of harm's way without lagging. A noisy altercation between the saddle horses would only remind her sire of her earlier sin of delaying their departure.

Only when they paused to ford a narrow stream did

Druyan have leisure to look about—Tavitha was being led across, the jennet having balked at the water and refused to obey its rider in the matter of crossing—and saw the flick of a jet-black tail, back behind the third sumpter horse. She turned her head sharply to count noses, but just then her pony chose to enter the stream, almost unseating her as it leapt down the bank. When she could look back again, there were only the baggage horses, none of which possessed a black tail. Druyan shoved her idle fancies ruthlessly away.

It was well after nightfall when they reached home. Her father was testy, and everyone—even her lady mother—walked carefully wide of him, not wanting to call down attention certain to be unwelcome. Supper and bedtime crowded one another, each hectic because Druyan's two eldest sisters and one older brother had not only temporarily returned to the flock but had spouses with them, as well, and the usual sleeping arrangements would have to be altered with only fair success. Druyan ate a bit of bread and cheese, retired to the pallet she'd been shuffled to in the corner of Tavitha's chamber, and thought no more of horses, no matter how swift.

She slept badly, being both hungry and uncomfortable on the ill-stuffed pallet. At foggy first light Druyan escaped outdoors to the orchard, hoping for a ripe apple to stay her appetite till the hour was more propitious for trying to filch a loaf of cinnamon-sprinkled bread from the bakehouse. The sisters and their husbands would be departing for their own homes by sun-high. Things at Glasgerion would settle down. She'd get her own familiar bed back, and probably her father would have forgotten why she was in his bad graces—he'd have been vexed by a dozen other matters ere then.

There was a horse in the orchard. That would vex Ronan for certain, whether only this one horse had been nibbling the fruit, or the younger groom had been careless with the latches and let all the stable stray free if it wished. Druyan strode carefully through the dewy grass, peering through the drifting mist. Unless this was one of the coursers, which were high-mettled and hard to handle, she could probably lead it back to its stall without fetching a rope first. Most of their horses—excepting the coursers—were like pets to her and did her bidding. Of course, this one might belong to one of her sisters' husbands, but she'd seen no black horse in their trains.

He nickered to her, wishing Druyan the best of mornings. She froze stock-still, staring into those sparkling eyes, full of colors where they should have been merely dark. Merry and ever so familiar. She saw high cliffs, wheeling gulls, apricot trees . . .

How her stray from Keverne had found his way into Glasgerion's orchard, Druyan couldn't guess. The palings were purposefully high . . .

He tossed his head at the weathered boards and snorted deprecatingly, obviously having no high opinion of fences.

"Well, excuse me! I'm sure you jump very well, but we'd really better get you out of here before anyone else sees you. The gardener will have your pretty hide."

She might need to fetch a rope after all. No reason this horse should lead as tamely as their own did.

He rested his soft muzzle against her chest, as if he were the gentlest of old pensioners, docile and sway-backed. His breath smelled of hay, and his eyelashes were longer than her own. His manners were impeccable. Two of her fingers twined in his mane were enough to guide him wherever she wished, Druyan found. "Valadan," she whispered, daring to name him aloud, if only with her lips muffled by his mane.

There was no more a stall for the stranger than there had been a bed for Druyan—not till the overnight guests had safely departed. She tucked him into the corner of the sheepfold, with apologies to both stallion and disconcerted sheep. When she left him, to see about her own breakfast, Druyan knew better than to babble indiscriminately about her good fortune at being followed home from Keverne by a splendid horse. No one would believe he'd trailed her all the way from the duke's castle, much less that he'd seemed to claim her. At supper, she confessed offhandedly to discovering a strayed horse in the orchard, wondered aloud whether that meant a fence needed tending, and offered to ride to their near neighbors to inquire whether anyone had lost a black horse.

She did exactly that most faithfully for a solid fortnight, though she knew perfectly well that he belonged to none of them. No one minded—had she not offered, Robart would have been made to undertake the inquiries, to his annoyance. By the end of the second week, her family was so accustomed to seeing Druyan riding the black, no one remembered where he'd come from, or how recently. She began to call him Valadan aloud, not only in secret.

For a stallion, Valadan was impeccably behaved in the company of other horses, never the least trouble. One coolish breezy day, the two of them trailed Druyan's elder brothers to the downs that lay beyond the farm and the pastureland. It was a fine day for riding—there were a score of horsemen already assembled with their best mounts, neighbors racing one another various distances over the gently rolling ground.

There'd be races run at the market fair, with prizes and wagering, and every lad with a fast horse was eager to gauge his competition ahead of the day, to adjudge the results of breeding and feeding and careful conditioning. Mostly they were testing the horses over the regular galloping spots, which varied in length and were well known. But where the soil was sandier than was general, long poles had been mounted upright, to make a course for those who wanted to test nimbleness rather than sheer ground covering.

Druyan eyed the setup with interest. She knew how fleet Valadan was on the straight—she thought there was no horse in all of Esdragon that could match him—but she didn't want to trumpet the fact. Proud as she was of him, she deemed some caution was in order. If she allowed him to run away from every horse on the downs, someone was apt to "remember" losing a black horse and come claiming him. Best she did not show him off too boldly, till he'd been seen in her company long enough for folk to accept him unchallenged as her property. But running the poles was another matter, because success there depended upon skill and nerve as much or more than fleetness of foot. The swiftest courser might not be handy enough to navigate the tight course without striking a pole.

There were six poles, set roughly equal distances apart, in a straight line. The goal was to dash along them, weaving in and out, then whirl and return so as to pass each pole on its opposite side. A horse that was stiff to one side, or unwilling to listen to its rider about where and which way to turn, wouldn't be successful at it. Some began very well, but got going too fast to hold tight turns and went bouncing stiff-legged off the course, fighting their riders with their nosed poked at the sky. Some turned well to the left but not to the right, and lost advantage with every other pole. One high-headed chestnut got so excited that he sent two poles flying when he crashed heedlessly into them, then took his rider for a mad run out over the downs till he finally got winded enough to answer to the curb bit in his mouth. Each run was attended by cheers, shouts, groans, screams of encouragement from spectators and riders both.

Valadan danced, eager for his turn. Druyan wondered if he'd run poles before, or was only excited by the activity. She'd know at the second pole, probably, whether he knew his business or was going to depend on her knowledge of the game. She patted his shoulder, begging him to settle a bit—if he became *too* eager, he might just bolt straight through the course the way the chestnut had. He did love to run and might forget all else.

The stallion snorted and dipped his head, playing with the bronze bit. *This game is played on the beach, at Keverne,* said a clear amused voice in Druyan's head.

She looked up from her reins, startled, to see who spoke to her. No one was near. Druyan's lips parted softly, as she stared at the tips of Valadan's ears. He turned one back toward her, in case she should have something to say to him.

But there was no time. Their turn at the poles had come. She sat deep, shortened her reins enough that she could guide the stallion with the least motion of her smallest finger. And then the word was given, and the first pole was hurtling at them, as Valadan thundered toward it.

They passed to the left of it, then swung right to take the next. Left for the following pole, the flying strides as measured as the steps of a dance. Druyan leaned with Valadan's turns, keeping them balanced, anticipating the next change in course. Sand showered away from them, flew up like wave spray. Surely they were the fastest yet! No one had done this well, sustained such a blinding pace.

Almost to the last pole, already leaning into a turn that must be nearly a full circle, Druyan felt a sudden rush of fear. The pole wasn't where it should have been! They were flying at it, in perfect accord, as they'd rushed at all the others, but they were going to hit it, for it was a yard farther away from the previous pole than any of the others had been set. The ground must have proved too hard where it ought to have been planted, and so the boys had set it where they could—no *wonder* most of the riders had gone wide on the final turn, lost speed or accord with their mounts!

If she couldn't drag him wide of it—Druyan had an instant's cruel vision of Valadan's slender legs entangled with the pole, of him crashing to earth and never rising again, all because *she'd* wanted to race.

She clamped her hand on the right rein, not caring if she made him veer straight off the course in disgrace, so long as he was safe. The wind they made whipped her hair over her face, blinding her. She shook it off and hauled with all her might at the rein.

She might as well have been pulling against a tree. Valadan heeded neither the rein nor the bit in his mouth that the rein was buckled to. He paid no mind to Druyan's frantic shift of weight, or her left hand's joining forces with the right to haul him out of the turn.

Instead, though hampered by his rider's attempts to save

him, Valadan dug his hooves into the sand for an extra stride and swung about the pole so closely that a breeze could scarcely have slipped between it and his hindquarters. He went back up the course, dancing the measure alone half the way, till Druyan managed to regain some feeling of being in harmony with him.

They exited to cheers and jogged off to compose themselves while the next horse went at the line of poles.

Very tricky course, a dry voice observed.

Druyan slid to the ground and flung her arms round about the glossy neck, loving the horse with the whole of her heart. He was safe—and wonderful. Valadan reached over her shoulder to nuzzle her back.

Their bliss was interrupted by the arrival of a horse and rider. Robart swung down from his roan gelding, which had once more disappointed him in the matter of racing speed. Stepping over to Valadan, he patted his flank, ran a hand down each of the stallion's legs. He glanced at Valadan's nostrils, which were flared still but not indicating any distress to his breathing. Indeed, they promised great endurance.

"He'll do. Give him here." He held his hand out for the reins.

"What?" Druyan stared.

Robart shook his head at her, smiling. "You don't want to ride a horse like this. He's no lady's jennet." He gestured impatiently for the reins.

"I do so want him!" Druyan tightened her hold on the reins and wished futilely that she hadn't dismounted. Now she could not simply ride away, as she longed to, before the discussion turned dangerous. She was trapped, caught afoot.

"Well, you can't have him!" Robart laughed. "Father hasn't said anything because he hasn't paid much attention, but if you fall off this black thunderbolt and hurt yourself, he most certainly will. Now give him here."

"Valadan came to *me!*"

Robart laughed again. "*Valadan?* Because he's a black horse? This isn't one of Grandfather's prize steeds, just some chance-bred that wandered in off the moors. Your nurse told you too many legends, when you were cutting your baby teeth. What did you think you were going to do—go off hunting chimeras on him? Let go of those reins!"

Druyan was weeping, tears of frustration that she knew he mistook for fright. "You can't take my horse!" she wailed.

Robart patted her arm. "Look, Dru, ladies don't ride this sort of horse. You weren't going to keep him anyway. Now let me see if I can win some silver. I'll give you a split."

He slid his hand down her arm, then opened her fingers one by one. Druyan turned her face away as her brother gathered the reins and shoved his foot into the stirrup. She was choking on tears, her head was aching with misery and loss. *No one would have let me keep him. At least Robart won't hurt him*—she tried to console herself, and failed.

The sight of her Valadan meekly bearing Robart away did not ease the lump in Druyan's throat. She stared with burning eyes, trying not to hate what had been inevitable.

And stared wider yet as Valadan's head plunged downward fast as a stooping falcon, ripping the reins from Robart's unready fingers. As the stallion arched his back and bucked, his hind legs kicking out one way while his rider went flying in the opposite direction.

Robart rolled to his feet and went after the stallion at once, keeping a careful hold of his temper as he caught up the trailing reins. Despite a white-rimmed eye, Valadan stood still to be mounted once more. Robart glanced back at Druyan, half pleased at his victory, half saying he'd told her so and had been right to relieve her of the unruly stallion before a like disaster befell her.

And no wise ready for the run Valadan abruptly gave him. No warning dip of the black head this time. No buck to shed an unwelcome rider. Valadan simply seized the bit and bolted, and nothing Robart did troubled the stallion in the least. The boy tried to sit deep and be ready to regain control the instant the horse slackened his pace, but Valadan put on a burst of speed instead that rocked him hopelessly far back in the saddle. Two more bounds and Robart slid off over the black tail, to land scrambling.

He nearly kept hold of the reins, but he stumbled in a rabbit hole as he came to his feet and lost his grip. Druyan watched the ensuing pursuit, as Valadan danced ever nearer to the spot where she stood and Robart grew ever redder in the face as the horse continued to elude him. Finally they stood on either side of her, and she held Valadan's reins.

"Give him here," Robart panted obstinately.

She'd lose him in the end, no matter how she struggled. There was no other outcome possible. And the stallion would get the beating of his life if he kept fighting. She wouldn't be able to prevent that.

"Go with him," she wished, and turned her face away as Robart swung up once more and gathered the reins in an iron grip that pulled the stallion's mouth wide open. Fool horse, to come back to one who hadn't the power to protect him. A little bitter wind curled about her toes, through the long grass.

She heard the thud of hoofbeats—Robart was ready this time and had sent Valadan away at a gallop, teaching the horse who was master. In a moment he'd reached a cluster of four other riders, who waited upon him beside one of the courses.

Druyan decided that if she was fated to walk home, she might as well begin the journey. There'd be rain later—the cool wind pledged it. She could have taken Robart's cast-off roan, but she preferred to leave it for him to cope with—he'd have a job ponying either it or Valadan home, and richly deserved the trouble.

The racers were dragged into a raggedy line. Someone shouted the signal to begin. Hooves thundered, like a presage of storm. Dru told herself not to look back, but she could not resist watching Valadan run, even with another rider on his back. He carried himself so proudly, his sculptured head so high, his tail an outflung banner . . .

He leapt to the lead, like a black wave breaking on the

shore. So lovely he took her breath, and for a moment Druyan forgot her loss in admiration. There was no horse his equal!

A black-legged gray had its pink nose at his flank. Druyan waited for Valadan to accept the challenge and draw away with quickened pace—instead, the gray unthinkably gained ground with every stride. Valadan ran steadily, but now the gray's head was at his neck. And a dark chestnut was overhauling the stallion from the other side, with a bald-faced bay gaining ground on all of them just behind.

They raced over a full league, and Valadan was the last to make the distance. Druyan watched open-mouthed as he came jogging slowly back, tossing his head. The expression on Robart's face was one of the purest disgust.

"Hasn't got the staying power of a sheep," he snarled, flinging the reins toward his sister as he vaulted down. "You might have said so." He walked away.

Druyan looked into the stallion's dark eyes, saw swirls of rainbows like laughter deep within. Valadan nuzzled ticklingly at her palm and blew upon her contentedly. He wasn't even sweating.

"Smart horse," Druyan said dryly.

The black head dipped in agreement.

The Widow

SPLAINE GARTH WAS as much salt marsh as cropland. Druyan could ride half a day—on any ordinary horse's back—and never be off her husband's land. The marshes looked wild beyond hope of farming, but in fact a substantial quantity of hay was taken from them each year, and cows, pigs, and sheep throve alike upon the spartina grass pastures. Waterfowl were plentiful, too—a heron turned its spear-beaked head to watch Druyan ride by, and she heard a swan calling overhead.

Many a husband would have found objection in a young wife's riding out alone as often as Druyan did, but Travic had trusted her. It had not been a cynical assessment that an old horse and a less-than-attractive woman were unlikely to come to harm or mischief—it had been her husband's respect of her need to take the air for an hour or so most days, his kindness in allowing her a pleasure from the very first days of their marriage.

And now Travic was dead, of duty and a stray arrow.

Dalkin had brought the news that morning, after walking alone a day and a night alongside the horse that bore his master's lifeless body. He was the only one of the little company to return—the rest of Splaine Garth's men, without a living lord to order them home after a reasonable period of service, had been conscripted into the duke's army for an indeterminate span of months. But Dalkin was barely ten, old enough to accompany his lord and run messages for him, not grown enough or expected to fight. So home he came, on one last service to his master.

Seaborne raiders had been harrying Esdragon's dangerous coasts for the past hand-span of years. Darlith had mostly escaped the attentions of the men in the long black ships, boasting few towns where riches would be clustered for easier plundering; but eventually even quict Splaine Garth's luck had run out. It was late in the season, they had begun to hope themselves spared for another year, but the ever-prudent Travic had not relaxed his vigilance while there was still sailing weather and danger to come with it.

Ready for trouble, he and his farmhands put the raiders to flight in wonderfully short order, and penned those they took captive within the farm's root cellar. Then Travic had marched every able-bodied man beholden to Splaine Garth downcoast to join the ducal army defending one of Darlith's scarce port towns, expecting to return in a sevenday. Instead, he met his fate, fletched with goose feathers gray as the sky. Ironically, the arrow was a stray come from his own side—the raiders were not even thought to fight with bows.

Druyan twisted her big hands tight into Valadan's mane, bent low over the horse's neck as a lump swelled in her throat. *I just buried my husband.*

Probably few folk would expect her to mourn Travic with an extravant, hair-rending grief, but they had shared married life for eight years, and his passing left a great empty place at the center of her world, as if a tree had been torn from the earth by storm winds. Part of her could not even accept the news. Another part of her looked ahead and saw worse disasters to come. Already she missed what she knew would never return. That was fool's business—Travic had often been gone from home a fortnight, and she had not then been in an agony of loneliness. It had only been a span of days since he'd ridden out—if all had gone according to plan, he wouldn't have been back yet anyway. If someone had known how to aim his bow, how to allow for wind and distance drop . . . how to shoot over his own lines . . .

Their marriage had been arranged by her father, a year before Ronan died. Travic was nearly her father's age, married once already to a woman who had given him no child, though she had eventually died attempting that wifely duty. Druyan had not given Travic an heir, either, but he had never spoken of setting her aside, or otherwise ill-treated her on that account. If they had not loved one another with passion, they had lived agreeably together, considerate of each other, partners.

And now Travic was dead, and this barren widow faced the bleakest of futures.

If only she'd had a child! That old ache cut deeper than the fresh pain of Travic's death, but Druyan had long since shed all the tears she was able to on that account—each spring as every female creature in sight brought forth young, and her arms ached with the burden they were not fated to hold.

But if she'd had a child—even a daughter—she would have been allowed to hold Splaine Garth in trust, and she'd have had a home there while she did that. As it was . . .

The land would pass to some overlooked son of one of Travic's great-aunts, and Travic's barren widow would have to leave. Go back to her family, which no longer had a place for her. She'd been settled, dealt with, married off, and if she returned now it would be in disgrace, having failed at the most basic of womanly tasks. Druyan pressed her face into Valadan's silky mane but could not shut out that desolate future.

She could marry again. Certainly her family would try to arrange that for her. It would, of course, be a very hard bargain for them to strike, with any man having half his wits about him.

She had no lands. She had no looks—not with her long, thin nose and her grandmother's square jaw. Not with hair the color of dead salt-grass and eyes that were pale gray without even a hint of blue—and there were lines at the corners of them, from gazing out over the marshes, from being out in the weather and not caring. She freckled if Esdragon got sufficient sun, though that was rare. And her hands were still too big for grace, though they were deft at spinning and weaving the wool from Travic's sheep, where more delicate fingers would not have served so well.

Worst of all, she was *barren*. What sane man wanted that in a wife, with naught of looks or money to offset the defect? She'd been fortunate with Travic, he had not reproached her or beaten her. Perhaps that was why she hadn't especially grieved that she'd had far more in common with her husband's farm dogs than she'd had with the man himself—they shared her devotion to the sheep. She had no reason to expect such forebearance of another man. Outside of Splaine Garth she had nothing, no place, no life.

Druyan dismounted and looped the reins over Valadan's neck, out of his way. He followed at her heels like a dog as she walked over her land—which was hers no longer.

They hadn't cut hay here—too near the winding stream that clove a lazy way to the sea. They'd have had to carry it too far, to spread it for curing or even to load it on a wagon. The grass rose to her waist, held secrets of bird nests and rabbit runs among its roots. They were far enough upstream that the salt tide did generally not invade, so purple-flowered mint clothed the streambanks. She should cut a bundle while she saw it, to dry for winter tea. Physick for digestive troubles, pleasant simply to sip with a bit of honey . . .

Druyan halted abruptly. What was she about, planning as if she'd be there when the mint leaves were dried, much less come winter? Hot tears blurred her sight again, and she put her big hands over her eyes. When Valadan nuzzled her arm, she flung both arms about his neck and soaked his shoulder with her grief.

When must we go? he asked her. The wild swan called a question of its own.

"I don't know." Her voice was thick. Druyan swallowed hard to clear her throat, blew her nose into a mullein leaf.

"I hadn't thought that far—" She patted his shoulder. "Not today."

Nor next day. Travic's body was barely carried home, scarce committed to the earth. Nothing would or could happen at once. There'd be a search for whoever stood heir to him. Time would pass.

Who'd search? Druyan suddenly wondered. The question hung in her mind, like the afterimage of a lightning bolt. She listened to the wind sighing through the tall grass.

The reality was, Splaine Garth was a backwater farm on the edge of nowhere, not a great landholding. Travic's lands didn't include a town and its population, just the marsh and the cropland and the few unremarkable folk who dwelt thereon, none of them his heirs, all of them waiting as she did, for whatever happened next. Suppose nothing happened? Suppose no one came from afar to claim the land?

Travic had taught his wife to care for Splaine Garth, had shared the stewardship of it openhandedly with her. There were few parts of its management Druyan did not have some knowledge of. Day to day, the farm would go on exactly as before, though Travic was gone. Day to day, little would change unless the nature of the world itself did. Plowing and planting, harvest and gathering, making and marketing—all that she could see to. That was the reality, no matter how dark the future might look from her vantage. Day by day, she could go on, and so thereby could Splaine Garth.

And taking into account such realities, there was a hallowed custom. Should a man die childless, and with no issue from previous marriages, if his widow could thereafter hold the land for a year and a day without remarrying and with all crop tithes timely paid, then the land passed to that widow, became hers to hold in her *own* right.

The swan called again, as if to underscore the point. Druyan gave a whoop of her own, spinning around with arms spread wide to Valadan, who threw his head up in startlement but stood his ground.

"The wool tithe was paid after the spring shearing!"

He snorted at her, trying to understand. The sun was on the far horizon, and most of the vast sky was the color of a ripe apricot. Druyan looked like a part of the marsh—her hair catching rosy-golden lights as the tall grass did, her eyes the silver gray of the shallow pools scattered among the rushes and sweet flag.

"There's the barley tithe, when the crop comes in. And after first frost, we have to send part of a cider pressing. Then that's it, for the year. If we send the crop tithes on time, there's no reason anyone would think to come here. It'll be winter, no one will want to travel—and by spring, the year's half done!" She was touching her long fingers, one by one, assuring herself of the count. "We can do it! A year and a day is nothing!"

She rammed a boot into the stirrup and vaulted onto Valadan's back. He caught her excitement and reared playfully against the pink-peach sky.

"We'll do it!" the lady of Splaine Garth cried to the swans and the sky and the salt marsh.

The Prisoner

ENNA WAS A childless widow, too. The winter before Druyan had come as a bride to Splaine Garth, an epidemic of lung fever had raged through Darlith and, by the time it had passed, claimed Enna's husband and two small sons. Enna herself suffered from joint evil, and though she was barely a handspan of years Druyan's elder, she seemed most often twice that age. The coiled braids of her dark hair were well laced with silver. When the weather turned wet or chill, movement became a torture for her, and her hands swelled till she could scarcely use them for the least task. She had kept the house for Travic after his first wife's death and continued the service after his remarriage—to expect her to do farmwork would have been a cruelty none of them were capable of. The house was snugger than a farmer's hut, and even there Enna suffered piteously, especially come winter. That she never submitted to her affliction did not ease it.

This day, howbeit, had been a good one ere Dalkin came to the gate. After a stretch of dryish weather, Enna had been able to knead the bread as she ought, to set it to rise, and later to shape the loaves. The upsets of the recent raid had faded. She had started a proper meal cooking for her lady, a joint of mutton roasting slow and late berries stewing into a savory sauce for the meat. Then came the news, and no one at Splaine Garth cared a whit for food, which was proper but such a waste of good cookery. And her hands and neck and shoulders had begun to ache from the instant she had seen the burdened horse behind the boy, as if there was rain coming off the sea.

The lady had ridden out after the burial was accomplished, to have her grief in private, Enna supposed. In the sanctuary of her kitchen, she listened for the sound of the horse returning and heard old Valadan's hoofbeats just at dusk, when she'd have otherwise begun to fret. She hastened to set out a meal to tempt her mistress to eat. The poor thing might need Enna's coaxing—the news had hurt them all, but surely the Lady Druyan had first claim to the grief.

Splaine Garth boasted a lofty hall, a pretention to grandeur by one of Travic's ancestors, but the great room was impossibly drafty at any time, never pleasant for lingering over meals. Food would freeze to the table in winter. The family had always dined at one end of the kitchen, where a carved wooden screen shut out the common sight of the cook's work but not the welcome heat of oven and vast hearth. Druyan came in from the stable, scraping her boots clean at the doorstep, and Enna brought her lady water and a linen towel.

"I should have sent that roast straight to stew," she fretted aloud as Druyan washed her hands. "I'm sure 'tis dry as bone now."

Druyan glanced at the wide board, with only the one place laid on the well-scrubbed wood, a new reality that stabbed her to the heart. "You couldn't ruin a meal if you set your heart on it, Enna. Did you feed Dalkin? Did the girls come in?" Pru and Lyn tended the sheep and kept an eye on the other beasts pastured in the marsh. When the weather permitted, the sheep stayed out nightlong, their shepherdesses sheltering in one or another of the little huts built for that purpose.

"They took bread enough yesterday to last another day or so. And Dalkin ate fit for three," Enna added, complaining.

Druyan settled herself on the bench. "He had a long walk, Enna. And boys that age—" She broke off. Enna's sons would have been only a little older than Dalkin. "Won't you eat?" she asked lamely.

"I did, a bit." Enna started around the edge of the screen, back to her domain, both women thinking of losses.

"Sit with me, Enna?" Druyan begged suddenly. To sit alone to a meal only underscored her situation. Travic's empty place loomed large, a pity of shadows.

"My lady? What's ... going to become of us now? Without the master?"

Druyan lifted a portion of roast mutton onto her platter. "Well, next thing's bringing in the barley crop."

Enna watched wide-eyed as Druyan calmly sliced herself some bread. Deranged by grief, might she be? The master gone, and she spoke calmly of harvesting?

"You don't think Travic intended to let it sprout in the field?" Druyan raised a thin brow. "Well, I don't, either. We are going to tend this farm, Enna, exactly as Travic would have done if he'd lived. That's what's going to become of us."

"But, my lady—" Enna's face twisted in consternation.

Druyan began to eat her dinner. "This is very fine bread, Enna. You always do wonders with it." She returned to the matter at hand. "A man's goods and lands pass to his children." She chewed a bite of mutton, then swallowed carefully. "But sometimes there are no children. So the law says, if the widow can hold that land, it belongs to *her*. That's what I intend, Enna." It sounded impossibly bold, said straight out for the first time. Not to be unsaid, or stepped back from.

It must have sounded so to Enna, too. Her dark eyes went very round, and the lines around them smoothed out. "But you'll remarry." Not a question, but a stated fact.

"If Travic had close family, they'd demand it. And I could not say them no." Druyan shook her head. "But there's no one, Enna. Some far-off cousins, who never came here, who've forgotten us. No one will force me."

"Would you have to be *forced*? Was being wed to my lord such an awful state?" Enna huffed, prepared to dodge back into the safety of her kitchen, away from the payment due her impertinence.

But her lady was not angry. "Travic was a good man, Enna, I don't deny that. But no one asked me if I wanted to wed a man old enough to be my sire," Druyan said, pleading for mercy. "They just arranged it for me. Well, no one's here to arrange another such marriage for me, and *I* won't seek one. I will not remarry. I will hold Splaine Garth, and we can all of us stay here."

"You could go back to your family." Enna presented the option uncertainly.

"They saw me provided for once. They won't thank me if they have to do it over again." The gray eyes implored. "Enna, the only place I have in this world is here—if I make it mine."

"Well." Enna sighed deeply. "Who knows what sort they'd give this place to, Lady? I think you'll be doing right, to try."

Druyan felt greatly comforted, though the victory was surely after the smallest of the battles she'd face.

Next morning, Splaine Garth's mistress went out to study her barley fields, to gauge them and try to guess what the next week's worth of weather would hold—or could be made to hold.

Splaine Garth enjoyed every advantage of weather come harvest season. It wasn't a thing Druyan wanted generally known, but she was more than competent at weather-witching. Holding off rain till a hay crop was ricked was no simple matter in Esdragon, where the sky opened up nine days out of ten. Timing a week of sun to coincide with the grain fields' ripeness rose to the realm of fine art. The nearby sea tempered the air, the lofty mass of the Promontory mostly broke the force of storms. Still, it took a lot of work to avoid disaster. Basic weather lore was learned in the nursery, in rhyme and riddle, but Druyan's skills soared

far beyond those. She did not merely observe and react—
she steered.

Her grandmother Kessallia's gifts had never been a topic
of family discussions, and outsiders did not consider the
duchess' witch powers a safe choice of light conversation.
All the same, adjusting the weather to local advantage was
a time-honored custom in Esdragon, and there had always
been plenty of crumbs of such knowledge for Druyan to
nibble as she would. When she came to Splaine Garth she
knew already that she could whistle up a wind—and knew
equally well that she must not, for she found the force unleashed impossible to control. She clung to safer pursuits.
She could disperse a raincloud, or chivvy it aside as a
sheepdog might an unruly wether, so that its load of moisture enriched a river meadow rather than ruined a cutting of
hay. Splaine Garth's dark soil was quick to warm in the
spring, and the fall frosts did not strike heavily enough to
kill until the last fruits had been gleaned from the raspberry
canes. It was more a matter of timing than of strength, a
knowing of what to nudge and when to do it, to get the best
result she could. A subtle art—Druyan was positive even
Travic had not suspected it of her. She grew more adept at
it as she came to know their particular bit of land more
thoroughly, and Splaine Garth prospered by unremarkable
stages—but it did prosper.

Now their fortunes all depended upon her skills. She
dared make no mistakes, this season. She needed perfect
weather.

Druyan bent an ear of barley, testing its weight. She
plucked a kernel and chewed it, frowning in concentration.
The grain must be ready, but not so ripe that it fell from the
ear and was lost during the reaping. She looked from the
green-gold field to the sky, which seemed farther overhead
than usual, whitish bright. The air felt stagnant and oppressive, solid as earth.

At this season, when such heavy weather shifted, 'twas
to intervals of very fine weather. But between those lovely
spells came fierce thunderstorms, sometimes accompanied

by hail that could destroy a barley field in a quarter of an hour. The grainheads were heavy, ready for reaping. If they were beaten down and soaked, by hail or heavy rainfall, the seeds would begin to sprout, which was well enough if the barley was in the malting vats but a disaster while 'twas yet in the field. The present weather, unpleasant as it was, was better to have, better to hold. They needed to begin cutting at once. That very day would be ideal, the next day vital. Travic had expected to have the men home for the task. He'd said so, riding out.

Well, Travic was already back, but Druyan had no expectation of seeing his farmhands in the next week. Dalkin had said that the duke's army was swelling. He'd seen no groups departing for homes and cropland, though harvest loomed everywhere. He'd reported talk of heading farther downcoast, where towns were richer and even more at risk from the raiders.

If the men didn't come back—and she dared pin no hopes on such a chancy thing—then there was no one to do the harvesting. Well, there was herself, and the sheep girls, and Dalkin. But they couldn't reap three fields in less than three weeks, Druyan judged. She remembered how much the men had cut in a day and knew for certain they could never match it. Enna wouldn't be able to grip a sickle, possibly couldn't even climb up to the wagon seat to drive the sheaves back to the threshing barn, however willing she was to try.

Her little crew had been hard enough pressed just to bury their master. Druyan had set the three youngsters to digging a grave in the orchard's relatively soft earth, while she and Enna washed Travic's cold body and wrapped it in his best cloak, gray and scarlet-dyed wool from his own sheep and Druyan's own loom. She had used the threshing sledge, with Valadan to draw it, to convey Travic to his resting place—and had found that three children could not be expected to dig much of a hole. Indeed, either of the farm dogs could have bettered them at the task, given the inclination.

They had done their best—and used stones, after, to make a proper cairn over the barrow. Travic was decently buried—but the weaknesses of the workforce remaining to Splaine Garth were laid plain before the farm's mistress. If they could scarcely bury one man, how could they harvest three fields?

Druyan wiped her forehead with the back of her hand and squeezed her eyes tight shut. Were her hopes to be blighted the instant they took form? All her fine words to Enna came stinging back. There *had* to be a way. Go to the duke—her uncle, after all—and ask for her men back? Travic might have demanded that boon, but if *she* went to the duke, Druyan would only draw attention to a situation she desperately wanted overlooked. Was there *no* way out? Must she yield with the battle unfought? The gently waving barley offered no answers, and Druyan finally left it.

Walking slowly homeward, her thoughts rebounding from futility to hopelessness and back again, Druyan hardly took note of her surroundings. But her gaze snagged on the shattered farmyard gate, which the raiders had battered down less than a week gone. There'd been no chance to repair it properly yet—the splintered boards had been jammed back into shape in the gap between the drystone walls and bound together with hanks of twine. They needed new boards sawn, and there was no one to do that, either, with the men gone and the saw needing two of them to wield it.

Might be there was a plank or two, set aside to season in one of the outbuildings, Druyan thought. She ought to look. She and Dalkin could manage the repair between them, if she could but lay hands on a board.

The raiders had come in the predawn darkness, and all Druyan had seen of the fighting had been a shadow-dance, mostly obscured by the shutters fastened tight over the kitchen windows. She'd heard more than she'd seen— shouts, screams, and curses. By sunup there'd been little sign of the mayhem save for the gate—and all her attention then had been on Travic and the men, helping to pack provisions for them while they saddled horses and made ready to ride out. She'd had very little sleep, and a lot of details to keep atop of. No time to suggest that someone pause to nail the gate back together, or even note that it should be done. Well, she could take the task on now, and hope that by sympathetic magic the rest of the farm chores would bend to her hand, as well. She could find a board and master one piece of chaos.

The board wasn't in the shed, though there was a mark in the dirt where something very like it had recently lain. Druyan cudgeled her memory. What had anyone needed a plank for lately? She walked out of the shed still unable to come up with an answer. As she passed Valadan's paddock—maybe there was a plank *there* she could borrow: He didn't truly need to be fenced, and she often let him wander the barnyard at will—she finally spied the elusive board.

It was jammed across the shoulder-high passage that led into their root cellar, built half under the barn. Now why on earth was that? The turnips weren't dug yet, there was naught in there but cool, damp air . . .

And the prisoners Travic had taken in the raid. He'd mentioned them, in the midst of hasty instructions for the farm and foolish—as it turned out—assurances of his swift return, had touched on the possibilities of ransoms being arranged. "We got four of them," he'd said, proud. "The others ran like coneys."

Nigh a week ago, and Druyan couldn't swear that anyone had fed the captives in that time. No, surely they had not, for Enna couldn't have dealt with the plank alone. She'd have needed help. Druyan frowned and chewed at a fingernail. Travic had been a practical man; perhaps he'd thrown some stale bread in after the men, a barrel of water, so no one would need to risk dealing with them till he got home. She might even remember him saying something about that. But fed or not, Druyan knew *she'd* have been screaming to be let out by now—yet she couldn't recall hearing a sound. Of course, the cellar's walls were thick earth and stone, meant to keep out the summer's heat and the winter's frost. Sound wouldn't carry far . . . She nibbled at her finger again.

Four men, penned so, ought to be more than ready to come out. Maybe also ready to bargain for their liberty.

Four men could harvest a lot of barley.

Valadan snorted disapprovingly and pawed the earth of his paddock.

"You're right," Druyan yielded, glancing at him. "I'll tell Enna what I'm doing."

What she was doing. That she'd gone mad, Enna would say. Druyan steeled herself for another battle.

Kellis had seen the hand, coming toward his face. Only at the last instant—when one steel edge caught a glimmer of light—had he realized that there was a sword in that punishing fist.

He had expected the blow, the moment he heard the shouts that told him his luck had run out, that they had been discovered when he had sworn to the captain that they would be undetected. It had been certain to happen sooner or later—he was blindly guessing when he claimed to be foreseeing, and not much caring about the outcome. It was inevitable, too, that he'd pay a price for falsehood and betrayal. He might not understand what was screamed at him, not every word, but he knew enough of the Eral tongue to get the sense of it. The attack was a failure, but there was just time to deal with the scout who'd sworn foreknowledge that it would succeed . . .

He expected to be struck, but not with cold iron. The blade's edge flashed like lightning, right in front of his eyes. Kellis heard no thunderclap—there was only darkness.

"Enna, there's no other choice! Those fields have to be reaped before the next rain, else we're ruined. We won't be able to salvage enough to pay the tithe, much less for seed and flour and market."

"Lady, you're grief-crazed." Enna's brow creased. Tears came to her eyes. "To trust those men—"

"To *use* them, Enna." Druyan noticed Enna did not dispute their inability to harvest the barley alone.

"They'll use *you*! What's to stop them getting on with what they came here for, the minute you let them out?" By her tone, she should have been wringing her hands, but so far Enna had resisted self-torture.

"For one thing, they don't have weapons. And I will carry Travic's hunting bow. I can't hit a deer at forest's edge the way Travic could, but they won't know that, and I'll take care to stay within range I *can* hit from." Druyan frowned, feeling the plan somehow inadequate even before Enna challenged it. "There's Valadan, too. He's better than a squad of the duke's troops; they'll never challenge *him*. I'll stay mounted, I'll carry the bow, and I'll watch them every minute. All they've got to do is reap, the girls can throw the sheaves onto the wain, and we can handle the threshing ourselves, once the grain's in the barn." That was sounding better, a scheme that could succeed. Or was at least no madder than all the rest of it.

Enna was wringing her hands, after all. "Lady, please don't do this! Don't let them out, with the men gone—"

"If I don't, we'll lose the harvest." All the weather-witching in the world wouldn't hold rain off more than a week. Esdragon would never bend to her will so long. And if she had truly thought the farmhands likely to return ere then, she'd never have bothered with the prisoners. She knew what a risk it was. "I've got to take them food, anyway. I won't starve them to death, even if they are thieves."

"Their kind killed your husband," Enna persisted, while Druyan shoved stale bread and half a ball of cheese into a carrysack. "There's no difference between one of them and another."

"Then they owe me a blood debt," Druyan retorted. "They can work it off cutting my grain. Otherwise we'll have to feed them forever," she added, appealing to Enna's frugality. "This way we get a crop in and get rid of them."

Enna trailed her to the door, clutching the kitchen broom—which had a stout ash handle—as if 'twere a weapon.

"What are you doing?" Druyan asked, eyeing the broom.

"You aren't going alone, my lady."

"Enna." Druyan smiled, and shook her head. "If they see just the two of us, and you ready to defend me with a *broom*, they'll *know* it's only women here. If I go alone, they'll see I'm not afraid, and wondering why I don't need to worry will keep them in line."

"Lady—" Enna's nostrils flared.

"They've been in a dark cellar for days, Enna, maybe with no food." Druyan tugged at the drawstring that closed the sack. "That will have tamed them."

"Or driven them mad," Enna pointed out.

"Then they'd be screaming, and we'd hear. I'll take one of the dogs, will that content you?"

Druyan whistled for Rook as she marched across the yard—despite her Otherworldly blue eyes, Meddy was too trusting to offer any sure protection. Even the sheep got the upper hand of her sometimes. Rook's nature was more suspicious, and she had a fine deep growl. The black and tan dog arrived at Druyan's heel and sat patiently while her mistress faced the root cellar door and gathered her nerve.

Likely she'd lose it if she thought longer about the business. She was not half so bold as she'd forced herself to be before Enna. *I will not let them out now,* Druyan thought, to hearten herself. *Nothing so final. Only make the offer and judge their reaction.* She set hands to the plank, dragged it mostly aside, and tugged at the door. It always stuck—but it didn't get opened often enough to merit being rehung. It moved, finally, till it bumped the plank. The opening was narrow, too narrow to allow much out save speech. The pitchfork she'd fetched from the barn would prevent any of the prisoners trying to escape. She hoped.

Show no weakness. That was vital. The illusion of strength was her secret to preservation. Druyan swallowed hard, shifted sweaty palms on the fork's handle. The door-

way was black as a slice of night, the day's light only lapping a short way over the packed earth of the threshold.
There'd been no reaction to her unsealing of the impromptu
prison.

Enna had feared the men would come rushing out at her.
But nothing within the cellar stirred, and Druyan trusted
Rook's vigilant presence to keep matters under control. She
licked her dry lips.

"You in there!" she called sternly, keeping back from the
door. "You trespassed, and you stole! My husband is dead
because of your thievery, and you owe me the blood debt
for his life. I will allow you to settle that debt and depart
for your own homes. What say you? Will you work for
your freedom?"

Only a silence for her answer. Rook whined and lowered
her ears a touch.

Kellis thought for a horrible distorted moment that he
had only one eye. That terror distracted him at first from
the person half framed in the bright doorway—he did not
take in her words at first, or truly recognize that 'twas a
woman who spoke them, till his fingers had determined that
his right eye was only swollen shut by the blow that had
split his world apart into darkness and fire. At least he
hoped only swollen shut—he could feel clotted crusted
blood, but the region about his eye hurt considerably less
than the matted edge of his hairline, where he thought the
blow had landed.

Cold iron. Kellis whimpered, low in the back of his
throat. He had the stench of it still in his nostrils, mingled
with the scent of his own blood. He was lucky to be alive
after being struck so, but not certain he was entirely grateful . . . He began to make out words, through the roaring in
his ears.

It wasn't the first time he'd heard voices, lying there in
the dark, sick and dizzy, not sure whether he was dead or
alive. But the words weren't Eral words, and it was the first

time there had been light, as well . . . he struggled to his knees, trying to listen.

"I have a crop of barley standing in the field, ready for reaping," Druyan continued. "Help my people bring in the harvest, and I will let you go free when the last sheaf is in the barn. You have my word on it."

No response. Druyan frowned and took a hesitant step forward. Why didn't they answer? Were they dead? Surely they hadn't starved? Even if the unrelieved darkness had driven them mad, they should have managed to make some sort of answer. She signaled Rook to rise, and they went forward together.

Her first thought was that the little cellar did not smell nearly so foul as she'd expected. Oh, it stank, but not with half the odor you'd anticipate when several people had been forced to remain in a confined space for several days without benefit of latrines or washwater or even fresh air. Druyan could still make out the aroma of damp earth, under the other less pleasant odors.

She could see more of the cellar's interior, too, as her eyes grew accustomed to the gloom within. There was the mound of loose earth at the back, and the stacks of old baskets they used to confine the turnips and the carrots. Had she brought a lantern she'd have seen them plain—but she really shouldn't have been able to make them out at all. There was a faint squarish glow at the back end of the cellar, adding its illumination to the bit of light that spilled around her and Rook, through the door.

Someone had pushed out one of the stones of the wall and made a gap big enough to wriggle through. The root cellar was empty.

Druyan sagged, the tension going out of her. They were *gone*, must have been gone most of the while, maybe that first night. They'd escaped before anyone even remembered them. No wonder they hadn't been screaming to be fed, to be let out . . .

"Lady?"

Startled by the croaking word, Druyan leapt back. Her left shoulder caught the door jamb, her head bumped the lintel, and she cried out, bruised and held fast. She thought she'd faint; she couldn't tell against the cellar's darkness whether the rest of the world was dimming, too. Rook began to bark thunderously.

The cellar wasn't *quite* empty. Druyan saw, as her sight unblurred, a dim shape stir against the faint backlight. Her heart pounded. She couldn't move. Rook's furry shoulder pressed her knee. She stared at the prisoner. There wasn't room for him to stand upright, but he didn't try anyway. He was kneeling among the empty baskets.

"Why didn't you go with the others?" Druyan demanded fiercely, trying to cover her fright. She shushed the dog, finding the barking more a distraction than a protection. "Why did they leave *you*?"

She could just make out the pale blotch of his face as he raised it. It changed shape—from his answer, she realized he'd put his hand up to it.

"I got hit on the head." His speech was thick, halting. He coughed feebly, as if his throat pained him.

"When did they go?"

No reply. Either he didn't know, or he couldn't understand her. The light hadn't increased, but her eyes were more used to what little there was of it—Druyan could make out a dark patch on the right side of his forehead, which might have been blood, dried and crusted. The raider was touching it with his fingers, but with what looked like great care.

"I don't know, Lady." He coughed again and groaned when the spasm jarred his head.

Likely he'd been unconscious, Druyan thought. Someone had given him a solid clout—the farmhands had been armed with rakes and hoes and shovels, any of their stout handles good as a quarterstaff in willing hands. Not likely he'd be able to tell her much, even if he wanted to. Assuming the injury wasn't feigned, to deceive her.

"I heard them talking . . . I think I did . . . but I

couldn't . . . I wasn't awake. I'm not surprised they left me."
Kellis was, however, surprised they hadn't killed him first.
And with every heartbeat sending stabs of agony through his
skull, a little disappointed they hadn't.

"Gone," Druyan said bitterly, accepting it at last. She
shut her eyes on the useless tears. No matter how hard they
worked, there was no way they'd other than fail to get the
crop in. And if they missed the crop tithe, someone would
come to see why.

"Lady?"

She startled again, having nearly forgotten him until that
croaking question. Rook growled.

"I am not four men . . . but I can work. I want to pay my
debt to you," he added in that ragged voice that made her
own throat burn.

"You want to get out of there, for which I certainly don't
blame you," Druyan said tartly, straightening her spine.
Hurt, abandoned, captured, he'd likely agree to anything
that promised him release. She backed a step away. "All
right. Come out. Keep your hands where I can see them."
She lifted the fork just a trifle.

Druyan retreated farther from the door, into the sunlight.
Even if he was shamming his injury, she and Rook could
deal with him, no question. One to one was a world different from four to one. She heard him scramble to his feet,
groaning something that was possibly a curse.

The man had to stoop to get through the door; and when
he had come under the lintel and could stand erect, he clung
to the frame for dear life. No chance he was aiming to deceive or lull her—he had a palm-width cut on his forehead,
and by the bruising around the wound, it had been a solid
blow, no trifling scratch. The skin looked seared. Could he
have been hit with a torch? Druyan wondered. His drab
clothing was splotched with dark-brown stains, and he
had—by the smell—been sick all over himself. He kept his
eyes tight shut, as if the daylight pained him.

Rook was growling still, her hackles rising. The man
tipped his head toward her, squinting in what must have

been a glare to his half-closed eyes. "No need, little sister," he whispered. "My fangs are very well blunted."

"I'm not your sister," Druyan said testily, wondering if the blow had bitten into his brain. He might be willing to work, but he didn't sound as if many of his wits remained to him. And now that she'd let him out of the cellar, just where was she going to put him? Could she force him back into his prison if she offered the food she'd brought? Where else was secure enough? She tried to tally their outbuildings in her mind, to recollect the strengths of walls and doors.

Come to that, was he even well enough to work? She recalled one of Robart's friends, ailing and useless for most of one summer after he'd taken a tumble from his horse and split his head open on an inconvenient rock. Maybe the raider was only cramped and unused to daylight—but just as likely he was too sick to do even one man's work.

She assessed her prisoner as heartlessly as she would have a stray sheep added to her flock. He did not, in the light of day, have quite the terrifying aspect the sea raiders were getting a name for. He didn't look as if he could raid a henhouse on his own. He wasn't much taller than she was, and his build was on the slight side. But that meant nothing. Armed, hale, he'd be another man entirely. She should remember that, not be deceived by pity.

From a distance she'd have reckoned him aged, by his ash-color hair and the pale stubble on his jaw, but close-to Druyan could see he wasn't age-gray. His brows—one of which was presently caked with his blood—were very dark. His weather-tanned skin was smooth where it wasn't bruised: not an old man's skin. His battered face was lean and narrow, with a long nose pushed out of line from right to left—he hadn't been born with it that way, but the damage wasn't recent, either. His teeth, blunted or not, were very white, and he had all of them, at least those that showed. A villainous face, Druyan told herself as ruthlessly as Enna would have.

He looked back at her, managing to drag his right eyelid open a trifle. That eye—like the left—was gray with flecks of gold, as open and startlingly honest as a dog's. *That must be useful,* Druyan thought, sternly distrusting them. No reason he couldn't be trying to put her off her guard. She held out the sack of food, the bottle of water, but she kept the pitchfork in her right hand.

"Eat that, while I ready the wagon," she ordered. There was still better than half the day left to work with. They could make a start on the nearest field. She'd see if he could work.

He looked first at her face, then at the sack. Smart enough, maybe, to resist a grab that would set the dog on him. Rook was still tense, her back hair standing up from neck to tail.

"Go ahead," Druyan insisted, shoving the food into his hands. "And don't even think about trying to escape. Rook won't let you stir a step."

He unstoppered the bottle, put it to his lips, and gulped the liquid down as fast as he could swallow. Too fast—he began to choke, and coughed till Rook's growl told him to desist, to behave himself. Stifling the spasm, he put the bottle down, juggled the bag around, and investigated the bread.

The door jamb was still holding him upright, Druyan noticed. She did not discount the danger of him, but it was very hard to believe there was much worry about him for the next few minutes, while she hitched the wagon and brought Valadan out. She could risk it.

Druyan made the hand signal to Rook: *Hold.* One sheep or an entire flock, 'twas all one to the dog, who knew her business. Rook settled happily and fixed the man with her best stare. Halfway to the barn—a dozen steps—Druyan turned back. The man had sat down in the doorway. The bread was gone, and there were crumbs from it dusted down the front of him. He had the cheese clutched to his chest. Rook was watching him alertly. Probably she wouldn't have torn his throat out if he'd tried to run, but he'd never have got past her, either. Especially not with the cheese.

Her fine scheme was seeming less and less a workable plan. Druyan sighed. Only a single man to aid the harvest, and already she was losing her fear of him, which was foolish and did not bode well. The hope—that she could hold Splaine Garth, make herself a place, seemed more and more a dream, from which she must wake and rise to unpleasant reality. What use to struggle so over bringing in a tiny crop of grain? Her husband was dead. She'd no child of his to carry on for.

Yet go on she must—Druyan knew no way to simply lie down and cease breathing, not on her own. So she'd go on, day to day, hour to hour, as one did, and not think about it, if thinking hurt. She'd bring in her crop, and this pathetic scoundrel would help her, since he professed himself willing. She looked back at him, sitting now a bare yard from Rook's eager face, not moving except to tear the cheese with his alarmingly white teeth.

"What are you called?" Druyan asked, wondering why she troubled with the courtesy.

"Kellis," he answered, almost choking again on a mouthful too large and too little chewed.

The Barley Harvest

THE CAPTIVE WAS clumsy at farm work. Perchance he'd never been good at such honest toil and so had taken up the more congenial career of raiding. Or maybe his wound made stooping to sever barley stems with the iron sickle a problem. There was no knowing—he didn't complain or try to shirk, just went on slowly, with dogged concentration, striving to cut grain and not his fingers. Dalkin had needed to show him how to wield a sickle—pleased as a cock robin at owning a skill a grown man didn't possess. The man didn't know how to bind a sheaf, either, and Dalkin puffed still more as he demonstrated.

The boy was less willing to be sent off to fetch the shepherd girls, but Druyan was adamant and she was the mistress, the giver of orders. It was fairly obvious by then that she was in no real danger of being overpowered by her prisoner, even granted that he was armed with a sharp-edged tool; and necessity pressed. Every able hand on the place had to be set to reaping. Every hour of dry daylight had to yield something for Splaine Garth. The sheep could feed unobserved, other chores could be ignored or postponed, but the grain must be cut.

Of course, Druyan herself couldn't be reaping if she stayed primly atop Valadan, keeping Travic's bow carefully trained on her prisoner, but Enna wasn't at hand to protest when she abandoned that ill-conceived promise. Any fool could see it made no sense, not now there was only one man to consider in place of four. The prisoner wasn't going to attack anyone—he could judge the odds weighted so heavily against any success. If he tried anything, it would be running, and between Rook and Valadan, that wasn't likely to be so much a danger as a delay. And there was no-where he might run *to*—Splaine Garth was a pocket farm, surrounded by moor and marsh.

Kellis misliked the iron sickle. Dislike was not at all a strong enough term—the tool terrified him. The boy laughed when he didn't know how to use it—but Kellis didn't *want* to know how. He didn't *want* to grasp barley stalks in one hand and then swing a fell crescent of cold iron—keener and more deadly than the best flint knife—at them with the other. He wasn't even sure his shins were safe.

There was a smooth wooden handle on the tool, but Kellis could feel the iron tang buried not very deeply under the wood—it wanted to bite his fingers, just as much as the sharper blade did. More, because it thought to take him un-awares. Kellis blinked sweat out of his eyes, struggled to make the pale grain stalks come into focus. *I'm going to cut my hand off,* he thought helplessly. His head was pounding, and every movement made the world dip and sway around him, as if viewed from a ship's deck in heavy weather. It was not the time to be learning to use a deadly instrument . . . but he had no choice. He had pledged he would work, and this was what he was set to do.

Even if he set aside his pledge, escape demanded that he be able to run, and he could barely keep himself upright. He could smell the sea, but reaching it would avail him nothing. All the other directions were equal mysteries to him, and unreachable ones, as well. The horse was hitched to the wagon, and looked stolid and slow. He'd be too slow stealing it, that was certain. He'd be stopped.

There was another horse, this one only saddled. His nose brought him scents of well-kept leather and sweet hay, and horse sweat in smaller measure, because this horse had not been pulling a wagon. His eye found it eventually, grazing at the field's edge. It was black as the edge of a storm, saddled but otherwise unencumbered. Trusted, it did not even seem to be hobbled. Kellis drew in a longing breath.

The horse looked at him. From across the tossing grain, its eyes met his, and it seemed to know very well what Kellis was hoping to do. It made him a promise in trade—a fall likely to part him from his body entirely. His for the asking, if he came near it. In the darkness of the horse's eyes, lightnings flashed.

Kellis looked away. He frowned at the wavery grain, grasped a handful, cut at it, his lips shaping a prayer to Valint—though he no longer believed that there was any protection for him, whether the Wolfstar shone upon this land or not.

There were five of them bending and stooping in the golden field after the girls arrived, amid the gently waving grainstalks, cutting and binding sheaves. After a time, Druyan moved the wagon closer and started throwing sheaves onto its bed—the man came and helped her with that, looking a question at her over his armload of grain first, moving slowly and obviously intending there'd be no misunderstanding. He was sweating heavily—but so were they all. It was a sweat of exertion, not the nervous wetness of deceit. She looked to Valadan for confirmation of that— she had sent Rook to the sheep that the girls had been forced to leave. The stallion flicked an unconcerned ear. All was well.

Druyan nodded permission, and when they had loaded the last of the waiting sheaves that dotted the stubble, the prisoner went back to reaping, with never once a covetous glance at Valadan or the horse hitched to the wagon. Not that he'd have gotten far essaying a horseback escape—the gray mare was elderly and had never been known for her speed—but if he'd used the sickle to cut the traces, he'd have ruined the harness and they'd all have wasted time more profitably spent reaping.

Nightfall was a gradual affair at that season—with the sun far away behind the shielding overcast of the sky, the reapers had no clues of sunset color or twilight. Eventually they simply could no longer see what they were cutting, and Druyan's belly complained that it was well beyond the supper hour. They had sheared a ragged third of the field— Splaine Garth's lady felt a twinge of hope, under her weariness. They'd have seed grain, at least.

Dalkin ran ahead, to assure Enna they were alive and tell her they were coming in, so she'd set the food out, ready for them. The girls would get a hot meal before rejoining their flock for the night, and Druyan would have let them ride back on the wagon, but they were used to walking and better content to swing along beside it, easing kinks out of backs, flexing tired fingers, and casting sidelong glances at the stranger.

She'd probably have done better to make him foot it, as well, Druyan suspected, but the man looked done up, and since the wagon wasn't full laden, there was no telling herself the mare couldn't or shouldn't pull the load. One man's weight more or less made no matter. Druyan gave him a surreptitious glance herself, as the wheel negotiated a deep rut and they both swayed on the broad seat. Roomy enough that they didn't need to ride shoulder to shoulder, she was glad—if he'd smelled before, he was twice as fragrant after a few hours of hot work. The odor reminded her that the root cellar would need cleaning once the barley was in, before the turnips were dug. It was a hard place to air out.

The prisoner's sweat had pushed out through the older dirt, then trapped an uneven layer of gray dust and flakes of chaff. His pale hair was threaded with green-gold barley stalks, brown bits of weed. His brows and lashes were dust-powdered—he looked, all in all, rather like a badly made corn god, left to winter in the field. His stillness bolstered such fancies—save when the wagon rocked him, his only movement was of his fingers, which were clenched tight around the edge of the seatboard but would shift sometimes for better advantage.

Pru dragged open the barnyard gate for the wagon to pass through. The wheels rattled on bricks laid to prevent mud puddles near the well.

"Kellis."

He didn't react. *Did I mishear his name?* Druyan wondered. She shook her head. *I can't be that far off.* She reached to tap his shoulder. *"Kellis."*

He gave a surprised start, throwing his head up like a shying horse, and Pru giggled. *"Asleep!"* she crowed, and doubled over the gate, hooting. Her brown braids danced on either side of her averted face.

The man ignored her, fixing his attention on Druyan with what dignity he could. "Lady?" His eyes looked muddy brown in the dimness. They were red-rimmed, from chaff and salt sweat and pure weariness, and the right still hadn't opened fully. His mouth drooped.

"Get down," Druyan said, too gently to be an effective order. "This is as far as we go."

The man didn't seem likely to exploit her weakness—he had his own to contend with, evidently. Merely obedient, he dropped off the side of the wagon. Druyan couldn't be sure, over the creaking of the wagon's springs, but she thought he groaned. "Lyn, please tell Enna we're here and to send something back with you for him to eat. Pru, you can help us unload the wagon."

They off-loaded the grain into one end of the barn, spreading the sheaves in a wide heap so they could dry a bit—easier to thresh later. Piled up in the vast space, the barley looked even more insignificant than the shorn end of the field—so much work, so little result, Druyan thought, but refused to be discouraged. Five folk had done what they could. Travic had mustered a score of reapers, so of course a day's yield had been greater. She was too weary; to judge their efforts now would be unfair. That they had done it at all, she must reckon as success. And see to it that the performance was repeated, day by day till all the barley was cut.

When the day's sheaves were all stowed, Lyn came back with Kellis' food—a wooden bowl of mutton stew. Druyan frowned when she got it into her hands. If there was a single bone left anywhere in the rest of the pot, she couldn't imagine it. And the bread thrown atop it had got too close to the oven wall, and was half charred, half soggy. As mistress of Splaine Garth, she was ashamed that even a thieving prisoner should be fed so meanly in her sight.

Her prisoner was trying not to cast too eager an eye on the bowl, she thought—or waiting to be led back to the root cellar and locked inside. He leaned against the wagon, shoulders drooping, his expression neutral. *Damn.* She had meant to tell Dalkin to plug the hole at the back of the cellar, and it seemed rude to give the order now, right in front of the man. Though why she should concern herself with manners—security should be her only interest.

She made Kellis help her park the wagon so its wheel spokes would bar the opening on the outside. Hopefully the man wouldn't realize that he'd just shored up his own jail, or figure out a way to escape in spite of the barrier. Likely he would not—he looked as if he'd be asleep on his feet, except that he kept smelling the food. His nostrils flared, and he sighed, very faintly.

"You did a good job," Druyan said heartily, handing over the bowl as if it was a fair payment, gesturing to indicate the cellar, that he should go in. "Tomorrow will be a longer day, but by week's end the harvest should be in, if this weather holds."

He nodded, too weary to show much interest in a freedom promised but still days away—and maybe never granted. How did he know whether he could trust her? He was as alone, as vulnerable, as she was. Druyan put her hand on the root cellar's door, ashamed.

"Lady?"

Oh, gods. Pity flared into panic. *He wasn't going to go in!* And she had made the mistake he had waited for, she was alone with him! The girls had gone, Dalkin was off feeding the horses. Had she counted the sickles? Rook was off in the marsh, not by her side. Druyan stared at the raider, her heart lodged choking in her throat, trying to keep her fear out of her face. She heard Valadan give the back wall of his stall a mighty kick, and wondered whether he could tear his way out to rescue her. She ought to have left him in the paddock, close, instead of letting Dalkin put him inside. She should have had some weapon handy, and instead all the tools were in the barn . . .

Kellis could see how frightened the woman was the instant he spoke. She tried not to show it to him—wise of her—but he could read it in her eyes, her whole body, like the one deer in a herd that was prey, when all the rest could safely run. It didn't matter, he was in no position to take any profit from it. And if he panicked her, she might hurt him, he thought.

There was meat in the bowl he held—or there had been meat near it. He could smell gravy, and cooked vegetables, and his mouth began to water, helplessly. He was glad she hadn't flung the bowl at him, made him eat out of the dirt, even though he was hungry enough to manage that, aching head notwithstanding. Yet starved as he was, there was something he craved more than food . . .

Showing her fear would be the worst thing she could possibly do. Druyan lifted her chin, stalling for time, trying to look confident, keeping an eye out for a purloined sickle. Someone would come, see what was amiss . . .

She was startled to see that the raider was standing stock still, his hands where she could see them both, holding no more than his supper, making no move more threatening than drawing a breath. Their scared glances skittered nervously, met again. Then he dropped his gaze to the ground.

"I was wondering if I could . . . have some water? To wash," he explained hesitantly. Then he ducked his head disconsolately and went into the dark of the cellar.

Druyan couldn't decide whether the sickness she felt was relief or shame. The chaff inside her own clothing scoured at her skin, like furious fleas. She, of course, could rid herself of the irritation, and would, in her own tub in her own clean room, before she slept in her own clean-sheeted bed. She snatched up the wooden bucket, dipped it hastily into the horse trough, thrust it half filled and slopping at the man, then shut him into the root cellar for the night, out of sight and guilty thought.

The kitchen was too warm, as it often was in summer, and mostly empty. Pru and Lyn had bolted their food and returned to their flock. Damn. She'd wanted to tell them to be back at first light, so she wouldn't need to waste Dalkin's time fetching them in. Maybe they'd know that, but that didn't mean they'd appear without a direct order.

"Oh, Lady, thank the gods you're safe!" Enna turned from the oven. "Dalkin said there was only one of those brutes left still alive, and him a frightful villain with a scar, and only one eye—"

Druyan sank down wearily into her chair. Her bones felt very ancient, the rest of her no younger. She wondered if this was how Enna's bones ached, if she had finally caught the malady from living near it so long, like a cough spreading from one of them to the other. She shut her eyes and saw uncut grain waving to the horizon, like sea billows. So tired she was, and such a little of the task done. So much still to do. *We've begun. But if it rains? Storms? I have to be sure that doesn't happen, and I'm too tired to think how to do it.*

"Did they kill one another, Lady? Like rats in a trap?"

Druyan blinked at the dish of stew set before her, conjured there out of thin air. Not a single white bone could she see, only tender chunks of mutton swimming in a rich gravy. A lovely loaf of bread lay sliced beside it, almost glowing in the candle's light. She ought to eat, before she fell into sleep . . .

"Lady?"

Druyan shook herself awake and found her tongue to answer. "No one's dead, Enna. They pushed out part of the wall and escaped, probably the first night, right after they were put in."

Enna fumbled at her full skirt. Probably she'd hidden one of the carving knives there, for protection. Druyan was too tired to smile at that—and could she call it foolish, in truth? A knife was a very fine weapon, even if it was meant for slicing bread. It could slice raider flesh just as well.

"They aren't still here, Enna," she said reassuringly. Ironically, when they'd needed to worry, they'd been blissfully unaware of any danger. "Probably the ones who got out went back to the sea, and their boat, and they're gone. One was wounded, and they left him." She sighed. "I suppose they're like that, don't even care about their own. He says he'll work, so I have promised him that I'll let him go when the barley's in. It's not much, but it's one more pair of hands."

Enna's lips pursed at that, still not sanctioning such madness, an offer hardly better for being extended to only one murderous stranger in place of four. "Why'd they leave him?" she asked apprehensively.

"Probably too much trouble to take him along." Druyan stirred a spoon through her stew, trying to summon energy to lift it to her lips. She was hungry, she knew. She'd discover that as soon as she tasted a bite, and eating would not be a burden. "He got hit on the head with something, and woke only after they'd gone. Maybe they didn't want to be bothered carrying him."

"Or maybe he's such a nasty wretch they were pleased to be rid of him," Enna said coldly. "There's always that. Nice for us to have around."

"He can cut barley. I don't care about his character, so long as he can do that!" Druyan smacked her spoon down onto the table—then let it go and stared at it, aghast. She should beg Enna's pardon for her loss of temper, for the bad manners of shouting. For spattering stew on the tablecloth.

And of course her husband should have been sitting across the table from her, and all his men should have been taking their suppers around a trestle and boards set up in the dooryard, and a very great deal of the grain crop should have been stowed safe in the barn, not standing still uncut in the fields, going further past ripeness each minute and prey to every sure-to-come hailstorm. And tears she could not stop should not have been rolling down her dusty face.

Druyan woke well before dawn, but the birds were calling already in the pear tree outside her casement. She slipped out of bed, relishing despite aching limbs the only coolness the day would likely know. She went to the window, trying to guess what the brightening sky would show.

If its uniform gray broke up into high-piled white towers of cloud, then soon or late there'd be a storm, probably at day's end. Hail, lightning, the disaster of battered fields. Therefore, the gray must continue undisturbed by shifts of cold wind off the nearby sea, while too-few hands reaped barley. She dressed hastily and went to the barn.

Valadan bore her bareback and in secret through the dawn to the farthest-off ridge of the last barley field. With a small silver-bladed knife, Druyan cut a palm-size square of soil, with the barley plants still rooted in it, worms wiggling and trying to hide themselves from sight. She carried the treasure carefully home, to a corner of the orchard, by the wall where it fronted the lane. So no breath of air might brush it, she put an upended basket over the replanted tuft of barley. It must stay just as it was, her tiny grainfield, and its larger fellows would thereby do the same. If no rain touched the smaller, then by sound magical principle none would fall upon the larger. No wind would harm either. She held away wicked thoughts of how much more exciting— and how much simpler—'twould be to raise a wind than to quell one.

Her hair clung damply to the back of her neck. Druyan forebore to wish for a breeze, as she drew from her pocket a hollow ball of yellow glass. She held the sphere so that it caught the light, like a tiny sun. The day was brightening—in the barnyard the red and green rooster crowed to welcome the dawn.

Druyan reached into her pocket again and found a lock of grayish, unwashed fleece from the spring shearing. Quickly she teased the fibers out to fluff with her fingers and wrapped the cloud of wool about the ball, swaddling it, shrouding it. The golden glow on the horizon transmuted to silver. Above the farm, the sky was overspread with a static gray blanket of cloud. The cover settled in. Wind could disturb it, tear it, destroy it—but there was no slightest hint of a breeze. All was still. Druyan lodged the fuzzy ball in the gnarled branches of an apple tree and left it there.

The sun's fiery face might be veiled, but his heat was in undeniable evidence, and there was hardly a breath of breeze for comfort. On the one hand Druyan rejoiced—her weather spells were so far effective. But on the other side, it made tiring work sticky, as well, and added salt sweat to the barley chaff making her skin itch. She twitched her shoulders against her shirt, but found no ease for the spot she could not reach with any of her fingers. She wanted to rub herself against a fencepost, like a horse.

They worked their way toward the end of the field, the trees that bounded it drawing ever so slightly nearer, the raggedy mess of stubble widening behind them. The wagon trailed them, ready for the sheaves to be thrown onto it. At the first Druyan had moved it wherever she wanted it—but somehow after a time the wagon always *was* where it was needed, without her fetching it. True, the mare was browsing as she walked, seeking tasty fallen grains among the stubble, but on her own she'd have been as likely to wander over to the hedgerow to forage, or into the uncut grain. She did neither.

Druyan cast a glance toward Valadan, who was nosing for a little grain himself, a ways off. He caught her looking and pricked his ears at her, though he did not raise his head. He was keeping the mare where he wanted her, and where he wanted her was wherever his grateful mistress needed the wagon to be. Druyan gave him a pat next time she went by to the wagon, and wondered whether there were early carrots to pull. He deserved one.

Kellis eyed the horse again. How hard would it be, he wondered, to fling himself onto it as he passed and whip it into flight? He'd need to ride only a couple of miles to be safe away—the woman and the children had no easy way to follow him. If he could just get out of the field . . .

Which he could not, probably. A measure of his dizziness had abated after food and sleep, but much remained, courtesy of the sword blow. Sometimes when he bent to grasp a handful of grain stalks, the black spots swirling in front of his eyes merged into one vast darkness, and his ears filled with sea sounds. What would happen if he tried to run, to wrestle with a startled horse, and one of those fits of weakness claimed him?

He did not see those odd lights in the horse's eyes just then, but Kellis did not think he had imagined them, or what the horse had promised him if he tried to steal it. And the beast was still warning him—with subtle changes of posture that he read with perfect clarity—not to come too close to it. It did that whenever he took sheaves to the wain, even when he thought it could not see him considering it. What it would do to him if he tried to throw himself onto its back, Kellis did not like to guess. But then, he did not really have to guess, for he had its promise.

And he had the other promise: If he worked, till the unending grain was all sheared off and bundled, the woman had said she would let him go. Kellis decided to be patient, to try to bear holding the iron sickle awhile longer. Maybe she would keep her word. It was no worse a bargain than others he had made lately.

The wagon was full. The prisoner hesitated before throwing his latest load of sheaves on top of the precarious pile. There was a puzzle—just what was she to do about *him*,

Druyan wondered, while she and the wagon went back to unload? If he decided to leave, he could just *walk* away. Two young girls and a younger boy wouldn't give him much trouble. Tie him? All she had with her by way of rope was the thin twine they were using to bind the sheaves. Wouldn't hold him a minute. Well, he could help her unload as well as anyone, couldn't he?

"Right," Druyan said to the man briskly, putting confidence into her tone whether she felt it or not. Sometimes, feigning sureness would calm a fractious horse, and control could be gained merely by acting as if one had unquestioned control. She hoped that would prove to be the case *this* time. "You come back with me to put this load in the barn. Pru, leave the sheaves just where you tie them, we'll throw them on when we get back." She made encouraging noises to the gray mare, and the wagon began to roll barnward while Kellis was still scrambling onto the seat. Valadan followed after discreetly.

Kellis settled himself, and they tried not to watch one another. They were each filthy from working, but he had started off the day nearly clean—or as clean as a man could make himself with half a bucket of stale water, in a dark cellar. He hadn't been able to do much about his garments, which were—and maybe always had been—the color of dirt, but he'd washed his face and gotten the caked blood out of his hair. He had a sark of thinner stuff under his woolen tunic—Druyan could see a raveled edge where he'd torn the strip that was now bound about his forehead. It kept the sweat out of his eyes, besides protecting the cut as it healed. He had tied strips around his palms, too—protection from the blisters of work he wasn't used to, she supposed.

The contrast between his pale hair and his dark brows was now startling. It wasn't a coloring one saw in Esdragon, and Druyan wondered whether the other raiders shared it. She hadn't seen any of them, only heard their battle cries. Travic would have known . . .

It hit her full force, that her husband wasn't going to be

coming home, to be pleased with the news that she'd brought his harvest in for him. That she could never now give him the child he'd wanted to pass his farm on to. He'd been fretting about having to leave at harvest—now, to him, it no longer mattered.

They said her grandmother had taken her own life, to follow the mate she'd loved. By such a standard, Druyan didn't suppose she'd loved her own husband. She might have died *for* Travic, trying to bear him a child as his first wife had—that was always a hazard of wedlock. But she didn't quite feel she wanted to die *because* he was no longer with her. She didn't feel that way at all.

Well, few wives knew that sort of passion, from all Druyan had observed. Nice if you had it, probably, but neither expected nor regretted—a childhood passion for romance, not much to do with the reality of a marriage. Travic had been a decent man, and now he was gone, and she missed him, because any person you were with day in and day out for eight years would leave a hole in the routine of your days, for a time. But though she mourned Travic, the empty feeling was not very much worse than it had been after their old blue merle sheepdog had passed on, summer before last. And shouldn't she mourn a husband more deeply than a dog? *There* was regret. *There* was grief, for what she did not feel.

She told it to Valadan, later. There was no one else to confide in—Enna's loyalty to Travic would have judged her even more harshly than Druyan's own conscience did. So, falling-down tired as she was, Druyan stood by her horse's shoulder in the dark and let the words tumble out when she'd surely have been better abed—a bed wherein she'd only have felt fresh pangs over her relief that she was alone in it, with no other body to trouble the rest she needed with movements of its own, to add its heat to the stifling room.

She rode to the second field, which rippled unbroken and half as wide as the sea. They'd finally finished the closest field by dusk, but the nearest also chanced to be the smallest. She tried to guess how much more time they'd need, to harvest the bigger fields. She didn't know how much longer she could hold off the cold wind from the sea—she could feel it stalking all about, like a cat in the tall grass—and the pall of muggy heat she'd draped over the farm was so oppressive that part of her longed for it to break free of her control. She *loved* storms, with a passion that she had never shown Travic—it was very hard not to yearn for one when she felt it close by, willing to come to her call. The white flashes of lightning, the resounding crash of the thunder, the cleansing wind, the slashing silver fall of rain . . .

Valadan dipped his head to her, snorting. Hardly thinking, Druyan grabbed his mane and leapt again onto his unsaddled back. The instant she had a leg on either side of him he was away, swift as the wind she craved, as exciting as any storm. They rushed through the heavy night, and his hooves were the thunder, his whipping mane stinging her cheeks like rainfall.

That night, she slept soundly.

From sunup to twilight, they bent and cut, bent and cut and tied. A dulled sickle brought a brief respite from reaping while its edge was whetted anew, a full wagon brought a longer relief, at least for the two taking the wagon back to unload it. Druyan had her suspicions about just how hard the girls worked while she was out of their sight, but she didn't blame any of them—it was cruel hard work with so few of them to share it. Her hands were blistered, her back seemed permanently bent. When she fell into her bed at night, all she saw behind closed lids was barley, endlessly waving.

Ironically, it was a huge crop. They'd be putting sheaves in the winter sheepfold by the time they'd harvested half the last field, Druyan was certain. She relaxed a little once she reckoned she had enough barned to pay the barley tithe *and* keep seed for the next planting—but she couldn't let her workers stop or slacken, not so long as the weather held. Each grain brought in was more to sell at market, or to fatten more animals upon. They had been blessed, but that blessing didn't make them free to waste the bounty.

After the first days, though, she did beg Enna not to send barley bannocks out for their midday meal. She saw barley, smelled it, and tasted it, even in her dreams. Eating it as well was too much to bear. Come midwinter she might relish the taste once more, but surely not before then. She passed her unwanted portions on to Kellis, who—since Enna refused to send him much of a breakfast other than a bowl of cold porridge—was actually happy to have it. Not that Druyan felt thieving murderers deserved viands fit for the duke's own table, but she'd have to speak to Enna about feeding the man better—he was working doggedly all day and hardly deserved to be starved by way of reward.

Kellis tried not to look at the grainfield as a whole, ever. If he did, it was a nightmare—barley, unending as the sky or the sea. If he cut a handful of it, it made no difference to the field. If he cut all day—and he felt a vast portion of his life had now been devoted to doing just that—it made not much more of a dent in the standing grain. One day blurred into another—nights, as well, since the field intruded on all his dreams, and he arose feeling he'd been working all night or that he had only imagined sleeping.

He was past dreaming of escape. All that was real was the grain and the iron sickle he slashed at it with. He cut himself a dozen times a day, and the slashes burned like fire, their edges puffed and turned black. That was his left hand, which held the stalks for the cutting. His right hand, which gripped the sickle, ached more cruelly, though there was no mark of hurt visible upon it. He had wrapped scraps of cloth about the wooden handle, others about his palms, but the added protection did little to shield him from the bane of the iron—not when he must grasp the tool for ten hours a day, from first light to last with little relief. He had heard that iron could eat into the very flesh of his folk, and he believed it—he just couldn't do anything to prevent it.

He reaped, ate, slept—and arose to do it all over again.

Or thought he did. Perhaps he was dead and paying eternally for his crimes. Kellis brushed salt sweat out of his eyes, leaving dirt and chaff in its place. Probably he was dead. That made sense. The bright flash of light, when the sword hit him ... then darkness, and when he woke, he was in the afterlife—exactly the sort of afterlife a man who had done the sorts of things he had done could expect.

One thing puzzled him—the woman gave him water, from the jug kept in the shade at the unending field's edge. If he was dead, why did she bother doing him that kindness? Kellis looked at her through the dancing spots that filled his vision. She was damp with sweat, and had barley stalks in her hair. She moved with the same dogged weariness that he did. Was she dead, too? She seemed to care very much about the grain. Did the dead care about such things?

Kellis had never seen a corpse that seemed to care about anything. And he had seen plenty of death.

Just when they were at their weariest, most hopeless point, they began to see signs of an end to their labors. They passed the boundary stones that marked the halfway point of the long, narrow third field. Dalkin began at once to fuss over whether there'd be a proper harvest supper to celebrate. Lyn teased him that they were so late at the barley, they'd have to go straight to digging turnips, with no time for any party. Druyan intervened with reassurance— Enna had already begun soaking dried cherries so she could bake pies, and next day before he came to the field, Dalkin was to kill and pluck two chickens for her, so she could be about roasting them. There were less mouths than usual to feed, but they'd eat as fine a harvest supper as ever at Splaine Garth—and certainly a well-earned one.

The edges of the wooly sky were beginning to show ragged patches of darker cloud, next morning. *There will be a storm tonight,* Druyan thought, looking at it. *No matter what I do about it.* She exhorted her crew to work faster and have a whole day's rest next day, not letting on that they'd not reap next day even if grain remained uncut.

It did not seem possible that they could work faster, but they could keep steadily at it. In some ways the last bit was easier, simply because it *was* the last bit. Sickles whispered through stalks, rasped on whetstones. Sheaves sprang up like mushrooms after a rain. The trees at field's end came closer, ever so slowly as the day waned—by sunfall the reapers had finally reached them. There was no more uncut barley.

Druyan pressed a hand to the small of her back and stretched to get a cramp out of her shoulders. Standing upright felt wrong, after so many days of continual stooping. The girls began dancing about, as Kellis handed the last sheaf to Dalkin, who bound it specially with a length of scarlet cord and perched it precariously upright atop the load, to ride in with all honor due the barley maid, spirit of the grain.

We did it, Druyan thought, almost too stupid with weariness to take the achievement in. She shut her eyes.

She heard a whisper in the stubble beside her and looked down with some alarm, expecting a snake, hoping she wasn't blocking its escape, which was all the poor thing would be wanting. The flashing sickles must have terrified it.

Kellis had collapsed onto his face in the pale-green stubble almost atop her feet, the sickle still clutched in his outflung hand. He lay motionless, save for the breeze riffling his barley-colored hair and the trickle of blood running from his cracked lips.

The Prisoner's Tale

UNABLE TO WAKE him, they finally contrived to wrestle the man over Valadan's back—there wasn't a bit of room to spare in the wagon—and fetched him back to the farmyard that way, with his head hanging down on one side and his feet flopping on the other.

Druyan couldn't fathom what ailed the prisoner. She'd have suspected sunstrike, which *could* occur even in rainy Esdragon—but none of them had so much as seen the sun in a sevenday, thanks to weatherwork that still made her head ache. He displayed none of the symptoms. His skin wasn't dry and flushed, he hadn't been noticeably confused. He hadn't complained of feeling ill. He might, by appearances, have simply fainted, but they'd thrown enough water on him—the river was conveniently near—to almost wash him clean, and he'd never even slightly stirred, much less revived. Duryan lifted one of his eyelids again and still saw only the white. Some sickness? That notion scared her. They might all take it, and she wasn't much of a healer, even against common maladies. She felt his skin—warm, but she couldn't tell whether that was fever or hard work. He was sweating, she thought, another sign that his trouble probably wasn't sunstrike. His hair was still wet with river water and dripping down Valadan's side to pock the dust.

"Is he dead?" Enna asked hopefully, drawn out of the

kitchen by the commotion for her first close sight of the enemy.

"No. But that's all I *am* sure of." The makeshift bandage about his head had slipped, and Druyan pushed it farther back, into his hair. She ought to take it off—it was filthy and useless. The wound was ugly as ever, the bruised flesh surrounding it going yellow and green at the edges, the scab over the actual cut seeping bright fresh blood. Yet it seemed clean enough, despite the available dirt. No sign that it was festering, gone bad enough to render the man unconscious.

"I wouldn't look much farther for his trouble than that head clout," Enna said professionally, following her thought. "Split his skull, maybe. Someone caught him a good one," she added proudly.

Druyan was less certain. "He got this a fortnight ago. I didn't think it was still bothering him." She felt for the beat of his heart, pressing her fingers under the edge of his jaw till she located a pulse. His heartbeat was a touch rapid, but there was no faltering. That was good.

"Made him dizzy," Dalkin volunteered brightly. "He bent over to pick up a sheaf and went right on his face. And then he was sick," the boy added, with relish.

Where was I? Druyan wondered. The man hadn't complained—he'd just done whatever she'd ordered, without comment. But then, did you confess the truth to your enemy, your captor, if you were sick and all but helpless? She'd told him to work, he'd worked—it wasn't as if they'd conferred on each other's health, asked how the day was going. He'd managed not to fall on his face in front of her. For a while.

"What's the matter with his hands?" Pru asked suddenly. The girl had stepped near—now she retreated hastily, without the poke at him she'd intended.

"His hands?" The last place she'd expect to see trouble that would make a man swoon and not wake was his hands, unless they clutched a wine bottle. Druyan looked, saw what Pru had noticed, and felt a sick twisting in her stomach.

The frayed strips of rag wrapped about Kellis' palms were sinking into the flesh. His fingers were puffed like black sausages, cooked to bursting. The color wasn't dirt—the skin itself was darkened, almost seemed burned. The right hand was the worst, but his left hand was bleeding from a dozen shallow cuts, and it was swollen, as well, if less severely.

His hands hadn't looked like that, in the barley field.

Enna, whose own hands swelled and altered color with the weather, if less dramatically, looked stricken with instinctive sympathy. That lasted a wide-eyed instant—then she mumbled something about marsh fever making bodies swell, and that they ought to get him off the place before the malady started to spread.

"I can treat marsh fever," Druyan said uncertainly.

"But, Lady—"

"I promised him he'd be free when the harvest was in, Enna," Druyan answered harshly. "I didn't intend that to mean he'd be thrown out on the road, free to die just the other side of our gate!" Something was nagging at her—the iron moon-crescents of the sickles, which had to be kept sharp by hand, with a whetstone, because you dared not wreak a charm of keen-edge on any implement made of cold iron. She had heard work charms for virtually any situation—some performed truly, like her weather charms, while others did not seem to—but there were no convenient little magicks worked upon iron. None. Cold iron spoiled magic. It was a firmly held belief that wizard-folk could not abide even the touch of the metal, that it could function as a protection against bewitching and bespelling, even a bit as small as an old horseshoe nail. She touched the prisoner's right palm gingerly.

Why had he bound his hands with rags? The discolored skin was calloused, he was well used to work. The sliding cloth was more apt to *produce* blisters than prevent them—

unless he had been trying to keep from touching the wood-cased iron haft of the sickle.

Which he had not been able to manage, in the end. To reap grain, he'd been forced to grip the sickle firmly all day, every day, for the best part of a week.

The wind was rising. White castles of cloud were sweeping in from the unseen sea. Their flat bottoms were dark with rain, black as Kellis' hands. Druyan felt every hair on her head lift at the root and knew there would be lightning, too, white fire out of the heavens. Beside her, Valadan stamped fretfully, bothered more by the weather than his burden.

"Dalkin, get the wagon over to the sheepfold and get that barley under cover! Unhitch and shove the wagon right in—I'll come help you in a minute. Pru, I know you're tired, but go make sure Meddy has the flock in a sheltered spot—*above* the tideline. Enna, I think we'll need to eat indoors. Lyn can help." Druyan jerked her head at the building sky and knew she need offer no more explanation. They were all bred to Esdragon's climate.

The entire population of Splaine Garth scattered, but Enna was close to her kitchen and could afford to linger a moment more. "What are you doing about *that?*" She inclined her head at the unconscious man draped over the horse.

Druyan frowned and thought again of faint suspicions. "Put him in the barn, for now," she decided.

"What if he's sick?" Enna jabbed a finger, careful not actually to touch him. "What if it's plague?"

"The horses won't catch plague." Druyan took hold of Valadan's bridle. There was a small box stall, where they put the weanling colts till they got over wanting their mothers. It was very secure, nearly as secure as the root cellar.

Enna fluttered after her like a sparrow. "But *you* could, Lady! Leave him—"

"Where?" Druyan asked, exasperated. "Out in the marsh? It's going to storm, Enna. I can't just throw him out into it—I can't even see how we'd get him off this place, short of dragging him!"

"My lord wouldn't like this—"

Probably not, Druyan agreed dismally, glancing sidelong at Valadan. But even assuming that Travic would have had the stomach to knife the man, so as to bury him and be done with it, she didn't herself. And *she* had to make the choices for Splaine Garth now. She urged the stallion to walk faster, till Enna fell behind and had to give up.

They clopped into the darkness of the barn. Valadan halted before his stall. It was not habit—the empty loose box was next to his, and with the weanlings now pastured, a few flakes of hay were now kept there. Druyan spread the fodder into a more or less bed-size pile, retreiving an egg one of the hens had left there. Not so bad a bed, once she threw a bit of sacking on top. She slept on straw herself, in summer.

What if he dies? she wondered suddenly, thinking of the trouble of burying him.

Yet not much more difficult than juggling the man from Valadan's back to the makeshift bed. She came around Valadan's off side, because Kellis' feet were on that side, then reconsidered. Probably she could not pull him down without dropping him, so at least she shouldn't drag him off to land on his head. He outweighed her, she wouldn't be able to hold him. How was she to manage?

The stallion pawed the dirt restlessly—then all at once folded his knees and lowered his forequarters delicately, until he knelt by his mistress and the mound of cloth-covered hay.

"Oh! That *is* better," Druyan said. She got a firm grip on Kellis' belt, gave a tug, and eased him onto the sacking with nary a bump, as Valadan nimbly arose.

She did not expect the motion to revive the man—not when many deliberate attempts had done nothing—but he moaned as his face slid over Valadan's shoulder, low in his throat, like a sick dog. Druyan felt a pang of relief. That was that, then. He'd come out of the faint, eat and then sleep, and be on his way come the morning, soon to be no more than an incident among other incidents.

She filled a pail with water and put it where he would be able to reach it, then, as an afterthought, used a little to bathe his face—and his hands, which were beyond comprehension, inexplicable. She pulled the rags away—they were cutting into the swollen flesh, and there was no use leaving them in place. His eyelids twitched when she began working, and he whimpered that starved-dog whine, but he must have decided coming awake was not presently a good idea—after a moment he was still once more.

When she went out, Druyan dropped the crossbar into place, to hold the door from the outside. True, the man was free to go when he chose—but not to wander off into the building storm.

The rain didn't formally arrive till after they'd feasted themselves half sick, made skeletons of two fat pullets and memories of three dried-cherry pies. They drank ale, danced raggedy dances before the wide kitchen hearth, and sang ancient harvest songs to the barley maid. It was a dismal shadow of other harvest celebrations, yet a brighter time than any Druyan had anticipated. For all the missing faces—those apt to return and those fated never to—they'd done it. The weather had held long enough. There was more back-breaking work ahead, threshing, but not that night. She would not need to cut another stalk of barley for a whole year. It was a moment to savor.

Thunder jarred the ground under her feet as Druyan dashed across the yard, head ducked out of the wind and the fat drops it was slinging. Safe in the doorway, she halted, letting the cool wind brush her hot face before she pulled the portal closed after her. Rain or no, it was refreshing, a delicious feeling after the long run of stifling days and ovenish nights. The storm was fiercely welcome. Enna was abed, almost pain-free thanks to ale and cider, and her mistress felt free to roam her own farm, to enjoy the cool wind and get her feet wet if she chose.

She'd just been to the orchard—the wool-wrapped ball had tumbled from the tree fork and was nowhere to be found. The basket had blown away from the little clump of barley plants, and she had found it only when it bumped her ankles, like a friendly cat.

After the rush of the wind, the barn's stillness was striking—the thunder was muffled by the roof and the hay-mow overhead. Druyan could hear horses munching hay, the milch cow stamping at a fly. Chickens fussed sleepily from their roosts among the roof beams above.

Druyan lit the lantern that hung by the door and walked with it to the box stalls. Mostly she saw the bay and chestnut rumps of drowsy horses, but Valadan left his hay and came to gaze and blow a soft greeting at her. She fed him an early apple, letting his lips brush her palm, knowing her fingers safe from teeth if not from tickling.

He has waked.

Druyan peered through the bars into the next box, while Valadan licked her now-empty palm, his whiskers teasing her skin again. She could see the man lying much as she'd left him on the bed of hay. "Are you sure?" she whispered. "I brought some food—"

There came a rustling from the pallet. Slight—he might only have turned his head. She hadn't seen movement. It might as easily have been a mouse, running through the bedding. Druyan hesitated, then lifted the bar and went in—careful to leave the door standing wide, and Valadan's, as well. That way she had both an escape route and a rescuer ready to hand. She did not expect she would need either.

"Are you awake?" Druyan knelt and began to open her bundle, folding the napkin back from about a wooden bowl full of scraps of chicken and bread soaked in gravy. Straw whispered once again—the prisoner had turned his head toward her. His eyes were open.

The last thing Kellis expected to wake to was amber lamplight and the comforting smell of food. He blinked slowly, his eyelids heavy as if they had been weighted with coins for his burial. He found himself in a little room, a most curious room, and he was lying on the floor. He had no idea why. After a while he recognized the snort of a horse feeding close by and decided that the inexplicable thing he could see partway up one wall must be a manger. He was in a stall, then, lying on soft straw or hay rather than the damp earth of the cellar, with what looked like a vast space above him—the lamplight did not pierce it well, but he could see that there was room for him to stand without bumping his head against the roof.

He could remember—assuming he hadn't dreamed it— that the barley was all cut, every stem of it in every field. Therefore, thereby, he was free, though that didn't explain why he was in what must be a barn or byre.

Free—and crippled, thanks to the cold iron sickle. Kellis did not have to glance at his hands to know that. He did not need the confirmation of his eyes, when every beat of his heart sent a throb of pain through his hands, lightning flashes into all ten of his fingers. The rest of him ached, from work and possibly from being dragged to wherever he was from wherever he had been, and even as he lay quite still his half-seen surroundings seemed to move gently to and fro, like weeds underwater. A fever sensation, probably, very like the aftermath of dream trance, unpleasant but not lasting. The hands could be another matter; there was no knowing.

Kellis was afraid to look, terrified of what he might see, so he watched the woman instead, as she fussed with the food she'd brought for him. He had no appetite for it, but as she moved the lamplight gleamed on her hair, and he could watch that, trying not to think of anything else save the play of gold on that red-gold . . .

It was hard to remember to be properly wary of the raider—he looked so afraid of *her*, and so ill on top of it. Druyan felt pity, whether dangerous or not. "I've brought you some supper, and some aloe for your hands," she said. Wind lashed the barn wall, little cold rivers of air raised dust whorls inside, made the lantern light flare and waver before the gusts got smothered in her skirts. Druyan considered whether she'd need to feed the man. He hadn't reached for the food, and she doubted he could grasp it, now that she got a better look at his hands.

He let her lift his head and give him a sip of water. "You fainted," Druyan told him, though he hadn't asked what had befallen him, or where he was. Perhaps he wasn't well enough to question good fortune or to know he wasn't back in the cellar and out of his head with fever. He didn't *look* very well, and her fingers' brief contact judged his skin as too warm for the shift in the weather. Gone dry, too, which was fever, or too much work in the heat, or both together.

He couldn't swallow well enough, lying flat, to quench his thirst. After a moment he struggled to hitch himself into a sitting position, and Druyan let him, offering the cup again when he could drink more easily. He shook his head weakly at the food, so she set it aside for the moment and turned to the cloths and salve she had brought.

She stroked aloe sap onto his appalling hands and wrapped them all round with clean rags to hold the healing juice in place longer. The treatment must have hurt him, but the man gave no sign beyond a single flinch when the sap first touched his darkened skin. The swelling was so bad, Druyan couldn't feel his knucklebones, and she was glad when the bandages hid the worst of it from her sight. Some part of her dinner wasn't lying easily in her stomach. She wished she knew healing charms as well as she did those for weather.

He had handled cold iron, and his hands had puffed up after, like a cow dying with the bloat. What did that mean? That question had brought Druyan out, into the night, as much as any love of the weather or concern for a sick man. What else *could* it mean, but what she suspected? Druyan offered more water, and he drank with his eyes shut, carefully not looking at her.

"What was your job, in the raiding?" she asked him when the cup was empty.

"I was ... the scout, Lady," he confessed reluctantly, watching her warily now.

"Hard to scout a place you've never seen." Druyan swallowed, then risked, "Does being a wizard help with that?"

There was real fear in his eyes, instantly. Panic, even, as if she'd shown him a weapon. He tried to scramble back from her and to stand as he did it. He collided with the wall before he'd gone ten inches and sat helpless on the pile of hay and sacking, his breath coming hard and fast, his swaddled hands fumbling to either side of him. "I'm no wizard," Kellis said unconvincingly.

Druyan shook her head. "Of course not. What happened to your hands?"

"I'm not—" He seemed to think hard about that, as if his life depended on his answer. Maybe he thought it did. "I'm not used to the work," he settled.

"Neither am I." Druyan looked him straight in the eye, then lifted her two hands as evidence. "All *I* got was a broken blister and a few cuts from a fresh edge."

"Lady, you said I could go when the harvest was in—" He spoke desperately, reminding her of their bargain, buying time to gather himself for another attempt at rising. His skin had gone the color of brown eggshells, the only blood in it around that nasty cut on his forehead. His eyes looked dark as stones, unfocused. "You said I'd be free."

"That's so." Druyan cocked her head at the persistent drum of rain on the slate roof above the mow. "You might want to wait for daylight. The rain will probably have stopped by then. You might even want to wait till your hands heal. You've worked hard. I'll feed you till you're well enough to go. Seeing as how you aren't a wizard," she added.

"I should go now, Lady." *Better for both of us,* his gray eyes suggested.

She couldn't sanely dispute that. This was a stranger, come to steal and do murder—that was what she knew of him. Dangerous. If he was willing to go, that was surely a fine thing. It did away with a lot of problems. Anyone would agree with that—the storm must be warping her judgment, making her wild and foolish enough to suggest that he stay. She'd had too much cider, toasting to the barley maid.

Druyan numbly watched the man get his legs under him and struggle to his feet, watching him pressing a shoulder against the wall till he found his balance and could step away, cradling one hand with the other. She knelt frozen and watched him walk to the door. She'd never have wagered that he'd achieve three steps in a row, but he did. Over the partition, Valadan's sparkling eyes likewise observed.

Thunder cracked just overhead. With every window close-shuttered to keep out the rain, there wasn't the usual warning of a flash. Just the appalling noise, as if the sky split, the earth cracked. Druyan saw the man startle at the explosion of sound, miss his unsteady footing entirely, and try frantically to get his balance back. He couldn't do it— Kellis went sprawling headlong, landing helplessly on his outflung hands. Druyan thought he screamed, but more thunder drowned lesser sounds and shook the rafters.

He didn't try to get up again. He didn't make another sound, just lay there like a discarded doll wearing odd white mittens. Hail began to hammer the roof. After a moment it was plain enough that he had fainted, and that he would be going nowhere anytime soon, whether he should or not, no matter what was best. Druyan dragged him back to the pile of hay, rolled him onto it, and fetched a blanket to throw over her uninvited guest.

Kellis had taken a fever, whatever else ailed him, whatever he was or was not. His forehead was blistering hot when Druyan took a few moments after breakfast to check on him, and he would not open his eyes, though he mumbled and turned away from her touch. It was difficult to get food into him—he spent most of the next three days drifting in and out of wakefulness, quite uninterested in his surroundings. Druyan brewed every tisane she knew in an

attempt to bring his temperature down again—feverfew
blossoms and willow bark, comfrey leaves—but no remedy
seemed to work. He had no spots, no cough or other sign
of plague. The fever might have to burn itself out, Druyan
thought. She hoped he would survive the conflagration. She
salved his hands each day with fresh aloe and wrapped
them with comfrey leaves and clean linen, but there was little improvement to be seen. Mostly the man slept, as if
waking or dying were equally too much trouble to bear.

Enna upbraided her mistress for wasting time and energy
nursing a wretch she should have been thankful to see dead,
but Druyan ignored the criticism. More work to bury him
than to nurse him, she said wryly, and put an end to the discussion. No one else took sick, depriving Enna of an argument; and before she could try out others, there was a
change at last. The third night, the fever broke, for no cause
Druyan could fathom and no credit at all to her herb lore.

Had he been sufficiently aware, Kellis would have willed
himself to die—it seemed the only escape left open to him.
But he lay adrift on a sea of heat and pain, prey to unpleasant dreams that robbed his sleep of any true rest, unable to
think with clarity enough to put an end to his misery.

He knew, of old, that courting death hardly guaranteed
achieving it. It was monstrously unfair, but true. His spirit
was firmly bound to his body, and he was too confused by
illness to remember how to sever the link deliberately. The
irony of that made his cracked lips twitch into a smile—he
knew so many who had found their way along the trails to
the afterlife so easily, without any effort on their parts at all.
His family, for instance. His clan. In his burning dreams
they all lived again, all died once more, and he was helpless again, unable to follow his people on their final migra-
tion, abandoned and cast out and alone. He howled as he
had then, screaming his grief to the darkness that surrounded him—and woke drenched in sweat, still tasting bitter medicines on his lips.

He wept scalding tears till sleep swept him up once more.

No one in Esdragon had an outdoor threshing floor. Some farmers built special barns for the purpose of processing grain—Splaine Garth used the large floor space of the main barn, where the cattle were penned during the worst winter weather. There was room to drive the threshing sledge around in a tight circle atop the spread barley, its weight beating the ripe grains loose from the straw. Usually one of the draft horses provided the power, but Valadan's nimbleness made him apt to the work, too—his strong legs stood up to the constant circling with none of the strain and swelling the more massive drafters suffered betimes.

The sledge bumped merrily over the fanned-out sheaves, weighted with as many bodies as would climb atop it. This was great fun—at the outset. After a couple of days every soul on the farm was heartily sick of the process. The girls complained that Meddy was letting the sheep stray and Rook was not preventing her; Dalkin was eager to begin winnowing the threshed grain once the rain had stopped, while the wind held strong. Myriad farm tasks pressed, offering opportunities of escape and respite.

Druyan was as bored as any of them. She had never threshed before, only seen it done, but it wasn't hard work for the driver, and it wasn't enthralling. It just went on, endlessly, numbingly. Sensing impending mutiny, she released her crew to other tasks and wondered what she might use to weight the sledge in their place. Rocks would do, of course, or barrels, but something that could get itself on and off the sledge bed under its own power would be nicer. Enna was enduring a bad spell thanks to the wet weather, and the bouncing would be sheer agony for her. One sheep didn't weigh enough to help and more would be impossible to manage. A pig was unlikely to cooperate.

Druyan felt eyes watching her, and saw them, in the open doorway of the box stall. She'd been leaving it unbarred—what use locking up a man too sick to stand? A notion teased at her. Kellis was just well enough to navigate from one side of the stall to the other—the fever had left him wobbly as a wormy kitten. But he could sit—and he was close by. She halted Valadan—and the sledge—with a quiet word, a twitch of the reins.

"Kellis, come over here." He looked startled, probably because her tone made it as much an invitation as an order, but he stepped through the doorway after only the barest hesitation.

The slippery grain stalks were tricky footing, but he managed, frowning at the effort it cost him. "Lady?" he asked, arriving at her side a little out of breath.

"Climb on. Better sit down," Druyan recommended, amused by his perplexed expression. Maybe he was expecting her to order him out of the barn, off the farm before she had to feed him another meal. When he had settled, she started around in another circle, fairly slowly. His added weight helped, she could tell by the way the sledge rode.

"What does this do?" he asked after their third circuit, bracing against the bouncing, then yielding to it as he realized his stiffness let the motion jar him.

The query was startling—hadn't he been watching, and hadn't they been threshing right under his crooked nose? Had he never seen such work before? He seemed serious. He was watching intently, waiting for her answer.

"There are rollers under the sledge," Druyan finally explained. "Dragging them over the barley loosens the seed heads, beats them off the stalks. The more weight on the sledge, the better it works."

He digested that gravely, shifting again to a more secure position. Hard when you couldn't use your hands, Druyan supposed. He was trying to hold on, also trying not to hurt himself.

"Don't your people farm?" she asked, wondering how they threshed their grain, assuming they grew any. By beating it with flails, by hand? That would be even more tedious than sledging.

A startled, wide-open gray glance. "No."

Small wonder he'd had to be shown how to use the sickle. "City-born?" Druyan guessed.

"No, Lady."

There'd been much speculation about where the raiders hailed from but precious few firm answers. Captured men had proved reluctant to talk. The bandits came, stole, and vanished, leaving only destruction and anger behind. Druyan wondered if this man might tell her now, not realizing what he did. Worth a try. "Where *are* you from?" Clever of her, if she could find out.

"Vossli." His answer was muffled, as if he were struggling not to put feeling into the name.

"Where's that?" Druyan asked, genuinely interested. "I never heard of it." Certainly it wasn't a place anyone had guessed, gossiping.

"Across the sea." He inhaled sharply, let the breath out slowly. "It isn't called that anymore. The name means 'the purple grassland.' " His gray eyes slipped out of focus, as if he looked over a far distance, rolling waves of lavender and green.

Over the sea. That meant none of his people would be back till the next spring, Druyan realized. They were entering into the season of storms, out upon the Great Sea. Even Esdragon's bold coastal fishers stayed in sight of land during those foul months, and no ships crossed the sea roads. Kellis had been left behind, abandoned, and must know that. It was too late for him to get home. He was still every bit a prisoner, whether of hers or merely of sea reach and weather.

"Kellis—" She put a hand out, almost touched his shoulder. "Come sailing weather, you can send word. Your family will ransom you."

He turned his head away, rather than shaking it. "I have no family," he said softly. "There's no one to pay to have me back. And if there *were*, they wouldn't do it," he added bitterly. "The sea raiders swept over my people long before they found yours. I am not one of the Eral, and when I joined them I made myself an outcast from my own clans."

He rubbed at his forehead with the side of his hand. "I don't want to go back."

The sledge bumped and bounced. "There are probably better ways of winning a welcome in Esdragon than scouting for a band of murdering pirates," Druyan observed wryly.

He shot her a look, out the tail of his eye. "They have all the ships. I needed to get across the Great Sea."

"Why?"

She could tell he wasn't going to answer. He'd said more in the last circle over the grain than he had the whole while he'd been with them. After a moment she observed: "Your hands are better."

He could not deny that, she'd seen him using them to hold onto the sledge, however gingerly. "Yes, Lady. Thank you for the aloe—there's nothing I know of that could have done more to heal them." He flexed his left hand—she could tell he didn't have the full range of its motion back, but it was coming, and obviously using it hurt him less than it had a few days earlier.

"Last time I saw a hand swell like that, it was snake-bit," Druyan said. "And it had to be taken off, in the end. You're lucky—but then it wasn't a snake that bit *you*."

She was beginning to suspect that he wanted to get off the sledge, away from her interrogation. Druyan deliberately drove a little faster when she saw Kellis shift, so he'd have to think harder about jumping. Finally he nearly *fell* off, and she took pity and halted. She turned toward him, so he could not as easily look away from the confrontation.

"I asked you flat out whether you were a wizard. You said *no* with your lips, but every other part of you screamed *yes*, loud enough to wake the stones. They say wizard-folk can't handle cold iron, and *you* don't seem to be able to touch it without some cost. Am I wrong about that?"

He still looked trapped, although the sledge no longer moved. He looked a touch green, as well. He might not feel able to stand, Druyan supposed. She pressed on, undeterred by mercy.

"Look, if I haven't killed you yet for a murdering scoundrel, what's to fear? If I wanted you dead, don't you think I had chances enough while you were sick? I told Enna it would be too much trouble to bury you, but it really wouldn't have been that bad. I could have fed you to the pigs."

He took what she meant for a jest as literal truth, and went as pale as he could. His dark brows looked as if they'd been painted on with lampblack. The gray-gold eyes went dark as wet slate.

"Don't faint on me," Druyan ordered sternly. "I need you to help fork this straw out of the way and spread more sheaves. Can you do that?"

He flexed his hands again, then nodded reluctantly.

"If you have to be sick, try not to do it in the grain. The fork's wooden, it won't poison you." She pointed at the pitchfork, leaning among the waiting sheaves. "You want to eat, you work. Got that?"

He nodded again, looking confused. He got off the sledge, took two steps, stopped, and turned back to face her. Druyan unhitched Valadan. She'd let the horse go out into the open air awhile and have some grass while they did work he wasn't needed for. It was raining again, but he'd never mind that. The horse had been foaled in Esdragon, rained on every day of his life.

"Lady?"

Beneath her hand, Valadan's shoulder quivered. His sharp ears flicked back. Druyan froze. She was afraid to look—a pitchfork made a weapon, even if unskillfully held in crippled hands. *What have I done?*

"You guess rightly about my people—cold iron *is* a poison to us," Kellis said. He wasn't moving, she could tell by the distance his voice carried. Druyan relaxed as she felt Valadan settle under her fingers.

"When the Eral came at us, we tried to fight them. We even learned to band together, all the clans—though that is far from our nature and was a great wonder—but we found we could not stand against their iron swords and axes. We would have yielded them the cropland, we are not truly a farming folk. We had no fixed homes to defend. We were used to moving with the flocks, the herds. Summer after summer we did that. But we would come to our summer pastures, and there were strangers camped there. The Eral. There were more and more of them. And then they began to drive us away. They hunted us like deer, slaughtered us without mercy."

"So you came here, with your enemies?" That didn't follow. Druyan turned and arched a brow at him. "That's a very odd thing to do, you'll agree."

Kellis looked unhappy—a different shade of a continual misery. "I am not what *you* call a wizard. I know herbcraft and a scattering of charms—such as I have seen you use yourself, Lady." The challenge was plain. Was *she* witchbred? "Beyond that . . ." He shook his head. "I can foresee, a little. Nothing very useful. And that's all. But long ago my people learned that even so little is enough to get a man killed. Yes, I lied to you—I was afraid. I didn't want to die here, especially not the way some folk kill witches."

She knew what he meant. Fire and cold iron weapons.

Valadan stretched his nose toward Kellis, snorting gently. The man regarded him nervously, as if expecting to be bitten. He held very still.

"Some time after . . . when I had been alone for a while, I heard a tale, of a place where other people like me were banding together. Wizards and charmers and healers, protecting one another, studying, learning, sharing their knowledge out with one another." He shrugged. "My people don't do that. I was apprentice to our shaman, but really we have each of us just whatever we're born with—no more. We don't take from one another or build on what someone else has learned. I would never have gone seeking such a place, I would never have thought I wanted it—but I had no clan. They were all dead, and I was alone . . ."

Valadan was nuzzling his fingers. Kellis looked at the horse as he spoke, as if that made the words come easier.

His fingers began to scratch under the horse's mane, then beneath the harness, where sticky sweat had dried. "I sold my services to an Eral captain gathering a raiding party for the sailing season—it was the only way I knew to get to this side of the Great Sea. I told him I could foresee, that I would warn him if there'd be resistance, tell him ahead which places weren't prepared for an attack, where the plunder would be rich. The Eral may despise us, but they'll use us if they see an advantage. You can imagine for yourself what *my* folk think of such transactions." Valadan was leaning into the scratching now, since he could not roll to ease himself while he still wore collar and harness. "I am an outcast. I sold myself, to come here."

"Something went wrong," Druyan said dryly.

She saw Kellis' mouth twitch slightly, while his fingers worked beneath the headstall. "I was lucky, at first. Or as clever as I thought I was. The captain had no idea that most times the divining bowl doesn't show me much of anything. I didn't have to do it all that often, mostly just say whether there'd be fog in the morning—and I could guess *that* without the bowl." He rubbed behind the stallion's ears. Valadan tilted his head a little toward him. "Then he split off from his partners. I was just about ready to slip off when that happened, and I got trapped into predicting for real. I looked in the bowl, I saw your farm, all peaceful and quiet. I swore to the captain that there'd be no trouble." Valadan sighed as Kellis scratched the top edge of his cheekbones.

Druyan remembered the doughty resistance Travic had put up to being robbed. "You're right, you're *not* very good at foreseeing."

Kellis nodded, taking no offense. "The trouble is, when I look in the water, I may know *what*, but I don't know *when* I'm seeing. It's seldom more than a day, but which? It matters. Tomorrow? Yesterday? I don't always have a point of reference. So I flat-out guessed." He adjusted a buckle that seemed too tight against Valadan's hide. The hair was rubbed a bit, the skin beneath untouched.

"And guessed wrong?" Druyan asked.

"I must have been seeing the past day, the day before we'd landed. When all those armed men met us at the gate, the captain was . . . displeased." Kellis touched his bandaged hand to his forehead. "He gave me this personally. You might have thought he was yelling war cries—that was about my people, about shifty treachery being bred into our bones. The last thing I remember of that night is seeing that iron blade coming at my head."

"And that's why they left you." It made absolute sense, finally.

"They could have done worse," Kellis said pragmatically. "They probably would have, if they hadn't been able to get out right away." He gave Valadan a last pat and went slowly to the pitchfork. "Where do you want the straw?"

Druyan gestured at the golden pile. "Over there, for now. This place you heard about—where was it? Did the stories name it?"

"It is called Kôvelir." Valadan had followed Kellis, butting his head against his back, so that he staggered and used the fork for a crutch. "And it's on the bank of a very big river." He put an arm over the stallion's neck and stayed upright. "You're supposed to be outside, I think." He steered the horse toward the door with a nudge or two and urged him through it. Valadan went to the trough, sipped a few sips, then blew across the water playfully.

"If you mean the Est, and I think you do, that's a long way from here," Druyan said. "All the way across Esdragon. Your raider didn't take you far enough."

"I can walk. It's not the same as the sea. It's just land. I can get across it." Kellis began forking straw aside, bending his fingers carefully about the fork's handle.

"You'll be very well advised not to try it in the winter. It rains twice as much then, it's cold, and the roads are hip-deep in mud." Druyan fetched a second fork and set to work alongside him.

"I'm a good walker." Kellis stated it seriously, though they both of them knew that at present it was hard work for him to stand, and she was shifting twice the straw that he was.

He was an honest worker, though. Even half sick as he was, he didn't quit and he didn't complain. Druyan glanced around the barn, contemplating running the farm with the hands she had at her command—her own, and Enna's swollen ones, which did not yield to aloe. Lyn's. Pru's. Dalkin's. Most times she could not imagine succeeding, and so she tried not to look ahead much beyond the next day. It made her nervous. One barley harvest was not a year-and-a-day success. If the duke didn't release her farmhands, possibly she could hire others—assuming she could find any. But surely that would call attention to her precarious position, might even cost her any hope of secrecy and success. Too much to risk.

Kellis was something of a risk, too, but a lesser one, a private one. "I am freeholding this farm," she told him carefully, throwing down fresh sheaves of grain in front of the sledge and feeling she threw all caution to the wind with them. "If I do it for a year and a day, it's mine—so long as no one catches me at it before the time's out and forces me to remarry and leave. I have the apple crop still to get in, cider to press, plowing come the spring, planting, and all the work with the animals. My husband died fighting the sea raiders, and I am owed a blood debt for that." She threw another forkful. Kellis was too winded to copy her. But she had his attention. His brows were knitted into one.

"I'll admit, you had nothing *personally* to do with Travic's death—but you're the only raider around for me to collect the debt from. If I wanted to be sticky about it, only a life can pay for a life, but you're no use to me *dead*. I made you a promise—work the harvest, for your freedom—but that was when I thought there were four of you. Now I want to propose a new bargain, one that suits the realities for both of us."

The dark brows knit again. He said nothing, though.

"You can try walking all winter, to a place that might not

even exist. You can starve, you can freeze, and every sword edge out there will have your name on it. Or—" She leaned on the fork.

She couldn't tell if she was scaring him. She didn't much think so—he was used to worse. Valadan strolled back into the barn, nosing at the straw. "Or you can work for me till the farm's mine. When that day comes, I'll give you a horse, and you can make your way to this dream city of yours easily, before another winter catches you. If the city's there *now*, it'll be there *then*, and you'll stand a chance of reaching it."

She could see him weighing his chances. And trying to stay on his feet.

"Well? Don't keep me waiting. I'm risking just as much as you are, and this may start to seem like a bad idea to me again in a minute. Better grab it while you can."

"Why would you trust me?"

There *was* no good reason. Not desperation, certainly. Not a mad hunch. Never that something in him seemed to call to something in her, the way a distant storm did. Best bury *that* fancy deeper than the sea's bottom. "My horse approves of you," Druyan said, and stroked Valadan's neck, while the stallion nudged her new farmhand halfway out of his cracked boots.

Kellis lay on his back, staring toward the underside of the barn roof. Somewhere beyond that, Valint the Wolfstar coursed the moon-deer. He couldn't see the hunt, of course. If not the roof, then there'd have been clouds to hide the familiar night scene from his eyes. It was always raining.

He might never see it again.

What have I done? he asked himself, shifting on the pile of straw. He'd had the chance to go, to get on with his chosen journey—instead he had agreed to stay, in this place he had passed through only by sheerest chance. Why? He was well enough to travel—barely, but he knew he could manage, this way and that.

Because one place is just like another, his sick heart

whispered darkly, the answer echoing inside his head as if he were nothing more than an empty vault of bone. Or a tomb. *And for all you know, the Wizards' City of Kôvelir is no more than a fever dream. Stay or go—it's all one.*

Combing Out Knots

"I DON'T THINK I care to have *that* in my kitchen."

"I don't recall asking whether you did, Enna," Druyan observed, placidly threading another warp through the second heddle of her great loom. "Surely you don't expect Kellis to chop the vegetables in the barn and then carry them back over here so you can start the stew?" She was pleased with the pale-blue thread in her hands—privet berries stewed for hours to make the dyebath, from her own recipe. The color was mild as the inside of a mussel shell, but once dried it faded no further, come sun or years. It was a flattering shade, too, light yet not showing dirt readily, and cloth woven of it would sell swiftly.

"And to give him a knife—Lady, he could do for us both and no one the wiser till Dalkin missed his supper and thought to wonder about it. He—"

"It's just a little brass blade. He can't very well chop carrots and turnips with his teeth, Enna. And you can't chop them when your hands are bad." Druyan counted carefully, chose another hole to thread. "You keep telling me it's not *my* place to be cooking—"

"And it is not! If my lord looked back and saw—"

"I'd like to think Travic would be proud of us, Enna," Druyan said. "We paid the tithes. We even managed to get some of the cider laid down for brandy. The root cellar's bursting with potatoes and turnips, the smokehouse is

87

stuffed with hams and bacon. Considering that Duke Brioc decided that his summer army ought to spend the winter building a seawall and never sent our men home, I think we've done wonderfully well."

Enna's eyes flashed. "So well that I've got to have a murderer holding a knife right in my own kitchen?"

Druyan threaded another heddle. "Surely you aren't afraid of him, Enna? Not with that iron horseshoe sewn into the hem of your skirt?" she added slyly.

"My lady, you'd do better to copy me than to mock me for that."

Druyan shook her head. "I don't think I could stand bruising my shins on it all day."

"Make fun! But he's not sick and hurt now. He's dangerous, Lady, that's the plain truth!"

"You think I trust him too much, too soon." She'd heard the accusation a dozen different ways, most of them unsubtle in the extreme. "Should I trust Kellis *less* than he's earned? He didn't have to work so hard to bring the barley in, Enna. Or do all the slaughtering and butchering. Dig turnips till his hands bled. He could have quit. He didn't. He's never given us less than a full day's work."

Enna had the grace to fall silent—many a day her swollen fingers prevented her doing much in the way of work. Druyan inspected a snarl in the thread, hoping to avoid a weak spot apt to break halfway through the weaving, at great inconvenience. Someone had been careless in carding the wool—there was a bit of burr spun into the core of the yarn, making the bump. She discarded the offending length and put in another. "I feel quite safe enough with a nail in my pocket." Truth to tell, she'd have felt safe enough *without* that tiny bit of cold iron. If Kellis did no harm, 'twas hardly because everyone at Splaine Garth carried some object made of iron to ensure his behavior. She'd set him to gathering apples, digging turnips, spreading manure on the fallow fields, tending the pigs and butchering those they'd salted down for winter. He'd never once tried to run away—not that there was anywhere for him to run *to*. And she had trusted him with all sorts of tools, most of them lethal if he'd wanted them to be. He was unfamiliar and unskilled with some, but never dangerous to anyone other than himself. She didn't fear a kitchen knife in his hands, whatever Enna said.

They both heard the door close.

"Where's he gone?" Enna asked, voice too shrill.

"I asked him to bring in a bucket of water when he'd done with the vegetables," Druyan said patiently. "He can put the kettle over the fire for you—it's heavy when it's full. Then ask him to come to me here—I need someone to hold the warp ends while I wind the back beam."

Enna's sharp intake of breath spoke volumes. The corner of the hall, where Druyan's loom stood, was farther into the house than Kellis had yet been permitted. "M'lady, let me."

Druyan shook her head firmly. "You have the cooking to see to, and it's too chill for you in here, even with the fire lit. Kellis needs to be in here anyway—I'm going to have him card wool. There's still most of the spring shearing to be dealt with, and it's not *that* long till next shearing, when you think about it. It's past time that fleece was spun and dyed. I've got the dyestuffs, it's only waiting on the spinning—and that waits on the carding."

"Dalkin—"

"Dalkin leaves too many stems and burrs in the wool." Druyan forestalled the next argument. "Pru has no interest in wool once it's off her sheep's backs. Lyn *never* did decent carding. The truth is, they're not children any longer." Carding was children's work, while those children were young enough to think of teasing and combing the raw fleece with the teasel carding combs as a sport or at least one of the more desirable of winter chores. Its delights palled as one grew older—Druyan herself preferred spinning the combed wool into yarn, she could not deny that. And she liked dyeing and weaving still better. The best carders were those too young to rebel. Or those like Kellis, who'd do whatever he was asked, and not protest that the task wasn't properly his.

She looked up a few moments later to see him standing in the doorway, as if uncertain about his orders, his right to venture farther into the room. Probably Enna had blistered his ears with a description of the fate he'd earn if he overstepped the letter of Druyan's instructions. His hands were red from a long bout of scrubbing, peeling, and chopping vegetables for the stewpot. Druyan motioned him closer and thrust a bunch of warp ends into each fist.

"Just hold these firm. Don't pull on them, just hold on. I need to keep an even tension while I wind on, but that's my worry."

"You're a weaver," he said, as if surprised.

It had not, Druyan supposed, been much in evidence ere then. The busy weeks of the harvest, the necessity of undertaking tasks she'd had only a touching knowledge of in other years—she'd had no leisure for her usual work. And she'd not have been doing it where he'd have seen. "Yes. Most of the cloth for the household, and some to sell at the market fair. Good thing wool keeps—I'm behind, this year." She cranked the broad back beam slowly, taking up the slack in the warps, ensuring that all ran straight with her free hand. "You can step closer to the loom when that gets tight." He nodded his understanding. "Do your folk weave?" Surely they must—he wore cloth, not tanned skins. She'd never heard tell of a folk who didn't make some cloth.

"Our looms are smaller," Kellis explained. "Not in a great frame like this—and upright. Our weavers hang the beam from a tree, tie rocks to the warp ends to keep the tension."

"You'd need a very tall tree to get much length," Druyan observed.

He nodded. "They don't weave *beltrans* unless they're near the forest. The loom's easy to transport, though—and it needs to be. We move with the flocks, follow the herds whenever the grass fades. A loom must travel easily, because it's often."

"So you know how to card wool, then?" Druyan asked

craftily. She'd wound on all the way, and now she took
the ends from him, deftly tying them in little bunches to the
clothbeam, one after another. Kellis glanced about the
room—shadowy the farther one ventured from the one unshuttered window. He could not help but see the sacks of
rolled fleeces, a half score of them, waiting. He shut his
eyes.

"Yes," he said wearily. "I'm afraid I do know how to
comb wool."

"Good," Druyan answered brightly. He didn't bother
with the stupid things some men would have said. He
didn't plead that he was a warrior, that the task was beneath
him. She approved of that. "You can start anywhere."

She watched out the corner of her eye as he walked to
the sacks. A set of combs lay atop the nearest, and a sheaf
of dry teasels stood ready to hand, to refresh the combs as
need be. Kellis untied one sack, unrolled the fleeces within,
and inspected the creamy wool, sinking his fingers deep to
gauge the length of staple.

"Lady, do you want me to sort as I go, or should I card
the tops first and leave the coarse stuff for later?"

The question fairly stunned her. Dalkin would have
carded all the wool together, the choice and the so-dirty-
'twas-next-to-useless, Druyan thought—at least till she'd
caught him at it. She considered how she'd *want* the job
done, not merely how she was likely to get it. "There's
plenty of room in here," she finally decided. "Why don't
you sort today while the light's good? Chuck all the belly
wool in that far corner—if we have enough of the better
fleece, then perhaps I won't spin that at all. Just boil it
clean and use it to restuff a few of the bed pallets."

Kellis nodded agreement and set to work, opening sacks
and picking through the fleeces within. Druyan took up her
shuttle and wove a few inches of plain weave to settle the
warp threads, beat firmly till she had a solid edge against
the clothbeam. When she looked up again, she was startled
to behold half a dozen fluffy white piles, growing in a
ragged circle about the sacks and Kellis.

He must actually know what he's doing, she marveled. Most folk—even many spinners—sorted fleeces crudely, into clean-enough and not-clean-enough to spin. If Kellis was making more than two piles, then he must be aware of such subtle nuances as length of staple, texture, the abundance or lack of crimps along the locks of wool. And when he began carding, he therefore wouldn't be mingling fibers fine enough for the lightest of summer gowns with those better suited to being woven into a hearth rug. While her mind chewed that over—beyond amazement, almost dazed by such good fortune—her shuttle flew back and forth like a barn swallow with chicks to tend. Thread by thread, she began to create the pattern of the weave.

She wasn't using a second color in this cloth, so Druyan had threaded three harnesses when she set the warp, to weave an intricate texture, subtle as the shadows of grass blades in a field. She lost herself in the work for a long while, and by the time Enna disturbed her the light was going and her shoulders were aching. She had, however, done better than a cubit of fine cloth, and set the shed patterns into her head so firmly that it would be second nature to her for so long as she required it to be.

"Lady, the bread's just out of the oven, and the meat's resting, ready to carve. Will you leave this awhile?"

Druyan straightened, putting a nursing hand to the cramp in the small of her back. "Before I starve or go blind?" she teased. She could hear voices in the kitchen; they'd all be waiting to hear whether they could eat yet. "Yes, Enna. The light's faded, we'd better leave off for today."

Enna nodded and retreated to her domain. A couple of sharp commands preceded her into the kitchen proper, and there was a sudden clatter of crockery.

Kellis got to his feet and laid down the combs atop one of the sacks. "Lady? Shall I feed the horses?"

He had made good progress carding, Druyan saw—there was a great heap of rolags lying ready for her spindle. After supper, she thought, by the kitchen fire's warmth and light. He'd been so silent, she'd forgotten his task while she was busy at her own—never noticed him sitting down to it, in fact, once he'd done sorting.

"Dalkin can help you," she said, giving her loom a last glance, trying not to be tempted back to it. "Get him out from under Enna's feet while she sets the meal out, he'll live longer." She smiled. "Mind he doesn't slip extra corn to that pony of his—we're eating hams from pigs that weren't half so well fattened."

It was pushing things just a touch, to expect Enna to tolerate Kellis at table with them. He made that reality less awkward by staying behind in the barn watering the stock after Dalkin had finished doling out feed and returned to his own supper. Druyan took Kellis his portion later, after angrily adding more bits of meat to the stew and the breadcrusts Enna had left cooling in the crockery bowl by the door. The scraps put down for the cats were more generous, Druyan noted. Not that carding wool was fieldwork, but the man was thin enough almost to see through—and with Enna bound that he'd not have one morsel more than would keep life in his body, likely to remain so, just when every other creature on the place was laying on fat to better withstand the winter cold.

She heard humming as she entered the barn and paused a moment to listen. Dalkin slept in the kitchen, but that was not to be thought of for Kellis—he still had a bed in the unused stall and seemed content with the arrangement. That door was shut, but Valadan's stood ajar, and she could see Kellis within, busy with brushes. He was humming as he worked—or perchance singing a song that was all but wordless—Druyan caught what seemed like a word now and again, the same one or two, repeated like a chorus.

The song ceased when Valadan pricked his ears at her and nickered softly. The stallion's winter hair was thick, but it shone no less than had his summer coat, in the lantern's buttery glow, and his mane and tail fell tangle-free as rain, testament to Kellis' diligence.

"I should think you'd be weary of brushing," Druyan commented lightly as she set the cloth-draped bowl down on a nearby bench. Kellis put the brushes carefully away and dusted his hands clean against his trews. He was clean-shaven—he'd presented himself for work that way one morning, with his hair cropped, too, at about the level of his earlobes. Druyan had no idea how he'd managed that. The hairline was ragged at the back, where he'd had trouble reaching. The shears they used on the sheep were bronze and were kept in the barn, but she hated to think of him trying to get right down to his skin with those.

"Easier to curry him than to comb burrs out of fleece," Kellis said, giving the stallion's neck a pat. "Different brushes, another grip, eases the cramps out. The wool grease is good for the hands, though. I should have asked before whether you had any."

Keeping clear of iron had done much to heal him, of course, but Druyan had frequently observed Kellis plucking herbs as he chanced upon them in field or dooryard, rubbing the crushed leaves and juices onto his skin, and knew by that token that his hands still bothered him. She was sorry she had not thought of the wool grease, either. She knew how soothing 'twas, if only on the surface. And there were herbs she might have added to it . . .

"It would help Enna's hands, too," Kellis offered. "My people fill mitts with fleece and herbs, warm them by the fire. The patient sleeps with them on, and usually come morning the joints are less swollen."

Druyan frowned, considering. "It certainly wouldn't harm her. It grieves me I'm not a better healer—all Enna's joints go stiff when the weather turns wet—which is most days, here—but her hands always seem the worst, and I have never known what else to do for her. She's in a lot of pain sometimes. Too much for willow tea to deal with."

"Hard to do without hands. You can't favor them like a bad leg—if they hurt, you just have to use them anyway."

He made the statement matter-of-factly and did not seem to notice how Druyan flushed. "If the wool grease helps her, I'll tell Enna whose suggestion it was," Druyan said lamely. "I'm sure you'd rather eat in the kitchen once the weather gets *really* cold."

"I'm fine here, Lady," Kellis said, and sounded sincere, even anxious that she believe him. Possibly he didn't want to eat close by the kitchen knives, any more than Enna wanted him there. Among the animals, he might feel safer.

But horses and cattle grew thick pelts to keep themselves warm. Humankind did not. By midwinter, the water in the barn buckets would be freezing right to the bottom of the pails, some nights, and you couldn't have a fire for warmth in a barn. Even if she gave him thick blankets, she couldn't allow Enna to deny the man a little warmth for part of the evening. There had to be some way . . .

Well, didn't she intend to do an hour or so's worth of spinning before the fire, that night and every night until the needful task was done? What with plying and skeining, didn't the work take most of the winter evenings? And didn't spinning go more than twice as fast as carding? Why should Kellis have his evenings idle? she might ask, if Enna pressed. No harm his doing a few more hours of carding, handy to where she and her spindle were.

Enna was predictably discomfited when Druyan brought Kellis back with her from the barn. Kellis wasn't much happier, Druyan thought—he hitched himself as far back around the edge of the hearth as he could manage, so that he was absolutely out from underfoot and where Enna's gaze would be least likely to fall upon him—particularly once she'd set Dalkin to sharpening the knives and cleavers. Druyan lodged a protest at that, unable to bear the noise of the grindstone and Enna's instructions as to how sharp she wanted the implements to be.

"Enna, I believe he'd get a truer edge if he did that when he could see. Tomorrow, and outside."

"I'd like it done now, Lady." She fixed Dalkin with a glare, to be sure he knew what the order was.

The grindstone whirred uncertainly to life again. Druyan's spindle twirled its way toward the floor. Metal screeched against sandstone. Druyan wound thread about the spindle's shaft, dropped it spinning once more. The thread thinned, broke. She cursed under her breath, then spoke aloud. "That'll do, Dalkin. If the cutlery's too dull to manage the breakfast porridge, there'll be time to hone the cleaver before you start chores. Take the dogs out to the sheepfold."

Dalkin abandoned the grindstone happily, whistling for the sheepdogs and making his escape ere the order could be countermanded. When the door had been slammed twice to close it against the wind nosing outside, the only sounds in the kitchen were the hissing of the fire and the soft brushing of the carding combs working against one another. The spindle traveled in hypnotic silence to the floor, trailing sturdy newmade thread.

Druyan began to hum, the comforting simple rhythm of an ancient carol. When that palled, she shifted tunes to a many-versed ballad about fate-crossed lovers, and stayed with that till she'd run out of verses in her head, even though every verse and chorus hummed just alike. By then the spindle was filled, and she wound the thread off into a skein, ready for dyeing. She thought about colors, mentally tallied the dyestuffs she had already gathered in. The room was still quiet save for the snap of beanpods under Enna's fingers, the whisper of the combs in Kellis' hands.

"Do your people sing, Kellis?" Druyan asked lightly.

He gave a start, and the right-hand comb scraped the inside of his left wrist rather than the wool waiting on the left-hand comb. The firelight washed his face with gold as he looked at Druyan, giving his nose back the straightness it must once have had. The wound on his forehead had finally healed to a pink line that ran crookedly from his hairline to the outer corner of his right eyebrow, and that brow, no longer prisoned by caked blood, raised when something surprised him, even if the rest of his face held carefully still. It did so now, went up like a startled horse's head. He glanced across the hearth at Enna, sorting dried beans and half turning her back, still put out about the matter of the grindstone. "If you ask it, Lady," he said, clearly reluctant, obviously preferring to huddle out of sight, overlooked.

Druyan marveled to herself, that Enna should waste so much of her precious energy safeguarding herself from a man who was manifestly scared to death of *her.* "Give us a tune," she said to Kellis, suddenly full of mischief. "To pass the time."

Sing, she bade him, and there was no way Kellis could tell her—not in front of the other, hostile woman—that his folk sang sometimes for a quite different purpose than passing the hours, and that he had not had a song on his lips for a very long while. She only innocently intended a little entertainment to lighten the work, and if he refused he'd be uncooperative, ungrateful, and deserving rebuke. She had no idea what she was asking. He couldn't say what it meant, when his people sang together, couldn't speak of the bindings made and reinforced within the clan, between families, between lovers. He couldn't tell her that the solitary songs were only for mourning, were so brimming with grief that a lonely person might die just from chance-hearing one . . . His wrist burned, where the misstroke of the comb had scored it, and he tried to let that little pain distract him from the greater agony.

He should sing her one of their weaving songs, she would like that. It was probably what she wanted. But Kellis knew none of those—weaving had not been his craft. He ransacked his mind for something safe, a tune that might not start his pain and loss pouring out of him in a flood he could not stem, a flood that would tear out his heart. He had refused to sing that grief out when he should have, refusing to let himself heal because that healing was an unearned comfort. He did not deserve it. He deserved much the reverse. The result of that denial, however it came about, was a chained wolf, mad from imprisonment and too dangerous to release.

Well, then, a song that could not touch his dangerous heart. Something he had learned by rote, something thereby safe, a song that only told a story, or better still merely played with sounds. Something he had known so long that he would not remember where he had first heard it, or from whose lips. A song sung so often that all the meaning in it had been used up . . .

Druyan couldn't understand a single word of what Kellis sang—pressed, he revealed 'twas a hunting song and did not translate it—but the sound made a pleasant background to chores. His voice was rich, full and expressive, never rough. Even Meddy, lying at his feet and worrying a bit of fleece into felt with her teeth, seemed to appreciate the diversion, and thumped her white-tipped tail when he got to what sounded like a chorus.

Meddy . . .

"What's that dog still doing in here?" Druyan asked, which was not exactly the sort of applause one accorded a performance.

Meddy, who knew very well what "dog" meant and knew trouble when she heard it better than any other creature on the farm, being so often the maker of it, strove to hide once more in the shadows, but Kellis snared her by the ruff without even losing the combs.

"Can't that boy even be trusted to count so high as *two*?" Druyan wondered, while Kellis rescued the bit of wool. Enna began exclaiming angrily as she discovered bits of dog-chewed beans scattered across her formerly immaculate floor. "You'd think Dalkin would have noticed she didn't go out with Rook. One and the other one—how hard's that to keep track of?"

Kellis was still holding Meddy's fur, looking down into her unrepentant blue eyes. "That was ill-done, little sister. I had already combed that wool." Meddy's tail brushed the floor in hopeful apology. "Shall I take her out?" Kellis asked of Druyan.

"That would be best." There was something odd about his expression, but Druyan couldn't name it. "When the animals are tended in the morning, come back to the hall—

where the loom is. Plenty more wool." He half smiled, and the puzzling glimpse vanished. "Good night, Kellis."

When he—and the brown and white wriggle of Meddy— had gone out, Enna dropped the door bar into place and added a new touch—an iron meat skewer thrust through the latch. There were already three iron horseshoes hanging above the door, and Druyan thought Enna might have buried a nail or two under the threshold—there was fresh-turned dirt there, less than Meddy left with her clandestine but irresistible excavations. None of that had impeded Kellis' passage through the doorway, but Enna remained hopeful. Druyan raised a brow of her own, when the older woman turned from the door.

Enna was as unrepentant as Meddy. "Now the dogs have got onto trusting that villain, I'm the only one can keep us safe from being murdered in our beds, seems to me." She walked past Druyan, and something in her skirt clanked faintly as she moved.

Half a Pail of Water

KELLIS PROVED TO be as handy with the sheep as he had
been at carding their shorn wool. As the weather warmed
into spring, the flock was let out into the marsh to forage
once more, but it was the shearing time and the lambing
season, too, so every evening the sheep were brought back
to the shelter of the fold again, lest lambs birthed into a
sudden last-of-winter storm be lost. 'Twas easy enough to
lose a ewe to a difficult confinement, so someone had to sit
watch with the flock through the night, ready to give whatever help was needed. Increasingly, that someone was
Kellis, even if he had spent long hours shearing by day.

Druyan's family had not kept sheep, Glasgerion being
better country for cattle. She had only learned to manage
the animals after Travic brought her to Splaine Garth. She
had loved the beasts from the first, and not merely as the
providers of the wool she spun and wove into her marvel-
ous webs of cloth. She rejoiced at each new lamb as if
'twas the child she herself had never borne, and mourned
every death among her flock as if the sheep had been close
kin. She would happily have delivered each and every lamb
with her own capable big hands.

Which of course did not befit the lady of Splaine Garth,
as Enna was never unwilling to point out to her. It was
farm hand's work, to sit up all night waiting for a nervous
ewe to decide to lamb. Pru's work, in fact, and Lyn's, and

the girls could send for help if they needed it, which they should not.

So Druyan would steal out to the fold in the small hours, when Enna was long safe abed and the ewes were most apt to begin their business. Increasingly she found Kellis there ahead of her, helping a wet wriggling creature to find its way free of its weary mother, drying the lamb with a bit of straw so it would not take a chill, being sure that it fed from its dam and that she accepted its attentions if the birth was a first for the ewe and she might therefore be confused about what was taking place.

He saved a set of twins that tried to come neck and neck into the world and stuck tight as a cork in a bottle, a hopeless tangle of legs and noses—Kellis sorted out the legs, then held one lamb back while he hauled the other out. Druyan was there, and marveled that the ewe was so calm under his hands through the difficulties—she had lost ewe and lambs, both, in a similar case the season past, when the sheep would not let herself be helped and had burst her heart struggling to deliver. Lambs that tried to come backward, arse-first, did not dismay the man, either—Kellis deftly turned them, then delivered them into the outer world, none the worse for the brief problem.

The only sheep he lost, in fact, was one that eluded the dogs, left the flock, and stayed out alone all night in a freezing downpour. Even Rook could not comb the marsh successfully in that sort of weather, and the tide was in, too—Kellis finally found the dead ewe at midmorning and carried her chilled lifeless lamb back stuffed under his clothing, while Rook trotted whining alongside. Enna swore the creature was dead, but they put it in a box of straw by the fireside, and Kellis rubbed its tight-curled wooly sides with warm cloths till even Druyan would have given up— just then the little orphan gave a twitch and a bleat, and they ended up raising it in the kitchen, on cow's milk and gruel. It adopted Meddy as its mother, to her consternation, but at least that kept it with the flock when it went to grass. By summer's end the gray lamb would be like any of the other sheep, no wise remarkable for its cruel introduction to life.

Plowing time arrived, just after lambing, when the chill was off the soil and the rains fell softer if as frequently. Druyan dragged forth the heavy plowshare and studied it a long while, trying to decide what to do with it. She knew as much about plowing a field as Kellis did—which was virtually nothing. Well, true, she knew which fields to turn and which were due to lie fallow that year. She knew they always used at least two horses and sometimes oxen—Splaine Garth's soil was heavy, and quite wet even though they planted crops on the best-drained ridges to prevent the seed corn's rotting in the ground.

Kellis had a healthy respect for the plow's iron-shod blade, which could do more harm to him than the reaper's sickle had—but the main part of the implement was safe friendly wood, and when he saw that he could keep well away from the blade, he grew more enthusiastic about figuring methods for plowing up a field to receive the seed.

They set their hands first to Enna's vegetable plot, and hashed out the basic procedure on a manageable scale. Next day Kellis swallowed hard, crossed his fingers, and took the harnessed team out to the small barley field, to mangle the soil there as thoroughly as he could contrive. Druyan and the girls broadcast seed onto that field next day, and Dalkin raked it in, while Kellis began on the next. His furrows resembled the tideline on a beach—all waves and ripples—but the work got done, and gentle rains set the seed sprouting almost instantly. There were gaps in the soft green cloak—places where the bouncing plow hadn't really turned the soil and the seed was eaten by opportunistic birds before germinating. Travic would have had a fit and thrashed his plowman.

But Travic would have had a plowman to thrash. His widow was just grateful to have the plowing accomplished at all. Crooked rows did not distress Druyan—they'd bear barley alike with the straight furrows. Two mares foaled. Cows calved. The sows farrowed. They put in the kitchen garden, once the weather was trustworthy. Fall-hatched chicks began to lay, and one or two elderly black-and-white hens went to grace the stewpot, their productive days over. The grass greened up, even faster than the barley fields. Blossoms burst open upon the apple trees and along the hedgerows, berry brambles and wild roses both. And Kellis, fetching water so Enna could wash up the dinner crockery, glanced down into the pail, went white as milk, and spilled water all over the threshold and halfway across the room.

Enna screeched and clouted him with her broom. Kellis scrambled out of her way by reflex and raced dripping to the barn, where Druyan was saddling Valadan for an afternoon ride, taking advantage of a gap in her chores and the clear skies that had followed the morning rain, thinking placidly that after that she'd gather pie-plant stalks and do a bit of baking.

"Lady—" Kellis slammed to a painful halt against the stall partition. Druyan looked at him from across Valadan's back, startled out of her thoughts. Valadan snorted and swung his hindquarters a little, putting his rump between his mistress, the stall door, and whatever trouble was apparently lurking on the other side. Dust the impact had shaken loose sifted down from beams overhead, gold when it entered sunbeams.

"What's the matter?" Druyan asked, trying not to sound anxious. She could hear Enna's voice now, pitched high in anger but not nearby. *Or was that anger?* Had she tried to lift a heavy kettle off the fire and burned herself? *"Is it Enna?"* She let go of the girth, ready to run.

Kellis stopped her, fighting for his breath. He still had the bucket in his hand, and it caught Druyan in the ribs when he reached out, before soaking her with the last of its contents. "Raiders," Kellis gasped out. "At the gate."

"What?" Druyan shoved past him, unstoppable. Kellis tried to go after her, tripped over the dropped bucket as he turned, and sprawled onto his knees. Valadan, bolting out of his stall in pursuit of his mistress, leapt nimbly over him.

Druyan pelted across the barnyard, scattering chickens.

She halted uncertainly. Everything appeared peaceful save for Enna, who was headed toward her, still brandishing her broom—and the chickens, already settling again, gone back to scratching for food as if the commotion was of no interest. Valadan skidded to a stop behind her.

"Where is he?" Enna demanded.

Druyan looked around, turning full circle. She could see the gate, closed across the lane that wandered toward a road that was scarcely more than a lane itself. There was no one near it, and nowhere a man could conceal himself, even behind the drystone wall. No sign anyone had tried. Valadan held his head high, nostrils and ears and eyes all working, evidently fruitlessly.

"He can just scrub the whole damn floor, since he's soaked it! Where is he?"

Kellis came out of the barn, with straw plastered to his wet clothes, straight into Enna's path.

"Get back to the kitchen, you! Playing games—"

"Wait," Druyan said, frowning, trying not to be distracted. She didn't think 'twas any game. "Kellis, there's nobody there. Not so much as a bootprint in the mud. What exactly did you see?"

"The inside of a cider barrel," Enna suggested darkly.

It sounded plausible enough, except Kellis didn't look tipsy—he looked terrified, scared half out of his wits. He stood staring at the gate, but Druyan was sure he wasn't seeing it. His eyes were dark as his brows—the pupils had spread, despite the bright sun he stood in, and covered all the lighter gray rims.

"Kellis?"

He staggered blindly past her, heading for the horse trough, and reaching it, dropped to his knees beside it. He took a grip on the edge of the trough, with either hand, started to lean over it. Kellis hesitated, shaking, lifted his head, and looked back pleadingly at Druyan.

"You have to understand—I don't *choose* to see things in the water. I *never* did. The bottom of the bucket would have been plenty for me—"

"But you *did* see something? Something else?" Druyan asked, suspecting understanding about to dawn. "In the bucket?"

Kellis nodded, like a puppet clumsily wielded. He was still trembling, unable to control his hands even while he held onto the trough. "The water swirled, and ... there were men with torches, at your gate. It was night. They had swords, spears. I could see the torchlight shining on the edges of the weapons." He glanced sidelong at the trough, bracing himself.

"Will you see more, if you look again?"

He looked as if he was choking and had to master that before he could answer. A long shudder wracked him. "I will try. There might be no vision—I'm far out of practice with calling them."

"Try," Druyan ordered, glancing uneasily about at the empty yard, the innocent gate. *Night,* he'd said. Well, it wasn't night, not for some hours. But it would come. Already the sun drifted onward from the zenith, and there was no staying its course.

Kellis nodded jerkily and bent over the trough. Druyan joined him. She watched his breathing slow, steady. His eyes went out of focus again, and sweat started out in tiny drops all across his forehead, like a dew. Very softly, beneath a whisper, he began to sing, leaning down over the water. With no idea how the business of visions worked, Druyan looked into the trough, as well, wondering whether she would see what Kellis saw, or must only trust his witness.

Actually, Kellis had quite forgotten that his visions could afflict him unbidden, that in fact they'd begun that way, when he was yet a half-grown boy. Such visions had twice the reality of the waking world, but he had forgotten that, too, and it had astonished him that he could walk out of the barn into daylight rather than darkness lit by torches and flashing metal weapons, hearing no screams, no shouts, no destruction. He tried to take hold of himself, steady his breathing at least, because he knew very well that prophets appearing to be lunatics were not listened to all that carefully. The vision was true, or it would not have come at him like that. He could trust it—and luckily it was not subject to any sort of qualifying interpretation at all . . .

His lips were cracked as old leather, as he began to sing up the vision again. He had tried desperately to forget how to call on his skill and had very nearly succeeded—but in the end, even having his head split open by a blow from cold iron had not been enough.

There was a fine film of dust lying atop the water, giving it the solid appearance of polished stone. A tiny breeze riffled the surface—no, that was Kellis, trembling, making the trough rock just perceptibly. The motion subsided. The singing took on a more insistent note. Druyan could see her own face darkly reflected, saw Kellis' alongside it, much distorted by the angle she viewed it from. She tried to look deeper, past the mirroring effect. She thought she could see the caulked greenish planks of the trough's bottom, but there was nothing else in the water.

Apparently there was nothing for Kellis, either. All at once he ceased his singing—in what seemed to be midword—and sank back on his heels, his head and shoulders slumping forward till he nearly cracked his chin on the trough. His right hand groped toward his forehead, he pressed three fingers against the red line of the scar, as if to assuage pain.

Druyan gripped his shoulder. "Kellis? Are you all right? What did you see?" Something *she* had not?

"Water," he answered dejectedly, his voice thin. "And I ought to scrub that trough out for you—*I* wouldn't want to drink out of it; the horses can't be much better pleased—" He lifted his head, blinking as if he came out of some dark place. "Lady, I told you before, I am not much use at foreseeing. I don't pretend any pride about it. I see when I don't want to, but I can look and not see, I can see and not know *when* I see. I can, for that matter, see and not know *where* I'm seeing. But it *was* your gate—I saw the new board."

She'd had him mend the gate properly, just the week past. The fresh unweathered board stood out like a blaze on a dark horse at night.

"And I never see much ahead, or much behind," he faltered on. "It was night, and the raiders were there. They weren't there *last* night, so what I saw must have been *this* night." He looked at her, begged her belief with those open, innocent eyes.

"If we believed you, you addled thief!" Enna broke in coldly. "Lady, go have your ride. I'll deal with this wretch. Honest work will chase these fancies out of his head, and there's plenty of that to be done round here."

Druyan looked at Kellis. He dropped his eyes and got stiffly to his feet, saying nothing. He'd added mud to the straw bedecking him. Had he lied? But if he had, to what possible purpose?

"They've never come so early," she said uncertainly.

"The winter was mild." A mere observation, nothing coloring it.

True. At the time, it had seemed a blessing. Now it might be something entirely less fortunate. There'd been fewer than the usual number of winter storms, and it had been some while since the last one. But that did not answer all her questions.

"Why would they come here? What do *we* have?"

Kellis looked slowly about the tidy farmyard, seeing with other, more desperate eyes. "Food. It takes many days to voyage across the Great Sea, even with the winds favorable. Even the Eral grow weary of salt-dried fish and damp journeybread."

"Towns are better to plunder." Thankfully, there weren't any such very near, only tiny local villages, two or three families choosing a common dwelling spot. Towns hugged the river mouths for the transport both coastlong and inland that the waters offered, and were easy prey to shipborne raiders. That had kept Splaine Garth safe, save for that one raid the autumn previous.

"Each ship and its men answer to one captain," Kellis explained, dashing her hopes. "That captain may join with others to sack a town, but he's on his own when it comes to getting his men fed. This place is rich enough."

It made sense, if you wanted it to. "Kellis, are you *sure* of what you saw?"

He looked long at her. At Enna. At the quite unremarkable farm buildings that had been his home all winter. At the mended gate, especially. "Yes, Lady," Kellis said, not hesitant any longer.

"Then we haven't much time," Druyan decided. "The tide is against them now, they can't have landed yet. But they can get in just about sunfall, which will probably suit them. They seem to like to come in the night." She had heard Travic say so. "I will move the horses and the cows out onto the moors. Kellis, I want you and Dalkin to drive the sows and the piglets down to the marsh. The *far* side, as much away from the river as you can get. Then find Lyn and Pru, and tell them to move the sheep as high up the headland as they can in an hour. After that they're to hurry back here—I don't want them alone out there." For all she knew, the raiders were slavers, too. "They'd better bring the dogs. Enna, chase the chickens into the root cellar."

"What, so these raiders of his don't need to catch the fowl for themselves?" She waved the broom in the direction of Kellis, who was heading for the pigpen at a trot. "You don't believe that mischief?"

"He has no reason to lie, Enna."

"None you know of! Unless he's maybe just crazed. Lady, don't listen to him! Who knows what deviltry he's up to?"

Druyan turned and walked away, having no answer to make. What was she to do? What had Travic done, when the lookout he'd posted on the headland had spotted black ships off their coast? She remembered no specifics, but the broad outline was easy. He'd gathered all the men together, armed them, defended the farm.

But she had no men, and a farm was not a castle, with great thick walls to slow an invader's progress. Most of their fences barely kept the cows out of the crops. Hiding what the raiders would be most apt to snatch was a fair beginning, but perhaps they ought *all* to take to the marsh. The salt grass wasn't so high as it would be by summer's end, but there were places where the ground itself would hide them, coves and twists of boggy ground no invaders unfamiliar with the place could easily penetrate . . .

And what if the thwarted hungry raiders burned what they couldn't take? If they put the house and the barns to the torch, there'd be nothing of Splaine Garth to hold, year-and-a-day notwithstanding.

Valadan was standing at the gate, still saddled, head high and nostrils flared, on watch for early signs of trouble. Druyan swung into the saddle. No idle ride now, but a swift tour to see what she might contrive to do before night and disaster fell upon them. She made for the top of the headland first, to scry the broadest reach of sea she could.

Defending Splaine Garth

DRUYAN SAW NOTHING untoward. But Valadan did not seem calm and unperturbed beneath her, despite the emptiness of the sparkling sea. The calm was temporary. In due time there would come a shipload of raiders.

Druyan studied the beach they would sail by, the river mouth and the lay of the land that would guide them straight to the heart of her farmland. The little ridge of higher, well-drained ground that ran along one side of the river and made such a handy path for them, a sure way to skirt the quaggy marsh, gave them away. One end was by the river, just where the water began to go shallow and a boat of any size had to anchor or risk grounding. The other end turned into the lane and finished at Splaine Garth's gate. The whole length was very obviously traveled, impossible to disguise. They were farmers, not castellans. They'd never thought they'd have to hide themselves . . .

It will be dark.

Druyan patted Valadan's neck. "They'll still find the path. They've been here before—or places just like this." It was the same story all over Esdragon—where a river met the sea, you found a settlement. Some were on the coast. Some were not. Go upstream, go as far as your ship or any other could, and there was the town or the holding, sited to take advantage of the river's access to both sea and land. On a cliffy coast, often that was the only place with room for building. Probably the raiders just looked for a river now and probed up it, needing no other guide to the places they'd plunder. Sometimes, as at Keverne, there was a fortress to defend the river and the town—but all too frequently there was nothing at all to protect a settlement. Attack could really come only from the sea, and till the raiders had begun arriving scant years ago, there had been none of that to fear.

It will be dark. Valadan repeated. The stallion pawed vigorously, sending heavy clods of earth flying back. *They will not see us.*

"That's what I thought," Druyan said. "We could hide—we know the marsh." Protect the folk that way, but not the farm itself.

It will be dark in the barnyard as well. Valadan raked the earth once more, eagerly.

Druyan realized he was trying to offer her a plan, beyond hiding in the mud and the dark. She pursued the logic of it. Could they, having moved everything they might to safety, trick the raiders away from the rest? Defend Splaine Garth as if they had great numbers and nothing to fear, making huge amounts of noise and confusion?

Should a dozen horses rush by them in the dark, strangers will not know that only I bear a rider, Valadan offered.

Add to that five people making noise from various directions, with two sheepdogs barking and darting and biting . . . It might work. "We should put the brood mares and the cows out far enough to be safe, but we could let the oxen loose, too," Druyan said. In the dark, a man run down by a bullock wasn't likely to know he hadn't been set upon by a horseman. The raiders would never guess that the defenders were almost all women and half-grown children—if they didn't see them. They'd not expect a fight from such; the helpless would give up and be robbed, so those folk who dared fight must, by logic, be formidable.

A bluff. That was all it came out to, in the end. Druyan wheeled Valadan about and headed back with all his speed, to do what she could to bolster the mad scheme before she reasoned her way out of using her only hope.

It was twilight when Pru and Lyn arrived, with the dogs in tow. Dalkin and Kellis were just back—Druyan had set them to moving everything vulnerable to fire out of ready reach. There was naught to be done about the thatch on the kitchen roof—they'd just have to hope that the morning rain had dampened it sufficiently to offer some protection. Every window was shuttered as if against a storm, and most of the doors were barred—one or two were designated as ways of retreat if such were needed. Every bucket and pail was filled and standing close to a wall, where it wouldn't be easily trampled or upset—Druyan was still thinking about firefighting, but Kellis said that if the raiders had torches, they might be able to douse them and further confuse men on strange ground by forcing them to approach in darkness.

The tide had been flooding in, and up the river, for an hour. Druyan rode for the headland again, lingered only an instant before racing back to tell Kellis he'd been right— even in the gathering gloom the river's surface sparkled, and she had seen plain the dark shape thrusting up against the current, with the tide. The raiders would soon be ashore. And once landed, it could not take them more than a few moments to find their way to the spot where Kellis' vision had placed them. Druyan expertly opened her gate from horseback, then closed and latched it behind her. She chased away the thought that she might never need to do that again—might never have a gate to shut or a farm to fence.

Enna and the others crowded close as she dismounted.

"They're here," Druyan reported tersely. She didn't wait for startled exclamations. "Here's what we're going to do about it. With this one thing said, first—I don't want anyone dead over this. We'll run if we have to. You all know the ways." They had blocked some of the spaces between buildings with barrels and such, to confuse the raiders, leaving always a retreat for themselves. But it might be hard to remember where that retreat was, in a confused fight.

"Lady—" Kellis touched her sleeve.

Druyan thought she could make out the glow of torches from the direction of the river. *Too soon,* she chided herself. *They'll hardly be ashore yet.* It was her own fear she was seeing. Valadan had his ears pricked in that direction, every sense straining, and more acute than her own. She could rely on him to give true warning.

"Lady, I can't do anything that will work upon their weapons," Kellis said. He shook his head disparagingly. "My people never could—it cost us dear. But . . . I can try something else, a charm that might help. If I can work a Mirror of Three, then whatever they see or hear of us will seem to them as if it is three times as great. In the dark—"

It will be dark, Valadan agreed, pleased, tossing his head in approval.

"They'll think we have the advantage!" Druyan exclaimed, hearing the two schemes mesh, seeing something like the possibility of hope. She leapt to catch it. "Do it, Kellis! Dalkin, fetch every tool we can fight with out of the barn—shovels, hoes—anything you'd hate to be hit with. Girls, Enna, get the pans from the kitchen—the big ones, the ones that will make a clatter when they're hit. Take them over behind the smokehouse, and when I give the word, run out beating them for all you're worth! Hug the shadows, don't ever let them have a clear sight of you. And watch yourselves—the horses and I will be coming from behind the barn. They'll follow Valadan, but don't expect them to dodge around you—keep clear, for your lives."

Now she *could* see torchlight, surely? Valadan snorted *no,* and Druyan realized the darkness was thicker than it ought to have been, so early—the sky had clouded over, and a low rumble informed her that she had mistaken lightning for the torch flames she anticipated.

Well, a storm would be one more weapon, and they needed every one. "Kellis, where are you going to be doing . . . whatever you called it?"

"Roof," he answered slowly, considering. "Kitchen, I think." He climbed onto the rain barrel and peered upward. When Dalkin staggered laden out of the barn, Kellis waved him over, said something Druyan couldn't hear, and Dalkin ran off again. Kellis turned back to the roof, scrambled the rest of the way up. "Hand me a bucket," he called. "I'll watch for sparks if I can."

Druyan grabbed a pail and lifted it up till he could reach the handle. Just then Dalkin fetched back, dragging a lumpy sack behind him. "Send that up, too," Kellis directed.

By the stench, she knew it for the last of the potatoes and turnips, not yet consigned to the compost heap. Missiles now, evidently. Kellis balanced the sack over the peak of the roof and knelt on the thatch, trying to secure a similar equilibrium for himself.

Druyan saw him begin tugging loose stems out of the thatch, breaking the straws so that each one became many. Another time she'd have been interested further, eager to see how the charm worked and what else he did; now all she could think was that Kellis would be lucky not to fall off the steep roof and break *himself* into many pieces, the moment his attention shifted from his balance to his spell-casting. There was no charm would work at all if its caster couldn't relax and concentrate—maybe that was why he wanted the vegetables to throw, a second line of offense in case the first proved unworkable.

Beside the gate, Valadan was plunging. Druyan saw again that distant glow. *Now it is torches,* the stallion said urgently.

"They're coming," Druyan relayed, loud enough only so her own nearby folk would hear. She saw no one. That was as it ought to be—it meant all her people were in their chosen places, hidden. She mounted and rode behind the great dark shape of the barn, where the dozen riding and plow-horses waited, and the team of oxen. She slipped off their restraining halters, one by one. Valadan could control them. She didn't want any of the beasts trailing a tangling rope.

Silence—save for another far-off roll of thunder. The storm might be deflected by the headland or the greater mass of the Promontory farther away, might not swing their direction. That would be a pity—wind and rain would be such a help . . .

The torchlight was near, and Druyan could hear voices, too, or thought she could. One of the horses stamped restlessly. And all at once she heard the commonplace clucking of a chicken, as a hen that had evaded Enna's roundup chose that moment to stroll across the barnyard, heading fussily for her roost. She hoped no one else heard the bird—it would be just like Enna to send Dalkin out to rescue it just as the raiders arrived.

The torches were very near. Druyan could see their light gleaming on metal edges, just as Kellis had said. Then the light went out of sight, blocked by the barn. Her mouth went dry. Her hands, tense on Valadan's reins, felt very cold. He shifted a little beneath her, as if to draw her attention to the moment, away from disheartening fear. Had it been like this for Travic and his men? she wondered. Or did she feel worse because women did not make war, and she was out of her element?

It is not wrong to be aware, Valadan assured her. She saw his ears prick sharply forward.

The gate shattered open, battered wide by a great blow that broke open the latch. There were shouts—some of them at least threats and bluster directed at the landholders, the owners of the ruined gate and the farm behind it. Now was the moment they should have appeared, first confused, then swiftly terrified, to be vanquished and pillaged, sent running before they had a chance to think about it.

"Who's there?" Druyan called loudly, bold as ever Travic would have been, angry about the gate, which would likely take a whole day to mend. Anger helped, she found. It was a hot strength warming her chilled blood. "What do you want?" she demanded.

"Hungry men," came a bold answer to her first question, amid coughs of laughter. "Come for our supper, mother."

"You can eat cold steel," Druyan said under her breath, and shouted the signal. *"At 'em, men!"*

On cue, the clatter started up behind the smokehouse, swirled into the farmyard. Druyan gave Valadan a quite unneeded squeeze with her calves, and he sprang into a gallop, neighing as he went. Eight draft horses, four palfreys, and two bullocks streamed behind him, thundering around the corner of the barn and across the yard.

There wasn't time to take a count of the raiders as they swept through them. The men hadn't bunched, but jumped in every direction to avoid trampling. Druyan had an impression of several, probably less than a dozen but surely close to that number. Big men, armed mostly with swords and round shields with shiny, light-catching bosses at their centers. They wouldn't need heavier weapons, against farmers. One raised a torch high, and Druyan took a swipe at him with the mattock she clutched in her right hand—it didn't chop flesh so well as soil, but it did well enough. There was a howl and the torch got dropped, which had been her objective. She knew her own ground in the dark. The marauders did not.

The wild-eyed horses created all the mayhem any general could have desired. Valadan tried to regroup them for another charge—Druyan, trying to keep her eyes everywhere at once, saw Dalkin slash a hoe blade across the ankles of a raider who had his back turned, then dart away into the noisy shadows where Pru and Lyn were clashing pots and screaming fit to rouse the long dead.

The bullocks, while not so easily excited as the horses, decided they nonetheless craved the safety of their normally quiet pen, and sought it at a lumbering canter. Druyan went after them fast, before the raiders could see that part of the "mounted men" were only a brace of plow oxen. She yelled every sort of cry she could think of, particularly the names of the men who weren't there but should have been, and took more swings with the mattock whenever she saw an opportunity.

The raiders were beginning to put their backs to the

buildings, which gave them leisure to look about. That would have been unfortunate, and the problem was dealt with by every shift possible. The dogs chivvied their legs, dodging sword blows as easily as they did cow kicks on a normal day. Enna slammed a frypan solidly into a raider's head and knocked him nearly off his feet, though she lost hold of the pan and had to scramble away without it. Dalkin rained blows with his sharp hoe. There was only one torch still alight, and that went out as Kellis got lucky with his water pail. He followed up that shower with a malodorous rain of turnips.

The horses were out of even Valadan's formidable control, dashing madly wherever they pleased, mostly wanting to escape the noise and the strangers and even each other. When one crashed a barricade, it did not return, and the others were apt to follow it and be lost to the defenders. Valadan's own charges were more effective—he willingly went at his targets with hooves and teeth, and 'twas all Druyan could do to keep in her saddle. They chased one raider as far as the gate and sent him flying over it, but they couldn't do likewise with the others.

Three of them had managed, Druyan saw with sinking heart, to group despite her efforts. The now-panicked horses were running around them instead of scattering them, and 'twas growing plain indeed that they were merely loose horses. A fourth raider joined his friends, and he had Pru fast by her collar despite Meddy's leaping and barking at his back. There was another downpour of vegetables, half-rotted potatoes this time, followed by frantic chanting.

Druyan rode to Pru's rescue, swinging the mattock like a sword. Out of nowhere a bullock came bawling, big as a cottage, and slammed into Valadan's near shoulder so that the stallion all but fell. Druyan shot helplessly off over his right side, to land with a great thump against the horse trough.

The impact drove all the breath out of her. Dazed, Druyan saw Valadan rearing and striking out with his forefeet, dropping down to avoid—barely—a sword cut. Strug-

gling to fill her lungs, she saw Enna dash for the kitchen
door—forgetting it was barred, not one of the several es-
capes they'd chosen. Druyan tried to warn her, but her
shout was only a wheeze. Enna tugged uselessly at the
door, then turned at bay, and Dalkin leapt to her side,
swinging a sickle in either hand, which was stupid—he'd
be more likely to cut himself than slash a raider. Druyan
tried to get up, but her limbs answered her sluggishly, as if
she was beneath deep water.

A fifth man joined his fellows, and they all held their
swords at the ready, impervious to attack from most directions now. Kellis' chanting from the roof had ceased, and
there was only Lyn still desperately clashing pans. Most
of the horses had either escaped or were clumped together
by the smokehouse. None was still running.

A tendril of wind brushed Druyan's bruised cheek. Tears
sprang to her eyes—the storm had passed them by. If only
they'd had its help, perhaps they wouldn't have failed.

A sixth stranger appeared from behind the barn, dragging
Lyn by her yellow hair. Meddy was barking as if she'd lost
her wits. There was a curse, and then she began to yelp.

Druyan put her lips together. She had barely been able to
draw a breath in, but she had enough air for one oddly
pitched whistle.

Valadan heard and swung toward her. So did something
else, farther away and swifter yet.

A great, icy gust of wind came howling through the gap
between the buildings. It had not even died before a coun-
terblast ripped through from the other side. Both gusts
raised dust—Enna dodged away under its cover, snatched
up a pan, and jumped back to Dalkin's aid. Rook's sharp
teeth found an ankle, and all at once Pru was loose. Lyn's
captor let go his hold of her as he turned toward his shouting mates. Meddy flung herself at him, sending him sprawling.

The wind howled like a starving wolf. Thatch lifted off
the kitchen roof, there were great stinging pebbles mixed
with the choking dust. Valadan reached Druyan's side, and

she scrambled back into his saddle. Two of the draft horses, used to working as a team, rallied to Valadan's call and galloped at the little knot of men. Dalkin was yelling and running toward them, too, his twin weapons waving.

Now the rain—not gentle drops, but a virtual sheet of falling water, as if the lightning that flashed above had ripped open the belly of the cloud. The wind drove it sideways as it fell, and it struck like slashes of a dagger blade. Thunder cracked, and Druyan flung back her head and screamed encouragement to the wind, squeezed her legs about Valadan to send him running with the storm.

Kellis yelled something from the roof—Druyan thought at first he was in fear of the wind, but he yelled it three times, and all at once there seemed to be thirty horses running with Valadan, and as they swept through the gate at the raiding party's heels, she wondered where the army had come from, with their swords and spears and clashing armor, fooled herself by Kellis' illusions.

Lightning hit the tree at the end of the lane just as they reached it—Valadan sat back on his haunches and slid to a desperate halt as branches fell in front of his nose, and Druyan felt every hair on her head lifting and crackling, like a cat's fur on a dry winter's day The crash of thunder—just overhead—deafened her for an instant. She steered Valadan around the shattered tree and began to gallop down the lane, but he halted again, in air so thick with rain as to be nearly solid water, ears flat against the lash of the wind.

They have gone, he said, sounding disappointed.

Mending

THE STORM THAT saved them cost Splaine Garth three venerable apple trees, one beehive, and half the kitchen roof—the last doubly unfortunate, as the storm took the best part of a week to blow itself out and considerable rain fell in the meantime. Kellis got blown off the roof with the thatch, and came out of the adventure with a lump on his head and a much-bruised shoulder. No one else was injured, though the wet weather made Enna pay dearly for her active part in the defense.

Before the sun had chosen to show his face that first morning after, the girls had rushed off to discover how the sheep had fared, and Dalkin had gone to the marsh to see whether the pigs and piglings were in any difficulty, then to fetch the cows home. As the rain eased, Enna began dragging things out of the kitchen to dry if they could, and Druyan rode out to round up horses and to assess damage they hadn't had leisure to notice.

Everywhere she pointed Valadan's nose, scenes of distress assailed her eyes. They had no very large trees along the Darlith coast, but most trees she passed had limbs a-dangle, torn entirely off or hanging by a scrap of bark, the leaves withering. The ground was blanketed with leaves fallen too soon, and bramble canes had been whipped about till they tore each other. Here and there bird's nests lay

120

overturned, the fledglings dead beneath them after a wild plummet earthward.

The birds would nest again, of course. Some of the trees would releaf themselves, and even the spots where the little streams had torn out their banks would be hidden by normal vegetation in a month's time, troubles forgotten. The grass, most flexible of all, stood cheerfully already, waving green fingers at the now-gentle breeze.

It was Druyan who could not forget or forgive. *She* had done this, unleashed this mighty force on her home and her people. And she had reveled in it.

The raiders would have done worse. Valadan pawed the turf as she sadly examined a dead badger. Where was its sett? If there had been kits, were they drowned, too, or merely orphans?

"The raiders would only have done it to the farm," Druyan said sadly. "*I* did it for leagues."

Valadan snorted deprecatingly. *Storms come.*

"I *called* it."

It chose to answer. He nosed the badger. *Male. Look for no cubs.*

Druyan leaned against his shoulder. "I called the wind, knowing I couldn't just send it away when it had done my will. Knowing it would do this."

The nature of storms. The stallion reached for a mouthful of grass.

I liked it too much, Druyan thought, watching him graze. *I cannot yield to that again. Not even a little. It's too easy.*

Small wonder the fisherfolk forbade women to board their boats, to whistle at all, ever. On the off-chance that one of those women was the one the wind would answer to. The seductive power carried a fearful price.

Returning, she found Kellis struggling up to the roof with fresh barley straw, the last from the previous year's crop and luckily not all stuffed into mattresses. Under Enna's protests, Druyan went up to help him.

Kellis seconded Enna. "Lady, you should not be up here.

It's too far to the ground." He took the bundle of straw from her and tried to spread it over the planking in a layer thick enough to keep out further rain.

"You'd know about that," Druyan agreed pleasantly, staying at the top of the ladder. "How's your shoulder today?"

He shrugged it a trifle and winced. "It complains but lets me use it. That was a provident storm, Lady. I thought it would pass us by, sweep up the coast—but it turned."

"It did," Druyan agreed, dodging his questioning gaze by descending for more straw. What exactly had he seen that night, from his rooftop vantage? Was he wizard enough to know?

Kellis did not press, but went on with the repairs. There was an art to thatching, in which he plainly lacked instruction—he was doing his best to make a watertight covering, but in the end it was still going to leak, and the roof was likely to be much thicker at the repaired end than at the other, unless he ran out of straw. Druyan, no better schooled at the craft, could only hope that Edin the thatcher was one of those men the duke sent home when the threat of the raiders was finally ended.

She said as much, and Kellis agreed cheerfully, not deceiving himself as to the permanence or the efficacy of the job he was doing, taking no offense as he pushed straw about and tamped it hopefully into place.

"Without you warning us, there probably wouldn't be a roof left at all," Druyan said. "Or any of us still here, likely. We'd never have stood them off, storm or no storm, without you helping." She laid a hand on his arm. "We're all grateful."

Kellis smiled lopsidedly. "I know. Enna put *milk* in my porridge this morning. Or else I got the cat's breakfast."

Druyan began to chuckle. "Next thing you know, there'll be actual meat in the stew. What a change of fortune!"

Or virtue rewarded. He *could*, Druyan knew, have used the raid for a chance to disappear, stolen a horse and gotten clean away in the ample confusion. Success would have been virtually guaranteed. Instead, he'd cast his lot with theirs, to succeed or fail as they did. It was such folly, to trust too far a stranger who'd come as Kellis had—but how many times over must the man prove himself?

"Will they come back?" she asked, suddenly alarmed, clinging to the top of the ladder, looking out over her cropland. It was so early, there was all the summer before them, and the autumn. All that time of peril and good weather, while crops ripened and stood ready for the stealing. "What do they *want*, that they have to steal from us? Where do they come from?"

Kellis inched his way up the slope of the roof, tucking straw into rows. Druyan had no idea what he was going to do when he got to the peak—she didn't see how the thatching was going to hold. The first fresh breeze would strip it away again.

"They all *want* to be older sons," he said, after she'd thought he either hadn't heard or had no answer. "There's not land enough in their homeland, to divide it among all the sons, so the younger ones get nothing at all, unless they're strong enough to take it for themselves. They grow up having to fight for everything—every song I ever heard them sing was about war, or raiding, or a blood feud."

"I always heard they took everything that wasn't nailed down and went away with it," Druyan said, puzzled. "There weren't more than a dozen of those men here. They couldn't have thought they'd just move in, keep the farm?"

Kellis laughed. "That lot? Not likely. They'd have stolen whatever they could carry and left with it. They don't want farms—they want gold and adventure. They're very simple-hearted that way."

"Younger sons *here* don't inherit much of anything." Not to mention daughters, who got less still, no matter where they came in the line of kin. "*They* don't go raiding over the sea."

"There probably aren't half so many of them." Kellis worked another row of thatch, and Druyan saw him pass his right hand over it, fingers cocked in a small binding magic. "I wish you had some tar—this isn't going to shed water very well. Any Binding I can put on it will wash away with the first rain."

"That's the reason it's so steep-pitched. Run the rain off the straw before it soaks through," Druyan told him.

"I'm trying not to think about that, Lady. This roof is anxious to shed *me* again." He made more hand-passes over the surface, sometimes with straw, sometimes with spellcraft. "Anyway, my folk tell tales of a wondrous golden time—my grandmother's time, I would guess—when the weather was so fair, there wasn't a winter you could notice. Lasted for years. Everything grew—crops, grass, and herds. The Eral, too, on their home coasts. I would guess that while they had plenty of food, they grew big healthy babies. Worst luck, lots of them were sons. And *they* all had big families when their turns came. More sons, so many that fighting among themselves didn't cull enough, and they started spilling out to plague other lands." He reached, lost his balance, and flung an arm over the roofbeam hastily. Straw showered down. "Lady, when you see me come sliding down at you, get yourself out of the way."

"You be careful," Druyan ordered sternly. The kitchen's roof was a story less lofty than the hall's, but still far enough to fall onto cobbles. Kellis had been lucky not to break his neck the first time.

"It's all right," Kellis assured her stalwartly. "I know how to fall off this roof! I have experience. I don't want to take you with me, that's all." He tossed out another tiny spell and frowned at the effect. "This is meant to keep sheep from straying, not straw from slipping. I don't know . . . So some of the landless sons go raiding for sport; and some of them go emigrating because it's that or starve, and they need to raise money first, to pay for the ships, so they go a-raiding, too. And if the songs are true—and I heard enough of those—any time one lord works his way to the top of the pile, there's a dozen others won't tolerate him, so they load up families and goods and go looking for other lands to settle on. All they do is fight, birth to grave. Compared to their own folk, my clans were hardly even an obstacle to them. Your folk might be another tale entirely."

"How so?" Druyan dodged another cascade of loose straw. "Are you sure you're all right up there?"

"Yes." But the word was gasped out. "Sorry. What about beeswax? Got any of that?"

"From just two hives? Enough for a roof? Maybe we could take something from the skep the storm upset, but those bees are very unhappy right now, and you didn't like them much when you looked in on them at winter's end." They'd opened the hives to see whether queen and workers had survived, whether they had reserves sufficient to feed themselves till blossom time. Kellis had been stung dozens of times and had made it clear he didn't intend to go near the bees again. "Last year's wax all went for candles. There's some tallow, I think."

"I'm thinking that if we coated some sacks with something to shed water, it would be a start up here," Kellis said abstractedly. "Watch yourself, Lady. I'm going to try to come down."

"There are some hides in the barn. Not sound enough for boots, but maybe we could drape them over. And you're six feet left of the ladder."

"Thank you." Kellis corrected his course, but Druyan didn't draw an easy breath till they were both safe on the ground, covered with sticks of thatch and looking like a pair of scarecrows.

"So, why is Esdragon another tale to the raiders?" she asked.

"Cities are harder to push aside than herds of sheep." Kellis brushed a hand through his hair, dislodging chaff. "It isn't just that cold iron doesn't poison you; your people stay put. Mine wander. That was what we did when the Eral first came at us—we just moved away from them. It didn't solve the problem, except that first year. I suppose they'll never get all of us . . ." He shrugged. "Some Clans will always be out of reach, on the fringes. We can't make the Eral leave, they can't make the Clans not exist. Nothing resolves. We'll go where they don't much like to be—the hills. It's hard to live there, but the Clans know how to survive." He pulled a barley stem out of his collar. "*Your* folk, on the other hand, will stand up to the raiders, and you won't leave it too late, the way my people did. Working together isn't the novelty for you that it was to the Clans."

"And we can fight them off?" Druyan asked, baffled, trying to take it all in.

"You already do." Kellis waved a hand at the dooryard they had defended so very well. "And if you do it long enough—well, the Eral still won't go away, but they'll change toward you. They'll roll over anything that shows the least weakness, but an equal—they'll trade with an equal, instead of trying to snatch whatever they want. They'll have to. It's not something they sing about on the raiding ships, but they do go places where the medium of exchange doesn't include fire and blood."

"When will that happen?" Druyan asked eagerly.

"Depends on how well you fight." Kellis rubbed his sore shoulder. "The better you are, the sooner they'll respect you."

Druyan's heart sank, seeing the impossible scope of it. How could she have hoped for immediate relief?

"Every captain's his own master and does what he chooses. The Eral follow the strongest. But the word will run back to the home shores that a land's too strong to be profitable for raiding, that it's too much trouble. Then they'll start to trade for what they want," Kellis consoled her.

"Meantime we break our necks watching our backs." Druyan showed Kellis where the hides were piled. He touched one and wrinkled his nose. "Travic got these in trade, I think," Druyan said, vaguely embarrassed. "We didn't cure them here." The hides from the early winter butchering were all salted down in a barrel, waiting for Mion the tanner to come home. They'd keep, and Druyan didn't feel desperate enough yet to teach herself tanning. "I remember he wasn't happy with them—the quality's poor, they're stiff and they stink—Travic never thought there'd be a use for them."

"They'll stop the birds from diving into the soup pot," Kellis said optimistically, ducking out of a barn swallow's flight path. "At least for a while."

They might add salt-grass hay to the thatch, too, later in the season. 'Twasn't grown long enough yet. "So, until we impress the Eral so thoroughly that they'd rather bring goods to our markets than swords to blood, the raids will continue?" Druyan wasn't sure she liked the implications, but she was determined to understand them.

"This place isn't *so* easy to find," Kellis offered, rolling the hides into a long bundle.

"It's been found *twice* in a handful of months," Druyan countered tartly. "The season's just eased enough to make sailing bearable. And half the settled bits of the duchy are this easy to find." She explained about the estuaries, the attractions river and harbor offered in Esdragon. "We might as well hang signs out: 'Rich pickings right here.' "

"You keep watch." Kellis shrugged, then bit his lip. "And your duke has an army in the field, does he not?"

"He took my men for it," Druyan agreed bitterly. "They'd have been better use here, seems to me. In case you didn't notice, no army showed up to help us the other night."

Kellis frowned. "You have a long coast. Raids are quick. How does the army know where it's needed in time to get itself there?"

"That's just it," Druyan answered. "They *don't*. They sit by the towns, and the rest of us are on our own." Her voice was bitter as black-walnut hulls.

"Keeping watch," Kellis repeated, "and having some thought for what you'll do when trouble comes, Lady. There won't always be a storm. Though there is always the rain." He lifted the rolled hides with a small groan and headed back toward the kitchen roof, accepting the realities of Esdragon's weather.

* * *

The barley shot upward in the fields. The sheep were sheared, the wool tithe paid. The apple trees set fruit. The kitchen roof leaked a little less with each rain, for Kellis took careful note of the weak spots and tended them, sometimes even while the rain yet came down. He fell off the roof twice more, but both times managed to catch hold of the edge at the last instant, so that he dangled a moment before dropping—a method of landing he reckoned to be far less hazardous than being lifted off helplessly by the wind.

He did, though, pause for a drink at the well before going back up to finish his work, and a moment later the roof was forgotten and Kellis off in search of Splaine Garth's mistress.

Druyan had gone out riding, returning home at dusk and riding straight into Enna's furious report that Kellis had vanished without a trace or a word, leaving the ladder standing where it might fall on any unwary soul trying innocently to pass through her own kitchen doorway . . .

He wasn't to be found. The amount of thatch scattering around the dooryard in the breeze suggested Kellis had been gone from the work a good while. There was straw torn from the lower edge—he might have tumbled off again and taken otherwise sound roofing with him. He might have hurt himself—but in such case, where had he gone? He wasn't in the barn. Had he landed on his head, then wandered off, dazed? Could he have gotten far, hurt? Druyan wondered. Or had he departed, quite healthy and perfectly ready to seize a chance?

Druyan remounted, in no small way confused. If Kellis had wanted to run, he'd had chances in plenty and could have gotten safe away with far more than the clothes on his back, which seemed to be all that was missing. Every horse save Valadan was safe in paddock or pasture—from the high vantage of the stallion's back, then, she saw the lone figure trudging down from the near edge of the headland. The distance was great, but she could not mistake that ash-pale hair.

Druyan touched a leg to Valadan's side and went cantering to meet him, as much to be out of earshot of Enna's grumbling as to discover what had made Kellis leave his work scarce half done. When she saw him starting to run, she urged Valadan into an effortless gallop and reached Kellis in what seemed an eyeblink.

"What is it? Did you see something?" Her gaze went to the river, frantic, trying to pull in information. There was no reason at all that another shipload of adventurers should not have found them. Bad luck so soon, but no wise impossible, from what Kellis had said. Maybe the first batch had never left the area, but had only retreated.

Kellis lacked breath enough to answer her, but he shook his head emphatically. "Not here," he gasped, to further reassure her. "I was trying to find you . . ."

And she and Valadan had been leagues away, on the moors. "Then you *did* see something!" Druyan rose in her stirrups and looked out over the fields again, searching in a panic. Whyever had she ridden so far? Fast as Valadan was, would she not have been sensible to stay closer to home?

"Can't see much in a dipper of water." Kellis drew in two more ragged breaths. "I couldn't tell *where*, except it wasn't Splaine Garth. A river, a village, a lot of ships—" He faltered, out of breath again.

"That could be anywhere!" Druyan cried, dismayed.

"I know." He pressed a hand to his side, waved away her concern. "I remembered what you said. And it wouldn't help if I'd had more water to look in—the only spot I can recognize in Esdragon is *this* one. But *you* know the others, Lady, and if I can show you—"

"You couldn't before."

"You didn't see because I didn't." Kellis shut his eyes and shook his head. "Lady, I don't want these visions! I turn my eyes away, whenever I'm close to anything that might reflect . . . but it's not helping, they're hammering at me. I can't shut them out. I have to see them. I think I can show them to you. And maybe if you see something that

tells you *where* the raid will be, you can send them a warning."

She reached a hand down to him. "Get up behind me.
Last time you *tried* to see ahead, it didn't work. Why's it
different now?" She urged Valadan back toward the farm
buildings. "You didn't fall on your head, did you?"

His explanation came in snatches, into her left ear over
the thudding of Valadan's hooves. "Always ran in cycles
. . . it would leave me for a long while. Then all at once it
would start up again, I couldn't tell where I was, what was
real, what was there and what was to be. It was strong as
this horse, Lady, only I couldn't ride it, couldn't control it.
It ran away with me, dumped me off when it chose. I want
to find that Wizards' City. Maybe someone there can tell
me, help me—"

"Was it like this all winter?" She couldn't recall him so
distressed, not ever. Not even at the very first, when he'd
been wholly an enemy and must have thought of her as
such, too.

Kellis laughed, as if he knew what she was thinking.
"You probably would have known, Lady! No, there was
nothing, nothing at all. I've never had such a long peace
from it—I thought it must have been something to do with
that knock on the head my captain gave me. I thought he'd
cured me of the cursed visions, and I was so grateful—" He
laughed again, a sharp bark like a fox's. "And so wrong, as
it happens."

Valadan halted beside the barn. Druyan slipped from his
back, dragging Kellis along by one arm. "What do you
need?"

"Water," he said, stumbling a little in her grip, then finding his balance.

Druyan let him go, snatched up a pail, and strode to the
well. Kellis heeled her. When she'd filled the bucket, she
thrust it into his hands. He accepted it, shivering, not looking into it directly.

"How do we do this?" Druyan asked doubtfully. "How
will I see what you do?"

"I am going to sit down, because otherwise I'll drop the pail," Kellis said unsteadily. He drew a deep breath. "Showing you—I don't think there will be any problem. So long as your skin touches mine, you should see whatever I do. It would probably be harder *not* to show you."

Kellis seated himself cross-legged on the paving tiles that kept the mud around the well from becoming impossible. He braced the pail against his right knee and hand, and reached his left hand out to Druyan. She knelt and clasped it.

It was the insistent visions that had made Kellis leery of conning the songs of summoning. Each vision he managed to call seemed to drag another, unbidden one after it, and that uninvited kind *hurt*. They were sneaky, too, often biding their time for days ere they struck, like storms lurking just over the horizon, rumbling but not breaking. When those finally arrived, at the very least they'd inflict a blinding headache on him. More than once he had fainted. The worst time he could clearly remember, he had seen double images for endless days and had felt trapped, stuck fast between vision and reality, terrified to try to move one way or the other lest he choose wrongly, frightened he might never come out of it. Wisir was no help—the old man's visions had never been painful, or so he claimed. Kellis had been compelled to learn to deal with the trouble all on his own.

To invite that again . . . already he felt the familiar coldness in the pit of his stomach, and the sweat was starting out all over him, in great drops. The day dimmed, as if he was about to swoon from lack of food, or blood loss . . .

I don't have to sing this one in, Kellis thought, dismayed. *It is coming, whether I ask it or not. If I invite it, will it be better? Or worse?*

You should know, he told himself. *You had two years before old Wisir died. If you'd wanted to learn, you could have. But by the time it got into your thick skull that it wasn't all a game, he was years dead; this is all your own fault.*

He unclosed his eyes and looked down into the water. For a moment the panic rose up, and he couldn't even see the pail—just black spots before his eyes. Then, all at once, he felt the pressure of other fingers against his, warm where his own were cold. His sight cleared. He found a breath of air.

Quavering at first, then stronger as his throat loosened, Kellis sang up the vision.

Druyan could see into the bucket easily—the water was rocking side to side from being set down, little waves that slowly dwindled to stillness. The surface caught little light—both their shadows fell athwart the pail, and the day was fading. Kellis shivered once, then began to sing, in words she did not know. The water rocked again, more gently . . .

And suddenly Druyan's sight was full of carnage. There were buildings aflame, and terrified children ran screaming. There were men with short swords, and those distinctive round shields, and so much blood . . .

"Look for something you can recognize." Kellis' voice grated into her ear. "The blood's the same everywhere—"

Druyan obediently looked beyond the struggling. Somehow it was no longer night, there was light enough to let her see the landscape round about. A coast, the blue sea, a roundish harbor tucked under the headland. Where sea and land met reared a great broken cliff, the most stubborn parts of which still stood as tall, isolated stacks of rock, unreachable by any save birds. Atop the greatest, a single pine still lifted its storm-torn branches.

"Falkerry!" she cried, and sprang to her feet, loosing Kellis' hand. He rocked back, reaching for the broken contact, slamming his bad shoulder against the well coping. His right leg flailed out and upset the pail. Awash, Kellis struggled to his feet, to Druyan's side. It took his eyes a moment to find focus again, and there was no blood in his face save a trickle from his bitten lower lip.

"Lady, what . . . where is that place?"

Druyan was distraught, as much as if the trouble had been at her own gate again. It took her a moment to hear the question.

"Falkerry? Where the Fal comes to the sea. I've kin there, an older sister, her family—" She thought of them in peril, real as if she'd seen their faces in the vision. Jensine, and four children she had never seen . . .

"Lady, they're still safe. It hasn't happened yet . . ." Kellis swayed, still chalk-white and hard put to stay on his feet.

"Unless you saw back!" Druyan remembered that possibility, horrified. "You *said* you don't know, you can't tell. What if—"

"Now you know," Kellis whispered miserably, and sat down bonelessly on the coping. "Why I tried *not* to see, all that while. It's never any help."

It helped here, at Splaine Garth, Valadan snorted, and stamped. Druyan gazed at him with wide, wet eyes.

"They're close to Keverne," she whispered. "The duke could get help to them."

"What?" Kellis was staring at her.

"I'm going to cry them a warning," Druyan said, determination taking the place of panic.

Warning Falkerry

KELLIS MIGHT NOT have the barest understanding of the distance separating the town of Falkerry from the farm of Splaine Garth, but Enna knew it very well, never mind that she'd never personally been better than a score of miles from her home.

"That's days of riding, Lady! And on *his* say-so?" Enna's eyes went hard. "This is what comes of refusing protection. He's witched you, just as I feared."

Enna had carefully introduced a nail into a seam of every bit of clothing her mistress owned, for safeguard against just such sorcerous mischief. Druyan had discovered and removed each one, amused and refusing to take the peril seriously.

"He didn't lie about them coming *here*," Druyan said, not really attending. Her thoughts were full of Falkerry. If she was too late . . .

"Proves he knows where his own bread's buttered, that's all! Even if he's telling true, you'll never be in time," Enna persisted.

"Valadan is swift as the storm wind," Druyan declared, hoping speed was enough. She donned sturdy clothing, plain breeches and tunic, woolen cloth of her own weaving, to stand a journey.

"In his day, Lady." Enna tried without success to hide

Druyan's boots. "But he was no colt when you brought him here, and there's eight years and more gone since."

"Then he's not fast enough to get me into trouble, Enna." Druyan was out of patience. "Believe what you choose. But I am going to Falkerry." She pinned her cloak securely.

"You might as well send word by the post riders!"

"I'm faster than the Riders." Druyan stamped her feet firmly into her tall boots.

Enna threw her hands up. "They'll *know* in Falkerry to keep an eye out for raiders."

"They won't mind getting sure knowledge." Druyan clattered down the stairs, across the kitchen, and out into the yard.

Kellis stood by Valadan's head, holding the reins, though the stallion wouldn't have moved had an earthquake struck, without Druyan's word. He had adjusted all the tack, added a saddlebag to hold a small amount of food for horse and rider. He held the stirrup for Druyan's boot, looking worried.

"Enna's right, they *will* have a watch posted," she said, leaning down. "I'll tell them to look sharp tomorrow, that I saw a lot of ships coasting their way. They'll believe that likelier than the truth." She gathered her reins. "Expect me back in two days, and work wherever Enna wants you. Do what she says—unless it involves putting your head into a noose."

Whatever Enna said. But all the woman gave him was a black glare, as Kellis slunk away to put the stone bulk of the barn between them.

She's right—what sort of villain sends a lone woman off into the middle of a raid?

He couldn't stop her going.

But it need not be alone.

There was need for haste. That black horse was fleet as a deer, and if he allowed it too much of a start, he would miss the way—and he *must* follow, having no idea of the land much beyond the farm's boundary stones.

Despite that urgency, Kellis dared not risk shifting any-where among the farm buildings. If anyone saw, they knew only too well how to hurt him. Sometimes the whole place seemed to him a field sown with iron—knives, tools, even pins. If he let himself think about it, the fear would stop his breath.

Away, then. He jogged silently past the far side of the smokehouse, out of sight of the kitchen yard, along the wall of the sheepfold. The pasture, that had to be it. The orchard was too nearby.

He halted for breath in a little swale, behind a thicket of raspberries. Running on two legs felt so awkward, Kellis knew he never had his full speed in that form. And he had no time to waste on it, truly.

Well, the spot he stood upon should be deserted till the bramble fruit ripened, and that was months off. It was as good as he'd get. Kellis dragged off his patched jerkin, slipped out of the tattered linen sark beneath. The breeze raised bumps on his bared skin. He tugged off his boots.

Before sane thoughts could bring him up short, his lips began to move. Kellis sang the wolf song as he skinned out of his trews, the song that had last been on his lips on the far side of the salt sea, water no less bitter than the tears that ran unheeded down his cheeks till he had fur enough to stop them. Farther off, Rook gave one sharp inquiring bark.

The song ended in a low, plaintive howl. *Wait for me,* the silver wolf wished, as it ran toward the spot where its keen nose could begin to track the black horse and his rider.

Druyan had been slow, herself, to believe what Valadan was. A horse who spoke into her ears alone—that was one thing, and perhaps only a fancy, but a steed who never aged, who could outpace a hawk on the wing—that realiza-tion had taken her a long time to come to. She knew he loved to run, but generally when she felt safe to let Valadan do his best, they were alone, and she had no gauge of the distance or the rate at which he covered it, save that 'twas easy for him. She had raced him long ago, with her brothers and their friends, but Travic had not had any acquaintances in whose company he would have encouraged his wife to ride at breakneck speed. She did not keep Valadan a secret from her husband by design, but the result was the same as if she had. All the folk on the farm thought the stallion old because he had been there long and did not dream what feats he was yet capable of.

The winding of the lane kept them to a fast canter till they reached the main road—then Valadan's tempo quickened and he galloped, his head stretching out before him, his body seeming to lengthen. As they reached the spot where the road ceased to be the shortest way of going, they left the track with a bound and struck out over the edge of the moor.

Then his four flying hooves seemed scarcely to brush the earth. Often Valadan *had* no hoof upon the ground, but was soaring like a swallow between footfalls, as free of all constraint as the wind that legend said had sired him. He swerved for nothing save deep water or bogs, and put to flight birds that could never hope to keep pace with him. The wind itself was pressed and could match him only in relays.

The sun broke the clouds just as it was settling into the sea. The vast sky went the color of the base of a flame. Pools of standing water shone like citrines among reeds and grasses so dark that they merged into masses like storm clouds.

Even cutting across the upland moors and shortening the distance the coast road would have cost, it should have been two days' hard ride from Splaine Garth to Falkerry. Druyan knew Valadan could shave time from that—and knew they must. She had seen Falkerry by daylight, in the vision, and feared that the hour had been little past dawn. They must therefore run through the night—and she could only pray that come dawn, she would not be riding still over the moors, out of time, having misjudged her horse.

Fear not.

She felt the warm body beneath her give another great bound, and the air rushed past her cheeks like a cold river. The hummocks of grass whipped past them like clouds harried by a storm wind. The river of air became a mighty flood.

Often Druyan would have halted to rest the stallion with a spell of walking—but whenever she drew rein, Valadan snorted and dragged on the bit till she gave in and let him go forward freely once more. His joy flooded through her, powerful as the wind, so that she forgot the reason for their running for long moments and rushed through the darkness without the least anxiety. Druyan *had* misjudged her horse—but not on the side of the scale she had expected. Time itself was left behind, as Valadan raced through the night. The drum of his hooves was like wind-lashed rain— only more rapid.

They fetched up at Falkerry when the sun had risen half a hand above the horizon, riding in a pale-yellow sky. The sea lay still in the cool blue shadows cast by the headland—the lone pine upon its lonelier stack was just touched with gold on its topmost branches, like a gilt windvane topping a barn. There was, Druyan saw with a pang of relief, no pall of smoke rising from torched buildings. There was a little fog, drifting over the sea. The land itself was clear.

Moor-pastured horses raced alongside them, inspired by their intrusion. Despite a night of running, Valadan was still in good form—none of the free horses stayed at his side for long. He did not deign to notice their shadowing—he did not so much as flatten an ear to warn them off. He simply ran on, till they dropped away, to pretend to crop the dewy grass as if there had not been a race but a coincidence in their courses.

Ahead lay a little round tower built on a high outthrust of land that would be a sea stack when another twoscore of winter storms had quarried it loose from the cliff. Druyan steered toward it. As she neared the gateway, one half of the tall portal was swung aside and two riders emerged, single file in the narrow way. They were clad all in sea blue, save for the gray cloaks of unwashed black-sheep's wool that protected them from the daily rains they encountered. Druyan halted and saluted the lead horseman with a question.

"Rider, are you bound for Keverne?"

"I am." The lead post rider smiled—Keverne would be the end of his circuit, and he could depend upon a few days' ease before setting out once more. Also, it was a short day's ride from Falkerry, one of the easiest stages in his rounds. "Have you a message?"

"I saw six black-hulled ships yesterday," Druyan said tersely. "Heading this way."

The Rider's easy good humor slid from his face. He turned to his companion. "Tamsin. Get the captain of the watch out here, *now*! Where are you from, Lady?"

Druyan dodged the question, for he would not believe her answer and might thereby doubt her warning. There was no time to waste on that nonsense. What she had said was true, but she must lie to support it. "My drovers and I are bringing a herd to market. I came ahead, to tell what I'd seen."

"Well you did. Six ships . . ." The Rider stood in his stirrups, trying to scan the sea. "If they come in here, they'll have the tide." He sniffed. "Maybe the wind, as well." There was a tang of salt in the air.

After a few moments, a stocky man came afoot through the gate. "Kernan, that idiot lieutenant of yours said you wanted me. Why aren't you on your way back to Keverne? My breakfast's getting cold."

"There's raiders seen," the captain informed him.

"What? I didn't hear any alarm—"

"They weren't seen *here*, Uwen, but you'd better look sharp. Six ships is too big a force to be content with stealing the odd pig from a steading. Six ships is trouble."

"Who says six ships?" The watch captain's eyes flicked about. *"Her?"*

Druyan nodded, swallowing the implied insult. Valadan was snorting and raking the dirt with his off forehoof, irritated for her. "Yesterday."

"You're *sure* 'twas six? You're sure 'twas *ships*, come to that? Not some village fishing fleet trying to get a catch in?" He yawned, and squinted toward the sea sparkle. "I don't see any ships."

"If you wait to prepare till you see them, you'll have left it too late!" Druyan protested. "I rode all night to warn you—"

"Our thanks for that, Lady," the watch captain said placatingly. "We'll keep a sharp eye out, no fear. You can go back home."

Even the post rider seemed to take Druyan's news in a less urgent light. "Sir, shall I carry a message to the town as I pass?"

"Don't bother about it, Kernan. Our usual signals will suffice—if we see anything out of the ordinary." He touched a finger to his forehead. "Lady." He strolled back through the gate.

Druyan was dumbfounded. There was no outcry within the tower, no extra eyes rushed to the ramparts—and no word of warning sent on to the helpless town below. They'd keep watch as they always did—and the town of Falkerry would be overwhelmed by sunhigh, despite her hard-run warning.

"*Captain.*"

He turned back toward her impatiently. "Lady, I've a day's ride ahead of me. I need to be about it." His horse tossed its head restlessly.

"Sir, will you at least carry a warning about the ships?"

He fidgeted. So did the horse. "You're *certain* they were ships? I can't be raising the whole coast just because a school of porpoise came inshore, Lady, no offense."

"It was *ships*! Rider, my own brother's a captain of post riders. Maybe you know him—Robart of Glasgerion."

The captain gave her a searching look. "I've ridden with him, Lady. He's no fool."

"Neither am I! I know a ship from a porpoise. My own farm's been twice-raided—" Maybe that was a mistake to say. He'd take her for an overnervous woman . . .

The captain chewed at his lip. "Tamsin! Is that beast of yours in his usual overgood fettle? Fine. Then hie yourself straight back to Keverne, and tell them we've tidings of raiders and that something better armed than the local watch would be a great help here. It's a risk, but the army might just get here in time to be useful, for once! I'll ride into Falkerry now, then likewise alert every farm I pass on the way back to Keverne." He turned back to Druyan. "There'd *better* be ships, Lady."

"I know," Druyan whispered.

The sea and the river Fal sparkled alike, empty. Druyan thought of how she had half disbelieved Kellis' first warning, how she'd waited to see the raiders' ship. It had been no less awful a time.

Six long, low ships came into the harbor on a flooding tide and a following wind, two hours short of sunhigh. They sailed right up the Fal, whose flow of water did not quite match the tide's. The watchtower gave its customary warning—Druyan saw the puffs of dark smoke rising up— but it would never have been sufficient had the town not been already roused and prepared for the invaders' appearance.

There was pitched battle, all round the harbor. If the duke intended to send men to Falkerry's aid, there was no time for them to arrive—five of the black ships lifted their anchors when the tide began to slacken, their crews leaving empty-handed lest they be trapped inshore by a lack of wind. The sixth vessel had strayed out of the Fal's channel and into very shallow water. It grounded in mud on its way to escape and was set afire by determined bands of townsmen. What should have been a fast-hitting raid came to nothing more than ashes on the wind, a score of wounded prisoners marched to Falkerry's dungeon.

Druyan rode homeward more slowly than she had come.

There were still five ships to harry Darlith's coast, but with every farm forewarned against the raiders, there was nothing more she could think to do. There was no way she could guess—on her own—where any of those ships would choose to land, whether they would stay together or separate. Her task was done.

She had been up all night and longed to drowse in her saddle. Indeed, she thought of halting to snatch a few hours of rest in the heather. The stems would be soft, so early in the year . . .

Valadan had other ideas. When she drew back on the reins, he bent hard against the bit, bowing his neck, and actually went faster for all her attempts to slow him. *Rain*, came the terse explanation into her head, and looking seaward, Druyan beheld a dark line of squalls sweeping in.

"That ought to give those raiders second thoughts," she said, pleased by Esdragon's own defenses. Maybe the storm would pound those five ships to pieces against the tall cliffs.

Hold tightly, Valadan requested. *I will run now.*

And the earth blurred away once again. Druyan, weary and sore, leaned forward and wound her big hands tight into the long black mane. She was too tired to watch sharp for obstacles, and doubted she was all that much help to the stallion anyway, at such a pace. The rushing of the ground made her head reel, so Druyan trustingly shut her eyes and rocked with Valadan's stride as his speed blended them into one being. It felt like being aboard a vessel carrying full sail, running before the wind, swept along with the spray sparkling behind, the seabirds falling back, unable to keep pace . . .

When she opened her eyes once more, her own mended gate was barring their way.

I would have jumped, but you might have fallen, Valadan said gently, apologetically.

Druyan slowly unwound his mane from her fingers and slid down over his left shoulder. The soft ground of the lane stung the soles of her feet like a blow, she had been in the saddle so long. Her knees ached. The first raindrops were just pocking the dirt as they reached the door of the barn.

An ordinary courser would have been furnace-hot after running so long—would have been dead at half the distance, like as not, Druyan amended. She fussed over Valadan for the best part of the next hour, rubbing his legs with cloths, massaging his back, currying him all over—before finally admitting what she knew in her heart already. The stallion ran like the wind he'd been sired by and took no more harm from such running than that wind did of blowing, though he found her attentions pleasant. She fed him his supper. She could have done it the moment they entered the barn and done him no harm, though such idiot-kindness would have killed any mortal horse. She left him munching hay and staggered through the rain to the kitchen. Her hips were aching, too.

First step inside, she stubbed a toe against the wooden washtub, which was pressed into service intercepting a stream of water falling from somewhere above. Enna, positioning a pail under another drip, looked around and exclaimed at her.

"Lady! You're home! And half drowned—not that you'll fare better in your own kitchen." She poked a finger at the ceiling. "That good-for-nothing thief Kellis has run off, the churning's not done, there's not a stick of firewood left, and this roof's leaking like a tea strainer!"

Druyan aimed herself at a bench, where she tried to sit without collapsing. "Falkerry's safe," she croaked.

"And look at you!" Enna ran on, unheeding of the good news—which after all did not concern Splaine Garth. "Were you off that horse for one minute?" Another puddle began forming by noisy spatters on the hearthstone—Enna went at it with a scream and a crockery bowl.

"There's not that much in here to take harm from the wet," Druyan protested. And the bustle was disconcerting, besides being useless. "Just let the roof drip, Enna. We'll mop it up tomorrow, after Kellis has the roof patched."

Enna narrowed her eyes. "I've seen neither front nor back of him since you rode out, Lady," she said, almost sounding pleased. "If he's within ten leagues of Splaine Garth this minute, I'll stand amazed."

"He's gone?" Druyan whispered, stunned. Somewhere she could hear another leak coming to ground—or onto a metal pot. It seemed loud as thunder.

"What did you expect? I'm only surprised the villain didn't manage it before this." Enna flung a rug over the flour bin, though it didn't appear to be in immediate peril of flood. "You let him have free run of the place. He's got two good legs under him, and no morals to speak of."

"Did he say anything?" It didn't seem the time to spring to Kellis' defense, but she didn't find a prisoner's escaping all that immoral. Just . . . inexplicable. "Take anything with him?"

"Nothing from the kitchen—he wouldn't have dared, I've knives in here!" Enna said with fierce joy. "I imagine if we count the chickens tomorrow, we'll be one or two shy. There's no iron round the henhouse."

Druyan stared about the dim kitchen, which was commencing to spin, ever so slightly. That new drip was sounding like a gong, or an alarm bell. *"Why?"* she whispered, not to Enna.

"We're well rid of him, Lady," Enna answered cheerfully, bespoken or not, then helped her mistress to bed.

Druyan was up—aches and all—at first light, to be sure the stock in the barn got fed and turned out. How she would manage beyond that, she did not know, and refused to think upon. She brought Valadan his breakfast while Dalkin guided the two cows and their calves toward their day's pasture. She stirred a treat of honey into the oats, and looked up at a noise from the doorway. Sometimes a cow escaped Dalkin's herding skills, though they seldom preferred barn to green pasture . . .

Kellis was standing there, the bright light at his back eating away at the edges of him.

Druyan gave the oats another stir round. "Enna said you'd left." Her heart banged against the cage of her ribs, denying her outward calm.

Kellis took a couple of steps into the barn. His clothes were soaking wet, covered with bits of heather twig and grass. His face was stubbled, his eyes red-rimmed. "Is the roof leaking?" he asked hoarsely.

"Yes, but I think she noticed *before* the rain started. Where were you?"

"With the sheep," he said inadequately. She could not let the lie pass, it was too obvious.

"That's Pru's job, and Lyn's. And they have the two dogs to help them. Who said you had to go, too?"

"I—" He struggled for something plausible to offer her, but came up empty. "It was because of me that you went. I decided it was better if Enna wasn't reminded of that every time she saw me."

"You didn't have to stay out in the rain all night to accomplish that. She can't climb up the ladder to the haymow." He was lying. Druyan knew it, and could see that he was well aware that she knew. But there would be no getting the truth out of him. It was plain as the crooked nose on his weathered face. Druyan finally stopped fruitlessly struggling to think of ways to do it. Kellis hadn't asked after Falkerry's fate, either, and Druyan was at an even greater loss to account for that disinterest.

Well, you don't know him, do you? Not at all, she coldly admonished her foolish self.

The Black Bowl

PATCHING THE ROOF failed to insinuate Kellis back into Enna's good graces, though he did a fine job of it—at least in the short run. He churned till the dasher seemed worn away—Enna pronounced the butter spoiled and fed it to the pigs. Kellis chopped firewood and split kindling till there was half a winter's worth stacked outside the kitchen—it made no difference, her hostility was unabated. The next rain could find no path through the thatch and had to be content with trickling down the chimney to make the flames hiss and jump, but Enna did not rejoice, or take it as anything out of the way. The roof had never leaked till Kellis went up there in the first place, and never mind why he'd done it. The various pots and bowls and pails that had caught the drips were all stowed in their usual storage places as a vote of confidence she loudly refused to share.

Druyan laid claim to a little basin of black-glazed clay as the other bowls went into the cupboards one by one. It was round and shallow, with a handle set on either side, and once it might have boasted a lid, she thought, though she had never seen it. The bowl had been at Splaine Garth, lidless, when she arrived there as Travic's bride. It was too fine for a cat's dish, too small to hold anything other than one drip too many for the other containers. She cradled it in her arms and took it to the kitchen garden, where Kellis was doggedly hoeing weeds into oblivion.

146

"You didn't ask," she said without preamble. "Falkerry beat off the raiders. They might have managed it anyway, but I saw the difference a warning made."

He eyed the bowl like a horse watching a grass fire. "So you want me to do it again."

"You're going to see things anyway. You said it worked that way. Why not do something about *what* you see?"

Kellis chopped viciously at a deep-rooted thistle. The garden tools were bronze-bladed, safe for him. "Lady, I would rather clean out your pigpen."

"This doesn't need to interfere with the regular chores. I want the flax seed sown this week, too," Druyan answered lightly, supposing that he jested with her.

"You think all I have to do is look in the bowl, and I'll see whatever helps you!" No, Kellis wasn't jesting. He had gone quite white, and his breathing was ragged. "It isn't like that! Most times there's nothing to see. And even when there is—the first time you go riding off to save some settlement that's already cold ashes, you'll hate me for not being able to tell yesterday from tomorrow. Let be, Lady. There are watches set all along your coast—they know the danger. You've done all you can."

"It's not enough," Druyan protested, shocked at his refusal. "No one can watch every harbor, every river mouth, every minute. And no matter how closely they watch, the raids are too quick. Half an hour's notice isn't enough."

"I can't give you better! You'll think I can, you'll rely on me doing it, and I'll fail you!" He went at a patch of bindweed, perilously close to the row of carrots he was safeguarding. The bronze blade rose and fell, as if he were trying to be no more than that, have no existence beyond the task.

"You didn't fail Falkerry," Druyan pointed out.

"A vision that demands to be seen is a different animal from one I deliberately go hunting, Lady." He kept chopping. "One's luck. The other flees and will not be taken without a chase."

"So chase it. A few minutes in the morning, before you

start chores," Druyan offered reasonably. "Or whatever other time of day you choose. I trust you not to take advantage and only pretend to look, and I'll tell Enna so—"

The hoe rang against a stone, and stilled. "You'll *trust* me. Lady, I have been *trusted* ere this." His face was nearly as white as his hair, immobile as a stone mask except for his darting eyes. "My family's dead. My entire Clan has ceased to exist because they *trusted* me to see clear enough to protect them from danger. And I saw everything peaceful and hadn't the wit to know I was seeing *back* instead of ahead. They didn't get a warning. That's what comes of *trusting* me."

If he'd leapt up and struck her, the message couldn't have come plainer to Druyan—she knew *nothing* of this man before her. Not his past, not his likely reaction to anything she might say to him—nothing at all. He was unknown and exactly as dangerous as Enna held, and naught but sheerest luck had kept her safe thus far. And luck could run out . . . She took a step back.

"I liked being the prophet," Kellis said harshly, staring at her. "Looking into the mirror of the water, singing the vision into being—not everyone could do that. Knowing every eye in the clan was on me while I did it. I liked the status—after the chief, they looked to me. I liked the attention. I could reassure the old people that all would be well, and the women would smile at me. The girls would be so grateful . . .

"But I never learned how to give them anything real. I never took the trouble to learn *how* to look, how to see past the surface and whatever would give itself to me easily. Our shaman was dead, there was no one to take me to task for it, no one even to know the difference—but *I* knew, knew I was only playing at it, for what I could get out of it. Respect, and fine goods, and women. I suppose I knew in my heart that I'd have to pay for that ease, one day— what I didn't know was, it wasn't *me* who'd be asked for the payment. I just had to watch."

Druyan wanted to break and run, from him and from his

confession, to put a safe distance between them. But that was showing weakness, and once she began, where would she stop? At the kitchen door? The twice-mended gate? The edge of the sea? She dared not run, and she would not.

"All right," Splaine Garth's lady whispered, her voice dry as sand. "I *won't* trust you. I'll weigh every word you tell me, and doubt it twice before I ride out. Will that satisfy you?"

That flying brow came down, level as a line squall over the waves. "We had a bargain, Lady. And none of this was in it, that I recall."

"I didn't *know* about any of this!" Druyan shouted, outraged.

"Now you do, and you think you can just add it in with the rest? Plow a field, fix a roof, shear a sheep, and order up a vision so you'll know where the raiders will strike next?"

"I don't expect it matters to you, if they do to Esdragon what they did to your people," Druyan accused. "It's not your home or your problem. You're only here till you can get to somewhere else. Well, I hope for your sake that the city you saw is *real*, that it's being built *now*, that it isn't so far in days to come that you'll never live to see it."

"It wasn't one of *my* visions," Kellis answered sharply. "I wouldn't have trusted anything *I* saw all the way across the Great Sea!"

"Probably you wouldn't," Druyan agreed. She set the bowl down at the edge of the garden. "You can have this for a shaving basin. I suppose if you happen to see raiders coming *here* again, you'll mention it? That's far enough in your own interest?"

He looked stricken. "I'm refusing for *your* good, not mine, Lady."

"Of course you are," Druyan said, and turned away, swirling her skirts about in a tiny, angry wind.

The flax field greened up rapidly under the light daily rains. They didn't grow a great deal of the fiber, but

Druyan liked to have the wherewithal to make her own household linen. Wool was warm and shed the rain wonderfully, but for comfort she wanted a soft sark beneath it, next to her skin.

Once fields were plowed and planted, the early season of the year held fewer urgent tasks than the harvesttime pressed with. Druyan took the winter's worth of saved wood ashes and rendered pig fat, and spent a week making soap, scented with a tisane brewed of last year's dried lavender blossoms. She worked daily with the three new foals, seeing to it that they learned to lead while they were still small enough to muscle if they proved reluctant, knowing they needed to learn early to do as humans told them if the habit was to hold when they were grown. Same for the new calves, though not to quite the same extent, as leading would be all they were expected to do. Playing with the lambs was a temptation she struggled to resist—'twas foolish to make pets of creatures you expected to eat. She felt a little safer about the orphan lamb—it had particularly silky wool and would be kept for its fleece.

Druyan seized the chance to dye the accumulation of winter-spun wool, working the craft in around cheese-making and the last of the soapmaking. She held back no skeins—there were dyestuffs she could not gather at that time of the year, but there was the wool from the spring shearing still to be dealt with. She colored her yarn with the skins of onions, the shells of black walnuts, the first green coltsfoot leaves, and the last of the wintered-over beets. By the time she had finished with all the possible colors, 'twas time for a first cutting of salt-grass hay.

In an ordinary river-bottom field, they'd have cut and left the stems to dry and cure in the sun—but that was not to be thought of in a marsh soaked twice daily by the tide. The hay would have molded, or been clotted with salt, or turned to peat like the natural edges of the marsh. Instead, they cut wain-loads and hauled them back to a hilly pasture that caught a good breeze and whatever sun there was, and hoped for a few dry days in a string. Druyan did what she could to ensure a lack of rainfall, but she would not risk whistling up a breeze.

She had not tasked him further about the bowl.

She had not taken it away with her, either. She had abandoned it on the dark earth, hard by the feathery tops of the new carrots. If he left it there, the rain would fill it to the brim, till its surface was a perilous mirror for his unwary eye to fall upon while he was at his chores.

It belonged in the kitchen, probably. But Kellis dared not step foot therein—Enna was having a bad spell with her joints and never left the shelter of the room for any sure length of time. Her knees were hurting her nearly as badly as her hands, she could not walk far, and her temper was exactly what one would imagine it to be under those circumstances.

He could put the bowl in the barn. And Kellis did, but he could not put it from his mind. He hoped a hen would choose it for a nest. There was one that prowled the barn, obviously broody, plainly not trusting the daily raided nestboxes the lady provided for her fowl. Her fluffed feathers would hide all of the bowl from him, from his sight. He would be able to forget.

Days, that goal was possible. His work took him far from the barn and the bowl, and the regular movements of his arms and legs could lure him into a sort of trance, when Kellis thought of nothing but the ground underfoot and the air about him; he could be mindless as a beast.

They cut hay in the marsh. Kellis dared not be mindless about *that*—he was required to wield a scythe with a wicked crescent blade of which he had a morbid fear—or a healthy respect, depending on one's point of view. Fortunately, the scythe's snathe was wood, and long, which meant he was able to keep the cold iron at some distance from his shivering flesh while he worked. But reaping required constant tense vigilance if some disaster was not to overtake him. Kellis could not carry the tool to the marsh, over his shoulder with the iron crescent pointing down his

back as Dalkin did. Nor dared he hone the dulled blade on
the bit of sarsen stone Dalkin had for that purpose. He had
to ask the boy to tend the tool for him, to carry it and
sharpen it.

And then, if he narrowed his attention down until his
head ached and his shoulders twitched, Kellis could cut hay
without slicing his own legs out from under him.

In a broader field, he would have been so slow as to be
useless. But the marsh was his friend, its twisty channels
and narrow ribbons of grass rewarding rather than punishing the care he took in cutting. Had he embraced the
scythe like a brother, he could have cut the salt grass no
differently, no more swiftly.

Come night he should have slept like the dead, worn out
by strain and exercise. But Kellis lay nightlong in the dark
cave of the barn, listening to the horses breathing and sighing and nibbling at their fodder, wide awake. And in the
blackness there was one spot of greater darkness yet, and
an empty space at the center of that darkness, a cup to
catch and hold all the overflowing misery in his heart.

He shut his eyes. It didn't matter—he wasn't seeing the
bowl with them. That was why the farthest corner of the
barn was not half far enough away for it. That was why
covering the bowl with hay did no good. Probably smash-
ing the fragile crockery would be no use, either, though he
had not yet tried that last resort, since there was no retreat-
ing from it if it proved faulty.

*You were quick enough to look into the water for those
murdering savages,* his dark thoughts accused him.

The answers didn't matter, he responded, flinching. *All I
had to do was tell them what they wanted to hear. And
hope I was right enough for my own sake. Never for theirs.*

As a plan, it had been stupid, and it hadn't worked for
long—but he'd done it, without a qualm, without this ago-
nizing. Means to an end, using the Eral to ferry him over
the sea, that broadest barrier on his quest for the city where
wizard-folk gathered, where he might find a place.

Night after night he felt the bowl's presence, like a bad

tooth that would not hurt him unless he bit upon it, but would not leave him in peace, either. What sleep he did find was tainted by dreams of uncomfortable intensity, worse than any that the iron-sickness had ever given him.

If he looked into the bowl—even once—there was no going back from it. If he asked to see, he *would* see. See, and be once more cursed with the conundrum of sifting truth from deception, today from tomorrow, with always the chance that it might as easily have been yesterday. He couldn't do it. He knew too well what the responsibilities were and that he was not equal to them. His clan had died to prove that to him.

Better, anyway, that he not tell the Lady Druyan what she wanted. She had shown him kindness, she had more than likely saved his life—mixed blessing though that deed was. He did not think he would fairly repay her by giving her a cause to ride that wonderful, terrifying horse of hers into danger. He was right to refuse her, if only for her own good.

Her good—or his cowardice?

The straw stuffing his pallet felt like so many bundled sticks. Kellis arose, unable to bear it longer. Morning must come, sooner or later, whether he slept or not. Time always passed, however distorted his sense of it. The nights were shrinking as the sun rode higher into summer. He leaned wearily against the wall that separated his stall from the next.

Warm air brushed his cheek, startling him. The boards creaked as Valadan rubbed his shoulder against them, perhaps soothing an itch. He blew another breath in Kellis' direction, through the narrow gap betwixt the boards.

"Am I keeping you awake?"

There was a snort for an answer. Horses dozed much, but did not sleep deeply nightlong. They preferred to spend the hours attending to their hay.

"What would *you* do?"

Kellis had heard the lady speaking to this horse as if he were a human soul, able to make her answer. He knew the stallion had speed beyond that of any mortal steed—had it not hopelessly outdistanced him when he tried to follow their shared mistress to Falkerry? And in the dark, Kellis could see the stars glowing, the uncanny constellations that filled Valadan's eyes. But the horse did not speak to him, the horse who was not afraid to be entirely whatever he was.

It was Dalkin's task to turn the hay over with a wooden fork, so it would dry evenly. The final stage was to spread the fodder on the barn floor for a while, before ultimate storage in the mow above. There was a contraption of rope and pulleys and a platform for lifting the fully cured hay up to the loft—good work for a rainy morning.

The pulleys were squealing like pigs at slaughtertime as Druyan ventured into the barn in quest of the overclever hen who'd made a nest in the henhouse but had steadfastly refused to lay in it—Druyan knew she had a true nest somewhere, and suspected an overlooked corner of the barn. Or else the fresh, inviting hay. Either way, the hen was destined to lose her clandestine brood.

Kellis lowered the platform carefully, then came down the ladder to load it once more. Druyan inquired whether he'd seen a hen.

"I didn't. She gave herself away when she pecked my ankle—I had almost stepped in the nest." Kellis indicated the general direction with an inclination of his head. "There's just the one egg, Lady, and she seems most determined not to give it up."

Druyan sighed. "I suppose she might as well hatch it out. Do you think we're finished with this cutting?"

Kellis glanced roofward, cocked his head to listen. The pattering of drops was less steady than it had been an hour before. "There's more I might get to, just the other side of the main channel." They only cut from the upper edges of the marsh—go too far in and the wagon would mire hopelessly. "Worth cutting if we get another dry week for the curing."

Druyan took stock of her weather charms, a review to help her decide whether she could entice a few days of rainlessness out of the sky. A breath of wind would break up the clouds . . .

Or invite a storm, like the last wind she'd whistled up, destruction and inconvenience because she'd played with powers she didn't in the least understand. Not a risk she should take, just for a bit more hay. Still, the wind had been shifting on its own, doing exactly what she would have asked it to do . . .

"Start cutting in the morning, even if it's wet—we're due some clear weather," she said, and went off to see about it.

Druyan was half through a charm for fair skies when she sensed she was no longer alone. The far side of the orchard had seemed private enough—the cows and their calves paid her no heed—but Druyan felt eyes at her back and turned to see Kellis standing by one of the gnarled apple trunks. She arose, leaving behind on the ground a little blue bowl. She had just poured water from it, wiped it carefully dry with a linen cloth, then breathed upon the grass gently, to simulate drying that, as well. It was too soon to tell whether the tiny mummery would have the desired effect on the greater stage of Splaine Garth, but she thought the sky was lightening.

"Is this how your people witch weather?" she asked Kellis, curious about her homespun technique. If there was a surer way to obtain her ends . . .

Kellis shrugged. The day's-end light filled his eyes, making them shine silver as his hair. "Hard to say. We're mostly concerned with having the rains come on time, so the pastures don't burn up. I don't think I've ever seen anyone trying to *stop* rainfall."

"I can't stop it, either," Druyan admitted. "Just hold it off for a bit, or chivvy it on its way. Steer it around us. Not much. Of course, the weather's generally a bit drier this time of year. That helps."

"You don't want much more magic than that, Lady. It's

no use, and a lot of trouble." His tone, like his expression, was bleak.

"You mean not to be able to touch iron?"

Kellis didn't answer. His eyes were empty, his thoughts and meaning impossible to guess.

"They say my grandmother Kessallia was a great witch," Druyan mused. "No one could keep anything at all from her. Every secret, hidden thing was open to her. But she didn't pass the witchblood on—they say she examined every child, every grandchild, and never found a trace. It must have been bred out of us." To her lady mother's relief, probably. But Druyan's own regret shaded her voice.

"Or she was looking too soon." Kellis' attention came back, if it had ever been absent. "You can't judge witchblood in a baby—they're too busy with everything else, walking, talking. Teething. The power crops out later, when childhood's being left behind."

An old man points a finger at you, picks you out of a crowd, and nothing's ever right after that—only you don't know it, he thought. Aloud, he tried to reassure her.

"If it's weak, and you pay it no heed, that power might even damp off, like a seed that sprouts but doesn't grow. Or it might curse every part of your life." Because maybe she shouldn't regret her lack as she seemed to.

Druyan blinked at the sudden shift in the wind. "Then perhaps I'm glad I don't have it," she said.

"If we get fair weather tomorrow, will it be an accident, then?" Kellis raised a brow at her. "There are plenty of weather charms, because no one can escape wanting weather that favors what he's doing. Most of them don't work. Yours do."

"It's a good thing," Druyan answered tartly, looking at the brown cow and her calf, grazing nearby. "We need a deal of hay out of this summer—that's a fine heifer there, and if I keep her to milk, we'll be making cheese enough to take to market in a couple of years. But if I can't feed her, I'll have to salt her down or sell her. The moors don't offer pasture enough for the horses and the cattle. Easier some ways when the year's calves are all bullocks."

"You could pasture year-round on that marsh," Kellis said, born of a herding people and knowing good pasture just by the feel of it under his boots.

"The winter storms take too much of a toll. When there's a storm tide, we don't dare let even the sheep into the marsh."

Kellis nodded, pulling a stem of hay out of his sleeve. "I see your point. I'm supposed to be telling you that Enna has your supper ready."

Druyan bent to gather up the bowl. There was a little breeze teasing at the ends of her yellow-red hair, where it was slipping free of its braid. Aloft, the winds would be greater yet. The clouds would break up, and they'd delight in clear weather for perhaps as much as a week. The hay would be made—and she'd probably manage to add another milking cow to the herd. The coursers who had gone with Travic's men were eating elsewhere . . .

The bowl in her hands brought another bowl to mind—she hadn't seen it since she abandoned it in the garden next to a row of carrots, but it had often been in her thoughts.

When he slept, Kellis dreamed of his homeland, the purple grassland of Vossli. At first all he saw were wind ripples that brushed the land's surface into waves like the sea's. And his heart lifted with a ridiculous joy, that all his troubles had been no more than a night of evil dreams, that his home was still there when he opened his eyes to the dawn.

But as he gazed with his wolf-eyes, he saw the black smoke, and the acrid tang of burning tingled in his nostrils. It was no natural fire—there had been no lightning storm to kindle a blaze of renewal. And there were the tall shapes of men behind the flames.

In an instant more, the charred land was being ripped open by iron-bladed plows. Kellis sobbed low in his throat, feeling the land's pain as if the rent flesh had been his own.

Crushed by the weight of the stone houses that sprang forth behind the new-plowed lands, the lines of stone walls that divided one bit from another, like unweaned pups torn from their mother's belly. Flinching from the tread of the strange feet that tracked the dust where once purple-tipped grasses had grown . . .

Kellis opened his eyes to the darkness. His cheeks were wet, and his throat ached as if it held fire-coals. There was no stench of burning, except in his heart.

But I have driven a plow, he thought. *It was hard work, but not a calamity. Not a desecration . . .*

Not for Esdragon, no. The invading Eral had made Vossli cease to exist in a generation. They could not wreak that upon Esdragon simply by farming—but they could do worse. And they would.

Unless they were stopped.

"I can't stop them," Kellis whimpered. "My clan is gone from every memory save mine—"

A snort came from the adjoining stall.

"I *can't*—" Kellis insisted. And glanced with a shudder toward the corner where the hidden bowl lay.

More salt hay was spread on the pasture, and Dalkin was set to making sure the sheep and the coneys left it alone. Druyan oversaw the planting of the turnips, the onions, and the leeks, a whole new patch of carrots in a sandy spot discovered accidentally. In the hedgerows, roses and blackberries and raspberries were shedding their white petals and beginning to set fruit on their long canes.

The sun lifted his shining face over the moors a heartbeat earlier every day and tarried a moment or two longer each evening before dipping into the water of the marsh. Druyan started Kellis digging peat—it was none too early to think of winter's fuel, as they had thought of the fodder. The turves needed a considerable drying time at the edge of the marsh, ere they could be carted in to stack and store—ready to supplement precious wood in the winter fires.

Kellis fed the stock and then went straight off to his digging unless she instructed him beforehand to tend to some other chore. So Druyan was startled, while she sat coaxing milk from the brown cow with her big, gentle but not a gentlewoman's hands, to see him appear at the cowshed door. The calf bawled at him, wanting to be loosed so it could go to its mother.

"You can keep digging," Druyan said, pressing her head lightly against the cow's soft flank, inhaling her warm animal scent. "You'll be long gone before any of that peat goes on the fire, but we'll bless your name, every fire we sit by, come winter."

"Lady—"

"What?" More milk swished into the pail, in time with her moving hands.

"This is . . . good sailing weather."

"We don't have a boat, Kellis. I suppose we could float the peat up the river if we made a raft, but the wagon works as well. If we pick dry weather—"

"The wind's from the sea."

"It always is, this season." She tugged gently, easing out the last of the milk. "The sunfall winds. Every tree on the Darlith coast will tell you that—they all lean inland." The cow lowed softly, and her calf, tethered so it would not impede the milking, answered her with another bawl. Druyan stood, set the pail safely out of the cow's way, and made ready to drive her to her day's grazing. Not the orchard again, she thought. That grass was thin, lush enough but easy to overgraze.

Kellis was still in the doorway, though he stepped back out of the cow's path. Something in his expression—which was unhappy, to say the least—caught Druyan's full attention. *"Are they coming again?"* she whispered. Her hands went cold. She forgot the cow.

For answer, Kellis walked slowly to the well and hauled the bucket up, hand over hand, not troubling with the slower winch. The black bowl sat waiting on the well coping; he poured into it from the bucket until it was brim full.

The water was clear, but within the bowl it looked like

a puddle of tar. Kellis leaned forward and blew one breath across it. Ripples spread, then stilled once more. Druyan could see the bottom of the bowl then, the faint ridges the potter's fingers had left, their circles growing ever smaller as they spiraled in to the exact center of the bowl. Remembering the last time Kellis had shared a vision with her, she reached to take his left hand. His fingers were cold as dew-soaked grass, and near as damp.

He would need to woo this vision—though his dreams had been tangled and vivid for far too many nights, those had been memories, never prophecies. No insistent visions were battering at the barrier behind Kellis' eyes—the well had not been emptied, but enough had been released that the visions no longer spilled out unstoppably. It was his normal state, when he could choose not to see, not to risk pain and confusion, failure and embarrassment—it had been a fatally easy choice for him to make, once before.

Kellis crooned the summoning so softly that he could not hear the sound with his own ears. His throat was tight with fear, he had to force the sound through, and it was far louder in his mind than in the air. One could entreat the visions, but they did not respect whining—they wanted a submission that came of respect, not fear. *Concentrate. Focus. Believe the foreseeing would come . . .*

Pain stabbed his temples. With better practice, he could have ignored it for the trifle it was. He must pay it no heed, must certainly not dread that the pain would increase if he persisted. If he flinched, it would only be worse.

You have to want to do it worse than you don't want to do it.

Wisir hadn't been much of a teacher. *He* hadn't been much of a student. And they hadn't spent time enough together for their mutual dislike to be refined into a useful I'll-show-him hatred.

Be a channel for the vision to flow through.

His stomach twisted, counterpoint to the throbbing behind his eyes. It wasn't going to work . . .

Kellis felt a reassuring pressure, other fingers intertwined with his own. The contact was so startling, so unexpected that for a moment Kellis forgot his dread in wonderment.

Light flashed across the surface of the water. It was white wave-foam, breaking over a shingle beach. Cliffs rose up almost at once. Druyan looked harder and saw ships rounding a rock the height of the duke's castle at Keverne, entering a harbor that much resembled a keyhole—narrow at the entrance, widening out inside to a safe, sheltered anchorage. There were a lot of buildings clustered behind its stone quays, rising up the sides of the hills as if they'd been pushed there by the crush at the harborside.

"Do you know it?" Kellis asked harshly, his pupils pinpricks in his silvery eyes.

"That's Porlark," she answered, unhesitating. "Fishermen call it the Mousehole, because of that harbor. But that harbor's a trap, you can hold its entrance with half a dozen men—"

Kellis tore his hand free and rose abruptly. The images in the bowl slopped over the edge and vanished. He dumped the remaining water unceremoniously onto the ground, the stream wavering with his trembling.

"It's not as far as Falkerry," Druyan said, feeling in consternation at her muddied skirts.

"Aye, you'll weigh every word I tell you, twice and thrice," Kellis said bitterly. "You won't trust me." He backed a step away.

"There's no harm to ride that way—if the raiders have been there already ..." Druyan gave her head a shake to chase that fell thought. She faced him. "Suppose they haven't? Should I *not* warn the folk of the Mousehole? I couldn't live with myself, if I knew and said nothing."

But he would not look at her. And she did not know what was amiss, that he should out of nowhere offer his help, then complain because she believed his warnings. When she went to saddle Valadan there was no sign of

Kellis, nor when she rode out to cry her warning to the folk who lived behind the Mousehole.

To the natural blessing of their harbor's narrow approach, the citizens of Porlark had added a great bronze chain, which lay at the bottom of the channel, running from far side to near. They kept a sharp watch, too, and when Druyan gave them her warning, that chain was winched up till it rode just below the surface of the waves, ready to rip the keel out of any ship that dared the passage without the watch captain's leave.

Simple defense, but scarcely an instant one—the winching required a full hour, and a dozen men working each capstan. Signal flags had to be unfurled, to warn off Porlark's fishermen and to alert incoming trade ships that they must choose other ports. Druyan watched uneasily all that while from Valadan's back. Her word of seeing ships upcoast had been believed—but if the ships did not come? If Kellis' vision failed, no one would listen to a second warning from her—she hadn't said how she knew, she'd said she'd *seen*, and failure would brand her a liar.

The flags warned off Porlark's ships. But what warned nearby villages and settlements? Anything upriver from Porlark was safe, but what of up- and downcoast? Druyan had asked and did not care for the answers she was given along with thanks for her warning. She could see no reason why the raiders, refused Porlark, should not simply nose into another harbor or river mouth, a place unwarned and unprepared.

Valadan carried her eagerly along the clifftops, where they paused at many a steading ere turning back for Splaine Garth. And on their homeward course there were settlements to alert, as well—it was long after dark when Druyan fetched Darlith once more, despite Valadan's speed.

The wolf waited atop the headland, from which vantage he could mostly keep the woman and the black horse in sight. That was far easier to do once they had stopped running—he had been hard-pressed to keep close enough to track them as they galloped, and his lungs had been afire for far too long a while after that race. Wolves are fairly tireless, but he was not wind-sired.

Thankfully, there was no present danger for him to fend off. The incoming ships would not get close enough to Porlark to fight for passage—in the narrow way, they could not offer any fight at all. There was no peril to the woman from the raiders—he had not sent her into danger, this time. He did not allow himself any relief over that.

When she rode out once more, he mistook the way, assuming wrongly that she would be bound for the farm. He looked over his shoulder and knew alarm—there was no sign of any horse, any rider. The wolf loped back the way he had come till he spotted them at last, going in what he felt certain was the wrong direction, but after the second steading was visited, he saw clear enough what the game was and relaxed. Unless they stumbled across raiders strayed from the main pack, there was no danger. He paid more heed to staying out of sight, too, after a farm dog scented him and came snapping after him, turning back only when the poor brave beast came close and saw plain what it had so rashly challenged.

Druyan snatched a few hours of sleep before 'twas time to rise for milking. The sun was just up as she crossed the yard, to see Kellis at the well, the dark bowl balanced percariously on his lap, his head drooping over it. A shudder went through him when Druyan put a hand on his shoulder. He raised his face to hers, and his expression was despairing.

"Far up a river, somewhere," he whispered bleakly. "I couldn't see open ocean, only the river winding out of sight."

"Show me," Druyan ordered, weariness forgotten. She had not expected another alarm so soon, but surely that was foolish. She had denied the raiders the Mousehole; they had to go somewhere else.

Kellis shook his head. "I can't get it back. I have been trying till I'm dizzy." He had not wanted to look at all, worn out and short of sleep as he was, unlikely to succeed at understanding—but the vision had demanded his attention, just as he had feared it might. "They burned something, Lady, I could see that much." Nothing to go on, except 'twas trouble for someone, somewhere.

"If it was a long way inland, it would need to be one of the deeper rivers," Druyan speculated. "Most of them don't run more than a few leagues before they're too shallow or too rough for ships. Maybe they got up the Fal. If they left Falkerry itself alone, maybe they could slip past the watch. If there was fog . . ." There often was, on the coast.

"There was a town," Kellis declared. He frowned, trying to sift out more details, significant landmarks. Whatever those might be. He'd only had an instant's glimpse. "And a lot of rocks in the river. The water went white."

"The Fal's known for its rapids," Druyan mused. "It's broad and it's deep, but you can't ship as far upriver as the merchants would like, because ships can't get through the rapids. The river runs a long way after, but it's no use to ships from the sea. There's a cattle market, they drive beasts there, so ships can take the beef—"

She arose and went to fetch her saddle. Kellis staggered after her, full of foreboding. "Lady, be careful. This one feels different." He could not have said how, but his head was near to bursting, and the edges of objects were haloed with light, though the sun was scarcely over the horizon. His hair clung damply to his forehead and cheeks, but he felt cold all over. When last a vision had repaid him so for viewing it, what had it meant? Future or irretrievable past? He should *know*. He should have learned. "I don't think there's very much time."

In fact, there was no time at all.

Teilo had been a prosperous cattle market, where beasts were gathered, sold, slaughtered and butchered and salted, then shipped down the Fal to many markets. There were tanneries to begin making use of the hides, a whole guild of leatherworkers to finish off the process. There were saddlers and harnessmakers by the score. Many a rich merchant dwelt there, in a home well appointed by his wealth. Druyan caught the smell of smoke from those homes on the sultry wind as she neared the river. The glow of the flames had been invisible, obscured by the new-risen sun. The same sun now showed the disaster plain. Her broad hands tightened on Valadan's reins.

Perhaps the raiders had fired only a building or two, for a diversion while they plundered. But the fire had spread while Teilo's folk had struggled to chase off the thieves, and in the end the flames had taken most of the town. Smoke-smothered cattle choked the holding pens. Others, fortunate enough to escape through weak fences, had run bawling through the streets, adding confusion, trampling folk fighting the fires. Everything of any value had been carted off, along with a few of the women. Fifty men were dead of the fighting, and the tally of those caught in the flames would run near as high when there was time to number them. Somewhere a dog howled disconsolately.

As Druyan was turning for home, heartsick, she spied two riders cantering over the moors and caught a glimpse of sea-blue tunics. She legged Valadan toward them, urging him to make good speed to intercept them.

The post riders caught sight of her and swerved to meet her the more quickly. Their faces were grave—the smoke rising from what had been Teilo was unmistakably ill news.

"How soon may word be got to the duke?" Druyan asked, when the Riders had taken a few moments to gaze upon the destruction. She had told them of the attempt on Porlark—though she pretended only to have heard of it from another. They would never have believed that she could have seen it, then been at Teilo next day. Even used to Valadan's swiftness, she herself still marveled at it.

"We will carry the news to our next way-station, Lady," the senior Rider said. "A message can be sent direct to Keverne from there. It should reach the duke by sunfall."

"For what good 'twill do," the second Rider interjected bitterly. "Those who did this deed are back on the sea roads, where the army can't touch them. Brioc has a thousand men armed and in the field—and still *this* happens!" He gestured wildly at the wreckage on the banks of the Fal, and his horse reacted by flinging up its head and plunging against the bit.

"I know," Druyan said, smiling without humor. "All the men of my freehold are kept with the duke's army—meanwhile my farm is raided. Those men would have been far more use to me than to my uncle."

The senior Rider squinted at her. "Lady, I think I should know you."

She should perchance have known his name, also, but did not. "You are acquainted with my brother, I suspect. We are colored something alike, and Robart's one of you."

The Rider's face split with a grin. "Of course! I'll say this, though, Lady—the captain's not so well mounted as you."

Valadan arched his neck, playing with the bit till it jingled, accepting the homage. Druyan patted his shoulder indulgently.

"See you stay aboard him," the Rider advised soberly. "I'd arrange you an escort home, if I could. There's no knowing where those bastards will strike next."

But there *was*, Druyan mused as she jogged homeward under a glooming sky. Teilo notwithstanding, she had the means to know what they must guard, where and when. And the post riders, faster than any army of a thousand footsoldiers, had means to spread that knowledge quickly. Surely twoscore of Riders could accomplish more than one solitary rider—even if they could never be mounted on Valadan's equals.

Next time Druyan rode out from Splaine Garth, she was bound for Keverne.

Audiences at Keverne

THE BUNDLE TIED securely behind her high-cantled saddle contained a gown made of Druyan's own weaving—its soft wool dyed a pale green with lady's mantle, embroidered about the hem with a pattern of blue waves. It was her best gown, and nothing less would do for an audience with her uncle.

That interview was a frightful risk—if it led to the discovery that she was attempting to freehold Travic's land, there was yet ample time for Splaine Garth to be taken from her. The duke himself could urge a marriage upon his niece if he apprehended the situation, and he would surely do so. There were always men about people and places of power expecting payment in land for their service and loyalty. Druyan could easily be used to settle such indebtedness, and would be utterly helpless to prevent it.

Still, her uncle might not guess how matters stood. Travic's rank had not been especially high. Other men had fallen when he did, and there had been great confusion afterward, as the army was gathered and moved about. Perchance the duke knew naught of his death. Perchance he knew, but had not connected it with one of his numerous nieces. Certainly Druyan was not about to inquire and give up the game while she still had a chance to win it.

She let Valadan canter when they reached the broad beaches that flanked Keverne. There had been no need to use the utmost of his speed—if she arrived at Keverne too soon, no one would believe she had been at Teilo, and her report of it would be suspect. Even the men who had seen her there would be confused, and 'twas risky enough explaining why she'd been there at all. She had rested for three rainy days at Splaine Garth, telling Kellis what she proposed to do, leaving orders for the work to be done in her absence.

Kellis was carving a spoon out of a branch from one of the wind-downed apple trees. It had an ordinary roundish bowl, but he was leaving the handle fat, shaping it to fill a hand so that sore fingers need not grasp tightly to have a secure grip. When his own hands had been at their worst, small objects had given him a great deal of misery—he'd been able to manage a hoe better than a spoon. He had seen Enna weeping that morning, as she struggled to stir the cooking porridge. If the tool helped her, he would make others, spoons and ladles and forks. He could make knife hafts, as well, he supposed—but he didn't much care whether Enna could grip iron weapons painlessly.

His little bronze knife teased fragrant shavings from the wood. Every part of an apple tree smelled pleasant, not only the blossoms and the fruit. Kellis was glad that even the ruined tree would have a use, beyond brief winter fires. A spoon was more lasting than a little heat, a swirl of smoke up the chimney . . .

Smoke like that from the town he had seen aflame, too late to save it. Well, the worst he had feared had come to pass—he had given a fruitless warning. The lady had at least not reproached him for it. She knew how little he liked her riding out with warnings on the strength of his predictions—now she knew *why*, as well.

He watched the spoon taking shape under his knife, with pauses now and then for sketching the charm of keen edge onto the bronze blade. The grain of the applewood made a pattern like an eye, looking back at him out of the bowl. Kellis became uncomfortable with the scrutiny and turned the spoon to shape the backside, which had no eyes to watch him, to see his thoughts.

If I go, she wouldn't ride out into any more trouble. True, an Eral captain might chance upon Splaine Garth itself again, but that risk was less likely, less constant. There was no doubting it—she would be safer if he went.

He had given her his word that he'd stay—but set against his other sins, oath-breaking scarcely seemed to matter. His clan would not sit in judgment upon him. And if he reached the Wizards' City, no one there would know.

If he went, he would be doing it for her good as well as his own—it was perilously easy to convince himself of that.

Kellis had been distressed by her determination to continue riding out with warnings, but he liked better her scheme to ask her uncle for mounted patrols, Druyan thought. No real wonder there—a force with scope enough to do what the army could not against a fast-striking enemy didn't hinge so tightly on depending upon what Kellis himself did not trust. Still, there had been a haunted look in his eyes when she'd told him, and Druyan had no notion whether he'd be at Splaine Garth when she returned. He'd be out from under her eye, and if he chose to break his pledged word, there was nothing to hold him. There was nothing she could do about it. The man would stay, or he would go. She could not solve his riddle, could not guess what his choice would be.

Seabirds wheeled overhead, crying mournfully. Valadan outran them, leaping a snarl of driftwood as if he had been winged with feathers, too. Druyan laughed as they landed. She missed riding full tilt along a strip of fine white sand—at Splaine Garth sea met land in a tangle of quaggy soil and twisty river channels, and to ride through at other than a careful walk was insanity. Glasgerion, where she was born and raised, had broad beaches such as these, and she had regretted leaving them, all these years.

She had missed them rather more than she missed her husband, so much more recently reft from her. She never thought of Travic now, except to wonder how he would have done a particular chore, and she found that faintly shocking. She could scarcely recall him as a living man. The timbre of his voice was gone from her memory. Her skin did not recall his hand's touch. When she strove to bring him to mind, all she could manage was a sort of general shape, and never a face on it at all. The dirt and stones heaped over his burial place had begun to sink, and he faded from her memory as swiftly, as inexorably. And she must go to Keverne as if he yet lived. It seemed impossible.

Valadan galloped through the frothy edge of the water, sending spray flying high. Druyan pulled the stallion up—she needed to catch her own breath, to compose herself before she reached the castle. Her face was wet with saltwater—the sea's tears or her own, she could not tell.

If he was going, the soonest start would buy him the most time, the greatest distance. Time and distance were his best insurance against being run down by that incredible horse.

No use to think of taking food with him—he'd need to wait for nightfall to sneak into the kitchen larder, and he'd lose too many hours, risk aside. Kellis filled a sack with barley from the horses' bin and threw in a few lumps of coarse salt. That was all the food available outside the kitchen itself—the vegetables in the garden were weeks or months away from harvest, and the smokehouse was too near the kitchen. He might be seen. With the lady gone, Enna would have an especially sharp eye out. He stuck the bronze knife through his belt and on consideration rolled up the most threadbare of the horse blankets. The nights were yet chill.

Slipping out of the farmyard was far simpler than slipping into the kitchen would have been. Kellis walked away as if he intended to dig peat, wooden spade over his shoulder—and changed his course once he was safely out of sight, abandoning the tool where Dalkin would surely find it. He headed steadily uphill, intending to cut through the edge of the pastureland, where it ran into the moor. He knew the way well enough, from having followed the horse. That familiarity would help him, though he would need to strike out into the unknown if he would not chance meeting horse and rider, returning from Keverne. He would steer by the sun, to keep himself very well inland—

A sharp bark caught his attention, as it was meant to. Rook stood in front of him, ears pricked, tail outstretched. The posture of suspicion. As Kellis watched, her ears slowly lowered. Her head came down and forward, and she took a step to close a little of the distance between them.

Kellis kept his eyes away from her amber ones, so as neither to challenge nor be beguiled. She'd work him like a strayed sheep if she could, perhaps bite him if she could not. He would rather it had been Meddy stumbled across him—she'd have let him pass with only a foolish, happy wag of her tail. Rook knew her business, read his intention to stray just from the way he walked, probably. He watched her black and tan body coming closer, crouching a little as she did before the sheep. Now the tail was down, curled upward only at the very tip, the rest of it following the double curve of her lowered haunches.

He had let her come close enough—she wasn't backing off, and if he did not make some move to obey, she might spring at him, though she never would at a sheep. Or she might bark again, and Meddy might be near. *She'd* wake the rocks under the earth, Meddy would, once she got started, and for certain bring the sheep girls, maybe Dalkin, too.

Bending slowly, slowly, Kellis tore a hank of grass from the tufts at his feet. Carefully whispering the formula, he broke the grass stems into three parts. The Mirror of Three did not work well under sunlight or against cold iron weapons, but against a lone sheepdog—if she saw three of him, Rook would never be able to sort it out before he escaped her. He didn't want to be forced to shift to wolf—Rook would certainly attack then, and he might hurt her—and as a wolf he could not carry even his own clothing, far less knife and blanket and scraps of food.

Three times he said the spell, and as the third died away, Rook's head came up. She whined uncertainly, no doubt wondering at the trio of raggedy men suddenly spread before her. Kellis smiled and took a step backward. To either side of him, his mirrored selves did likewise. He took two steps sideways, crossing paths with one of the fetches that was moving mirrorwise, opposite to his direction.

Rook stood stock still, as baffled as he'd hoped she'd be. Kellis turned his back and strode boldly away.

The only warning he got was a single *sniff* just as he took his fourth step. There had been other sniffs, he realized as Rook's sharp teeth seized his ankle to detain him. She had been scenting all the while, like all dogs trusting her keen nose over her ordinary eyes. He had only heard the single noise because that was the one closest to him, as she caught him, the one that verified her quarry. He froze, obedient to her.

She had him by flesh and bone as well as cloth of trews, if she chose to clamp her jaws. But Rook merely held him as she had been taught, with that grip which would not lame a sheep or damage a fleece. He could feel her fangs pressing, but she had not broken his skin, and she would not unless he forced her into it.

"Little sister, you should let me go," Kellis pleaded hoarsely. "It really would be best—"

Rook growled, cutting him off, the threat muffled by the cloth in her mouth. He had to look back and down at her over his shoulder; and when he did, their eyes met, amber to gray-gold. He had dreaded that. Kellis lifted the corner of his lip in a silent snarl. The teeth on his ankle tightened. Rook's mesmerizing gaze never wavered. He took the deliberate warning to heart. They stared at one another.

When she saw that he was no longer minded to run, Rook released him and watched with satisfaction as Kellis trudged back toward the farmyard, pausing along the way to collect the spade.

* * *

Druyan did not desire that her mission should become Keverne's public gossip, so she asked the chamberlain's leave to greet her uncle informally, and in private. Therefore it was long past the supper hour when she was admitted to Brioc's private apartments, and very late when she stood without the ducal door once again, her back pressed tight to the smooth stone wall in a mostly vain effort to control the trembling that had seized her.

Ten years separated Brioc, the eldest, from Druyan's father Ronan, Kessallia's youngest son. Druyan had been prepared to find an old man awaiting her. She had seen her uncle seldom since his accession and not at all since her marriage, but Brioc appeared little changed by the years— his hair had gone all white about his long face, his stature seemed a little less lofty now that Druyan was grown herself. He favored his brothers enough in the face to not quite seem a stranger to her.

They greeted as kin—she was a vassal to Brioc, as well, but where women were concerned that was seldom discussed, since women did not bear the charge of supporting a liege lord with arms and armed men. They spoke of family, of births and marriages. Druyan asked after Brioc's grandchildren, for he had half a dozen and was flattered by any mention of them that he had not needed to coax.

When she was sure she had his favor and attention, Druyan told the duke of the increasingly frequent raids on coastal farms and villages, and tendered her remedy for the problem—a swift mounted force to protect what the army afoot plainly could not. Esdragon was blessed with fine horses, surely such a force could be easily mustered?

For answer, the duke inquired whether Splaine Garth was in any part forested, and if so of what height, what girth were the trees? Would they do for ships' masts? Druyan, thrown off her stride, could barely answer that she in fact had no trees of timber quality—there were very few such in Esdragon. Much of the land was treeless moor. Along the coasts the scattered trees leaned from the steady offshore breezes and grew too crooked for ship lumber. One had to go to the hills that made the border with Clandara before there were true forests. So it was that Esdragon had fishing boats and smallish merchanters, but no ships of war such as the raiders sailed. Timber was scarce, large logs for long keels difficult to come by.

The duke knew that. Her uncle told her at great length of the raiding problem, of how a fleet of warships would be their salvation, how the threat of raiders came from the sea and could therefore be stemmed only upon the waves. His eldest son, Dimas, was anxious to captain a force to make the sea roads safe—only first the difficulty of getting ships had to be resolved, some way.

Druyan's trembling increased as she recalled the words, alone in the torchlit passageway. *Ships,* she thought, pressing her spine to the cold wall. *He wants warships, never mind we don't have them, have no timber to build them, no men skilled to crew them. The raiders have been battening on us for ten years, and it will be ten years more ere any fleet of ours is truly able to take them on.* Even if no raider stepped foot in Darlith during those years, how could she keep the farm alive with only the folk Brioc's rule left her? Probably he'd be after boys like Dalkin in a year or so. She needed her men back, not pressed into service as lumberjacks and sailors. *What will be left of us in ten years?* The wall was no colder than her heart.

In less time than *that*, Kellis' people had been dismissed as weaklings and shoved to the bare fringes of their own land. Ten years was time a-plenty for some bold Eral chieftain to choose to winter in Esdragon, to decide he liked the situation of a fortress by a river's mouth. Time enough for him to take it, improve its defenses, move in with his own people—burrowing into Esdragon like a tick into a sheep, till finally there was a festering wound that no physick could cure. Then the plague would inevitably begin to spread . . .

Small wonder Brioc's army didn't defend the people

even when given the chance of a warning. They weren't meant to. The duke wanted ships. He'd sent his standing force to the mountains, to fell trees for masts and keels! Never mind that for most of the length of its coast, Esdragon was as hostile to ships—even its own—as any land could be. Sheer cliffs and a vicious surf, the only possible anchorages where rivers cut paths to the sea—easy enough for intrepid merchant captains to slip into such harbors on a favorable tide, easy enough for raider captains to dare for their rewards—but how did one patrol and protect such a treacherous sea, day by day?

One did not, but Brioc probably would not be confronted by his folly in his own lifetime. Dimas would be duke by the time the extent of the disaster was shown—and since the scheme was more his than his father's, he might not recognize it even then. As for the rest of them? Druyan shuddered again.

Was *that* why Kellis had found it so difficult to look ahead? Because his people had lost their future, lost their hope? Whatever his gifts, he would not allow himself to see more than the short view of the day to come, and by preference would look back to the day just past, in which evil was at least over, done with, and known.

What was she to do? Work her farm and ignore it all, hoping to be spared? Continue riding out to warn the coast, every time the sunfall wind swept in over the sea? Saving scraps in her hands while the whole coast went to ruin about her? Her gorge rose in a sudden wave of hopelessness, but she had not dined, so after a moment or two, Druyan swallowed hard and abandoned the support of the wall. Suddenly she longed to be out under the open sky, the clean wind cooling her face, lifting her hair . . .

A little draft made the floor rushes rustle, brushed her ankles like a cool invisible cat winding about her feet. The torches flickered, streamed smoke in their holders. Druyan unpursed her lips, with great care, and began to walk.

She aimed herself for the ducal stables, where Valadan was housed in surroundings certainly not unfamiliar to him.

She had made no arrangements for sleeping space for herself, not really thinking ahead beyond the need to speak with her uncle. By that oversight, she was free—she could ride for home within the hour, be at Splaine Garth ere dawn—but Keverne's great gates would be shut, there would be commotion if she tried to leave. She would be better for a few hours of rest—Druyan felt worn and distraught. She didn't require a chamber. If there was an empty stall near to Valadan, as there had been when she'd left him, then she had all she needed, for she'd only tarry till first light made leaving possible.

She needed, though, to discover the route to the stables. The chamberlain's usher had conducted her to the duke, and doors that had been open earlier were shut fast now that 'twas night, altering routes. A winding stair took her to a courtyard, but there were many such, and Druyan had no idea which she had entered, where it lay in relation to the stables or aught else. The hour being late, few folk were about. She might, Druyan thought with distaste, need to make her way back the entire way to her uncle's apartments, where there were guards posted, so that she might ask her way.

The situation struck her as absurd. The most twisty trail through head-high grass in Splaine Garth's salt marsh never confounded her, yet now she was lost in a warren built by her own ancestors' hands. She could look into the bowl alongside Kellis, glimpse any bit of Esdragon and know where 'twas—but she had no least idea how to reach Keverne's stables, certainly less than a thousand paces distant from her.

Voices, and then torchlight approached. The yellow flare of light revealed two young men clad alike in sea-blue wool, doublets and breeches, with gray cloaks thrown casually over all. Druyan smiled and stepped forward. Post riders would of a certainty know the location of the stables.

"Riders, may I impose upon your kindness?" she bespoke them politely.

"How many we aid you, Lady?" asked the one who held

the torch, smiling back at her. He had dark-red hair, unless the torch lent it color, and a countenance that would have graced a statue. The other, grave-faced and less flamboyant, stopped in his tracks, staring at her.

"Druyan?" He named her as if 'twas beyond his belief.

"Robart?" Druyan held both her hands out, and her brother took them in his own. "Oh, well met! Let me look at you!" Her surprise was as great as his, though she might have expected him to be at Keverne from time to time, and by chance at the same brief time she was there.

It had been years since they had seen one another—Robart's youthful softness of face was replaced with a leanness, the bump on the bridge of his nose, broken in a long-ago scuffle Druyan well recalled, was more pronounced. His skin was weather-browned—darker even than Kellis'—the same shade nearly as his wavy hair, which was cut chin length and pulled back into a tail. Her brother's eyes were unchanged—dark blue, the left one bearing a very distinctive fleck of gold amid the azure. His cloak was pinned back at the left shoulder with a brooch of bright silver, shaped like a breaking wave. Druyan touched it lightly. "We were all of us proud when we heard, Chief-captain."

Robart colored slightly, pleased. "It's not such a great matter as all that, to rise to a captaincy," he said modestly.

His companion—who likewise wore a captain's badge—laughed, and Robart scowled at him through the torch glare. "What brings you here, sister?"

"Valadan brought me here," Druyan answered, for the delight of watching his brows shoot up.

"You still have that old fellow? But he must be—"

She could see him trying to reckon the years in his head. "He must be what I said he was, all along, else he would be too ancient to amble from Splaine Garth to the sea, much less bear me cheerfully all the way to Keverne. You can judge for yourself—I stopped you intending to ask the way to the stables. I knew Riders would know. I had no idea 'twas you."

"You're leaving at this hour?" Robart frowned at the notion, ready to forbid it reflexively.

"I only came to chat with our uncle," Druyan said hastily. "And I didn't expect I'd be here long enough to bespeak a bed. As matters stand now, I believe I'll sleep better out on the heather."

"You'd rather that than the duke's roof?" the red-haired captain inquired pleasantly.

"I'd rather get homeward before my farm's raided and robbed again," Druyan answered, not wanting her dissatisfaction to tempt her into indiscretion with a stranger. For all she knew, this captain was one of Brioc's sons, a cousin she knew too slightly to recognize without his name.

The furrow between Robart's brows deepened. "Did you sup with the duke? No? Then forget this foolish talk of riding out in the middle of the night." He took her arm. "Come with me now, we'll talk while we have at some food. There are reports of raids coming in from up and down the coast, but Darlith is remote—we hear little. Whatever you can tell us of matters there would be useful." He gestured toward his companion. "This is Yvain of Tolasta, one of my fellow captains."

Yvain gracefully inclined his chestnut head. The torchlight caressed him. "Your servant, Lady Druyan. Your churlish brother has too seldom mentioned you, and never done you close to justice with his less than nimble tongue."

"She's a wed woman, Yvain," Robart warned.

"As if I'd no manners," Yvain observed with a wry smile, ignoring him. "Let me light the way, Lady. These cobbles are treacherous even to those of us who know them, and not so clean as they should be. The duke himself never comes this way—"

Robart retained his hold on her, though Druyan couldn't fathom why she might require the supporting grip, unless he intended to prevent her escaping at such an unseemly hour. Robart was right, come to that—she was too used to being her own mistress to remember that she was among folk apt to judge her actions by their own notions of propriety. To ride out of Keverne alone, at night, was unthinkable. Even an escape at dawn might not be permitted.

The captains led her across one court, then two others, finally up an outside stair to the second story of a slate-roofed building snugged against what—by the sound of the sea faintly carried through it—must have been one of Keverne's outer walls. The door was unbarred, and opened at Robart's touch.

There were a dozen men, all blue-clad, within the chamber. The scattered remains of a meal covered a long trestle across the far end. "I'll fetch us food," Yvain said, while Robart guided Druyan to a chair close by the warm hearth.

"My sister, the Lady Druyan of Splaine Garth," he announced to the company, lest any form a false impression and taint her reputation with it.

One or two of the men nodded pleasantly in her direction. Druyan returned the greetings with what she hoped was a gracious smile, feeling out of place and awkward. Yvain returned with a platter of meat pies in one long-fingered hand, three mugs of cider juggled somehow in the other.

"We don't keep quite the same state Brioc does," Robart said ruefully, looking at Yvain's meager burden. "Especially once we're down to scraps. I could send for more—"

"Rather plain food and plain talk here than marchpane swans and folly at the duke's board," Druyan declared, and took a sip of her cider. She had not eaten all that day and was famished, but she thought despite all that she would have choked, been unable to swallow a single bite of the daintiest fare at her uncle's table. She saw his face in her mind's eye, as he prattled happily of warships being Esdragon's salvation, and her outrage almost brought the cider up again.

"What did you and our uncle talk about?" Robart asked softly.

Druyan told him—exactly as she had the duke—about the attacks on Splaine Garth, the other raids she had learned and warned of. "The army's never in time to be any use—

before it even hears of trouble, the raid's over, the ships are
back at sea looking for another town or farm to rob. But a
mounted force could be where it needed to be more easily.
He *has* the horses—"

"Not for long," Yvain interjected bitterly. "Brioc's making ready to sell all but the breeding stock, to raise money."

"Money for ships?" Druyan asked, not really a question.

Yvain nodded elegantly. "I see our liege lord has mentioned his passion to you. 'Ships will save us—' " he
quoted, in a wicked approximation of Brioc's habitual tone.

"They might," Robart answered reluctantly, as if he
wanted to be fair about it.

"They never will." Yvain waved his mug disparagingly.
"You know what Meegran suggested?"

Robart made a face. "I hadn't heard. What's Councillor
Meegran's latest wise scheme?"

Yvain's face and voice were devoid of expression. "Hire
one of the raider captains and his companions as mercenar-
ies, to defend our coasts while Dimas puts a fleet together,"
he deadpanned.

Druyan choked on a mouthful of pie.

"Exactly my opinion," Yvain said, patting her delicately
on the back. Robart scowled at him. "Well, Chief-captain,
do *you* suppose it's good policy to set the wolf to guard the
sheepfold?"

"You *are* joking about this, Yvain?" Robart offered
Druyan his own cider, to wash the offending bit of pie
away.

"I assure you, Robart, I am not. 'Twas seriously proposed and considered."

"Brioc's our duke," Robart's face went sunfall red.

"He's *wrong*," Druyan said, shocking even herself, putting it so bluntly. "A-anyone can be wrong," she faltered
on, wondering if she could back down, if she should try to
qualify what she'd blurted out.

Another Rider crossed the room to join them, making a
little bow to Druyan as he arrived. "Well met, Lady, once
more. I don't know that we had one another's names." He

pulled up a chair. "I'm Kernan. We met at Falkerry. I did pass on your request about sending soldiers, but 'twas not acted upon." His expression said he was rather used to that outcome.

"What were you doing, at Falkerry?" Robart asked, looking sharply at Druyan.

"I just told you—carrying warnings—"

"She was at Falkerry," Kernan agreed. "Told them about the ships upcoast, and the alarm was raised in time to save the city. There was fighting, but they were ready, and prevailed."

"She was at Teilo, also," said another grim-faced Rider, entering into the loose circle before the fire. "Though not quite in such good time. And she knew about Porlark. Your pardon, Lady, I know you said you only *heard* about that, but there is no way you could have known about it so soon, if that was true. You warned them, as well, I think."

"So *that's* how they knew to hoist the chain!" Yvain exclaimed delightedly. "I wondered at that—they mostly use that marvel to keep captains *in*, who'd otherwise skip out on port fees." Two or three other men drifted closer, into easy earshot. Another joined them openly, deeming the talk no longer private.

"How did you know where they'd strike, Lady?" the grave man asked. Druyan's skin prickled—she did not think she dared give him the truth.

"Never mind that," Robart cut in. "How could you possibly get all the way from Splaine Garth to Falkerry? Where did you see the ships?"

Druyan mock-frowned at him, lifting one corner of her mouth. "All these years, and *still* you won't believe me about Valadan!"

"Valadan!" The name ran around the room like a trail of fire across the night sky. It was repeated with familiarity, with nostalgia, sometimes with wonder.

"It's just a black horse she's named that," Robart insisted into the hubbub.

"Of course," Druyan agreed sweetly. "And never mind how I got to Falkerry in one night."

"I don't much care what she was riding," Kernan said, refusing to be distracted. "She was there, in time, with a true warning. That's what interests me."

Druyan felt as if she'd been trapped against the wall. If she confessed to them about Kellis and his talents, she might be putting his life at risk—but if she did *not*, she would lose their confidence, which was now her sole means of spreading the warnings Kellis gave her. These horsemen would never believe she rode widely enough—even upon mage-created Valadan—to see every shipload of raiders approaching. Chance could not account for her knowledge, she would never dupe them that way. They might not even accept the truth . . .

"When my farm was raided, we took prisoners," she said, the inevitable choice abruptly made. She looked from one face to another, trying not to let Robart's eye catch hers. "One of those was wounded, left behind when the others escaped. We needed harvest hands, the duke had all Splaine Garth's men—*still* has them, come to that! Kellis agreed to work, to pay for his release."

"What does Travic think he's doing?" her brother asked, outraged.

Druyan refused to be lured off onto a tangent and ignored Robart. "Kellis turned out not to be one of the raiders' own folk—the Eral took *his* people's land, overran it years ago. He told me what he'd learned about them, where they come from, and why—"

"We all know *why*!" a tall Rider blurted. "They're thieves and murderers. I saw Teilo—"

"The Eral despise weakness," Druyan reported seriously. "What they want, they take. If they can beat us, push us aside, they will. If they *can't*, if we stand up to them, they'll learn to respect us. Then the raiders among them will look elsewhere for their plunder, and the traders will come in their place, with goods to sell."

"They won't respect us very much if we pay a few of them to keep the rest away," Yvain observed cheerfully.

"None of this explains how you knew where they'd be," Robart persisted, hammering away at her like a raiding ship. "Little bands, striking each at their captain's whim— how did *you* know where and when?"

Druyan swallowed hard. "Kellis saw it. He . . . has a gift of prophecy. He looks into water and sees what's to come." No sense telling them the rest of it—that yesterday and tomorrow were indistinguishable.

"You said they beat his people. And *he* got himself captured, didn't he? He can't be very handy at foreseeing." It was as if what she sought to hide was written across her face, Druyan thought. And Robart's objections seemed so logical.

"His people couldn't fight iron weapons," she said, fighting back. "Even *we* say iron poisons magic—for his folk it was worse than that. Iron poisons *them*." She shuddered, thinking of Kellis' hands after the barley harvest, what he had suffered trying to hide that flaw from his captors, his presumed enemies. "They dare not touch iron, much less stand against it in battle. And they don't farm, not to any extent. Most of them follow herds of cattle and migrate with the seasons. You can't defend grassland the way you do a coast, a town."

"We're not doing much of a job of defending a coast either," Yvain observed. He wasn't smiling.

"We've been dismissing the raids as an unpleasant fact of life, like winter storms," Druyan insisted. "A nuisance, but with an end coming. We can't do that. They'll only get worse."

"Particularly if our duke begins inviting some of the villains for extended visits," Yvain said under his breath.

"From what Kellis has told me, they'll test us till we make them stop. The Eral rob any folk they can—but if we fight them, stand them off, they'll turn to trading instead. They'll do whatever brings in the profit. Whatever we make them do."

"You trust this man?" Robart asked incredulously. "He was one of them, Druyan!"

"He was *with* them," she corrected, not waiting to let him accuse her of splitting hairs. "Using an Eral ship to carry him over the sea, away from a place where he couldn't live any longer. I believe him about that. As for trusting him—Kellis has never betrayed me, and his prophecies have always been true."

"*So far.*" Robart's hands were white-knuckled fists.

"So far's as far as we've gone," Druyan said stubbornly. "Ask at Falkerry. And Porlark."

"You let him send you riding into the middle of a raid?" Robart slammed his right hand, palm flat, onto the table-top. The sound was as loud as a shod horse kicking his stall. "It's a wonder you didn't get yourself killed!"

"What choice, except to let other people die?" Druyan cried. She wanted to protest, to say how careful she'd been—all the while outraged to be censured so roundly for simple good deeds.

"She needn't risk that again," Yvain interjected smoothly. "If *we* do it in her place."

"We?" Brows shot up, on every face. A few pulled back down into frowns. Other mouths smiled. The cider was making Druyan's head buzz. Perchance she was not the only one so affected. She found herself agreeing with Yvain, but wasn't quite sure what the captain was about.

"We have the means for passing news quickly," Yvain explained, sweeping an arm about to indicate the room. "It is our function, after all. There are a lot of us, tolerably well mounted, so we can get about quickly. We are armed. If we were to stumble upon a raid in progress, even our fearless duke would expect us to pitch in and shove it back out to sea."

"You're talking about seeking the raiders out, though," Robart said, before emotion could sweep sense away. "Aren't you? And doing it without orders. You're talking treason."

"I am talking about stopping trouble, if we should happen to hear of it. Swinging a bit wide of our routes to do it, perhaps." Yvain gave him an ingenuous grin.

"Happen to hear of it?" Robart queried, shaking his head.

Yvain turned the full force of his smile upon Druyan. "What do you say, Lady? Will you help us? Be our ears?"

Catching the Wind

DRUYAN COULD HAVE had a bed—any one of the post riders would gladly have slept in an empty stall to give his sleeping pallet up for her—but she wanted to return to Splaine Garth before her nerve failed her. Or something else, less under her control, did.

"What if he's gone?" she whispered into the black ear cocked back to catch her speech, while she and Valadan flew through the last rags of the night. The ends of the stallion's mane fanned her cheeks, like sable moths' wings.

If he has gone, I will trail him, the stallion assured her, unconcerned.

"He may have taken one of the coursers," Druyan fretted. "I promised him a horse. The fastest ones went with Travic, and the army's got them now, but—" She could not relax. Too large a portion of the new-hatched scheme depended upon Kellis. If he had considered their bargain early concluded and vanished, what would she do?

If he is on a horse, he will only be easier to find. Valadan sounded amused. The long run had put him in a good temper—as had Yvain's exclamation at the sight of him. Robart might be steadfast in his dismissal of the stallion as just a nobly named black horse, but Yvain and the other Riders had been willing to see the truth that stood munching hay in the ducal stables, and had made much of him.

When they turned down the familiar lane, the sun had

186

risen just high enough to throw their shadows before them. There was a dew halo about the shadows—Druyan started at the sight. Their dark shapes were clothed in a moving rainbow. Was that a blessing on the task they'd set themselves to? A portent of success?

The beneficent light dimmed—thin clouds were crossing the sun's face. Druyan dismounted and undid the gate, then led Valadan through. She pulled his saddle off at once and turned him out into the orchard to take his ease. As she left him, he was already lowering himself to the ground, indulging in a back-scratching roll, his legs waving in the morning air.

It felt strange to have her feet on the ground, as she walked toward the barn—she and Valadan had been one creature for so much of the past day-span of hours, and when she was astride him she had not felt the uncertainty, the trepidation that she felt now, alone on her own two legs.

The saddle needed to be cleaned and oiled. The stirrup leathers had developed a squeak as she came homeward. It could wait. She set the tack aside and went to find Kellis.

She found him stacking the turves he'd cut from the peaty edge of the marsh, arranging them into roof peaks as Dalkin had taught him, so they'd catch a drying breeze more surely and would shed any rainfall quickly. It would be autumn ere all the moisture was out of them and the turves were ready to burn. The bricks of soil would have become light shingles of fuel.

The sea was the color of the post riders' garb, and the marsh was mostly a gently rippling green. Kellis' eyes picked up touches of both colors, as if the goldish gray was but a mirror to whatever his eyes looked upon. Shadows crossed them, like clouds, as Druyan told him how matters had gone at Keverne.

"I have their routes and schedules from Robart," Druyan said. "So I can reach the nearest, whenever there's a raid to warn of. It'll be faster than guessing where they should be."

Kellis said nothing. His left eyelid was twitching like the hide of a horse pestered by flies.

"The Riders have been passing news about the raids all along," Druyan went on, wishing he'd make a conversation of it with her. She couldn't tell what the man was thinking—all his face showed was his unhappiness. "Trying to help the army get to the trouble in time. It never helped—now we know why that was! Brioc thought it useless, he never tried. He sent the army away to cut trees! So the Riders will turn now to rallying whatever local support there is."

"And you will go with them, Lady?" His voice was carefully neutral, and his eyes were on the limitless sky overhead.

"I'll help them as I can." *If I ask him, I think he'll refuse,* Druyan thought. *It's no part of our bargain, but I must not let him see that.* She used her best weapon. "I don't want to see another Teilo."

He nodded, resigned to it, and did not shift his eyes to hers or return his gaze to the sky. The wind stirred his thistledown-colored hair.

"If it makes you feel any easier," Druyan said, "my brother Robart's no happier about trusting you than you are about being trusted."

"Lady, don't mock me."

"I'm not." The bleakness of his tone made her falter, like a stumbling horse. "I swear to you, Kellis, I'm *not*. But the raiders will come, whether I trust you or I don't trust you. And if a warning comes too late, it's no worse than if it didn't come at all." She sighed. "I don't see the dangers the way you do, and I don't think you can teach me to. Right now, I'm going home and to bed."

He raised that brow at her.

"I don't need you to tell me that it's safe, no. There's no smell of sea to this wind." Druyan lifted a hand, letting the air pass between her fingers. "There's rain in it, though. Finish this up by sun-high, and then find yourself some work to do in the barn, if you don't fancy a soaking."

* * *

Kellis stayed at the edge of the marsh long after spatters of rain had turned to a steady fall. The wind was not particularly chill, and it was clean to his nose and his lungs. The barn would smell of chickens. No use to think how he should have gone when he had the chance. He knew very well that he could have outwitted the dog, had he chosen. He knew very well that he was bound to Splaine Garth now, as if with fetters of cold iron.

He watched the falling drops pock the surface of the rivulet he sat beside. No danger of visions in it—the top layer was too roiled to mirror even the real world about it. All the surface gave off was a sparkle, now and again. The water danced to the prompting of wind and tide, accepting new water from the falling rain without a qualm—Kellis wished he could be more like that water, taking whatever came, untroubled beneath. He could not. He was too much aware of consequences.

She asked too much of him. No, that was wrong. She did not so much ask, but assumed his compliance, because *she* could never see a creature in need and pass it by. Now, suddenly, her plan was greater by a score of human parts, and his responsibility had grown correspondingly heavier. If *she* rode out into peril, he could slip after her, protect her with every considerable skill at his command. Kellis knew himself a much better wolf than a prophet, he did not feel inadequate for the task. But suddenly there were a score or more of other lives involved, too many for him to safeguard even if he wanted to.

His woolen clothes shed much of the rain, but his hair was plastered flat to his skull, dripping into his eyes. Kellis tried very hard not to remember why that hair had all gone silver, every lock of it, in one single night.

He had no success. After a while, he trudged back to the farmstead.

The rain lay like a soft gray blanket over Darlith for a week. Druyan applied herself to the never-ending tasks the farm's life required. Spring planting had been the first claim on her time, then the matter of the raiders—but now the clamor of lesser chores could no longer go unheard. Much of it she could delegate—feeding, milking, thinning the rows of new-sprouted vegetables. Pru could churn, Lyn could take the new-made soap and launder clothing, Dalkin was fine about doing whatever he was specifically bidden to do. Kellis could handle any heavier work and the less pleasant necessities—making wethers out of surplus ram lambs, mucking out the henhouse and the pigs' sty. But Splaine Garth had been worked by a half-score of men, men who had done more than tend their own garden plots and thatch a roof as needed. Hides could wait untanned, packed in a barrel with moist wood ashes and borax till there was leisure to deal with them, but few other tasks were likewise accommodating. Every crop had a series of things that must be done to it, each in its proper time and not *too* much later, if they were to keep the farm going at all. When the cows needed their hooves trimmed, they didn't understand that the pole beans needed to be encouraged up their poles just then and that the beehives urgently required attention.

Most such work had never been Druyan's province. The household chores *had*, and there were fully as many indoor chores as outdoor. Some could wait, some could not. Falling-down weary she might be, but Dalkin must have a new sark and trews before his outgrown, outworn clothing fell off him entirely. Enna could not grasp the slender needle, nor even hold the shears to cut the cloth. So Druyan cut and stitched in the firelight, struggling not to think of ships upon the seas, out beyond the mist that settled in with the evenings all along the coast of Darlith.

Kellis hauled up a bucket of fresh water and poured from it into the black bowl, while Druyan waited anxiously. He sat down on the well coping, took a deep breath, and began the crooning that sang up the vision. Druyan took up a position at his right side, her left hand resting on his right shoulder, the bowl where she could look down into it as easily as he could. The song went on, for a very long while. Kellis' breathing showed strain.

"Rain," he said, interpreting what she could see for herself. It rained every day, in some part of Esdragon. The sea brought it. By itself, useless information.

There was quick movement on the bowl's surface. Druyan peered intently. Was that ships, or armed horsemen?

"Are those your pigs?" Kellis asked. "Wait. Yes, I know that fence. They got through there just the other day. Either I need to mend it again, or we're seeing them go through that day. I can't—"

He put a hand to his head, suddenly, with a sharp intake of breath. The bowl tilted precipitously, and most of the water spilled out, splashing Druyan's skirts. "I'll check the fence again," Kellis said faintly. He was still holding his head, pressing his fingers against the light furrow of the scar on his forehead, and his eyes were tightly shut.

"Are you all right?" Druyan asked. His shoulder, still under her hand, felt hard as a stone, not like living flesh at all.

"The summoning always gives me a headache." Kellis shook off her concern, opening his eyes again. "One reason I never cared much about practicing it." He got up unsteadily, almost missing his footing entirely.

"Careful!" Druyan snatched at his arm. "Don't fall down the well. Maybe there's just nothing to foresee," she added, trying to comfort him.

"But there's no way to tell, is there?" His eyes went narrow. "You've loaded too much of this on me! I *told* you—"

"Not to trust you," Druyan conceded. "A dozen times, at least. This isn't sailing weather anyway, Kellis. Trust yourself a little."

He stood still a moment, doing nothing more than breathing, possibly thinking. "I am still going to see where those pigs are."

He was trying, Druyan thought, to make light of the failure, for her sake. Kellis was failing at that as badly as he'd failed to capture the vision. His eyes were bleak as the middle of winter—he knew what the failure meant as well as she did.

He didn't *want* to see. Didn't want to send the post riders—and worst of all Splaine Garth's lady—into the teeth of whatever was coming. That was the trouble, Kellis thought. He was not empty of visions, he always saw *something* in the bowl, but he could not see what he needed—and feared—to. He kept watch every day, so sure there was a danger to be seen—if only he could manage to glance at the proper spot at the right moment—that he tended to lose himself in his quest until a familiar hammer-blow of pain brought him back to himself.

Sometimes the pain was real. He caught a nasty blow from the edge of the horse trough, and suspected he might have fainted and fallen against it. He made the boy Dalkin finish watering the stock, and went about his other chores with one eye swollen shut and the other averted from anything that might cast a reflection.

"Once a day's enough," Druyan said sternly when she saw the blacked eye and learned how he'd gotten it.

"You're optimistic," Kellis retorted bitterly. "It's not like riding a horse, always there when you want to do it. It's more like sailing a boat, catching the wind. Sometimes there *is* no wind."

"Sometimes you have to tack across the wind," Druyan told him firmly, coastline-bred where he was not and well able to bend his metaphor to her own use.

"Lady, I am *trying*—" He clenched his jaw on whatever else he was going to declare.

"You're trying till you fall down," Druyan said. "Wanting's not always enough."

She recalled all at once how desperately she had longed to give Travic a child. And how she had failed at it, while being reminded of her failure monthly for each of eight long years. No other's reproach could have been half so foul as that which she heaped upon herself. A tear slid hotly down her cheek.

Kellis was right—tack as you might, sometimes there simply *was* no wind.

It was an indulgence when she returned to her loom, which had stood idle since the end of winter, but Druyan needed its solace, even for the bare snatched moments when she ought to have been abed. She could not make a child, but she could make cloth, to keep another's children warm. She set up a warp of blue threads and green, and wove a pattern like the shadows among the sea waves, seen from the clifftops. She had a fine store of cloth laid by— perhaps she would offer some for sale at Falkerry's autumn market. Most of the cloth had been woven for her pleasure, not for utility, and the woolens were finer than any of them would wear about the farm. They'd sell to city folk and fetch decent prices.

The rain was good for the crops. They could take a second cutting of hay in another month, and the barley harvest promised to be bountiful once more. One ridge she'd sown with oats was growing better than that grain generally did in Darlith, evidently not quite drowning in the field. The lambs were thriving on the lush grazing, and two of them were black sheep, promising darker wool for her loom without the chores of dyeing it first. Druyan suspected there'd be little time for nonessentials like gathering dye-stuffs that autumn.

Enna came in, flustered, to report there was a visitor in the yard. Druyan laid down her shuttle, possibilities making her heart pound.

"Who is it?" No one ever called at Splaine Garth—they had few neighbors, none near and none sociable. The road ran many leagues between towns, drawing no more than local notice. Druyan strove not to fear the worst—that her visit to Keverne *had* somehow drawn notice to Travic's heirless passing. Her heart thudded nonetheless, from canter to gallop, running away with her.

"It's a post rider, Lady," Enna said.

"Just one?" She had not thought of Riders. "They ride paired." Maybe 'twas Robart, passing by. "Show him in here, Enna. It's not so drafty this season, and Kellis swept it out last week." She ran a smoothing hand over her skirt, as Enna gave the room a doubtful glance. It had been long years since Splaine Garth's hall received any sort of guest. It looked nearly as much like a barn as the barn itself did—not an obstacle to Druyan's weaving craft, but hardly what one wished a guest to see.

"Can't be helped, Enna," she said, acknowledging the problem. And if the caller was her brother, perhaps it didn't matter. "Show him in."

Enna went, frowning. *I can't help it,* Druyan thought. *We work, here. I have no time to keep company-best.*

"Lady Druyan!"

She *had* been assuming 'twould be Robart, so to see red hair and a more sculptured face confounded Druyan far more than it should have. After all, surely Robart would have given Enna his name and stated his connection to her. "Captain Yvain? What brings you to Darlith?" Her face felt flushed. She hoped he would not notice. And hoped, too, that there was not dust smeared across it, or slubs of wool caught in her hair last time she scooped it impatiently back.

"My route, Lady. And then my social instincts, which led me a little way off that well-ridden track, to call upon you here."

"More than a *little* way off, Captain. I hope you will take some food—or is thirst more pressing? You will be weary from riding." At least he wasn't wet. The rain must have ceased. Her duty as hostess was bred into her, Druyan thought, as her lips spoke of themselves, her brain still spinning.

Yvain lifted her hand to his lips before she could guess his intent. Druyan winced inwardly as she saw his nostrils flare—bad enough their uncouth size, but her fingers were tainted with grease from the wool she wove with. The eye might not catch it, but the nose certainly did. She made light of the matter.

"I assure you, Captain, my hands may taste of the outside of a sheep, but we don't put the wool into the soup pot along with the lamb! Enna crafts fine fare."

"If only Keverne's court ladies with their rosewater lotions but knew the virtues of wool, they'd all turn weavers, Lady. Your hands are soft as a babe's cheek."

Druyan blushed and was discomfited by her reaction as much as by his words. She withdrew her hand. "By your leave, Captain, I will go and wash them."

"Don't stop your work on my account, Lady," Yvain begged, stepping smoothly to place himself between her and the door. "I have intruded upon your peace without warning, which makes me no better than a raider. And I may not tarry for a meal—my horse is fleet enough to gain a bit of time on my companion's mount, but I knew as I came that I dared not steal more than a moment."

"For courtesy?" Druyan asked in wonderment.

"For courtesy, Lady." His smile flashed bright as sunlight on wavecaps and suggested something more than good manners. He finally allowed Druyan to slip past him, escape out the door into the kitchen and thence the farmyard, her face still too warm for the season and the weather.

Druyan saw to it that Dalkin watered the captain's big-boned bay, which had indeed worked hard for his master's whim. "What have you heard of raiders?" she asked Yvain, while they watched the horse drinking.

"Naught—but the weather's been especially foul downcoast. I think it spared us." He hesitated, then spoke low. "All the Riders know now, Lady. We are of one mind in this matter. Should you receive any . . . news . . . you are safe to take it to the first Rider you can get to. He'll do the rest." Yvain smiled once more. "There are not so many of us, but that only makes it easier for us to agree together. There's no man among us thinks we'd do well to sit back while our duke sells our remounts to buy himself useless ships." He swung lightly into his saddle, gathered his reins expertly. "Good day to you, Lady Druyan."

"Safe journey, Captain Yvain."

He made her such an extravagant bow, Druyan felt she had no choice but to watch him out of sight. Sure enough, he put his horse at the wall rather than waiting for Dalkin to run and unlatch the gate, then turned to wave once more as he proceeded at a handgallop toward the road. The bay's black tail and Yvain's red locks streamed in the wind they made.

"Is he known to you?" Enna asked disapprovingly, as they stowed away the untasted food she'd prepared, the new bread sliced but unnibbled, the cider unsipped in the mugs.

"He serves with my brother Robart," Druyan said blandly, as if disinterested.

"Had he a message?"

Druyan gave Enna a hard look—and got one back. She dropped her gaze. "Th-that's what post riders *do*—carry messages," she faltered, trying to remember that Enna really had no right to ask.

"Aye." Enna poured the cider back into the pitcher and set the crockery in a cool spot. "Likely he'll be back, with more messages."

Druyan felt it would be beneath her dignity to deny or agree with that speculation, so she returned to her loom, too aware that her cheeks were flaming once more.

Swords and Wolves

PEBBLES RATTLING AGAINST the shutters waked Druyan sometime prior to the midpoint of the night. At first she took the noise for rain, but she heard wind whistling and, fearing hail, she rose from her bed hastily. When she flung the casement wide and thrust a hand out, the air was dry. And the whistling wasn't the wind. It was Kellis.

"*Lady!*"

He stood below in the gloom, his face tipped anxiously up to her, and what she could see of his expression looked tense. Druyan whirled from the window without troubling to latch it, snatched clothing randomly from pegs on the wall, and donned it hurriedly. It might be that a horse or a cow had colicked—emergency enough—but she thought Kellis had been cradling something in his free arm, the one not flicking pebbles at the shutters. Something like a bowl.

He was just outside the kitchen door when she tugged it open, and did indeed have the bowl clutched to him. Most of the water had slopped out of it to soak his trews and the ground around his boots.

"Why are you bothering with that *now*?" Druyan asked, more amazed than cross. "It's the middle of the night."

Kellis shoved his hair out of his face, distractedly. "If you call a thing long enough, it will come to you—at the least convenient time, just for spite. One true thing my master taught me. I woke up with a headache so fierce, I couldn't bear to lie still. It got better—a little—when I went to the bowl, and I knew I'd been answered."

"You saw something?" Druyan asked.

Kellis nodded and winced in pain. "Lady, I *think* it was the first place you rode to, the one with the sea stacks outside the harbor—"

"Falkerry?" But he knew too little of Esdrágon to be sure, Druyan thought. Would they touch Falkerry again, having failed there? Would one captain know of a fellow's defeat?

"It looked the same. You can better judge." Kellis' dark brows knotted. "But there was something odd—they sailed—rowed, the sails were down—*past* the city, up the river."

"Surely they can't be after Teilo again? There's nothing left to steal." The Eral raiders worked independently, though. It came back to that. A captain might not know of other ships recently plundering the quarry he had chosen for himself.

"I watched awhile," Kellis said. "I was afraid when I broke away to fetch you, I'd lose my hold on it. I wanted to see whatever I could, to have that much—but I couldn't work out where they were going. Then the image was gone, I thought that I'd fallen asleep, let it snap, but—I'll try to show you. It doesn't feel to me like it's truly over, I can hunt it down . . ."

He gripped her hand and bent his head over the dark bowl. It was dark in the yard, even when your eyes were accustomed to gloom, Druyan thought. No light but from the stars. How could Kellis see anything, even with sight beyond that of his eyes? A black bowl, dark water within, and barely a few drops of that . . .

Kellis sang an insistent phrase. After a heartbeat's pause, he repeated the summons. The water in the bowl began to glow, faintly pink gold. Druyan could make out dark shapes against it, ships riding the current. Long, low ships, with their sails furled. Heading *downstream.*

"To take the town unawares," she whispered in horrified

understanding. "They'll come at Falkerry quietly, from a direction they *never* use, where no one expects danger, sails down so there's next to nothing for anyone to see. With the sun rising at their backs, Falkerry's watch will never spot them—if they're even looking in the right direction. The tower faces toward the sea. No one keeps a landward lookout."

Kellis' one hand shook in hers and the other on the bowl. The vision trembled, the dawn became merely ripples. The golden water went dark.

"But *which* dawn?" Druyan whispered, shivering as if his grasp had been a contagion she'd caught. "*This* one's only a few hours away."

"Did it rain yesterday, early?" Kellis was willing to grasp at any straw he could find, but he had said he felt there wasn't much time.

"Here," Druyan agreed. She looked skyward, to judge clouds and wind. "But at Falkerry?" There'd been no rain in the vision, that was sure. The break-of-day sky had been too vivid. Druyan started for the barn. "I can't take the chance—I'd better warn the Riders."

Kellis heeled her, like Rook after her flock. "Can they get there, by dawn?"

"They can try. At least—" Druyan swung her saddle down expertly from its rack. "They'll all be lodged for the night. I won't have to ride the routes trying to find the Riders closest to Falkerry. That will save some time." No telling whether Falkerry had even that much grace.

Valadan whickered a greeting to his mistress and stood rock-still while he was tacked—but Druyan could feel him quivering with excitement beneath the good manners, eager rather than distressed at being rousted out of his warm stall in the middle of a cold dark night. Bless him. The other horses shifted and stamped, snorted questions to one another about the commotion.

"How many Riders are close enough to come?" Kellis wondered, securing a brass buckle handily.

"Not all of them," Druyan admitted soberly. "I will ride

to raise one pair, possibly two, and the news will go from there by relay, Rider to Rider." The carefully arranged scheme no longer seemed likely to work—never had she supposed they'd have so little warning of need.

Let us make the most of what we have. Valadan flared his nostrils wide and looked with his sparkling eyes over Druyan's head, through the open door and into the darkness.

They soared over the dark moors, Valadan confident as if every inch he trod upon had been the grass of his home pasture. They had already raised the first of the farmsteads they sought and roused the post riders lodged there for what proved to be a short night. One Rider of that pair had made straight for Falkerry, while his partner sped onward to relay the dire news. Druyan's appointed task was to race inland to alert a second pair of Riders, so the news would be more widely spread. That done, she was to return home.

Instead, she turned Valadan's head toward the coast whilst the second team was still saddling their fractious mounts, and urged all speed upon him, striving to outrace the coming dawn. The summer nights were so much briefer than those of the winter. A few hours of darkness, and then the sky was aglow and the vision was being fulfilled as she watched helplessly . . .

They topped a rise, and the Fal shone below them, like a single loose silver thread among dark-napped wool. There was fog lying along the river's course, just over the water—another help for the bold raiders.

Panting as if she had run the course to Falkerry on her own legs, Druyan looked about, dismayed. Where were the silent ships? Where were the Riders? The first of them at least should have reached Falkerry, should he not? Had his horse come to grief in the darkness, less surefooted than Valadan? The town didn't look as if it had been warned. It slept, and on the headland the watchtower was dark as the sea stack a league seaward.

There, Valadan observed coolly, dipping his head to point the direction.

Druyan saw a horse gallop ghostly out of the mist, hard-driven, aiming at the watchtower. One Rider, at least, had arrived in time. But there was work aplenty to be done, and one Rider and a single warning would never be sufficient to save a town the size of Falkerry—not before the sun came up.

Indeed, a lone rider could raise no more than the watchtower—the one who was trying was at a standstill already, hammering at the portal, trying to attract the gatekeeper, who was likely asleep. The raid might be long under way ere word of it went down into Falkerry proper. The tower might signal, but who was awake to see? Druyan made a small moan of dismay.

There is a better way, Valadan agreed with a snort, gathering himself. He leapt into a gallop, his tail bannering behind him like a cloak flung out upon the wind. His mistress sat tight, breathing deep to be ready for her part.

They raced straight into the town, Druyan screaming, *"Raiders! Raiders on the Fal!"* at the top of her lungs, over the clatter of hooves on cobbles. She cried the warning over and over, as folk came stumbling out of houses in sleepy confusion. Most of Falkerry's citizens automatically looked toward the sea, the danger that most commonly bore down upon them, and saw nothing, and were yet more perplexed.

There were questions called, but Druyan did not halt to answer. If she drew rein, she'd be trapped at a standstill on the outskirts, useless to the rest of the town. Enough that folk were waked, they could see the danger when it came. Valadan thundered over the cobbles, leaving a drowsy babble in his wake.

Then there were shouts from the landward end of the town, where half a dozen blue-clad Riders were converging. Flame-glow contested with the first glimmers of sunrise to lighten the sky. Druyan turned to ride toward the noise of the battle and rejoiced to hear townfolk running behind her.

Falkerry was all at once wide-waked and angry as a hornet's nest pelted with sticks.

Four sleek, long-keeled ships rode at the quayside, their masts lowered so their crews might row them silently downstream. Those crews were ashore, looting the nearest warehouses when the Riders swept down upon them. Now a small, pitched battle raged down the twisty streets of the waterfront, and one thatched roof was aflame, perhaps a deliberate distraction crafted by raiders against the onslaught of defense.

Valadan plunged and then reared, as danger appeared in his path. Druyan had one frightening glimpse of a big raider as the stallion rose up under her, lifting her high—the man had long unbound hair, a beard full of bared teeth white as an animal's, eyes of as cold a green as the winter sea. One hand was hampered by a bulky sack of plundered goods, but the other was free to swing a short sword at her. Valadan squealed, and the stallion's forehooves slashed out viciously.

Hold on!

Druyan felt the impact through the stallion's body but did not see the raider fall. She heard him cry out harshly, in a tongue she did not know, and then Valadan was scrambling around a blind corner, where he bowled down another thief attempting to shoulder an unwieldy bolt of embroidered cloth back to his ship.

Suddenly a low dark shape flashed by, almost beneath his flying hooves. Valadan shied, stumbled, and recovered—by which time the shape had vanished.

"A dog," Druyan said, patting the stallion's neck and trying to secure her seat. Probably caught up in the fight and terrified, only trying to escape, only wanting safety.

A wolf, Valadan contradicted wonderingly—for what would a wolf do in a town, unless it was some wild beast tamed by the raiders, taught to do mischief. From out of an alley mouth came a snarl and then a high-pitched scream, cut off sharp as if with a knife. Or teeth. In the darkness, two yellow-green eyes gleamed . . .

"Well met once more, Lady Druyan!"

Druyan turned in her saddle, startled into forgetting those shining eyes and what they might belong to. A large bay horse nickered a tentative greeting to Valadan. There was light enough now from the sky to reveal his rider's familiar, comely face.

"This is, of course, no place for you," Yvain said confidentially. He legged his stallion nearer. "You should not have come into the town, but at least this unpleasantness is for the most part concluded." Flaming thatch fell suddenly into the street beside them. "They have fled to their ships—next thing for us is to get the fires out. Here, you had better have this, in case there are a few rats left that could not reach their ships."

He held out a sword, hilt-first. Druyan reached for it, was surprised by its lightness. What she would do with the weapon, she had no notion. She gripped it awkwardly as Yvain wheeled his horse and made for the quayside. Possibly the blade would make a useful pointer, as she directed the folk with buckets toward the fire.

The wolf came out of the alley, head low and nose easily sorting out the scent of one horse from another. He went after the black stallion, toward the hot odors of flaming straw and charring wood. He was unhappy—he could deal with an armed man, but if a flaming roof fell from a house, how could he protect the woman from that? He trotted over the uneven cobbles, dodging glowing embers with disquieting frequency. He was not a creature of cities. He hated the close streets, the walls hemming him about. And as the sun rose, there were fewer and fewer shadows to offer him even the tiniest measure of concealment.

Townsfolk were striving to combat the arson—already there were pails passing from hand to hand, between the fired buildings and the nearest water—in this case the River Fal, around the next corner. The wolf dodged past the bucket brigade, avoiding the pail swung deliberately at him by a man he passed too closely by.

Where had the stallion gone? The smoke confounded the wolf's keen nose, the maze of streets muddled his other senses. His lines of sight were short, the damned walls blocked them and bounced sound in many directions, making his ears less than useful. He whined nervously and padded faster. All at once, he had reached the quayside, with the river before him, and then he heard the woman's voice, shouting. He ran toward the sound. He'd be glad to have her safe in his sight again, even though his nose told him he was headed for her . . .

A gray horse backed in front of him unexpectedly. The wolf slid to a halt, caught in the open between the horse—which screamed as it saw and scented him—and the chute made by a warehouse wall to one side and the river on the other. If he tried to squeeze past, he risked a kick from a shod hoof, and he was not foolish enough to chance that. He lifted his lips and snarled a loud warning at the towering gray horse.

The horse would have chosen the prudence of retreat, but as he tried his rider heard the noise and looked down. He let out a snarl of his own and wrenched his long sword from its scabbard.

The wolf's retreat was cut off by fresh flames. The Rider noted that, and spurred at him, sword slicing down like a scythe at ready grain. The wolf barely got himself out of the way, between the blade and the hooves that wanted to stomp him. Valor discarded, he streaked full speed for the river. The Rider veered to cut him off.

And the gray stallion nearly collided with Valadan, who slid on his haunches and half reared so that the wolf passed safe beneath his belly. There was a splash as it dove into the Fal's dark water.

"Druyan?" Robart shouted, amazed.

Druyan snatched at Valadan's flying mane for security as the stallion reared again, snaking his head and lunging at Robart's gray. She had seen the shadow darting over the cobbles, but had no idea what it had been or what had become of it—she had seen Robart slashing at something as they galloped up, and had thought Valadan meant to help her brother; the rearing and challenging between the two stallions took her utterly by surprise.

Robart had to bring the gray's head hard back to its chest before he was certain the horse could not break his grip and bolt. It wanted no part of standing anywhere near the admittedly murderous black stallion. The creature had unnerved *him*, come to that—anger colored Robart's voice when he shouted at his sister, though her horse by then stood calmly, violence showing only in those weird eyes.

"Are you stark mad? You aren't supposed to be here."

"There wasn't time for many Riders to come," Druyan explained hastily. "I—"

He cut her off, as if her reasons did not matter. "You were to relay the warning! No more! It's not safe here." Robart glared about at the flaming waterfront.

"Valadan keeps me clear of the fighting," Druyan lied, hiding her new-given sword behind a fold of her cloak.

"It's not only the raiders! Half Falkerry's afire."

"I know!" Druyan wondered what her brother could think she'd been doing. "We need more men with buckets, up to the right. Pass the word."

Robart refused to acknowledge that she could serve a purpose or give an order. "And that was a *wolf* I was after! Or a wolf-dog—" He spun the gray in a tight circle, searching vainly for his quarry. "Gone! But it must have come with the sea raiders. It's not just men we've got to look out for. It's dangerous here. You get home, *now!*"

Druyan glared at him. Robart glared back. Valadan snorted and jingled his bit.

The only fighting now is against flames, he suggested softly.

True. Already the din of battle was ebbing. Armed horsemen had routed the raiders, and with no new fires being set, the old ones would be swiftly contained. At the center of the worst confusion, Druyan could have believed the entire city was afire, but she could see as she glanced about that the raiders had afflicted only the riverfront. They'd had no time for anything more. All was well. She could appease Robart and go home without weighing guilt over tasks left undone.

Another Rider was struggling to claim his attention, but the Chief-captain's eyes were still upon Druyan. Robart's mouth opened, and his sister knew what he was about—he was going to order her escorted home!

Let him try, Valadan snorted, and spun handily to a direction that would take him to Falkerry's edge and thereafter the open countryside.

The wolf's fur was all but dry—the long run over the moors had shaken away a good deal of river water, though he was still damp next to his skin, especially on his belly and haunches, where the fur grew thick. He halted in the sheep pasture, near a familiar rock, put back his head, and half whined, half howled.

A moment later, Kellis knelt in the long grass, his hands planted on the turf to either side of his knees, his head hanging. He started to rise, only to fall back at once, dizzy. His throat was raw, and he got his breath only with the greatest difficulty, and then not for long.

Of course, he had half expected to drown in the Fal. He was no swimmer—few wolves truly are. And once in the water, he'd had no way to get out even if there hadn't been iron swords waiting to spit him. He had floundered all the way to the salt sea in the wake of the raiders' boats, been nearly run down by one straggler coming behind him, ere he finally blundered by chance into a marshy spot and got ashore—if half a league of mudflat and marsh could well deserve the dignity of the name. By then the sun was very well up, the light was bright, and he dared not linger.

He tried again and got to his feet, ignoring the giddiness that swept over him in a chilly wave. Kellis shifted the rock a few inches, pulled his clothing out from underneath, and slipped it on—a much more laborious task than slipping into his wolf-shape. The wolf had greater stamina than he did—when *it* was exhausted, he was utterly done up.

Threadbare sark. Trews. A jerkin streaked with mud. Must have rained, while he was gone. His head still buzzed, and the edges of things shimmered.

He heard a surprised *woof* and looked up to see Meddy's blue eyes watching him, her silky ears pricked above them as high as she could get them. The sheep beside her looked equally startled—not that sheep are capable of overmany expressions.

Well, worse if it had been Lyn. or Pru. Or come to that, Rook, who might well have attacked him for true. "Not a word of this, little sister," Kellis begged the dog. One of Meddy's ears flopped down. She whined uncertainly.

Kellis made himself take deep breaths. It helped. Not enough, but eventually he could get all the way to his feet, could balance atop his unsteady legs and drag himself back to Splaine Garth.

His hair was still wet.

Druyan hid the sword in the barn, not wanting to hear what Enna would say about it. The woman had enough to whet her tongue upon, what with her mistress vanishing in the middle of the night without one single word, then dashing about the countryside in a quite unseemly manner, riding home brazenly in broad day, her skirts dabbled with blood, reeking of smoke . . . Travic would never have condoned such behavior.

No husband would, Druyan supposed, her ears still ringing with the condemnations she imagined. So an ill-blow for her had been good fortune for Falkerry. There was no understanding that, and she did not try. The weaver set the warp, but fate laid in the weft—always.

The sword was hidden from sight right enough, but Kellis knew where it lay the instant he stepped foot in the barn. He approached the pile of sacking with the same care he'd have used if he'd suspected it of harboring a nest of

copperhead vipers, and hesitated a great while before he
drew the dusty cloth back.

The short double-edged blade was of the sort he remembered the raiders carrying at their brass-studded belts. The
hilts were of the same metal as the blades, with wooden
grips fitted on and bound with gold wire for Eral chieftains,
leather thongs for lesser men. This grip was one of the
leather ones, but the short crossguard terminated in little animal heads of brass—the poor man's gold. The beasts' eyes
were chips of polished obsidian, dark and blank as any
snake's gaze.

There was blood dried on the blade, a brownish stain up
near the hilt. The Rider must have tried to wipe it clean before he handed it over to the Lady Druyan, but there was
only so much one could manage in the heat of battle. Did
he mean it for her protection, or as a jest? No knowing,
Kellis thought, sweating. It wasn't likely she would know
how to use it, and he didn't think he could show her. He
had once been a decent fighter with a quarterstaff, and his
clan had owned a bronze blade or two, but it was not the
same sort of fighting. He did not deceive himself on that
account.

Just seeing the cold iron blade brought chill memories
flooding back. He'd been surrounded by the things, after
he'd found a chief and a crew who believed his prophecies
could be useful to their enterprise, and joined them. All the
wave-tossed way across the Great Sea, out of reach of any
escape save into death, he'd been taunted endlessly with
blades very much like this one, threatened for the sheer
sport of it. If the Eral hadn't needed him, they'd probably
have gone on to burn his flesh with their weapons, because
it would have amused them endlessly, hurting him with
something they could handle harmlessly.

He had taken his revenge once they were safe ashore—
making no attempt at all to see ahead for them, just making
wild guesses and hoping a lot of the freebooters would be
complacent, trust his showmanship, and shortly be dead as
he wanted *all* the Eral to be. Once in a while he had tried

a true foreseeing, but mostly he'd guessed—and till his luck ran out that first night at Splaine Garth, it had served him well enough.

Kellis touched the scar on his forehead. A blade not much different from this one, where it counted. The hilt had been gold, with dragons twined together, but he hadn't seen that as it came at him, and certainly the blow had been no softer for the costliness of the weapon's appointments.

His Clan had died upon swords such as this. And he had survived one, and now went among others. And would sleep in the same room as this one.

But not sleep well.

Druyan took the sword along when next she carried warnings, for there was no sense she could see in riding un-armed into trouble, even in little villages like Penre, which she could not believe the raiders were troubling over, no matter what the bowl showed at Kellis' command. A barrel of salted fish was the most booty Penre could offer a thief.

Penre was probably someone's mistake, but it was fought over, regardless. Two Riders and a dozen fishermen, about even odds with the fierce men who'd thought to find them-selves riches there. They'd beached their shallow-draft ves-sel, and one of the fishermen had managed to fire it. Thus trapped, the raiders fought to the last man, vicious as cor-nered rats.

Penre's womenfolk and their children had crowded into the stoutest of the houses, huddling there like chickens in a coop. The raiders began going to ground anywhere they could, and the stoutest walls looked best to them. One or two forced a way in, like foxes. Some of the women came out at once, into danger and confusion. Still others were trapped within. Penre's outraged men laid siege to the building, and Robart and another Rider showed up to join the fighting. Druyan ducked out of her brother's sight, knowing she couldn't keep that up for long—Penre was too small, and Valadan too recognizable.

She rode escort for the women and half a dozen children

of varying sizes, guiding the little group out past the edges
of the village—they could hide themselves better in the
moorland where no raider was apt to venture. Night would
fall soon, adding protection.

Druyan wondered how many folk were still trapped
among the buildings. Shifting her sword in her hand, she
tried to decide what the best grip for the weapon she had
not yet needed to use might be, as she rode back to the village. Valadan trotted down a muddy backstreet, every sense
alert. He sidestepped something, and Druyan's breath
caught in her throat—she'd thought for an instant 'twas a
body, lying in the road. Every shadow, every shape she
could not instantly identify became a peril, a threat. The
blade in her hand weighed heavier than she'd expected,
making her whole arm strain and ache, her entire body
twitch with nerves. She might have to use it, and that
frightened her. Robart was right, she had no business there,
none at all. She'd given the warning, and she should
go, flee home to safety.

But if she did that, retired and retreated as was seemly,
who would shepherd Penre's women while their homes
were fought over? Druyan heard a scream and headed
Valadan for the noise, glad to act rather than fret, finding it
easier.

When it came, Druyan had no leisure to debate the mo-
rality of wielding her sword against living flesh. A desperate raider ran yelling at her from her right, waving a
short-handled axe at Valadan, and Druyan defended the
stallion without thought, even as she tried to turn him to
safety. Swinging her blade in a tight sunward circle, she
caught the man just as the sword's tip was moving forward
and up. The blade's direction of travel matched Valadan's.
His speed thereby lent weight to Druyan's sword-stroke,
then carried them past their attacker.

He fell, Druyan thought, trying to turn in her saddle,
struggling to pull Valadan up, to turn him, to see what had
happened.

The stallion ignored the bit. He could see as well behind him as ahead, and had no need to turn. *He is dead.*

"What have I done?" Druyan whispered. Her hands and feet went cold. She began to shiver.

What you must, Valadan assured her, warm and steady beneath her.

She still held the sword, ready for another blow, though she had drawn her arm back toward her. There was something dark upon its tip, a splash of blood across the back of her sleeve. *Blood.* Druyan felt sick. Her cold hands shook, her limp legs could hardly grip Valadan's sides.

Not your blood, the stallion reminded her. *Which of course is the point . . .*

Druyan thought she saw that darting shadow underfoot again as they turned, a distraction to be seized with alacrity, though Valadan did not shy at it this time, only swerved smoothly.

It *couldn't* be a wolf. That had been at Falkerry. Maybe the raiders used battle dogs. She would have to remember to ask Kellis when she got home, Druyan thought. When she was herself again, if ever she could be.

The wolf leapt at the sea raider, but the man was dead as he fell, the sword-stroke having cut his throat. The wolf's bloody lips lifted. No need to waste time over this one. He loped on down the narrow street, behind the stallion. There were not many raiders left living—he had torn the throats out of two, the woman had done for another, and the horsemen were harrying the remainder of the longship's crew through the streets with good success. Only these raiders could not escape, because their ship was ashes, and no prey is half so dangerous as a cornered predator. So he hastened to get the woman in sight again, for she might not appreciate the increased danger . . .

He skidded around the blind corner, into the open, intent on his pursuit.

No! was all he had time to think.

Not all the dangers came from acknowledged enemies. Not for the likes of him.

The last raider had been rooted out of his hidey-hole and dispatched on a post rider's sword. Druyan slid out of her saddle, reckoning nightfall as protection enough from Robart's disapproving eye. She'd stand a moment on her own legs and allow Valadan the rest he did not seem to require, before heading out for Splaine Garth. She wanted to see the village folk returning to their homes, rejoining as families. She wanted to know that what she'd done had at least had a good result, that she had not done murder in vain.

All at once Druyan saw him, staggering toward her as she stood beside Valadan, through the smoking wreckage of Penre. Her mouth dropped open. Kellis was the last person she expected to see in that place. He hadn't a stitch of clothing on him, and he was barefoot, but there was no mistaking that silver hair, not in all the world. Without further thought, Druyan snatched up a cloak from a sea raider who wouldn't require it any longer, ran, and threw the torn wool about his muddy shoulders.

"Lady?" His eyes tried hard to focus on her, but couldn't manage it. He blinked as if he couldn't see. There was dark blood all over his face, mostly around his mouth. "Are you well?" he asked her anxiously.

Druyan was well—in the way Kellis probably meant—if speechless. Not that her answer mattered. As she nodded woodenly, his knees buckled, and Kellis would not have heard any answer she managed to make, much less her own urgent questions.

Shape-shifter

" 'S ALL RIGHT," Kellis insisted faintly, lying prone in the sandy dirt while Druyan knelt by him, wide-eyed and distressed. "Always lightheaded after a shift, getting thrown out of form is just worse. Got dizzy, that's all—"

"Out of form?" Druyan bent closer, not sure she was hearing correctly. "What are you talking about?" How ever had he gotten himself to Penre? Had he followed her? Afoot? No, that wasn't possible—but what *was*? There was blood on him, but she had yet to discover a wound, and most of his skin was under her eye.

"Stupid," Kellis went rambling on, a little louder, obviously not answering her, maybe not even hearing her questions. He frowned, lifting a hand to his head as if to brush an insect away. "Got too close to that horse, knew I was. Couldn't get clear. Didn't see him in time. He didn't catch me solid, but of course he was shod. Iron shoes are no better than iron swords—"

Druyan's search for an actual injury was finally rewarded. Most of the blood on his face had no obvious source, but she found a nasty scrape just above Kellis' left ear, raw where the hair had evidently been torn out by its roots. She'd seen kick marks like that on pastured horses. The spot leaked blood sluggishly. "You're lucky that horse didn't kick you into the afterlife!" she exclaimed wonderingly. The flesh was puffing like rising bread, and she thought the blow had been solid enough, whatever Kellis judged. "He came close. How—"

"Not his fault," Kellis said generously. "Horses will kick at wolves, it's their nature. Nothing to be done about it."

A wolf? Was *that* what she'd seen and taken for a big dog? A wolf, loose in Penre? Of course, it was hard to put much stock in anything a man told you, when you knew he'd just been kicked in the head by a horse. A *shod* horse, no less! Druyan frowned. An odd distinction for Kellis to make. Had he been close when the horse struck at the wolf and gotten himself kicked?

Kicked him clean out of his clothes, did it? Valadan put his muzzle close and sniffed curiously. *Even I cannot do that.*

Druyan had to agree with the horse.

Kellis began making an effort to sit up. Druyan thought to restrain him, then took pity and helped him instead. As he came more upright he seemed to grow dizzy again, and drooped heavily against her, his left hand pressed to the side of his head. His skin was cold under her fingers, though not bumped with it, clammy, grayish as if all the blood Kellis had were splashed on the outside of him. Druyan was prepared for him to be sick, but she felt him draw in three deep breaths, one after another, and in a moment he was able to sit unsupported, though he slumped and looked extremely unwell. Too unwell, Druyan judged, to go on lying to her.

"Kellis?" She felt faint herself.

He looked at her sidelong, someone else's blood all about his mouth, for his own lips weren't cut. There was blood dried between his teeth. Sharp teeth, Druyan suddenly noticed. Sharp as a wolf's.

"Lady?"

"Is there something you forgot to tell me?" Druyan asked bravely, pursuing a conclusion she could hardly have named. Kellis saw it in her face, whatever was dawning, and understood it well enough.

"Some of my people are shape-shifters," he said hesitantly. "It seemed . . . unwise . . . to mention it before, with the rest."

The confession was unexpected. Druyan had no idea what she *had* expected. And it was true. She knew it in her bones, as sure as she knew that she'd taken that raider's life with her sword, not merely crippled or maimed him.

"That wolf was *you*?" She accepted it calmly, because nothing else made even nearly as much sense.

Kellis nodded, then hastily put his hand back to the side of his head, supporting it as if his neck hurt him, too.

Something nagged for Druyan's informed attention. "Not the first time, was it?"

Kellis rubbed at his scalp. "No. When you rode out—I couldn't let you go alone, unprotected. I followed you, or tracked you—if I could." His breath hissed, and he stopped rubbing. He looked across her, at Valadan. "That horse is too fast for me. Sometimes you'd be coming home before I ever got to where you'd been . . ." His explanation trailed off.

"And you were a wreck when I got back, of course. Enna thought you'd been into the cider."

That coaxed a lopsided smile. "I wish I had been, Lady—that headache's easier to sleep off."

"Where are your clothes?" A wolf had no use for garments, of course. They'd only be a hindrance, so he must have taken them off.

"Buried under a rock in your sheep pasture."

Druyan rolled her eyes. "And I wondered why they seemed to be going to rags so fast! Meddy probably chews them full of holes while you're out of them." She heard voices, and remembered that they were neither alone nor at Splaine Garth. "Think you can sit behind me on Valadan?"

"I will shift form again and go back the same way I came," Kellis argued. He set his mouth. "Just let me get my legs under me—"

"A wolf traveling out of here now might expect worse treatment than having his hair parted with a horseshoe."

Druyan was brooking no dissent. "You're coming with me, and no more fuss."

Kellis seemed set on protesting further, but he changed his mind when he was on his feet once more—Valadan was his chief support, and the hand he tangled into the stallion's mane went white-knuckled with the desperation of his grip. It was a long moment before his legs were doing anything to hold him up, and it took heroic efforts on all their parts before Kellis was seated on Valadan's back.

"*Gods above and gods below!*" The horseman's voice cut like a well-honed sword, from high above. "Would you care to explain this?"

No, Robart, I would not, Druyan thought, leaning against Valadan's shoulder with her eyes tight shut, feeling as weak as Kellis must. *I have just this day hit a living man with a sword and probably made him a dead man, and now I discover that I have been living all these months with another man who can shape-shift himself into a wolf when he chooses. No, somehow I* don't *think I want to try to explain that to you.* She said nothing, but her brother did not notice.

"Kernan *said* his horse took a kick at the biggest dog he'd ever seen in these parts—and when he looked back at it, he saw no dog, but a man's body. A naked man's. And evidently nowhere near so dead as Kernan thought, when he asked me whether the raiders might have sorcerors with them!"

Druyan could feel Kellis' leg trembling beside her shoulder. She'd have sworn he was growling, only she heard no sound, just felt the vibration.

"This is Kellis," she said matter-of-factly, as if they'd met one another at a market fair. "He's a shape-shifter." Offhandedly, as if 'twas scarcely worth the mentioning. Maybe Robart wouldn't notice, she thought, hoping vainly. She wished she was ahorse, not afoot and feeling at such a disadvantage.

"*A shape-shifter!* Gods, Druyan!" Robart's smoke-reddened eyes, then his soot-marked, outreaching hand, fell on the sword she had forgotten to try to hide. "Where'd you get a sword? That idiot Yvain? What are you even doing here? I told you at Falkerry—you're to pass the message! You aren't supposed to be riding in the thick of this mess!"

Druyan's protest that she'd been useful, that she'd been safe, died in her throat. There was still blood on the sword, like an accusation.

"Tell your men," Kellis interrupted harshly, "not to do this again." He waved an arm at the burned boat, smoking and steaming on the beach sand. "Trap them like rats, they'll fight to their deaths—or yours."

Robart ignored him, save for a glare. Druyan was better quarry, or else he simply had not finished with her. *"Where's your husband?"*

"Travic is—" Is *what*? Druyan frantically wondered. Nothing plausible came to mind. She hadn't a wit left. Home, tending the crops? Too dead to disapprove? "My husband, not yours," she said to Robart, amazing herself. "Not your business."

Robart's blue eyes fairly started from his head, whites showing all around. His horse, responding to his temper, to the hands tightening on his reins, shied back and tried to rear against his rider's iron grip. At once Valadan's head snaked out, his teeth bared to fend off the other stallion from his mistress, afoot and imperiled whilst he was burdened with a helpless rider and hard put to protect her. Robart's horse half reared again to escape him, was pulled back under control ruthlessly, the bit dragging his mouth wide open. His rider's temper was not improved by the battle.

"He doesn't ask where you go, when you ride out? Doesn't question? Travic must be in his dotage! And we're none of us any better, acting on prophecies from *that*!" Robart hissed, jerking his chin at Kellis as he dragged the plunging horse back to Druyan's side. "You know nothing about this creature—except that he took service with sea thieves who're stealing everything in Esdragon they can carry away!"

"He's right about the ship," Druyan said angrily. "You cut off their only escape. Nowhere to run—they *have* to fight. What else would you expect?"

"I don't need a lesson in strategy—certainly not from something that's barely human and probably all traitor!"

"He's trying to help us," Druyan protested, her voice gone thin enough to tear, like a cobweb.

"Help us?" Robart laughed mirthlessly. "You mean by guessing where his old friends will strike next? Once he's won our confidence, what's to stop him sending us where he knows they're *not*, so they can raid undisturbed? Or sending us all into a trap?"

"He hasn't done that!" No, only begged her, over and over, not to trust him—and all the while hiding what he was, what was inside his human skin.

"Maybe he hasn't found a way yet. Well, I am for certain not so trusting as your husband! If this shape-shifter of yours makes one false move, he'll face my sword. You said he can't abide cold iron? I'll use it on him. Shift him straight into a corpse." Robart pointed his weapon at Kellis' nose for emphasis, but spoke to Druyan. "You hear me? No questions, no *trusting*, no second chances. He'll be dead."

Druyan tried to speak, but there was only silence when her lips parted.

Robart whirled his horse, shouted back at her. "You remember what I said!"

As if she was likely to forget any of it.

Kellis was silent during the ride homeward, and Druyan suspected he might have slipped into a drowse. It was a longish trek over the moors, and she held Valadan to a gentle trot, out of consideration for the double load on the horse's back and the condition of the second of his passengers. She had ordered Kellis to hold onto her belt, and she could feel one of his hands pressing obediently against her backbone, but she did not think him apt to keep his seat long should Valadan go at his best speed.

All at once he sat up straight, brushing against her, and

Druyan realized she had been all but asleep in the saddle herself. She looked about. The sun was coming up mistily. The ground nearby had a familiar look to it. They'd come home, into one of the high, windswept pastures. She heard a sheep bleat, one of the dogs bark sharply thrice.

"Lady, let me down," Kellis begged her. "I'll fetch my clothes and come back to the barn."

Valadan halted without waiting to be reined.

"I can find you other clothes," Druyan said, her thoughts fuzzy with sleep. "The stuff you left up here is nothing but tatters anyway." She'd been thinking so each time she saw him, for weeks. She'd just never guessed *why*. She looked back at him, suddenly uncomfortable.

Kellis shook his head at her, then glanced away at the ground, which might look awfully far away if he wasn't used to riding. "It's been a nice, dry week," he said, explaining. "Enna's bones won't have been bothering her, she'll have attention to spare. Let me down. I've got a headache, I don't want to come in like this, with you, and be answering her questions halfway to tomorrow."

Or facing the kitchen knives, Druyan thought. She braced her hand against Valadan's neck as Kellis slid down from the horse's back, was relieved to see that the man was able to stand steady when he arrived at the ground. "That cut wants tending," she said. "I'll bind it up when you get back." It hadn't bled much—the dark smear in his hair was no larger than it had been.

Kellis shrugged, unconcerned. "Just a scrape. Woundwort grows all over up here. I can take care of it."

"It's over your *ear*, there's no way you could possibly see what you're doing."

Kellis only shrugged again.

"I could tell Enna you were with me," Druyan went on, working it out aloud. "She might just be relieved to know someone was looking out for me."

"What else will you tell her, Lady?" His tone was reluctant, but unshirking. In the morning light, his gray eyes looked clear as water running over limestone, shafts of golden sunlight striking through now and again.

"Oh. I hadn't thought about that." Now that she was forced to, Druyan had no idea what to do. She sidled up to the issue like a nervous horse. She could well imagine Enna's reaction to the truth about what Kellis was—probably not far off from Robart's, only the kitchen knives in place of a sword. Maybe she *shouldn't* be told—but was it fair *not* to tell Enna what she was helping to harbor? Was she sure how she felt about him herself?

Some of that dilemma surely crossed her face. Kellis was watching her, knowing every twist, every turn in the conflict of loyalties assaulting her, or guessing them. There was no vestige of hope in his expression—not for mercy or anything else.

"Are you dangerous?" Druyan whispered, wondering how she'd know whether he answered her truly. She remembered how guileless those changeable eyes of his could be, the size of the secret he'd hidden effortlessly behind them. There was still blood around his mouth—only now she knew how it had gotten there.

"Lady, you have given me shelter and kindness, where I had no reason to expect either," Kellis said gravely. "I swear to you, I will never do harm to you or yours."

"But you've warned me not to trust you." It was out before she thought, she couldn't help herself. Valadan jigged under her, restless, tense with her sudden unease.

Kellis looked stricken. "The *prophecies*. I told you not to trust the prophecies. You do it anyway, no matter what I say, no matter how often I say it! You've dragged all those men into doing it, too—"

"And I suppose if you weren't trustworthy—*you*, not your foreseeings—we'd have lost a sheep or two ere this?" She didn't want to bring the prophecies and the post riders into it, Druyan thought. That was only smoke.

She wanted an answer, and Kellis gave it to her, looking straight into her eyes.

"Wolves take sheep because it's easy, Lady. Or it's the

only food. I'm not lazy, and I am not starving. I'll do you no harm."

"I know," Druyan whispered, ashamed. "I shouldn't have asked. It was an insult."

"It was a reasonable question, and taken so," Kellis said mildly. "And I answer it. I *am* dangerous—but never to you."

"Then it's not anyway unfair to Enna—she's at no risk I can see if she doesn't hear about any of this. I won't tell her," Druyan said, relieved to have made the choice. "Now go find your clothes—I'm sure that cloak's lousy, and even if it isn't, it's mostly holes, and the wind's cold up here."

That right eyebrow lifted, then one corner of his mouth, just as she turned Valadan toward home.

He should not have told her. He *would* not have, Kellis told himself, except he had been dazed by the glancing blow to his head and the resulting loss of his wolf-shape. He had not been himself. His tongue had escaped his control and gone its own merry wayward way. She'd asked, and he'd answered, while his wits were still so scattered that he hadn't quite realized what he was doing—till he'd said it and it was too late to dodge back from telling her the whole truth.

Not that he likely could have managed such wordy nimbleness if he *had* been able to think about what he was doing. Feeling well enough on the horse, he had misjudged himself. Once he was on his own legs, matters were much otherwise. Kellis discovered it was all he could do to get himself down from the upland pasture—his balance was unsure and his sight as unreliable as his visions, showing him double the usual number of sheep in Rook's flock as he staggered through them, a fuzzy mist on the peripheries. Putting one foot in front of the other took concentration, seemed a miracle when he succeeded at it. He never actually fell, but there were near disasters and many a clutch at a fencepost or outbuilding, while sea sounds came and went in his ears.

Finally, the weather-silvered bulk of the barn itself swam before his eyes. There was a dark, cavelike opening in it—the door standing welcoming wide. Kellis made for that and held onto the jamb, getting splinters in his fingers and happy beyond measure that there was no sill to trip his feet.

Once he was inside, there was nothing more for him to cling to, just a vast dim space lit by the doorway at his back and slanting rays of sunlight that entered through gaps between boards. Kellis stopped, swaying uncertainly, staring at the light-lances. Somewhere within the maze lay his goal, the soft pile of blanket-covered straw he used for a bed.

He heard a horse nicker, part greeting, part question. For a long moment, Kellis could not determine which form he was presently in, man or wolf. He remembered dashing unwarily in wolf-shape past a corner and being surprised by a horse earlier. He had surprised the beast, too—the horse had kicked out in a panic. He had dodged, of course, but only enough to prevent the hoof's catching him square and shattering his wolf's skull. The blow glanced, but flung him a dozen feet and out of his senses . . . not to mention out of his wolf-shape, courtesy of an iron horseshoe. If this horse, now, had it in mind to stomp a wolf, he did not think he could save himself, man or wolf, either one.

He smelled horsehide and hair, right in front of his face. Warm, sweet air puffed across his skin as the stallion blew at him. "Good boy," Kellis said with relief, recognizing Valadan, the only horse he knew to be allowed free run of Splaine Garth. He patted the stallion's neck, then took an unsteady step forward, trying to decide if two legs were superior to four or in fact inferior. Less of them to manage, certainly, but 'twas so much easier to fall on one's face after a misstep . . .

A great, warm bulk came alongside him—the horse had circled around him, was walking with him instead of at him. Kellis put a grateful hand on Valadan's withers. Six legs were better than four, so long as he had to personally direct only two of them. He tangled his fingers firmly in the long black mane. "Where are we going?" he asked.

The stallion turned his head. His near eye was as dark as the night sky and full of twinkling stars. Kellis looked automatically for the green of Valint, but the Wolfstar must have set or else had not yet risen—he could not find it. The stallion snorted. When Kellis looked away, the sunshafts looked like a thousand sword blades, slanting all about him. He had lost his bearings, but he didn't much care. He didn't need to find his bed—if he could just sit down, somewhere out of the way, where nothing could step on him . . .

He smelled hay, and pearwood, shavings from the fork he had begun carving what seemed half his lifetime ago, with a thick handle that a woman with sore hands could comfortably grasp. Kellis put his left hand out and swung the half-door open. He'd made it after all, thanks to the horse's support. His bed was only three steps ahead, and he could hold onto the wall the whole way . . .

A racket of happy barks exploded behind him. Meddy had discovered he was back and was headed at him with her usual riotous greeting.

"No, little sister," he begged her, but she flung herself at him anyway, paws on his shoulders and warm tongue on his face. Falling, Kellis hoped he would fetch up on the cushioning straw, not bare wooden boards.

She will hate me.

He returned to the thought as the dark whirled about him. Kellis couldn't remember whether the sun had gone down. The Wolfstar had set, hadn't it? He smelled hay and horse sweat. Dust tickled his throat. He coughed, and pain stabbed alarmingly through his skull. Somewhere near, a dog whined.

She will fear me and, being brave as she is, try to hide it . . . Straw poked his cheek; he had either lain down or fallen. Either way, he need not fear a further collapse, and he seemed to have made it to his bed after all. But there were other fears to plague him. *She will hate me* . . .

"Kellis?"

Hands touched him, shifted him so that he lay on his side rather than his face. The process hurt. He had no notion why he was being tortured so. Kellis bit his lip till he tasted salty blood.

Truth was, he should never have come back at all. He should have taken the wolf-shape back, then denned up somewhere secret till he recovered. And then he should have vanished.

Of course she'll hate you. She saw you with blood all over your teeth; even your own womenfolk don't much care for that. And she's not one of the Clan . . . no reason to expect . . .

Blessed coolness touched the pain biting into the side of his head.

"Is that better?" Druyan asked, sponging again with the wet rag.

Actually, it was not. She was probing gently at the wound, trying no doubt to decide whether his skull was cracked, and Kellis thought he could not have borne a spider's walking across his skin just there, just then. But the lady was speaking to him, she had searched him out—his astonishment at that reality swallowed most of the pain. It would be ungrateful of him to groan at her touch, so he did not.

Ungrateful, too, to faint, but he had less choice as to that. His senses slid sideways, like a horse shying.

His hearing came back first, but only as a ringing in his ears, a bothersome buzzing, like flies round a carcass. Then touch reasserted itself, with the water's cool comfort. For one delicious moment, Kellis was in no pain at all, and he would have felt perfectly well, save that his heart was so heavy, like a great wooden weight in his chest, for some unremembered reason. He tried to hold the memory away, but it found him, sniffed him out, came racing home glad as Meddy to see him awake once more. Pain stabbed his head and his heart, both of them at once. He groaned. *I should not have told her . . .*

"Hush." A firm touch on his shoulder. "Lie still. You've had a bad knock on the head."

I know, he wanted to say. *I wish I'd died of it.*

"No, you don't." A chuckle. "Well, maybe you *do*, right now, but you'll feel better presently. Try to sleep."

Kellis opened his eyes instead. She was there. Truly there, not just put there by his half-dazed dreaming. He could smell the apple-blossom scent of her hair, the smoke smell of Penre still lying faintly atop it. "Lady, I am sorry—"

"So am I," Druyan said wryly. "I should never have let you walk back. *I* wasn't the one kicked in the head, I ought to have known better even if you didn't. I ought to have known not to listen to you." She dipped the cloth back into the water, wrung it out, and laid it on his forehead.

She'd been in the kitchen, with Enna, when she'd seen him come weaving and stumbling across the yard like a blind man, and she'd gone sick and cold inside. Druyan sponged the wound again, frowning. The bone was whole, but he'd slipped in and out of consciousness thrice at least since she'd run into the barn and found him lying on the floor, with Valadan standing over him and Meddy curled in a scared, guilty ball by his side. At least this time Kellis had his eyes open and made sense when he spoke. She squeezed his hand, to reassure him. "You'll be fine." *Willow tea,* she thought, for the headache—but willow tea made you bleed, for all it tamed pain. Better not, at least not yet. She wished she had some poppy sap. "Just lie quiet."

Kellis wanted to tell her how glad he was to see her, what it meant to him, that she had not forsaken him—but relief and sleep surprised him more decidedly than ever that scared horse had.

"I wasn't his first choice for an apprentice," Kellis whispered, not opening his eyes. Druyan had thought him finally asleep, but he was still drifting restlessly on the edge of it, like a boat with no hand on the tiller, at the mercy of the waves' whim. She felt his forehead—no fever. His wound had stopped seeping blood, and the wet rags had kept the swelling down as much as they were likely to. Come morning she could bind it up with herbs, to start the skin healing. She had been on the point of seeking her own bed for a few hours, leaving Meddy curled by his side for company. She sighed, stretched a little to ease her back. Not much different from the broken nights of lambing time.

"He didn't even *make* a choice, till the chief got nervous about it. Wisir was old, and if he wasn't training someone to be shaman after him, what were we to do when he died?" Kellis asked plaintively. "He lived all alone, out past the edge of the camp, he didn't have any family. No one to watch over him so he'd be able to watch over the Clan."

Druyan was not entirely certain Kellis was awake. His eyes were closed, though the lids twitched now and again. She made sure he was well covered by the blankets, that his bare toes weren't poking out into the chilly air. He had come back without his boots. She had no idea where he'd left them. She'd have asked, but didn't think he'd answer. She didn't want to risk waking him—he needed rest.

"So Wisir told us he'd picked, finally, and everyone felt better," Kellis said conversationally. "He was going to make a formal ceremony out of it, Wisir was. Dancing. Feasting. We were hunting deer, a whole pack of us, to have venison for it. The stag was a big one, and it was early in the rut. He was fierce as a catamount, and we should have left him alone. But we didn't, and the boy Wisir had chosen got an antler in his throat, and he bled to death, right there. So fast." He sighed. "Nothing we could do. We just stared. We couldn't take it in."

His dark brows knit together. "Wisir wasn't very good at foreseeing. Not to know that the person he'd picked to succeed him wasn't going to live out the week—it would have been a scandal if the Clan had known it." He sighed again. "Which they did not. Wisir made sure of that—he wasn't smart, but he was clever. He made another choice, right on the spot, as if that was what he'd had in mind all along. Just pointed his finger, blind—and I wish to all the gods there are that someone else had been standing in front of him when he did it."

Druyan had not been paying much heed—she had no notion whether Kellis was even speaking to her, if he had any idea she was there to listen. The implications of what he'd just said made her catch her breath sharply. He was explaining himself.

He knew she was there. His eyes were open, staring at her, and both of them were wet. The first few tears had already run down past his cheekbones.

"My qualification for being our shaman's apprentice, the talent he saw in me—I was *there*," he said brutally. "My training you can guess at—how hard either of us tried. Wisir was a fool and I was resentful. If I had tried at all, my people might have survived. They trusted Wisir. They trusted *me*." He shut his eyes again, on the shame of that trust betrayed.

"I don't think it's your fault," Druyan said unsteadily. "Not all of it."

Kellis didn't answer.

Constable of Esdragon

KELLIS HUNCHED OVER the bowl, scowling refusal at Druyan when she strode up and tried to prise it from his fingers.

"You don't have to do this *now*," Druyan told him angrily. "It's not likely there's a ship striking near again, so soon." The raids had taken on a discernible pattern—heavy, then nothing, after that a period of light forays, followed by another crest. They were due a respite, assuming they had learned to read the pattern accurately. And Kellis was due one even if they were wrong—she'd caught him trying to do the milking when she came back to the barn at dawn, and the stuff in the pail had more color than his face did.

"Better to *know*," Kellis said stubbornly, tightening his hold on the crockery. "We don't know that ship was alone. Or that it wasn't."

They did know that the sea raiders did not repair to their cross-seas homes upon meeting the setback of a defended village—more likely they fell back upon places they knew from past experience to be weak, along the Clandaran beaches. More than once the bowl had shown faint, misty images of places Druyan was certain were not in Esdragon.

"Anyway, one headache's no different from another." Kellis dismissed her concern. He looked wan and unwell, and was moving rather cautiously, but he was up and determined to resume his duties, including the prophecies he dreaded. Doing so without reference to those things he had confessed during the passage of the night—if he suspected he had revealed them. He wasn't staggering any longer, so Druyan let him have his way, however reluctantly.

She protested the bowl, he fought her on it, and she let him do as he pleased about that, too, but was not sorry when the effort came to naught.

"Waves on a beach," Druyan said a few minutes later, trying not to say told-you-so. "And fishing boats. Not much to judge by, but it didn't look like they were having any trouble."

"No." Kellis dried the bowl with a rag. His tone was neutral, but his movements were abrupt with frustration. "I'll look again later."

"You can look again *tomorrow*," Druyan corrected.

"We don't *know* that was a foreseeing!" he snapped back at her.

"I don't remember peaceful moments spent watching the waves, yesterday." She waved a hand. "Let it be, Kellis. Once a day's enough."

"I don't want to be wrong." His jaw tensed. "My head may have been half split, but my ears worked just fine. I heard exactly what the captain said."

So *that* was it. And, Druyan thought, a very legitimate concern for a man with Kellis' liabilities.

"The captain is my brother," she said. "I can deal with him. I got you into this, and I haven't forgotten that."

"There will be others feel the same way." He didn't look especially relieved.

"I don't say you're foolish to want to stay out of Robart's way," Druyan soothed. "I think it's a fine idea. Sensible as sunlight." She let her smile fade. "Now be sensible about this, too. You can't chase after a vision till you drop—you tried that before, and we both know it doesn't work. It's even less likely to work right *now*. You're tired, and your head hurts. Give yourself a chance. Catching the wind, I think you named it?"

Kellis frowned fiercely, but Druyan could see that he had

given in. "If you're worried about Robart's threats, the best thing I can advise is to keep out of his reach. I never said that you had to escort me." Of course, she'd never known he *could*.

"Does that mean *you'll* do what your brother asks, and come home when you've passed on the warning?" Kellis inquired sweetly, his wolf-gold eyes ever so innocent.

Not a few of the places they rode to warn were too small to own formal names, insignificant even to those who made their homes there and never previously visited by post riders. There were neither towns nor harbors for landmarks. Druyan might at best recognize a stretch of coast, perchance some rocks leaning back from the surf as if they hated being splashed by the tide. Hungry ship crews landed at such spots to steal themselves a meal, no more complex objective than that in their hearts. It was a hard threat to meet effectively—twice the Riders turned up too late to offer anything beyond sympathy and hopeful promises of future action. Twice in a row, that happened to be, and Druyan remembered with dread what Robart had vowed, what he'd promised Kellis about betrayals.

It was mischance, not betrayal, of course, but convincing Robart of that might have proved tricky. Fortunately, her brother had been riding the nether reaches of the post riders' route, working his way back toward the Darlith coast, and Kellis was as safe as he was likely to be—considering that a wolf continued to follow at Druyan's heels and go darting among cold iron weapons that would shed man's blood or a wolf's with equal ease.

The Chief-captain rejoined them during their defense of a hamlet grown up round a brace of tanneries, enterprises that had made their owners both prosperous and vulnerable. The place stank to heaven, even without the smoke of the fires the raiders had set to create confusion. Druyan saw her brother all at once through the haze, his jaw clenched because his eyes had just lit upon her face. The message was plain as any Rider ever delivered, even unspoken—she'd disobeyed him.

Robart came riding over to repeat it, flat out, in case she had not properly read the look. But as he arrived at Valadan's left flank, Yvain rode up on the right, with one salute for his senior officer and another for Druyan herself.

"I'm going," Yvain reported to Robart. "Questions asked if I don't. Our schedule has always been . . . flexible . . . hour to hour, but there'll be notice taken if it gets much more irregular, Captain."

"Aye." Robart nodded and sheathed his sword. He looked about, at scurrying townsmen. "This is over. Get yourself gone, to where you're supposed to be. I'm late myself."

Druyan held her peace and indeed her breath, in case the press of time should force Robert to put up his lecture to her as he'd just put up his weapon. Thankfully, Kellis was nowhere in sight. If he saw Robart first, he'd make himself scarce.

Yvain gave his stallion's sloping shoulder a pat. "This can't work much longer," he said in a conversational tone tinged with regret. "The horses aren't holding up. We're riding them farther—and harder, to make it look as if the routes are ridden just as usual, with no gaps unaccounted for. The difference is too much for the poor beasts to make up for, even if you don't take the fighting into account. They're losing condition. No one's noticed yet that the roads seem to be taking an unusual toll of our horseshoes this year, but that will come! At present the horses only want rest, but matters can go very much the worse in less time than I'd care to contemplate." Stressed horses could succumb to colic and founder overnight.

"You need remounts," Druyan said, daring Robart's attention to state the obvious. She wondered why they didn't have spare horses, and use them. She knew the Riders by their mounts as well as by their faces, and they all looked tired, dispirited.

Robart barked a laugh, but Yvain courteously answered

her. "That we do, Lady. But we shan't have them—our duke's bound he'll sell such 'excess' stock to pay for his ships. We're lucky to keep what we're sitting on. I own this fellow myself—else I'd not have him. And he's fortunate I've another courser to share his duties, waiting for me at Tolasta. Most of our beasts won't get that relief."

"Our uncle hasn't poked his nose out of Keverene in a year," Druyan said, wondering if they'd overlooked that. "Does he *know* how many head he's got in his herd?"

"No, but Siarl does," Robart said, squashing her hope before she spoke it.

"Siarl? Tavitha's husband?" Druyan asked, baffled.

"The Constable of Esdragon," Robart explained. "The duke's herds are in his charge."

"How do you suppose *he* feels about them being sold?" Druyan wondered aloud.

"He's probably not overly joyful," Yvain said wickedly. "Siarl's no fool."

Robart scowled. "What are you suggesting—that we invite him to put his head on the block for us? Maybe you two don't realize it, but we're talking treason."

Druyan looked around. The other Riders, four of them, had come up, though not quite joined their leaders' conference. There seemed a lot of men about, clad in sea blue and gray. "Isn't this?" she asked.

Her brother winced. "I'd like to think there's some way it isn't."

"Maybe Siarl would like to think that, too," Druyan said.

Tavitha's husband was a big man, extremely fair of face and hair. Constant exposure to weather in the course of his duties had left Siarl's skin a deep pink and bleached out his brows till they sat over his blue eyes like two tufts of shorn fleece. His lashes were pale and nigh invisible, so that his eyes looked oddly unprotected—particularly once the constable heard why his brother and sister by marriage had come to call on him.

"I'm under orders," Siarl said carefully, moving his

earthenware goblet about as if 'twas a chesspiece. "The brood mares stay, and any late sucklings at heel. Everything else is offered if there's a buyer interested."

Druyan was too shocked to speak. The duke's fine horses were Esdragon's greatest pride. To sell so many at once was not merely to wound but to destroy a breeding program that had run more than a hundred carefully recorded years.

"When's this grand horse fair to be held?" Robart asked, with sympathy. "Next spring?"

Siarl snorted, like one of his stallions. "The fair's always been held late in the spring—show off the new foal crop, the young bloodstock, that's the point—as soon as the winter coats are shed out and the grass has greened up, so they're fat and sleek and looking fine. Only *this* year there was no fair, by ducal decree. Brioc's shifting it to the autumn, so that this year's foals will be well weaned and ready for sale with the rest. He wants to keep nothing back, if 'twill bring him gold."

"Lucky for him the herds are pastured far enough inland to be safe," Druyan said acidly. "By autumn they might be the only wealth Esdragon has left."

"It's true, then? He's selling them all to trade for warships?" Siarl shook his head in wonderment, lifting his cup to his lips.

"He spoke of ships to me," Druyan said, "when I asked him for help against the raids. Brioc didn't mention the horses, just wanting the warships, to protect the coast. He asked me what sort of timber Splaine Garth could give him."

Siarl choked on his wine. "*Is the man blind?* There's never been a ship's mast grown in Esdragon. Our trees don't yield warships. We're lucky to have fishing smacks, and a lot of those are built of drifted-in timber."

"Ships are all Brioc sees, no matter what he looks at," Robart said disgustedly, running his finger through a puddle of spilled wine, which lay on the table like blood.

"How does he think to crew these ships, once he's built

them?" Siarl grumbled. "A fishing boat's a far cry from a warship; we've no sailors can do what he intends."

"I'm sure Dimas has some thoughts on that," Robart answered softly.

"That's where this comes from, then? Sell off my horses so Dimas can play fleet captain?" Another stallionlike snort—Siarl knew Dimas too well. "Sell them cheap at that, flooding the market that way. What happens when his fleet's sunk—and you *know* there'll be losses, those sea raiders are cruel fighters—and there's nothing else to sell?"

"There's the mines," Robart said helpfully.

"If those mines brought in that well, he'd be leaving the horses alone, wouldn't he?" Siarl shook his head. "I don't like what I see of our future, Robart. I would I was Brioc's age, and unlike to live as witness to the full disaster. And I've three sons . . ."

"Perhaps we can forestall that sort of future," Druyan offered. She spoke, carefully, of the work the post riders had done thus far, using their own resources to accomplish unofficially what Brioc's policies would not allow them to do openly, what the duke's army was not able to do. When she had finished, Siarl was looking at her with frank amazement, his white brows lifted up very high.

"You'd heard nothing about this, then?" Robart asked. "That's most reassuring."

"Nary a rumor. You've kept your secrets very well, Captain."

"Proves the saying, that it's only true tidings if a post rider passes it on."

"We want to continue," Druyan said, ignoring Robart's digression, though she smiled at it.

"If your uncle learns of this . . ." Siarl's white brows moved to meet one another.

"We're taking every care that he doesn't," Robart assured him. "That's taking an awful toll on our horses."

"So you'd like remounts from me?" Siarl frowned in consternation as he understood. "You know I can't let you have them. There's a tally stick for every horse in the herd.

f I gave you *half* what you need, the shortage would be
noticed. Most years, not a problem, but *this* year—"

"*Swap* with us," Druyan said coolly.

"What?" Even Robart stared at her, uncomprehending.

"You can't tell me Brioc knows one horse from another,"
Druyan went on earnestly. "All he knows is how *many* he's
got. So let us bring you our horses *before* they're badly out
of condition, and take fresh stock in exchange. It's a fair
trade. The post riders' horses mostly came out of the ducal
herds in the first place.

"So they did." Siarl smiled.

"Your tallies will balance."

"Assuming you don't lose a horse." Siarl looked concerned. "You're talking about horses hard-ridden, going
into fighting. And most of them aren't trained for it."

"None of them are trained for it." Druyan shook her
head. "Siarl, I won't put your head on the block—I won't
make Tavitha's children fatherless. If we lose a horse, I will
send you one to replace it from Splaine Garth. We breed
good strong stock—I wish you could see this year's crop!
Most of the older horses went with Travic and his men and
got swallowed up into Brioc's army, or we'd be using them
first, for the Riders—but we can send you something on
four legs to make up your numbers, even if it's only green-
broke. Depend on it."

"Does Travic know about that?" Robart asked, frowning
at her.

"Travic won't mind," Druyan said, quite truthfully.

The Battle for Sennick

THERE CAME A spate of quiet days, when Kellis saw nothing of raiders in the dark bowl of water—nearly a full sennight of them. Part of that blessed lull could be explained by the water falling out of the sky—heavy rains made sea travel in open boats less than pleasurable, even for men bent on plunder. If there were raiding parties bound for Esdragon, they might have put their boats in at some deserted, unsettled cove to wait upon favorable winds and drier weather. Those already near were unlikely to venture forth, either.

The rain made the crops prosper. The respite renewed everyone's hopeful spirits. Druyan threaded a new warp upon her great loom and nurtured a dream that there would be no more raids, that the fierce sea-folk should have at last learned from their many defeats that Esdragon would not lie before them with her throat exposed, that she was no easy victim. She wove stripes of blue, and gray, soft greens, and wet-slate black, all the shades of the Duchy of Esdragon, and the cloth grew by an ell a day, as if 'twere a magic web, a sorcery to safeguard them all . . .

But it was not.

The great fleet of raiders did not strike all at the selfsame place. Few spots in Esdragon were so rich as to offer spoils enough to content a dozen captains and their crews all at nce. The raiders split their forces and attentions, so that each dawn some new spot was under siege, or a port that had been visited once before knew trouble again. The Riders mustered every village watch and rode frantically to turn out any town garrison that would hearken to their warnings—or *could*. Splaine Garth was not alone in losing men to the duke's army. All along the coast, defenses were weakened by the measures meant originally to succor them.

There were too few post riders to stand and fight as they had done in those now fondly remembered early days, when merely to lift a sword had seemed enough to ensure their success and raiders were put to flight by any show of force. They were suddenly thrust back upon the tactic Robart preferred all along for his sister Druyan—warn, ride, and rouse local forces as swiftly as might be—and then they were forced back to fighting once again, because there was no one else to do it, in places like the market town of Sennick.

The "nick"—the valley that gave Sennick its name—was gentle-sloped to either side of the river that had cut it, and so there was room to either side for settlement and commerce. The banks of the river, the edges of the harbor where the river met the sea—the town had spread all along them. Unlike marshy places such as Splaine Garth, Sennick's land was underpinned with sturdy rock, and building was possible at any point.

There had been talk in past years of building some sort of a wall about the town, but no one had been able to devise a way of walling off the river that would not divide one half of the town from the other half, and 'twas Sennick's river that the raiders used, rowing up it boldly in the sunfall light, abandoning the surprise of the dawn attack in favor of the concealment and confusion that oncoming night would offer them.

Eight riders were there, lending mobility to the town forces if they could not offer strength. Sennick's narrow streets were no places to attempt massed charges—not that there were enough horsemen to ply that tactic anyway. The

Riders tried to stay in pairs, to use the height and speed their horses lent them to see trouble sooner and bring Sennick's fighting men afoot to bear upon it. They kept a watch for fires, as well, and sent parties with buckets where they were worst needed.

There was a plan to their work, conceived for the moment though it necessarily was. But in action that plan resembled chaos more than organization, at least to Druyan's eye. The Riders, beset from every side, were reacting as best they might, struggling to force the raiders back upon their ships, and one moment's seeming success might be proved a ruse the very next instant, as a building went up in flames just after they'd thought a whole street was swept clear of the sea thieves.

They were slow to recognize that the fires were now a more deliberate tactic than they had previously been. Some of the raiders had been lessoned by previous repulses, and now Sennick's defenders were kept very busy firefighting on several fronts. And while they sought to douse one blaze, its kindlers were a dozen streets away, hot at their work again.

With many streets aflame, the Riders could no longer make full use of their mounted speed. Streets not entirely blocked were nonetheless a terror to the bravest horse. Valadan would go anywhere Druyan desired him to, but none of the others had battled chimeras in its first youth, and though the post riders' mounts trusted their riders, they would hardly face flames for them. Kernan's black-leg gray disobeyed his master for the first time in five years, plunging sideways out of a street lined by dancing yellow flames, shying with such force that the post rider was unseated and sent sprawling onto the unforgiving cobbles, where he lay stunned.

Druyan hastily dismounted and raised the captain to his feet, while Valadan bullied the gray back toward them.

"They're learning," Kernan said, and spat blood out of his soot-framed mouth as he climbed to his feet. "We can't fight the fires *and* them—and they know it! There were torches through the house doors first thing."

"What about their ships? If we—"

Kernan cut off her plan with a headshake, trying to get a toe into the gray's near stirrup while it circled around him. "They've learned there, too. I just came from the river, the ships are left close-guarded. Best we can do now is go after any raider we see, nothing fancier." He gained his saddle and groaned. "No use trying to get men to the fires before they spread—these were *set* to spread, half Sennick's aflame now."

Valadan stood calm while Druyan remounted, despite the near crackle of flames, the waves of heat and billows of smoke. "I'll pass the word to Robart."

"You'll get yourself out of here, Lady!" Kernan snapped. "Carrying messages is peril enough when it works; trying to do it now is suicide! We've done all we can for Sennick, and the rest of the Riders will see that, on their own."

Druyan wheeled Valadan about and stared at him. Kernan stared back as best he could—his right eye was swelling shut.

"No, I am not abandoning them, Lady. What I can do, I shall—but one of those things must surely be to urge you to get out of the city." A house collapsed in on itself, sending flames high into the darkness. Kernan's horse screamed and plunged away. This time the Rider stayed with the beast, Druyan saw as she and Valadan rode away in another direction.

Be good, Druyan told herself. *Stay out of trouble. Stay out of the fighting. You only run messages. The sword was a bad jest of Yvain's. And a worse one, that you used it.*

"Out of the city," Kernan had said—but even if Druyan had considered herself bound to his sensible will, she would have been hard put to be obedient to it. There were fires everywhere, leaping from roof to roof, harmless on tile but betimes a spark would find thatch, and then the dark streets were suddenly too well lit. There were still concerted efforts to put the flames out—Valadan slid back on his haunches to avoid crashing into a line of women passing buckets frantically from one hand to another. Trying to ride around them, Druyan discovered that the file ran all the way to the river, down a slope and around a corner in the process.

Probably she could pass through the line without harm closest to the river. But should she then go upriver or down? Neither course would take her straight out of the town; she must ride the cross-streets instead, seeking dark and quiet as river water seeks the sea, mostly by trial and hopefully not often by error. The fires themselves would determine where she could go. Kernan was right: Sennick was lost now, they had done all they could do, and this time 'twas not near enough. Far off, Druyan heard a wolf's howl. She wondered if Kellis would realize she had left. She didn't want to leave him behind . . .

A scream tore the smoky night, very close at hand. Then a great splash—they were still only one street removed from the river. Druyan turned and rode hard toward the commotion, her sword ready in her hand.

The tail of the bucket file was in disarray. Half a dozen women were dipping pails into the river—or had been when they were chanced upon by a trio of sea raiders. One woman had been hurled into the chill water, where she floundered, screaming that she would drown, and the remainder faced the three men, armed only with their wooden pails. Two ran for it, choosing discretion over the unequal fight. One made it into the dark of an alley and escaped— the other was dragged back by a laughing raider who seemed merely amused by her desperate struggles.

All three men carried bulging sacks—evidently they were bound for their ship, with the goods they'd been able to carry off. And possibly trade goods weren't all they'd deal in, for as Druyan watched in horror, one of the younger women was suddenly felled by a fist to her jaw and slung swooning over a shoulder, while two of the others were summarily dispatched with dagger blows. The last woman swung her bucket in a mighty arc, but she stumbled over a body and went headlong with no damage done to her target. The raider snatched up the bucket and clubbed her with it, then seized her wrist and hauled her to her feet, where he struck her twice more before Druyan and Valadan fell upon him.

He heard the clatter of hooves on cobbles and turned. The woman fell when he let loose of her, so Druyan's sword had a clear path—down and back from just above shoulder height, sweeping forward in an upward circle, gaining speed and taking Valadan's momentum, reaching the raider's neck just as the blade began to rise once more.

Valadan's height let Druyan catch her target in the throat, and though the raider wore a leather collar for protection, with a torc of twisted metal over it for show, the blade sheared clear to his spine. Druyan would have lost her weapon, only she had its thong looped over her wrist against such a mischance. A jolt shot up her arm—as if, scything barley, she had struck a hidden stump left carelessly in the field. Valadan leapt over the falling raider, skidded, and spun back to the battle.

The sailor with the woman over his shoulder heard them coming and tried to sprint into a narrow spot where a horseman could not follow. Instead, he tripped on a loose cobble and fell, and Druyan's swipe at him missed by a hand's-breadth as he went down. She sent splinters flying from the bottom of a house shutter, recovered, and struck again to keep the man occupied, but his captive did not seize the chance to escape—she lay huddled where she had been flung, moaning.

I can't let him take her, Druyan thought. Nor could she keep riding at the man without trampling the fallen girl. The raider had his back to the house wall, where he could fend off any frontal assault with his sword, though 'twas short as any of the Eral blades.

And he could expect aid. But the man trying to creep up behind Valadan had little knowledge of horses—or else forgot a horse sees better behind than ahead and has ears attuned to hear the softest footfall.

Hold on!

The raider was nearly close enough to try the hamstringing he contemplated, when the stallion let fly with both hind hooves and introduced him rudely to the gods of the Eral afterworld.

Druyan had seen Valadan's ears go back and would have needed no more warning to secure her seat. But the action cost her a moment's attention, and when she looked back at the raider by the wall, he was coming at her, screaming words she did not recognize but could hardly mistake as to their intent.

He came at her left side, and she could only chop at him awkwardly from across Valadan's neck, her reach much shortened, while the stallion reared and struck with his own weapons, slashing hooves and crushing teeth. His hooves touched the cobbles, and Druyan hewed at the raider.

Again the jolt of the blow connecting solidly with flesh and bone. Except that this time something jarred against her hand, as well. The sword fell away with its thong cut, and the hand Druyan raised was running scarlet with her own blood.

Wolves, Running

DRUYAN FELL FORWARD onto Valadan's neck, clutching her right hand tight to her chest. Dimly her ears reported the doleful howl of a wolf, going on and on and on, till she could not have said whether it was truly some wild beast or only a scared dog—or whether the sound came from her own throat, which was aching and raw with the copper taste of blood in it.

Hold on, Valadan ordered, as he had when he kicked out at the raider, and when he felt Druyan's legs automatically obeying him, he began to run.

The world was all blackness, but that was only because 'twas night and her eyes were tight-closed, Druyan knew. The roaring in her ears was merely the wind, rushing past her head. The sparks behind her eyes were but fire-dazzle. She was not fainting—she must not, for she would fall, and Valadan was earnestly begging her not to. She must stay with him . . .

Her right hand ached, deep into the bone. *I'm cut,* Druyan thought, amazed, trying to puzzle out how that had happened. *What a nuisance. Cuts on the fingers never stay closed, and everything gets in them . . .* She kept the hand cradled tight against her breast, afraid to let loose, though she knew she should be trying to gather her reins. She ought to sit up, not ride lying along Valadan's neck, barely in the saddle. She was making it so hard for him . . .

So long as you hold tight to me, I can carry you, Valadan reassured her. *Only hold on.*

They weren't in the city any longer. Valadan's hoofbeats were muffled by soft turf. Still, they echoed loud as a heartbeat, and just as rapid. No, that was wrong, a heart should not beat so fast. But hers did; 'twas racking her bones apart one from the other.

Druyan could smell bruised grass, and mint, and sometimes the heather that cloaked the moors in a thousand shades of pink and white and lavender. But mostly the wind only smelled cold, and she fastened her senses upon that, and on the way Valadan's mane brushed gently against her cheeks, licking at her like cool flames. He had never run so fast, Druyan thought. She had not known he could. He could carry her away from all darkness, all pain, all fear.

I could, but I will not. Not yet, the stallion said calmly. *You have years yet to live.* And he ran onward, never slackening, like a cloud flying before a fresh gale.

Water splashed up to soak Druyan's legs.

I am sorry, Valadan said. *I dared not leap it.* He did have to scramble up the stream's far bank, and Druyan slipped back, but she managed to tangle the fingers of her left hand into his mane, and lying close to the horse's neck was the best way to ride up a steep slope. Her right hand was caught fast in her cloak now, awkwardly, painfully. Her whole arm ached, to the shoulder, but she was frightened to try to ease it, to shift it the least bit.

Brambles snatched briefly at both of them, could catch no lasting hold. They must be scattering petals in a cloud, Druyan thought, confused all at once about the season.

And dewdrops, Valadan said, but she could not open her eyes to look. The wind was too loud in her ears.

When they came to Splaine Garth's gate, Valadan leapt over it after all, for there was no one to open it before them, and he knew his mistress could never manage it. He deemed the action worth its risk, to save the last crumb of time, for he was confident he could leap gently enough not to unseat his rider, and he wanted to have her sooner to the care he could not give her.

A moment later he halted in the yard and neighed loud enough to wake the dead—certainly loud enough to bring Dalkin and Enna stumbling out of the kitchen, half dressed and utterly confused. They stood and stared at him, at his burden.

I must get down, Druyan thought fuzzily, her ears still ringing with Valadan's call. But how was she to manage dismounting, with her right hand for some reason useless and her left hand clenched around black mane and thereby likewise unavailable? Valadan was standing very still, but there was no more he could do to aid her. He might have knelt to let her climb aboard, had the situation been the reverse, but if he kneeled down now he would probably only pitch her to the ground, and he knew it. He could only stand steady, in an agony of distress for her.

"Lady, what is it?" A pale face, lifted up by her side like a fish's poking out of a pond. The words sounded far away.

She could not make herself answer Enna—her breath was come too short, Druyan had none to spare for speech. Slowly she eased her right boot from its stirrup and, with a mighty effort, shifted her left hand to grasp the crest of Valadan's neck. If she concentrated very hard, she could do this. She had to rise in the left stirrup, bring her right leg over . . .

"That's *blood*," Dalkin said, awestruck.

Now 'twas daylight, Druyan could see what she had before only dimly felt—the whole front of her tunic was over-dyed with scarlet, like cochineal. The ruby stain was going a dark brown at the edges, where the fabric began to dry. Not a true color, then. She ought to try a different mordant . . . She began to slide her right leg—which was heavy as a wet fleece—over Valadan's broad back. She needed to take as much of her weight as she dared onto her left hand upon the stallion's neck, so she might slip her left toe out of the stirrup and slide the rest of the way down Valadan's side, to the ground. It seemed a great distance, as if the horse were tall as a house. She could feel Enna's arms coming around her from behind, so she should not fall. But frail Enna would not be able to hold her . . .

Indeed, she staggered as she landed and shoved Enna off her balance. And though Druyan clutched frantically at her right hand with her left, still she had instinctively flung both her arms wide to save herself from falling, and as her right hand left the shelter of her blood-soaked cloak, the gentle morning light fell uncompromisingly upon it. She could not help looking at it.

Though her sight was darkening and narrowing, Druyan could see her hand plain enough. Or see what remained of it—for the last two fingers had been sheared clean away by the raider's sword.

This once, because there had been a more than usual need for haste, Kellis had sung himself into wolf-form inside the barn instead of at the back of the far pasture. He was desperately grateful for that alteration of cautious custom now—even as a wolf he was thoroughly winded, and to have run back from the pasture in human form would have been time-wasting—while to burst into the kitchen without his clothing would have been unthinkable.

The shape-shift itself all but undid him. He came out of it on his feet, but there was a roaring in his ears, a swirling darkness in front of his eyes which was slow to pass. Kellis reached for his garments, determined not to yield to the faintness. The Lady needed him—by the signs, needed him very badly indeed. Every step of the way to the farm, the scent of fresh-shed blood had been in his wolf's nostrils, and he knew too well whose blood it was. Kellis had heard her scream, just before he had reached her side—but as he had been tearing the throat out of the man who had maimed her, Valadan had carried his mistress away with a speed no wolf could hope to match, though he ran till his heart all but burst.

He was, for all his efforts, an hour behind her. And out of breath—Kellis gasped and panted as he crossed the yard, his lungs aflame like Sennick's streets. His legs tried to fail him, but by then he was at the kitchen door, and the jamb kept him upright, though it bruised his shoulder and his ribs when he fell against it.

The latch resisted him, till he collected wits enough to lift it rather than mindlessly shoving at it. No one would have locked it, he realized. Enna was too busy.

Enna was wrestling with the fire crane, swinging a kettle of water over the licking flames, when Kellis burst into the kitchen. The flames hissed like cats as water splashed onto them.

"You!" Enna looked around for the nearest iron implement she could lift, then settled for the poker as Kellis tried to edge past her. "You get out of here this instant!"

The woman took a mighty swipe at him with her chosen weapon, but Kellis was past her by then and no harm done, scrambling up the steep flight of stairs. The topmost step betrayed his weary legs, caught a toe he couldn't lift one last inch, so that he measured his length most painfully on the oak boards and got splinters in his hands and chin. Even so, Kellis kept his lead on Enna, whose legs were worse than his, and gained Druyan's chamber at last, there at the far end of the short passage. He had never been so far inside the house before, but the blood scent led him surely. He shoved the door open.

Splaine Garth's lady lay in her curtained bed, her skin much the same hue as the lavender-scented linen sheets, perchance a degree paler. Her right hand had been bound and was propped carefully upon a pillow. Even with the wrappings, there didn't seem to be enough of it, Kellis thought—the sword hadn't just cut, it had cloven part of her away.

The only color in the scene at all was the too-bright stain of red soaking through the white bandages. Kellis took a step toward her.

"Don't you touch her, you filthy pig! Sending her out to run into your foul friends—"

The poker whistled at him—Kellis dodged and the iron

tool hit the wall instead of his head. Enna shrieked at the impact, and the poker fell free of her hand, to clatter on the uncarpeted boards.

He had of course tried to stop her from going into that danger—Kellis thought he had, at least—but he had no breath to explain that to Enna, to say that Druyan hadn't listened to him, or that he had in truth guarded her as best he could. Kellis glanced down at his hands, which were still glazed with someone's blood, and thought with regret that he'd have done well to wash his face before he let Enna lay eyes on him.

He went to the bed and put one stained hand out, to feel for the blood-beat at Druyan's throat. Twisted fingers fetched him a slap that must have hurt Enna far worse than it did him, but this time she did not scream, except to command him. *"Get away from her!"*

Kellis retreated half a step, trying to discover whether Enna had recovered the poker. Though he supposed she'd have brained him with it already if she'd still had it. "I won't hurt her, Enna. I swear that! Let me—"

Druyan's eyelids lifted. Her gray eyes were clear as a sky with all the rain washed out of it. "You came back," she whispered, plainly astonished.

Kellis knelt down beside the bed, caring no more for Enna's wrath. "I was just behind you," he said, forcing a smile. "That horse of yours is so fast, he ran my legs off. Is it well with you, Lady?"

"I don't think so." She only moved her lips—no sound came to his ears, which were nearly as sharp human as wolf's. He had to decipher her words with his eyes. "My hand—"

Kellis looked at the bandage. Most of it was crimson now, as was the pillow beneath. He spied a basket of rags by the bed, the wadded contents stained, as well. He cocked his head at white-faced Enna.

"I've sewed the wound closed, and the bleeding's slowed, but it won't *stop*," Enna said, relenting out of desperation and speaking to him. She took a step closer. "I used yarrow, and lady's mantle, and shepherd's purse—"

"You did right," Kellis agreed. He could smell the healing herbs, but the fresh blood scent overwhelmed all else. Maybe they'd need to resort to cautery—he cringed to think of the burnt-flesh stink filling the little room. And the pain . . .

But that might not need to be. Kellis lifted Druyan's hand gently and held it up against his chest, which had at last ceased to labor. He captured her gaze, too, kept it locked with his own. "You know, if you uncork a bottle and lay it down, all the wine will run right out," he said conversationally. "But set it upright—" Kellis was arranging his fingers carefully, to bring pressure to bear on the wound beneath the scarlet linen without hurting her overmuch, letting her eyes be his guide. He could tell she was trying not to flinch. "I'm going to make it harder for the rest of your blood to drip out of you, Lady. Just lie still."

"No worse than I deserve," Druyan whispered, her eyes now tight shut. "I always thought my hands were ugly, they were so big. I was always wishing them smaller . . ." A drop of water squeezed between her lashes and slid down into her left ear.

"Shhh," Kellis said to her, with lips and eyes. "Only children have tiny hands."

By the day's end—so many hours later—Kellis was finally confident the wound was staunched. Druyan had been sleeping most of that time, which was fine so far as it went—asleep, she would not move about and reopen the wound. Presumably she was in no pain. Enna had at his direction bound new wrappings right over top of the old, so as not to start the bleeding afresh. She should heal, and even if the wound festered, a fever could be fought off. He knew plenty of simples to treat such maladies—when one lived by hunting, wounds were a commonplace.

Only Kellis greatly feared that Druyan would not live

long enough for a fever to set in. She slept, but it seemed more like a swoon. Her heart still beat fast as a caged bird's, and her pale skin was damp and cold despite the fire that warmed the chamber. Kellis had seen men take terrible wounds and readily recover, but he had likewise seen men suffer what appeared to be trifling hurts and die of them, once this same cold pallor had come over them, the same rapid, weak heartbeat manifested.

Fear was a huge portion of it. Kellis could feel the terror in her, even while the lady slept or swooned. She was frail and frightened and dying of the shock of her hurt, more than its severity. If only he could gift her with a wolf's courage, a wolf's strength and lust for survival.

There *was* a way, if he would risk it.

Enna had brought a fresh pot of medicine. The cooling liquid was a tisane of nettle leaves and dried briar hips, mostly. Kellis' nose sorted out the ingredients easily. Parsley, too, he thought, and a little honey stirred in. The sweetener and the rose fruits would scarcely overcome the other, less pleasing tastes, but each dried herb in the simple was a blood-builder. If Druyan woke, he would make her drink the brew, and it would do her good.

She drew in a breath a little deeper than the last, and her eyes unclosed, with no more warning than that. "Still here," Druyan whispered. Which of them did she mean?

Kellis nodded, and lifted her head so she'd be able to swallow the tea. He held the cup to her lips. A single sip, then he had to let her sink back into the pillows. She had not swallowed, and Kellis was fearful of choking her. A coughing fit might stop her heart. He wiped the corners of her mouth, carefully. Her lips were palest mauve, ever so slightly shading to blue.

"When's the turn of the tide?" she asked him then, those pale lips moving against his fingers.

"You know I've never figured the tides out," Kellis answered, smiling at her and getting the cup ready again. "I get a saltwater footbath every time I go near the marsh. I can remember the water comes in farther sometimes than others, but never *when*. Why?"

"Nothing that lives by the sea can die till the tide goes out," she breathed.

"You mean like snakes can't die till sunfall?" Kellis raised an eyebrow. "That's superstition. I have killed any number of snakes, and when I'm done, they're dead, no matter where the suns stands."

"When the tide ebbs, life ebbs," Druyan whispered, ignoring him, and shut her eyes.

Enna was determined to send him away, once the bleeding was staunched. She would not have him spending the night in her lady's bedchamber, no matter the reason. Kellis could not convince her of the danger that still lay waiting, though he scornfully thought that anyone with two working eyes should have recognized it. Second sight wasn't needed to know that future.

"When's the tide?" he finally asked her, exasperated.

Enna reckoned it up, though she didn't trouble about answering him—shorefolk knew the turn of the tide as they knew their own names. "What sort of trick is that? What are you up to?"

"Your lady thinks she'll die when the tide goes out—and if she believes it, she might just do it! Beware the turn of the tide—her spirit will follow, if we let it."

"You won't touch her again, you filth!" Enna said, outraged. "That's a stupid superstition. I know well enough that you're free if she dies."

I shall have to do something more than touch her, Kellis was thinking. He wasn't afraid to turn his back on Enna—she needed him able to walk out on his own legs, because she couldn't drag him, so she wasn't likely to hit him. He saw that Druyan's gray eyes were open again, and watching him. Her freckles stood out like brands against the bloodless white of her skin. Kellis thought he could see her heart beating, right through flesh and cloth and blankets, having a very hard time, and more than ready to surrender its fight, like a brave horse overidden. She looked past him.

"*Enna.*" Very, very faint. A hummingbird's wing stirred the air more loudly.

"Lady?" Enna bent close by the bed, ignoring Kellis beside her.

"Do whatever he tells you."

Enna started back and glared at Kellis. "I *have* done," she said. "The wound's well closed. You're fine, you'll mend, you just need to sleep. And *he's* not staying in *here*. I'm sure he's full of fleas, if not lice—"

Druyan's eyes went to Kellis' face, to the message his golden wolf's gaze sent. *Let me help you* . . .

"Enna, let him stay. Do what he says. *Whatever* he says—" Her voice was slight as wind rustling through grass, a shuttle through the warp threads. It was an order, all the same.

Enna gave him a look fit to stop a man's heart. Kellis swallowed hard, then found his voice. The time was come. He didn't know how the tide stood, but he saw ebb in Druyan's face.

"Just . . . heat me some water, please. Lots of it."

"There's tea brewed already—"

"Hot *water*," Kellis repeated firmly, and stared her down.

Enna hobbled out grumbling, and Kellis went at once to peer round the door, stepping softly on his toes. When he saw Enna start down the stairs, he swiftly barred the door with oak—for strength, and magic—for silence. Then, confident they could not be disturbed, he turned back to the bed.

"I feel so light," Druyan said wonderingly. "As if I could fly on the wind."

"That's the blood-lack," Kellis explained reassuringly. He sniffed twice. "You lost buckets. Don't fret. I won't let you die. I swear it."

"Trust you?"

He winced. "There's no help for it. You'll have to." He sniffed again.

"It was so confusing," Druyan said, not really hearing him. She frowned. "The battle. All that shouting . . . no order to it—is war always like that?"

"I can't judge," Kellis admitted, busy. "The first fighting—that sort of fighting—that I ever saw was right here, and I think having my head bashed in right at the start of it warped my perceptions a. trifle. It's more confusing than hunting deer. It isn't any harder, but it's muddled." He flared his nostrils.

"Deer don't hunt you back," Druyan said wisely. "What are you doing?"

He was searching all about the bed—between the sheets, beneath the blankets, along the head and foot, among the goosefeather pillows, in the seams of quilts and hangings, sniffing and then questing with his fingers. And it was taking him too long.

"Enna hides nails in all your clothes, to keep you safe from me," he said lightly. Iron scent led him to his quarry, a wicked long pin worked into the mattress edge.

"I take them out."

"I know, but she's persistent," Kellis said, easing the fell object free of the cloth gingerly, with his nails. "And I need to clear every last bit away, even the smallest pin. It's not quite true that my folk can't touch cold iron—you have seen." He flicked the pin away, out the open window, and blew on his fingers. "It's painful—sometimes excruciatingly—but it can be done, for a while. And we can be near it without much distress, though I do think my heart's been scared out of a beat, now and again. But I dare not work any magic upon cold iron—the results may be less than predictable, but they're predictably unpleasant. You're hurt already—I don't want to find out how much more harm I can do you by being stupid."

"Are you going to work a magic?" Druyan asked drowsily, like a child promised a treat.

"I'm going to sing to you. You like that."

But even as Kellis answered her, she had faded once more, beyond the reach of his words.

He sniffed out three nails dropped into floorboard cracks, and flung each one out the window, hissing at the brief contact. There was something sharp worked into the hem of her bed gown—another nail, Kellis thought, or a big pin. The only sure way to be rid of all such tiny traps was to slip the gown from her. He did that, gently. Kellis stripped the bedclothes away, as well, still wary of the linens despite his unrewarded search of them. And the warmth of woolen blankets no longer reached Splaine Garth's lady.

The firecoals gave the room its only light—all was darkness now, outside the unshuttered casement. 'Twas quiet, too, thanks to his lock charm on the door. The oaken bar would stop Enna short of reaching his magic with cold iron, try though she likely would, and he did not think Dalkin was strong enough to break down the panels by force. The wall beneath the window was sheer, he did not think it could be climbed. The chamber was secure. He could begin his work—and none too soon.

Kellis slipped out of his own garments and lay alongside Druyan on the bared straw of the pallet. If this desperate chance worked at all, it would only be while they were skin to skin.

He gathered her to him carefully, alert to her irregular breathing, the still-frantic hammering of her heart. She was so cold, only the rise of her chest offered him any hope at all. Kellis calmed his own lungs, calling upon all the care and control he had ever managed to learn, and then he sang them both into wolf-form.

Druyan dreamed that she ran lightly over the moors—not carried upon Valadan's familiar back, but on her own four legs. And though the world about her was all muted shades of gray and silver, lacking any stronger colors, it was rich beyond imagining in its scents. She could smell the grass, the earth, the rabbit that had crossed her path an hour gone, the birds wheeling in the air. She could read by scent the places the wind had visited, all the shores the sea had touched . . .

Something loped alongside her, at her right shoulder. A great silver wolf, with slanting golden eyes she knew she had seen ere then, somewhere, in another sort of face.

Fear not, he said to her, tongue lolling from his pointed muzzle. *You have the wolf-heart inside you—you have always had it. I am only showing it to you. You have more courage than you know, as much as you can ever need.*

The grass was soaking with dew—sparkling drops flew up with her every stride, were deliciously cool against her legs. Suddenly one paw flamed with pain, and she yelped, breaking her stride, nearly falling.

There is no loss you cannot withstand, the wolf told her, steadying her against his shoulder till she found the pace once more. *There is no loss that even matters, you are so strong, so brave . . .*

I'm not brave, Druyan said, confused, and faltered once more. It seemed to her that there was some reason she could not run so, some disaster of her own making that had befallen her. Something she should not have done—she ran faster, to get distance on the troubling thought. There was darkness at her heels, like a storm cloud on the far horizon, sweeping ever closer, about to overtake her.

The silver wolf still galloped beside her, easily keeping pace. *Your courage lies within you,* he said. *Only hold tight to it, do not deny it. Do not let it go . . .*

I don't know what you mean! she howled in utter despair. The darkness was sweeping closer. It was cold, so cold . . .

Be what are you, the wolf insisted, forcing her to hear him. *Not what others tell you!*

What you *tell me?* For some reason, the advice seemed ironic.

Now the silver wolf faltered, in a manner she found somehow familiar. Just for an instant he did not look like a wolf at all, save for those golden eyes. But in another moment he was by her side again, long-furred, long-legged.

Run with me. Run from nothing, but run in the night, for the joy of it.

And in her dream she did, beneath a huge silver moon and a sky of wooly tumbling clouds.

Kellis had not expected her to take to the wolf-form so eagerly as she did—he had sung her into it, but when she questioned he was startled into losing his own hold on the wolf-shape for an instant, and he should have lost his grip on hers, as well.

Instead . . .

He had been trying to give her courage, but the gift was not needed. He had not deceived her: She had bravery and to spare, *in* her, not forced upon her from the outside. She had been taught to hide what she was, to smother her nature relentlessly, but the lessons were all at once swept away, by the free wind that blew shatteringly through them both.

The moon darted through a sky of wind-tousled clouds, flirting with the two wolf hunters, sometimes only a faint glow, sometimes revealing her full glory to them against a starry gap. It was different from hunting deer—there was no scent of fear wafting from the quarry, and they were all of them, all three of them, reveling in the sport. It was a hunt, but the object was not a kill.

Tussocks of heather, rounded bellies of cloud. Patches of white blossoms, silvered edges on the huge shapes sweeping overhead. The wolves seemed to cross from land to sky at their pleasure, one instant heather stems beneath their pads, the next moment only springy moist air. The moon played at hide-and-seek, and they leapt joyously after every slightest clue, howled rapturously when She showed them Her full face for an instant. The great silver wolf coursed the sky, with the pewter-hued she-wolf ever at his side, running swiftly on her big, strong paws.

All at once he lost her in the windswept clouds. With a startled yelp, he sought her earnestly, keen nose to the ground, then thrust into the concealing clouds. When he did not find her at once, he put back his head and howled. *Where are you?*

He listened, but was not answered, and he quested desperately on. He dreaded to smell blood on the wind.

She lurked in ambush behind a hillock of faintly purple heather, and when he rounded it searching, she sprang out at him, mock-growling and boring into his shoulder with her muzzle, playfully snapping first at his forelegs, then his belly. Grinning with relief, he tried both to follow and to keep out of reach of her nipping teeth, spun and skidded through wet grass and came to a splay-legged halt.

Behind him, she yipped excitedly. He turned. She was crouching, forelimbs flat to the earth, rump and waving tail high in the air, bowing in exaggerated invitation: *Play with me.*

When he ran to her, she leapt to her feet and met him in a rush, yipping eagerly. He reared back to evade her, but she rose on her hind legs, too, and they crashed first together, then into the heather, rolling tangled through shades of silver, black and white and gray, all the dewdrops flying, little glistening copies of the great moon above.

Kellis had a hand on either side of Druyan's face, his fingers twined in the silvergilt and copper of her hair. He did not recall choosing to shift out of the wolf-form, and for an instant his senses swam indecisively between wolf and man, betwixt windblown night and still room. One was reality, one was healing dream, but he could not tell which was which. Only the moonlight, pouring through the open window, seemed constant and familiar.

Then he was firmly back in the bed, pressing his face against a face that nuzzled back at him as urgently as the playful she-wolf's had . . . her lips parted under his, welcoming. Her skin was warm, smelling faintly of apricots and heather blossoms. Her eyes had the moon in them, and the wind sighed in her blood . . .

Her arms were clasped about his neck, warm and strong, drawing him to her. He did not resist.

The Crow

KELLIS WAS ON the far side of the room, in his human shape and his tattered human clothes, when Druyan stirred in the morning light. She opened her eyes, half expecting to see waving seas of heather and the silver face of the moon. Instead she beheld dapples of sunlight on the pitched ceiling and a pale sea of bedclothes that seemed more disarranged than Enna would ever have left them. The wonderful palette of scents and sounds was gone out of her reach— she had only her normal senses now, in the daylight world. And her wolf-strength was fled as well, drawn within her, deep inside, to heal her. She recognized that but regretted its loss.

She ached in every bone, every sinew. She was gnawingly hungry, pathetically thirsty. And her right hand— Druyan tried to raise it, found the effort too great, and stared wide-eyed at the thick swaddling round about it from forearm to fingertips. Her hand hurt, but not with that terrifying, stupifying, guilty agony that she remembered too well.

Kellis knelt down beside her and cupped his hands carefully about what remained of her right hand. When she looked up, his gray-gold gaze captured hers and held it.

"It was a terrible wound, but a very clean cut," he said judiciously. "There's no fever in it. You will not lose the rest of the hand, nor the use of it."

"How many fingers do I still have?" Druyan whispered. Better to hear the worst and have it over.

"Two." He stroked her forearm, above the bandages. "And the thumb. It could have been worse."

"Yes." Her eyes were brimming, and Druyan agreed only in principle. If she thought about what it would be like to have no hand at all, would that help? She drew in a breath and felt how easily it could turn to a sob. She held it, a delicate balance.

"I have heard tales of maimed warriors given magic hands of silver, with fingers that moved like living flesh," Kellis said. "But I have not the skill to do that for you, Lady." He had stopped meeting her eyes, slumped till his forehead touched the rumpled sheets. "Lock charms and Mirrors of Three don't answer."

"Three fingers are enough, to twirl the spindle, throw the shuttle," Druyan whispered, reaching out blindly for the wolf's courage. "I can even hold a needle. Is that Enna at the door?" The sound was faint, but insistent as a fly trapped by window glass.

"Probably." Kellis shook himself, rose, and crossed the room to the door. The lock spell dissolved at his touch, and instantly Enna's voice could be heard plainly.

"—or I'll have Dalkin break it down."

Kellis lifted the bar, stepping nimbly back before the swinging panel could more than brush him.

Enna had the poker in her hand again, and the will to use it. She came straight at Kellis around the door, trapping him in the corner, and held off her attack only when she heard Druyan's voice, calling her name.

"*Lady!*" The poker's tip hit the floor with a *clunk*.

"Enna, I would like some breakfast," Druyan ordered calmly.

"Praise be!" Kellis was instantly forgotten. "And you shall have it—a new-laid egg, and some fresh bannock, with cream. I'll bring it up—"

"No, I'll come down." Druyan tried to swing her legs off

the bed and felt unexpectedly giddy. "Or perhaps not." She sank back onto the pillows.

Enna helped her to lie comfortably once more, plumped the pillows and fussed with the sheets, striving to reorder the bedding. "You'll not stir from this bed, and there's an end to it! You're bled white as a trillium, and it's rest and healthy food will mend you soonest. No flitting about! And some nettle tea, to build your blood up again."

"Yes, Enna," Druyan agreed mildly. "But no calf's liver, I can't abide it. Don't you dare go killing one of my calves for something you know I won't eat."

"And that blackguard Kellis!" Enna scowled darkly. "Bolting that door so I couldn't get in to see to you, not all night long! 'Tis a wonder—"

"All night?" Druyan asked faintly.

"Aye—as if he was some sheepdog, set to guard the fold. He tricked me! Sent me to fetch hot water for you and then locked me out, bold as you please. When I get my hands on him, he'll rue the day he ever stepped thieving foot here."

Druyan lifted her head to look past Enna. The chamber was empty, except for the sunshine.

Kellis had no notion how he'd come to be at the edge of the marsh. The first he noticed of his surroundings was a soaked boot, which squished till it attracted his attention. He looked down and saw he was standing in water.

All he'd planned was to take himself out of Enna's way, and he'd supposed himself bound for one of the upland pastures. Instead, he stood surrounded by waving salt grass, his ears full of the tiny sucking sounds the farthest reach of the tide made as it left the land. He stared at the green-gold grass, gemmed with tiny crystals of salt all along its stems. That was how the grass survived its twice-daily flood of saltwater—it excreted out the salt that would otherwise have destroyed it, and glittered with those wind-dried tears like a dragon's treasure trove.

Pain was like sea salt—kept in too long, it would burn

and eventually kill. He ought to have learned that, very long ago, Kellis supposed, stepping back to drier ground. He had held tight to his guilt and self-loathing, and there had been room in him for nothing else—until she had pushed it all aside and made a place for herself, however much against his well-intentioned will. It had let him help her—he was glad of that. That was the sparkle on the salt-gems.

Kellis looked up, and there was that black horse, with his uncanny eyes like a moonless night sky. The stallion stretched his neck, to blow a soft puff of hay-scented air across Kellis' cheek.

"She lives," Kellis told him. "And she will be safe." He could guarantee that, he thought. His term of servitude would soon enough be up. Splaine Garth's lady would be recuperating all that while and longer, and neither he nor the stallion would permit or tempt her again to ride into danger.

By the time she was truly well, he would be gone, on his way to the mirage of the Wizards' City, no more a danger to her. That was how it would be.

Valadan snorted softly, as if content.

After a week of lying patiently abed, drinking teas of parsley and spinach, sipping soups made from lamb's quarters and dandelion greens, eating pies stuffed with dried apricots and rhubarb, resignedly accepting black molasses by the spoonful, Druyan was at last permitted to descend the stairs. She might sit quietly in the garden, forbidden to rise from the chair that had been carried there for her use, but at least allowed to feel the breeze and the sun against her skin, while she sipped more of Enna's tisanes and potions. Dalkin was bidden to keep himself in earshot so Enna could inform him at once of any need Splaine Garth's lady had, and Meddy lay by her slippered feet, no matter how many times the dog was dragged off to her real job of helping Rook watch after the flock.

Kellis was, Druyan was reluctantly informed, stacking

the peat ricks into castles, the turves of fuel having dried enough for that step. And then he was putting new posts in, along the orchard fence; and how he and the iron axe and the iron spade were getting along, Enna did not know and barely cared, but whatever befell the wretch was surely no better than he deserved.

Next day Druyan refused the sun and settled under the apricot trees, with the industrious bees and Valadan for her company. Eventually she looked up from the pages of the book she had brought along to gaze at between dozes, and saw Kellis standing under the next-nearest tree, a fencepost propped jauntily on one shoulder.

"Do you have the *slightest* idea how to set a post?" Druyan asked him.

He shook his pale head in cheerful denial of the skill. "My people don't build fences. But your animals are very well bred, Lady, except maybe for some of the pigs, and the posts look fine so long as nothing bumps them too hard."

"I'll remember that, next time I'm walking by," she said, smiling.

"That will be soon, Lady," he predicted, smiling back at her. "You look well."

"I feel well. But I'm tired too soon—all I want to do is sleep in the sun, like an old dog." Just crossing her bed-chamber got Druyan out of breath, making her heart beat a frantic measure. It was most disconcerting—she had never had a sick day in her life, save for early childhood fevers that had long faded from her memory. "When you're done with the fence, the flax field needs to be pulled."

"Pulled?" His right brow rose at the mystery. "I thought we *planted* that field. On purpose."

"We did." Druyan nodded her head at a plant that had strayed into the orchard, likely assisted by a linseed-robbing bird. Its pretty blue flowers were gone, replaced by round seedpods. "You don't cut flax to harvest it, just uproot it and spread it out to cure. In a week, Dalkin can start rippling to get the seedpods off. Keep the best for next spring's planting, the animals get the rest, in the winter. The stalks get bundled and put in the marsh to soak. Pru will show you where—we've got stones there, to hold them under."

Kellis nodded carefully. "Sheep are a *lot* less work, Lady."

"And I haven't even touched on braking, scutching, and hackling, before I can spin and weave." Druyan rolled her eyes. "It takes most of a year, to turn flax into linen cloth. Worth it, too—much better next to the skin than even the softest wool. Speaking of which, there's a sark of Travic's in the press. You can't keep going around in rags and tatters, even if it is summer."

Kellis looked away, watching the lazy switching of Valadan's long tail. "I don't think Enna will like you giving me her master's clothes."

"I hadn't intended to ask what she thought. Travic was *my* husband, and *I* wove that linen and sewed that sark. I'll do what I please with it."

"Dead men's clothes are luckless."

"He wasn't wearing it when he died," Druyan said, exasperated. "The sleeve ends were frayed. I was waiting to darn them."

Kellis shifted the post on his shoulder. "I should set this, while I still remember where it's going."

He might avoid the shirt, but Kellis was not quick enough to escape Druyan's question.

"What does the bowl show?"

His eyes shadowed to a muddy amber, and then he frowned, his mouth going stubborn. "I have not looked, Lady."

"But if the raiders—"

"The only raiders I'll fret over are those coming *here*, and I don't need any bowl of water to spot them." His mouth was straighter than any furrow he'd ever achieved with the plow. "And don't be trying to trick me into it, or wheedling, either."

"Why?" Druyan laughed bitterly. "Do you think I'm apt

to go riding out of here like *this*?" She lifted her bandaged hand an inch and gasped. Valadan's head came up.

The notion fetched a wintry smile. "This horse would refuse to carry you, were you so foolish." Kellis reached out to pat Valadan's shoulder. The stallion snorted and returned to grazing the clover. "What's the point of seeking news of raids you can't do anything about? The visions have not been asking me to look at them, and I am not calling them, either. Let it lie."

"But if we get word to the post riders, it helps *them*!" Druyan protested. Was he deliberately being dense?

Kellis smiled again. "I'm none so sure about that—but assuming sending your Riders hopelessly outnumbered into danger *is* a good idea, how would I be getting word to them?"

"I could have told you the routes!" Druyan snapped. "You've followed me all over Esdragon, you know the country by now!"

Valadan snorted a grasshopper out of his next mouthful.

Kellis only raised an eyebrow. "And of course your brother—who's promised faithfully to see me dead—will listen to me if I go to him with a message?"

There was a silence, broken only by the sounds of the horse grazing, the breeze riffling apricot leaves. Druyan admitted defeat. "I suppose you have a point. And I should not be taking you to task, the first moment I lay eyes on you. I owe you too much for that. Enna told me you stayed by me all night when I came back hurt, never left me. Thank you."

Kellis shifted the post again, as if its weight was beginning to trouble him. "When I was hurt, you watched after me. No thanks is needed, Lady."

"I don't remember very much," Druyan went on, searching out the words. "Just dreaming about moonlight, and wolves running on the moors. But I'm glad you were with me, Kellis. Enna wouldn't have known how to help. I was so lost, so afraid—"

"Don't speak of it. It's over. Why bring it back?"

Druyan shook her head and let her eyes fill with the green orchard once more, instead of far-reaching blackness. The apricots were yellow and waxing fat. The apple fruits were starting to show touches of color. There would be, ere long, some harvesting to be done at Splaine Garth, and how that necessity was to be managed *this* year, she had no notion. She knew as well as Kellis did that he had no reason to care how much work it was to make linen cloth. He'd be long gone ere 'twas done.

Druyan called for combed wool and her pearwood spindle the next week and sat by the kitchen door beginning to teach the three remaining fingers on her right hand—which had always done most of the work anyway—to get along without the company of their lost mates. The wound was healing—she could tell that by the healthy itch, even before Enna took off the dressings to exchange them for a lighter wrapping of fresh linen that left her fingers free—and careful exercise would prevent the hand's going stiff and weak on her. Moving it pained her now, but it would hurt whenever she began, and likely worse later. She set herself to bear the discomfort, and found 'twas not so bad as she dreaded.

Her work was predictably clumsy—the thread came off the spindle thick and uneven, fit only for weaving a coarse rug to be flung over the puddle that tended to appear by the kitchen doorway, just by where she sat. That was fine— Druyan had asked for belly wool to begin with, not caring to waste better fleece while she was still stiff and unproductive.

She lamented her loss most when it came time to wind the wretched yarn off the spindle and into a ball. The ball kept escaping her grasp, and she'd have to reel it in, unwinding a deal of yarn in the process. The third time she dropped it, the by-then dirty ball went bounding clean across the yard, trailing thread, and Druyan let it keep going. The sun's warmth was agreeable, there were wild doves cooing from their nest in the roof thatch above her head, and 'twas pleasant to stop struggling with the spindle, just to sit idle for a while. She was weary, sleepy, and cross. When she'd napped a bit, she'd be ready to work again, and she could fetch the recalcitrant ball of yarn first thing, to stretch her legs.

Druyan did not suppose she had actually been asleep, but then she surely must have been —dreaming unawares of the very sort of day that was actually lapping round her—for she never even heard the horse trot up to her gate and cross the kitchen yard to the water trough. She opened her eyes when the ball of spun thread was laid gently in her lap, and blinked first at it and then at Yvain, who stood grinning at her, handsome in his post rider's blue and gray.

"I think such an occupation would have sent me to sleep, too, Lady! If 'twere left to me, there'd not be thread enough in all of Esdragon to weave a single cloak."

"I know I've lost track of the days," Druyan said stupidly, "but you shouldn't be anywhere near here, should you?" Too late she realized how ungracious her words sounded.

Yvain laughed. His teeth were astonishingly white, like the edges of clouds. She had never noticed that before. "You've lost track of nothing, Lady Druyan. By the official schedule, I should be riding above Glasgerion by now, but I exchanged routes so that I might come this way the sooner. You look well."

Druyan felt her face color—as best it could. She had very little blood to spare for blushes. "Flattery on that scale has to be bred in," she said. "There must be bards in your family."

"Dozens," Yvain agreed cheerfully. "But I was never one of them. I am glad to see you, Lady, all flattery aside."

"That's a new horse, isn't it?" Its blood-bay coat closely matched Yvain's own hair. Siarl had done the Rider proud with the remount. "Why not put him in the barn, out of this hot sun? If Dalkin's in there, he'll fetch you some hay—"

"I'm sure the horse will think ill of me, but I cannot

tarry so long, and I've not had him long enough for him to expect better." The captain hesitated. "I've grave tidings."

Druyan's eyes jerked toward Yvain's face. She marked the unhappy set of his mouth, masked only a trifle by the pleasantries exchanged a moment earlier. *"Not Robart—"*

"No!" Yvain said hastily, and breathed a curse upon his clumsiness. "Your brother's hale, Lady, last I saw of him, and none of us was dungeoned for treason, either, though *that* was a near thing." He swallowed. "We've lost Kernan."

"Lost? What happened?" Her heart began its too-familiar racing, and Druyan was glad she was not standing.

"It was . . . just after you were wounded. He and his partner were headed back to their regular route when they chanced on a party of raiders. Kernan sent his second for aid and went on himself to raise the town, alone. He was killed."

Druyan's eyes brimmed. Yvain went on, playing with the wave badge at his throat.

"The wonder is we've lost no Riders ere this—and lost them in places we can't explain away, places they shouldn't have been. Had Kernan been ten leagues off his route instead of merely two—" He sighed. "I don't suppose any of us thought we'd have to play this game so long, dodging our own duke to protect his lands—it's true, you know, about the army. Most of the men have been sent to fell timber, and they're a good month's march away. Brioc expects to have his fleet ready come spring."

"Will any of us be left by then?" Druyan asked bitterly. "There's plenty of good sailing weather still to come." Seeing the sun made the farmer part of her rejoice, but the rest of her quailed.

"Keverne will stand," Yvain said, shrugging. "There's a small garrison posted there. The coastal settlements are left to fend for themselves, despite the increase in raids upon them this summer. The larger towns have watches or garrisons of their own, lesser places may be assumed not to require protection. That's what I was told."

"My uncle is a fool," Druyan said harshly.

Yvain patted her left hand. "Well, don't let the defect run in the family! Don't come chasing after us again, Lady, well or not."

"But—"

"The Riders will still keep watch and aid one another when the word is passed. But the raids come too thick now, Lady. Being there to meet them isn't serving so well anymore. We tried, but we're done. We are messengers, not warriors." He still had hold of her hand. "May I pay my respects to your husband, before I depart?"

Never saw that coming, Druyan thought, reeling still from his tidings. She could only flush and stammer a stupid excuse that she thought Yvain did not for one instant believe, as he lifted her suddenly cold left hand to his chiseled lips. He was smiling—Yvain was always smiling—as he released her hand back to her. *He knows,* Druyan thought miserably. But what use would the captain make of his knowledge?

Kellis watched the birds. Easy to do—they were everywhere, filling the air wherever he chanced to be working. Most eggs had hatched out, and there were fledglings to be fed, so the parents were busy and always on the wing. He studied ascents, descents, takeoffs, and landings, soarings upon updrafts of warm air. He paid close heed to the swallows in the barn, the larks above the barley fields, the blackbirds that filled the marsh with song. He took note of hawks, herons, and crows.

It had come to him, as the raids from the sea increased, that the attacks were too numerous, too closely spaced, for each one to be originating on the far shore of the Great Sea. It just could not be, not from what he had seen of the Eral. Their captains threw together expeditions too haphazardly, every arrogant one of them obeying no will but his own. Coordination could not be coincidence.

Kellis remembered how it had been for his own homeland—a raid or two a year—then all at once a dreadful spate of them, unrelenting. Eventually it was learned that the Eral had established a foothold on a peninsula, a base from which they could launch forays in hours rather than days. He thought much the same thing must be happening in Esdragon. He trusted his nose more than his eyes, and he had smelled the same man-scents in more than one raided place. It was not chance.

So each night a wolf ranged out from Splaine Garth, once the Lady Druyan was out of obvious danger. Kellis trotted upcoast and down, putting his long wolf's nose into every secluded cove and inlet, stalking to the top of every spit of rock and sand, no matter how insignificant. Settlements he steered well clear of, not so much out of fear of discovery as because he had no need to inspect such places. Inhabited spots offered no concealment. And the Eral had a fondness for garlic in their cookery. He could detect a lack of the herb a long distance off.

He had worn his pads so thin that he limped even as a man, with his broken boots packed full of soft wool plucked on the sly from the new lambs. But Kellis found no sign of the raiders save their customary destruction. This was not a waste of effort—it told Kellis that the base, wherever it was, was likely not on the coast itself, but just off it. Easily reached by the Erals' sea-snake ships. An island or a peninsula that was an island at all save neap-tide times. Wherefore he turned to studying the birds, which could readily go where a wolf could not. Kellis could swim as a wolf, but not for long in Esdragon's pounding, shifty surf.

Some few of his people had the knack of shifting to more than one form. It was tricky work—the natural leaning tended toward the animal the Clan had long ago taken as its totem—wolf, or deer, or marten. There was a Hawk Clan, but they were very few, even before the Eral raids began to thin out or wipe out the Clans. Kellis had never encountered one of the Hawk shape-shifters.

To shift to anything other than wolf—which felt so natural, its long-furred pelt by long practice his second skin—required meticulous observation and careful concentration.

And even then he could hold the form only for a moment, because it felt so unwolf that he kept startling out of it. Kellis worked at it for a week before he could hold feathered form reliably.

He discovered next that he loathed heights, a nasty liability he had likely gained from his dealings with the kitchen roof. And there was a further handicap—he didn't in his heart *believe* that he could fly. And that was the whole point to his being a bird, besides flight being the very essence of the shape-shifted creature.

Without belief, action came very hard. Kellis climbed a tree, finally, and shifted there to his new-learned shape. That way he *had* to fly, however poorly. There was no chance for second thoughts about it, nothing to permit failure. He glided down, terrified, tumbling the last bit of the way till the ground caught him, but doing himself no lasting damage.

The next stage involved a seaside cliff, and Kellis got his shifted wings spread wide just as waves were about to claim him—and went skimming off above the water, master of the air at last. Beats of his wings gained him altitude, and when he reached the clifftops he swung inland and landed by crashing into a gorse bush.

He switched to daylight flights at that point, ready to commence his search. At first he was disoriented whenever he ventured out of sight of the farm buildings. He was used to orienting by scent, and as a bird his sense of smell was poor. But better vision compensated—Kellis methodically learned landmarks along the coast from his new perspective and went skimming from one to the next, surely the most timid crow in all of Esdragon. Each flight took him farther ere he was lost, and the practice made him a marginally better flier.

In the end, it wasn't all that much of a flight, once he got past the point of needing to hug the coastline closely to know where he was. Kellis flew high over the boar spine of the Promontory and saw the object of his quest lying below him—a jumble of stone with one rock bigger than the rest, a tiny island with its cliffs on the one side battered down by the surf so that there was room for a score of ships to be safely beached. It couldn't be seen from the shore—the rough anchorage faced the open sea. Only a bird could spy the black ships, the activity all along the islet's perimeter. There was no smoke. Somehow the Eral had agreed among themselves to forgo cooking fires that might have given the secret away.

Kellis howled in triumph, but the sound came out a croaking caw. He wasn't sufficiently master of his wings to risk a landing—even for much-needed rest—so the crow that beat its way back against the wind toward Splaine Garth was weary and windblown. Finally he spotted a familiar orchard and gratefully angled his sore wings for his descent.

"That crow looks big enough to take a sheep," Enna observed, squinting over the bowl of bramble berries Dalkin had just brought from the patch. "You want to keep that lot out of the fields, when the grain comes on," she instructed the boy. "Look sharp to it."

"It's early to worry about that," Druyan said thankfully. She did not want to think about the harvest's approach, or its problems. She filched a berry from the bowl and popped it into her mouth. It was tart and delectable, the essence of summer.

The black bird teetered on the top fence rail, spreading its wings for balance. Dalkin shied a pebble at it, in practice for his upcoming duties as living scarecrow. There was a startled squawk. The bird rose into the air. Loose feathers flew to one side as it tumbled down behind the fence. There followed a very loud thump, and a curse.

Druyan made a squawk of her own and rushed to the fence.

Kellis lay sprawled on the far side of the rails, blinking dazedly at the sky and green leaves above him. He raised his head and touched his shoulder, where a long graze had begun to weep drops of blood.

Enna, running after Druyan, shrieked at the sight of him—naked as the day his mother bore him, lying shamelessly in front of her lady. Dalkin babbled shrill protests of his innocence. Kellis felt of his head, winced, and shifted his whole attention to Druyan, who had ducked under the fence to kneel by his side.

"Lady, there is something I must tell you." He tried to sit up, and got as far as propping himself on his elbows before the edges of the day wobbled distressingly. "I—" He lost the thread of what he'd been trying to say. Something about flying? His arms and shoulders ached, it was all he could do to move them.

"I didn't know you could do birds," Druyan interrupted, amazed.

"I'm not sure I *can*. Did I crash?" His head throbbed. Kellis realized suddenly that the accident had thrown him out of his precariously held bird-form, which only redoubled his dismay. What had happened? Only a serious injury should make him lose control that way; anything else was inexcusable among his people. He felt sick to his stomach and was unsure whether the trouble was shame or too-rapid shape-shifting. If he'd been struck with cold iron—but all he could remember was trying to land. Try as he might, he couldn't get past that.

"Crash? Not without help! Target practice, I think," Druyan said. "From someone who plainly doesn't require any." She glared at Dalkin, through the fence.

"I didn't *know*!" Dalkin wailed again. "How could I know?"

"You indecent wretch! What sort of work do you call this?" Enna flung the berries, bowl and all, in Kellis' face. The wooden bowl missed, but the berries hit and left purple splotches all over him. He wiped some away and stared confusedly at his fingers.

"I just threw a rock at a crow," Dalkin whined. "I didn't know you were over here!"

"That was fine work," Enna answered. "Don't repent it. Go fetch me a stick, boy."

"No!" Druyan said angrily. She unclasped her cloak and swept it over Kellis, as much to silence Enna as to stop his shivering. "Are you hurt?" she asked him.

"No—" He didn't see how he could be. And if Enna wanted a stick, he could guess very well what she wanted it for. He needed to get up and get some distance on her— but everything seemed too dark to Kellis, as if masked by a pall of smoke, and he still felt on the edge of being ill, as if he'd fed on carrion too long ripened. He sat up, but that was as far as he could get. Escape didn't seem an option.

By the time the faintness had mostly passed, he and Druyan were alone—Enna sent protesting to fetch some herbs, Dalkin gathering blankets and bringing cold water from the well. Kellis took one deep, slow breath, then another. He sighed. The ground felt solid under him for the first time.

Druyan was parting his hair with her fingers, trying to decide whether he'd hit his head on anything more hazardous than grass-covered dirt. She pulled out two small feathers and an apple leaf. "Hold still. I won't hurt you."

Kellis sat still, to let his head finish clearing. "Enna's *never* going to forgive this."

"She'll get over it," Druyan said sternly. "What did you want to tell me?"

"Tell you?" Kellis frowned.

"You *said* you had to tell me something," Druyan prompted.

"I—I think I can remember saying that." Kellis began to feel sick once more.

"Well? What was it?"

"I don't know." He frowned again, but the memory was a cold trail, not a wisp of it left to guide him.

"Maybe it wasn't important. You'll have a bruise here, but I think that's all," she said, and took her fingers away. "When did you learn to do birds?"

"Just lately." Kellis shivered. "But I don't think that was it." He rubbed his forehead, trying to pull the memory out physically, as if it might be lodged just under his berry-stained skin.

Try as he might, he couldn't recall what he had wanted to tell her. He could remember that he had felt urgent about it, but that was all. The memory was out of reach, and whenever he stretched for it he felt a nasty plummeting sensation, as if he were falling from a great height. He wasn't going to fly again, Kellis thought, more relieved than sad. He couldn't imagine why he'd ever wanted to leave the safe solid earth behind.

The Horse Fair

SEVEN SUNFALLS NEVER passed without a horseman garbed in sea blue topped by black-sheep's gray appearing at Splaine Garth's gate—Riders pausing to pay their respects to one of their own, maimed risking what they had all risked, reassuring themselves that she was as well as might be and lacked for nothing they could provide. Finally 'twas Robart who rode up to the much-mended gate, with unwelcome tidings.

"A *horse* tithe?" Druyan asked, aghast. She could not stop her glance from darting toward Valadan, busy grazing down the grass that sprang up untidily between the yard's cobbles no matter how she tried to keep after it.

"This year only," Robart explained soothingly. "Two horses, and you're allowed to choose them. Though of course landholders are expected to choose well. Sacrificially well."

Druyan felt her muscles relax, though she had been unaware of them going twanging tight—they had done that in an eyeblink. She still felt a touch ill, as if the new-laid egg Enna had cooked for her breakfast had been week old and beginning to grow into a featherless chicken.

"Selling off his own herds isn't enough for Brioc?" she asked bitterly.

"No." Robart laughed. "Not nearly. He's just learned

276

what sail canvas will cost, probably. Don't fret about your Valadan—to any save the Riders, what is he but an old horse? Send two of Travic's coursers—they're bloodstock and should fetch a price to satisfy our uncle."

"The army still *has* some of our coursers. And nothing will fetch much of a price, with half the horseflesh in Esdragon put on the block!" Druyan's eyes flashed.

"Brioc's been told that—I spoke to Siarl myself, he told me. As you can see, our duke takes no counsel from it." Robart sipped the cider Enna had fetched. "Anyway, the coursers will suit, and I shouldn't think Travic will mind."

"No, he—"

"How long has it been, sister?"

Druyan's tongue went to stone, her lips to ice. She wanted to leap to her feet, but not a muscle would obey her. Or was she best to stay still and feign ignorance?

"Yvain told me what he suspected, what he learned when he made inquiries." Her brother's blue eyes transfixed her. The gold spot was bright as if shaved from a coin. "He said he thought you were trying to freehold."

Mute, trapped, Druyan nodded. So, the disaster had come at last. Her own fault—she had begun to hope, now that the time drew near to its close. That hope alone had attracted fate's attention, and she was undone.

"Well, you're doing a fine job," Robart said unexpectedly. "The farm looks just as Travic would have wished it to. How much longer do you have?"

"Travic was killed just before the barley harvest last year." It was difficult to admit it after hiding it so closely for so long, but Druyan felt a measure of relief as she said the words aloud. Seasons had passed, come nearly full circle. Already the green heads were beginning to bend the barley stalks perceptibly. There was barely another month to run, ere she and Kellis were both free, before she was safe and he was off to whatever fate he stubbornly sought. *I must keep back one decent horse somehow,* Druyan thought, remembering she had promised one such to him.

And figure out how to bring this year's crop in. At least they can't throw me off the land for failing this time.

"Yvain is planning to ask Brioc for you," Robart said casually.

Druyan's head jerked up so suddenly that her neck cracked. "He's *what*?"

"You have awhile—Yvain has to be careful, because there are those who'd claim you just to get the land, Travic's heirs. He's got to ride delicately around those, not let them suspect—"

"Travic didn't have much family." She had thought about that very carefully, to know where the dangers ahead lay.

"Amazing how blood-ties out, though, when there's land at stake. There are two possible candidates besides Yvain, and it will be a close race when it comes to it, sister." He sipped again. "You press fine cider here."

"Darlith's famous apples. All we do is gather them in, Robart. So, if I don't accept Yvain, I'll go to whoever's at his heels?"

"Not accept him?" Robart looked puzzled at that unthinkable choice. "Whyever not? We're talking of *Yvain* here. They sing songs about him, you know. Ballads of thirty verses."

Druyan sniffed. "They can sing all they want. Should I wed again for a song? Robart, I'm almost *free*."

"Free?" He snorted at that himself. "What does that mean? Do you fear Yvain wouldn't be good to you? That's groundless. He worships you. He's heads above anything the family could have got for your dowry, and he's not an old man like Travic. He's—"

"I suppose you'd buy a horse you didn't need and didn't especially want, just because the price was right?" Druyan pleaded, knowing he'd never see it her way, would never consider that it might differ from his own.

Robart frowned. "I might. Horses can go lame. I suppose that doesn't apply so aptly to husbands. But just you remember, Druyan, you really don't have the right to turn him down. And if you *do* somehow manage it, your hand

and this farm *will* go to someone. I'd not be so quick to spurn the likes of Yvain. Unless you've cause?" He cocked a brow.

"None you'd understand," Druyan whispered. To speak of her barrenness, even before her own brother, was impossible. She could not find words to tell him what having something of her own meant to her, nor to express the pain of seeing that goal so near when 'twas snatched away. Kinder if it had happened before Travic was cold in the ground.

Druyan chose to conduct her tithe to the horse fair personally. She had the past two winters' worth of fine-woven cloth to sell and no objection to finding a broader market for her work than the local market fair. She rode Valadan while Kellis drove the wagon with the tithe two long-legged dark chestnut brothers—tethered to its footboard. The horses were the best her holding boasted, save for Valadan himself—Druyan would not risk taking a tithe that might be rejected as unsalable and thereby call attention to Splaine Garth and its unattended lady. Yvain was enough to fret her.

The weather turned hot and close, unrelieved by the scattered rainstorms, and the nearer they drew to Keverne the deeper the dust lay on the roads. Those narrow ways were crowded, too—Druyan was hardly the only farmer forced to pay a new tithe that year and bound for the fair to deliver it. Valadan made a way for them handily—polite enough, his manners impeccable, but brooking no disrespect from strangers. Even so, their progress tended to be sluggish.

She had allowed them a full sevenday to reach the fair, so as not to take condition off the tithe horses by traveling too fast. They needed most of that time to contend with the choked roads. Druyan wondered betimes if the wagon had not been a foolish indulgence—she might have packed her cloth on a sumpter horse, and then they'd have been free to quit the roads when progress got too slow. She had dust powdering every inch of her, and Valadan's coat had begun to look dapple gray. Kellis' brows were as white as the hair on his head. They were both coughing. So were the chestnuts, but that passed off after they'd grazed awhile without breathing in more dust than they could snort out again.

The horse fair was always a huge event. This year there were more horses sent to it and more paying customers invited. The one notable difference was that every horse brought was sold by the Duke of Esdragon. The side sales that throve in other years were sternly prohibited. Not every horse trader had known that beforetime, and there was grumbling aplenty for Druyan to overhear, as she stood patiently waiting to turn over her tithe.

She remembered both the chestnuts as foals—indeed, she would have seen them come from their mother, save that the mare had been too secretive to deliver while a human soul was anywhere near. She tried not to dwell on the memories as she stood with them one last time, the elder nibbling at her fingers on his lead, rubbing his head against her, while the younger one took in every strange sound or sight with keenest interest. They were quite alike, copies save for the younger having three spots of white upon his face where his elder brother had but a single one. Whatsoever one had done, the other had done just the year after. They had never been apart in their lives, but she had no say in their fates now. Druyan hoped she'd be well out of earshot by the time the colts discovered themselves going separate ways.

After three tedious hours, Druyan's turn finally came. Her tithe had eaten every blade of grass within a horse-length of her by then. They were inspected by Siarl himself—the constable carefully did not look her in the eye—recorded in the tally book, which was signed with Travic's signet ring and the duke's seal. Then Druyan was free to return to her camp, which was a good long ride away—and no use could be made of Valadan's speed unless she was enough a fool to do such a thing under strange eyes. She cantered back slowly.

Kellis had a meal cooked by the time she finally arrived, and she could see he was trying not to look anxious. "Done," she announced, settling wearily on the tail of the wagon. "I've half a mind to go home this minute and forget about peddling the cloth. Only I'm too tired."

"Too many people here," Kellis agreed, warily sniffing the evening breeze.

"I just hate watching," Druyan said, pulling off the glove she had worn on her right hand to forestall casual stares and comment. Her hand looked like a bird's claw, and she did not want other eyes making her remember that. But the leather was hot, and the red scar itched. "It brings home what my uncle's doing, which is not a whit less foolish than cooking seed corn a month before planting time. Even if we build the ships Brioc's so set on, most of our folk just aren't sailors, not to match the Eral raiders. Fishing isn't fighting."

"No," Kellis agreed. He offered her some stew.

"How does it happen that you've got most of that road dust off?" There was still a powdering on his clothing, but his hair was clean, shiny.

He grinned lopsidedly. "It doesn't stay on through a shift."

Druyan nearly choked on her stew. "You be careful about that!" She was appalled at the risk he'd taken. The fair was better populated than most towns, and not a single wall to hide behind unless one counted canvas pavilions.

Kellis let his expression sober. "I was. I was fetching firewood, and there was no one else in the wood." He gestured with his chin, to the little smear of scrubby woodland half a league away. "There's a thicket of wild rose, where the rock comes through and even the little trees can't root. Safe enough, except for thorns." He sucked at a scratch on the back of his wrist, like a dog licking a hurt paw.

Druyan blew on the stew, to cool it. There was rabbit meat in it, she realized. He must have caught it. They'd brought a small ham and a flitch of bacon, but no fresh meat was among their provisions. "It's not like it's just Enna to fool," she warned him.

"Thank you."

Druyan put her spoon into the bowl with a click. "Why? For pestering you about things you certainly know better than I do?"

Kellis tilted his head. "Not for that. For what you *didn't* say, to Enna. For telling her the bird was only a magic trick, and never mentioning the wolf."

"I did that for *her* sake, Kellis. Can you imagine how she'd be if she knew the *whole* truth?"

"Oh, yes." He grinned. "I counted all your knives, you know. More than once."

"I'll bet you did!" Druyan's eyes sparkled.

"Lady?" One moment they were laughing together—then he had turned serious, like a cloud-shadow passing over a sunny meadow. "What are you going to do about your barley harvest?"

Certainly the man had not lost sight of his goal—he was trying delicately to remind her that he'd be free and gone when the grain was ready to cut, that his sentence was up the same moment Druyan's goal was won. In fact, whether 'twas won or not, for his fulfillment depended only upon time spent.

"I'll hire men," Druyan said calmly, ignoring a disappointment she knew she ought not to feel. She had set the terms. She had always known he would go. "It will be safe to do that, once the freehold's mine. I suppose there will be men to hire—unless my uncle takes them all to be sailors for his dream fleet."

There were the usual races run and games played, save now less as challenges between proud horsemen than calculations to catch a buyer's eye. Gone, the leagues-long chase after an old wineskin refilled with air, with upward of twenty horsemen to ride and few rules attached to the quest save possession of the quarry and nerves of iron. Gone, the displays of a stallion's get in contests of every sort, demonstrating that he was well worth his breeding price. While some coursers were pitted against one another for a mile or two, mares and yearlings were being trotted mere paces before those who'd come to bid upon them—and sold, shown off no further. It made for a surpassingly dull fair.

Besides charging the post riders to carry word, Brioc had sent forth messengers, paid men riding far and wide with tidings of the fair. There were horse traders come in from all the corners of Clandara—Radak, Lassair, Josten, and a near score of lesser places. Kinark was heavily represented, and there was one dealer Druyan thought had come even farther—from Fithian, or Asgeirr, far down the edge of the Great Sea. The fair was a very great event, 'twould be spoken of for years. And likely, in Esdragon, cursed.

The spectacle left Druyan heartsick, as she had suspected it would. She watched the racing for a time, but without joy—Valadan could have walked away from any of the winners, at any distance—and when she saw her cousin Dimas casting his appraising eye over the racers, she was too frightened to linger long thereabouts, even without entering the contests. Druyan did not doubt that a subject would be invited—for the good of the duke and the whole land—to part with any horse a buyer sought that day, whether that cherished horse was part of a tithe or not.

Sell me, Valadan suggested wickedly, rolling an eye back at her. *I know my way home, and there is no bridle can restrain me.*

She slapped his neck, astonished that Valadan proposed such a rank dishonesty. Then again, it exactly suited the occasion. Druyan sighed. Time she saw about spreading out her weavings, anyway. She could not be the only person at the fair weary of watching the decimation of the ducal herds. She'd lay out her wares, find buyers, empty the wagon, and then she'd go home.

The day was warm, and Druyan was thirsty. She didn't doubt the stallion would also relish a drink, so she jogged Valadan to the river, then rode upstream a little distance, where the water would flow unsullied. As she made to dismount, she discovered Kellis at her stirrup. He had a wooden pail in one hand—he'd come for water, too, evidently. Well, at least he wasn't following her about in wolf-form. That was something.

Druyan slipped down and parted the soft green reeds with her left hand, while she gripped Valadan's mane with the three fingers she had on her right. If the low bank proved boggy, she didn't want to sink, or slip and go tumbling into the water. Her eyes would go first, well ahead of her feet, because glancing into a bog didn't soak your boots. There was a little strip of yellow sand just past the reeds that might offer her a dry spot to stand, if 'twas solid.

"I want to move the wagon," she said to Kellis as she tested the footing with a toe. "Somewhere a little nearer to the crowds. I'll drape the cloth over it, get the weavings out of the dirt and up where they can be seen. The horses are going cheap, the traders will have coin to spare. That's a good turn for us, anyway."

Kellis didn't answer. Druyan looked to see why.

He had just leaned to dip the pail, and she thought he simply hadn't heard her over the noise of the water—when suddenly Kellis lurched and one foot went into the stream with a splash, betrayed by the soft edge of the streambank. Pitching forward off balance, he flailed out with one hand, which Druyan caught. She still had hold of Valadan, but three fingers' grip wasn't much to stop both of them falling. Druyan leaned back hard against the stallion, hoping Kellis could get his feet back under him before she lost her hold. The stallion's shoulder felt like a wall at her back, but her feet were slipping . . .

The vision ran through the three of them—the man, the woman, the stallion—like a whip of fire.

There could be no doubt about what spot this vision showed—it was all about them, they could behold it with outward eyes as easily as inward sight, one overlaying the other like transparent enamels on glass. The green and tawny moor, the milling horses and the spectators, the winding silver river that had permitted the raiders' arrival to be both quiet and secret. The duke had his own guards to protect his person, but there weren't many above twenty of them, not enough to protect anyone else. The carnage began, and scarlet overmastered the other colors . . .

Valadan reared back. Kellis lost his grip on Druyan's left hand as she was dragged away from him and toppled headlong into the river. A burning pain shot up Druyan's right arm, and she let go of Valadan. Springy reeds cushioned her landing. She sat up, looking for Kellis. Splashes met her ears, but she had to get to her feet to see over the reeds.

The river being more wide than deep at that point, Kellis floundered upright at once, coughing and spitting out water. The bucket tried to float way, then took on water and sank instead.

"Gray sky," Kellis choked, trying to scramble to his feet and retrieve the bucket at the same time, with much splashing and little progress. On the bank, Valadan trotted in a tight circle, snorting.

Druyan stared up at the white-spotted blue overhead, rubbing at her strained hand. "Tomorrow?" she asked, stricken.

"It wasn't yesterday." Kellis climbed up the bank, swore, and groped back for the boot he'd lost to the bottom mud. "The sun showed his face all day, remember?"

"What are we going to do?" Druyan wailed.

She could warn her uncle, as she had alerted the vulnerable river towns, the seaside farms and villages, all that spring and half the summer. But *if* she could get to the duke, and *if* he believed her—still, what use? Brioc's army was a month's march away, felling useless ship timber. Keverne itself, on its lofty headland with its mighty stone walls, could offer shelter, but not for the horse herds, nor likely for most of the folk who had come to trade gold and silver for those horses. Keverne could shield its master, but few others were likely to reach the citadel or be permitted to share its protection.

"We could go home," Kellis suggested. He raised that brow, up to his wet hair, and sighed resignedly. "No, I didn't really think so. Well then, where are the Riders now?"

"Spread out all along their routes," Druyan answered miserably. "I could get to them, warn most of them—" Valadan snorted, agreeing with her as to his speed. "But they won't all of them have time enough to get here. They'll be too far away, and by the time I get to them . . ."

Kellis nodded, clenched his jaw, and swallowed very hard. "Then it will be best if we both carry word."

It was Druyan's turn to stare. "How do you propose to do that? You said before the Riders wouldn't listen to you—" So he had, and she had thought he was very likely right, angry as she had been with him. Most of the post riders weren't pleased about having someone shifting shape right under their eyes—what else might such a person shift? How did you trust such a creature?

"Write the message to them and hang it around my neck," Kellis suggested. "Saves time, if I don't have to keep shifting back and forth to argue with them—I'm only good for three or four shifts anyway, before I'm too done up to move. Write it, and let them decide for themselves what they'll do."

Druyan steadfastly refused to allow her thoughts to dwell on what Kellis had risked, was risking—refused to let herself wonder what sort of success he might have had, if the Riders had heeded him or chased him away. She had ridden all night before turning Valadan's head back to Keverne at dawn. She had personally intercepted ten pairs of Riders, rousing the final three teams from their billets. Most had been startled but delighted to see her, and they had sped toward Keverne even as she was forging onward to her next destination. None of them had shown her a moment's dissension. Druyan thought she had never been so weary in all her life, though her own feet had not once touched the dark ground since she climbed up to Valadan's saddle.

The Riders wouldn't all be in time. For certain she'd overtake one or two along her own route back, and those would never be able to ride her pace, not mounted upon ordinary horses. Nor would Kellis have been able to run so far as Valadan, even shaped as a wolf, so if she managed to have eight teams of riders to the fair in time, he would likely have less. Druyan toted up the probabilities and winced. At best, there would be very, very few of them gathering.

There are always the horses, Valadan comforted her, under the insistent rush of the wind past his neck. *They will answer to me.*

As it had been at Splaine Garth. So long ago, when she hadn't yet known what consequences were . . .

Valadan snorted, cautioning her against dwelling upon such dark matters. Was the sun not rising behind them? Did they not seem to bear the dawn with them, tangled in the hairs of the stallion's tail? Did not the very wind cry their names?

Yet still Druyan's lost fingers throbbed and tingled as if they remained a part of her, hurt and fearing to be worse hurt when she overreached herself again, forgot her station and cast aside all proprieties, when she dared to do again as she had done before. *She* was no Duchess Kessallia, witchbred and equipped to venture such things, to flout every convention. She was but a younger daughter of a younger son, a farmer's widow, and her place was in her own farmyard, with her hens and her spindle and her butter churn. If she dared to step beyond her lawful sphere, what befell her was surely no less than she deserved. Any person in Esdragon could tell her that, would be glad to. Her half-empty right glove repeated the lesson.

There is always a price, Valadan said, pulling against the bit to get her attention. *That a thing costs does not make it wrong to have, but only more precious.*

"What if the cost is too high?" Druyan moaned into the wind.

That you must reckon, Valadan answered. *You know how to strike a fair bargain. I have never seen you deceived.*

"This isn't buying a new ram to improve the flock!"

Druyan snapped. "This is *lives*, not length of fleece staple and how many crimps to the measure!"

Not all costs are the same. Some prices only a hero can pay. His neck arched like a black rainbow against the dark land. She could see his left eye rolled back to her, full of sparkling lights. Druyan's mind's eye was given a brief sharp glimpse of flame and smoke, the intolerable brightness of a chimera's mane.

"But I'm no hero," she whispered, as Esdragon's cool wind replaced the burning vision.

No hero ever thinks so, Valadan said inscrutably, and galloped onward, never missing a stride.

Six Riders awaited her, dismounted to let their winded beasts recover, gently walking those most recently arrived and still needing cooling to prevent founder. Only six, and the sky overhead was thin gray now, as clouds had drifted in over the sun almost the moment it cleared the horizon. Druyan shuddered, seeing the stage set for the deadly play.

Six Riders. There would be others, and perhaps those would yet arrive in time—no way to tell about that. The vision had scarcely been precise. It had offered no glimpse of the sun's angle to guide them, since the sun could not be seen.

Two of the waiting men were not among those she and Valadan had alerted, which was a comfort to Druyan— Kellis had gotten at least that far, his message had been accepted by at least one team.

She remembered hanging the message pouch about his silver-furred neck. It seemed a month ago already. He had not allowed her to watch his transformation, but had gone discreetly behind some trees and then come trotting back to her in his wolf-shape, his yellow eyes troubled, as if he feared even she would refuse him, mistrust him. She had secured the message and he had bolted away at once, not waiting for her to speak to him. But what more could she have said?

She wished she had thought to tell him to go back to

Darlith when his round was finished. He'd surely be in reach of the farm, however weary he was. And if he tried to come back to her at Keverne he would burst his heart, and still likely be too late . . .

One of the Riders called her name joyfully. Druyan lifted a hand to acknowledge the greeting and rode to join her little company.

No use to try to take up a defensive position. They were too few to find it useful, and attempting it might only bring them to the duke's troublesome attention. Two more pairs reached them, the four horses sweat-soaked but sound. They lurked at the fringes of the fair, on high ground that offered them a slight vantage and the marginal concealment of a stand of scrubby trees. Druyan considered what they might do in such and such a case, if the raiders did thus and so. She discussed tactics with the captains—what they had found to work during other raids, in other places. Mostly they spoke because simply waiting for the disaster to overtake them was intolerable. They all knew there was no plan, however cunning, likely to grant them victory. They were straws thrown into a flooding tide—helpless, and knowing it. Some of them might never ride again.

Two more Riders pounded up, men who had been bedded down just the near side of Porlark when a wolf's howls had roused them from sleep. And the day was advancing, though the veiled sun did not mark it.

Druyan reckoned the progress of the tide, which was strong enough to counteract the sluggish flow of Keverne's river, at least along these lower reaches. She should have thought of that before, as a way of knowing what to expect! The raiders demonstrably preferred to row up rivers, so as not to show sails, which might be seen from far off. They might also prefer to have the tide's help, to make their rowing easier, she thought. And with the moon nearing full, those tides were high and puissant. They would not reach quite so far upriver as the horse fair, but one aware of the tide could judge when the raiders would find it possible to begin their voyage. Druyan strained her eyes against the gleam of the water, alternated that with glances at the horizon, watching for the dust hard-ridden horses would raise.

And all the while, small groups of horses were shepherded from holding pens to the great circle of well-trampled grass where the selling took place. The beasts left mostly singly, were led to picket lines that the buyers had set up, and kept there by drovers who had much to contend with, as old herd bonds were severed and nervous animals adjusted—or did not—to their new companions.

Bidding waxed spirited when the duke's great roan stallion, the king of his stables, took his turn in the ring. It barely faltered when the stud took exception to the excitement and began to display his temper in dangerous ways, hauling his attendant grooms wherever he wished, ungovernable. Eventually he managed to plunge into the crowd, though folk nearest had moved back to safety several times. There was chaos, and Siarl the constable waded in himself to take personal charge of the stallion, but the bidding never quite ceased. Duke Brioc looked well pleased. He was gaining a good deal of gold in return for his horses—gold that would soon be transmuted into long-keeled ships. A little of it would go to the coffers of one of the more tractable and practical Eral chieftains—his pay for keeping off his fellow pirates—but that was a temporary inconvenience. Once the ships were ready . . .

In fact, there were a score more ships in Esdragon, that moment, than her duke guessed. And most of those were beaching on the gentle river shores at that very instant.

The Riders

THOSE TRADERS ENCAMPED nearest the river were the first to realize that something was amiss. All at once their wagons were being rummaged through, their strongboxes located and smashed open, the coins within scooped up, thrown into carrysacks. Merchants who objected met short, sharp swords in the hands of men quite willing to use them—men brazen enough to attempt such business in the broad light of day. Picket lines were slashed, and loosed horses spread confusion with every stride, unwitting allies of the thieves.

Turmoil spread inshore, and the only folk not affected by it were those who'd caused it—and had expected to have to deal with it.

"There's a good fifteen ships beached in the shelter of that bluff yonder," reported one winded post rider, who had raced his mount round the fringe of the fair to scout out their enemy.

"And never less than a dozen men to a ship," Druyan reckoned grimly. "Probably they've crammed more aboard for this. For now we act together. There aren't enough of us here to split off and try anything fancy. Keep close, ride stirrup to stirrup." Below, she could see her uncle's bodyguard drawing up about their master, making no move toward the disturbance on the perimeter of the fair. "We'll ride straight through," she decided. "Aim for the river, and we'll try to push them back ahead of us. *Now!*"

The horses—even the weary ones—leapt forward eagerly. *"Valadan!"* someone shouted, like a war cry. Other voices answered him, and two horses neighed. The charge was under way.

The slope wasn't extreme, but it blessed them with momentum, and the horses, excited to run together, left weariness behind them like the dust they raised. The thunder of Valadan's galloping hooves was multiplied a dozenfold, as if Kellis had been working his Mirror of Three again. Druyan had never ridden so fast in a close-packed bunch before—sometimes pastured horses had run along with Valadan, but never for so long. All about her, manes tossed like seafoam, heads stretched out as teeth fiercely clenched bits. Nostrils were red as firecoals, wide as wine cups, and a roaring sound filled Druyan's ears, as Valadan led the charge. The ragged wave of sea blue and black-sheep's gray crested into the horse fair.

The fringes might have broken their charge upon picket lines still up, or deflected it around breakwaters of wagons, but the center did not much impede them. Loose horses dodged out of their path—others loosed themselves from terrified handlers and fled, only to attach themselves to the post riders like the tail of a comet, adding weight to the headlong rush as they followed it.

"Valadan!" The name was screamed, high and shrill.

"Druyan! Druyan!" Because there was not a man there did not feel she was the Riders' luck, their lodestone.

The shouts were all just at Druyan's heels—Valadan was forgetting to school his pace to something the others could hope to match. And they were not pausing to slash at the raiders they began to encounter—Druyan carried no sword, could not have held it if she had. Valadan was her weapon, her shield, as well, his white teeth and sharp hooves putting sea bandits to flight more surely than any blade ever forged. No raider stood before him.

The stallion veered from the river's edge, on the heels of

a yelling man with a sack slung over his right shoulder. The yells changed to screams as he went over the bank and into deep water. Druyan whirled Valadan about, his forehooves treading empty air, his quarters bunching powerfully beneath her.

Four Riders drew even with them. Three others pelted up, to re-form the line.

"Back across!" Druyan shouted, her voice breaking into a croak. "Try to push them on toward the right." Keverne lay in the opposite direction, and she knew there were already folk trying to make for the safety of the stronghold— they would do no kindness to send the raiders into them.

Now to charge was a struggle, uphill and without a running start. To stay in any sort of a line was nearly impossible. The Riders mired upon knots of struggling men— stray guardsmen and horse traders fighting back against those who'd sought to rob them. Afoot, they'd never have won to the hill to regroup—even ahorse some of the Riders couldn't get there, but were forced aside, sent wide and slowed.

They were the only mounted force on the field, but there weren't enough of them to matter. Druyan reined in, trying to decide whether another sweep through could possibly do further good—the horse fair was absolute chaos, and determining a course of action could be done only whilst one was on the edges of it. Once embroiled in the struggle, only the next instant could be judged—only the next instant would matter. She looked, and her head swam with the enormity of it. But everyone was looking to *her* for their direction, it was *her* name they cried . . .

Valadan snorted, stamped, and tugged at the reins. *Too few of us to keep the line,* he said. Three horses had not rejoined them after the last charge—they were together in a little knot downriver, their riders quite busy and plainly too far away to return. Choose to or not, their little force was split.

* * *

Esdragon's duke had never beheld an Eral raid at close hand, or even seen the aftermath with his own eyes. He had been willing to permit the coasts of his domain to be pillaged the rest of this season in order to better protect them the next—never had he imagined he would need his army to stand off such an unheard of, daylight, and not the least secret attack. His Guard alone should have been sufficient to keep order at the fair. So they had been, but were no longer. Two dozen men, even hand-picked, could not defend the traders and see him safe back to his fortress, as well; Brioc forbade them to try. He looked about for his son—Dimas was nowhere in sight, having made for the riverbank to report on the raiders' ships, and steal one if he could. He should have forbidden that, the duke thought—surely those ships were not left unguarded . . .

"Lady, I'll not ride into that *alone*, but if your Riders are game, I'll add my horse to yours," the trader said, speaking over the neck of a high-spirited gray he had purchased the previous day and managed to saddle ere the picket lines went to perdition and loosed the rest of his stock.

"Follow me, then!" Druyan shouted, and wheeled Valadan to face the worst of the fighting. She felt his forehand lighten, and all at once he reared as if he would touch the stars that hid out the day behind the gray clouds— reared and screamed both a challenge to the foe and a rallying cry to every ridden horse upon the moor. Druyan did her best to look as if the action was her own idea.

The riderless answered Valadan, as well, and the ground trembled with the thunder of thousands of hooves. If the earlier charge had been pounding surf, now it was an earthshake. And over the edge of the rolling gray-green horizon came half a dozen more blue and gray riders, with a silver shape darting just ahead of their horses' hooves.

"Valadan!"

"The Warhorse!"

"Druyan! Druyan!"

"Valadan!"

The raiders had been hard-pressed enough to keep out of the way of the early charges. Afoot, even a single horse running at them was a terror hardly to be withstood. Now, faced with scores of onrushing beasts, some few Eral stood fast, but most broke for their ships—if, in the confusion, they still had any notion where the river lay, whether they were up- or downstream of their beached craft.

"*Valadan!* Follow the Warhorse!"

A wolf howled.

Brioc looked over the shoulders of his guards, as wave upon wave of gleaming horseflesh swept past. Incredulous, he saw his post riders among them, wielding their swords at any sea raider fool enough to be trying to stand in their path.

"What a sight!" exclaimed Siarl, Constable of Esdragon. He recognized some of the horses hurtling by. "And this you'd trade for a paltry few barnacle-covered tubs?" He spat into the trampled grass.

The duke was speechless.

The horse at Valadan's near shoulder was a blood bay, with a white spot between its eyes. The Rider's hair matched the stallion's coat, though by then 'twas too dark to notice such details.

"They managed to launch all their ships, though they left a lot of their crewmen behind," Yvain reported.

Some had in fact been drowned trying to swim after departing boats. Others were cut down ere they reached water too deep to ride a horse through at speed. A few were taken alive. Most had not been.

Robart cantered up to them. "Brioc's safe back at Keverne. No one has seen Dimas, but there was hard fighting by the boats, and last anyone heard, he was headed that way."

"Did we lose any Riders?" Druyan asked hoarsely. She wanted to ask after Kellis, but dared not, not of Robart. All those iron-shod hooves. All those cold iron blades . . .

"Some wounded, none like to die," Robart answered. "I can't say as much for the horses. Some may never carry weight after this day's work. If they get through the night without foundering or colicking, I'll be pleased. And amazed."

There were horses everywhere one looked, most unmounted. Some were probably wounded or otherwise hurt. Most were upset and exhausted. Druyan had seen a sad number lying dead, the great roan stallion prominent among those. He had been surrounded by bodies, and Valadan had commented on his valor as they passed.

"We should try," Druyan said, "to send someone along the coast, to see where those ships dropped anchor. They won't be able to get far, not as they are now. They're still here. Somewhere."

"But not on the coast," croaked a familiar voice at her left stirrup. Druyan looked down, her heart leaping with relief. Kellis was swaying there, barely on his feet. He was clad in a shapeless garment starred with thistles and muddy hoofprints, which possibly had been part of a merchant's tent that morning. There was dried blood all over his face, but nothing red and fresh and *his*.

"I remembered," he mumbled. "What I wanted to tell you before, Lady." Druyan leaned down, barely able to hear him. Valadan looked back curiously. Kellis took hold of his mane. "The raids came too thick, I knew it had to be the same ships striking again and again, not always fresh fleets from over the sea. That meant they had a base here, an anchorage no one knew about." He faltered, put a hand to his head, and clung to Valadan's mane for dear life. Druyan reached for him, but he got his eyes open and shook his head at her. "That's how it was I set myself to learn birds, so I could scout your coasts the way a boat can't. That crash, though, going out of form when I wasn't ready—" He smiled ruefully. "It put most of it right out of my head."

"What's he babbling about?" Robart demanded harshly. Druyan waved him off and leaned closer.

"Kellis? What did you remember?"

He lifted his face to hers and gave her a clear sight of those innocent dog's eyes and a lopsided grin. "Where the base is," Kellis said, just before his knees buckled.

The Wind-Witch

"An island," Robart said dourly, while Kellis sucked thirstily at cider Yvain had liberated from some unfortunate merchant's wrecked caravan. "Can't be. Someone would see them. No place in Esdragon is *that* deserted."

"Perhaps not," Yvain answered thoughtfully. He nodded at Kellis. "He said the anchorage faces the sea. You'd need a boat to spot it, and if I was fishing off the Promontory, I'd be steering well clear of all such islands—the water's nothing but shoals, and the surf is murderous. I'd want to get safely by, not gawk at the sights."

"Yet the raiders stumbled on it?" Robart argued scornfully.

"Probably they were seeking such a bolt-hole purposely, Captain. No one's said they were stupid, besides having magpie morals."

Robart growled something indistinguishable, and Yvain laughed.

"You're both missing the point," Druyan said sternly, intolerant of the squabbling. "Most of us in Darlith have been clinging to the hope that the raids would end when winter came—living for that, truly. Now we know they won't stop."

"No reason they should," Kellis agreed cheerfully, waving the hand holding the cider.

Druyan took the just-emptied bottle away from him,

298

frowning. Too late she suspected he'd been parched enough to get himself silly-drunk in the space of two minutes, and she angrily wished that Yvain had found them water to quench Kellis' thirst instead of hard cider—she didn't doubt he could have managed it. Kellis looked aggrieved, as if he'd guessed her thought and resented her judgment of him.

"Today should convince Brioc that he needs cavalry more than ships," Robart said, with satisfaction.

"Brioc's guards found Dimas' body on the river shore," Yvain reported reluctantly. He fiddled with his dagger hilt. "We may not be able to count on much from our duke."

"He's got two other sons!" Robart protested, sparing no sympathy.

"Dimas was his heir," Yvain stressed softly. "And his favorite. You've been about Keverne enough to know *that*, Captain. And I am only saying that this might be a very poor time to call Brioc's attention to anything. Especially his post riders, whose lapses as regards their official duties can be called to account. We're easy prey."

Robart pounded a fist against his thigh. "We're heroes today and examples the day after?" He shook his head. "I'm not disputing the pattern, Yvain. I know my uncle quite as well as you do! So we lay low, lick our wounds, stay out of Brioc's sight, and the raiders do . . . what?"

"Hit us all winter long," Druyan supplied dismally. "No end to it."

"We can't *make* an end, Druyan!" Robart snapped, irritated.

Next to her, Kellis gave a little warning growl. Robart's eyes went wide, then relaxed. He schooled his voice to a more reasonable tone. "Look. Even if we could depend on Brioc's always chancy gratitude, we've nothing to do *with*. We rode the legs off our mounts to save Brioc's guests today—we have nothing left for tomorrow, or the day after. Siarl himself couldn't wangle us fresh horses out of this mess, without the duke knowing. Afoot, there aren't enough of us to hold off a town watch." He began to slide his dagger in and out of its sheath.

The moon was lifting over the horizon, washing the moor with silver. Kellis saw, tipped his head back, and softly howled a welcome to it. The sound was different coming from a human throat, but unmistakably wolf. It echoed weirdly, and horses snorted.

Druyan grabbed Kellis and muffled his lips hastily with her left palm, while Robart glared accusingly at Yvain.

"You had to get him drunk? A shape-shifting sorcerer wasn't trouble enough?"

Yvain spread his long-fingered hands in innocence, but his eyes smiled.

"Our own grandfather saluted every moonrise, they say," Druyan offered, taking her fingers away again. She frowned—they were sticky with cider. "Though not in quite that way."

"Sorry," Kellis mumbled faintly, ducking his head and rubbing at the bridge of his crooked nose, wishing his head would clear. He had been a fool, he thought, to make himself helpless when he was hardly certain of being among friends. Every Rider still had an iron sword, and he had just called himself to their collective attention. Foolish. "But it's so *big*." It was, he thought, a moon for hunting.

"It *is* close—almost near enough to lay hands on," Druyan agreed, staring skyward at the shining disc. "And not even full till tomorrow night. The tide's already as high as it normally gets, folk will be making ready all along the coast, the way they do when the moon's full and close, and the tide rises, too . . ." An utterly natural peril, expected, predictable. Nothing at all like a raid in the night, swords and fire and murder . . .

"Too much to hope, that any islands off the Promontory would be awash in a high springing tide," Robart said, beginning to dig idly in the dirt with his dagger.

"Probably so," Yvain agreed reluctantly. "Perhaps the winter storms will do for them."

"Or they'll carve themselves a stronger foothold before then," Robart groused. "Maybe ashore. As you say, no one's said they're fools."

Druyan had gone silent, her eyes full of moon-silver. Behind them, her thoughts swirled like a wayward breeze, then steadied. High tide . . . A full moon increased the tidal rise. A *close* full moon brought the water up a touch more, but coastal folk were used to that predictable event. Only when an ill-timed storm pushed the water still higher was there truly danger. Every estuary was vulnerable to disastrous floods of saltwater, if a storm wind got behind a springing tide.

A storm . . .

A breath of wind feathered across her right cheek, to slide beneath her collar and down her back like a chill finger. Druyan shivered and could not cease trembling.

There were always storms offshore on the Great Sea, far out from land, waiting restlessly to rush at the land. One such would come, if she called it. Druyan *knew* that in her bones, in her lost fingers. She had no need of hopes, or guesses. For whatever reason, a taint in her blood or her character, she had that power, unquestioned.

She could call a storm—if she dared. Call, and be answered, but scarcely control and certainly not quell. She could save her people with her forbidden, smothered gift— and she could drown quite a lot of them along the way to that salvation.

The trembling grew to a shuddering. Countering it, of a sudden Druyan felt the comforting steadiness of an arm about her shoulders. All at once she saw, in her mind, a tiny silver image, two miniature wolves running as one, shoulder to shoulder, bold and unafraid of what they were. As she stared the image grew, the wolves came closer and closer yet, until with a bound they sprang right through her, through her heart. She saw moonlight, but felt a splash of rain.

Do what you must, the great silver wolf whispered into her head. *Never fear what lies in your heart, for that alone can save you . . . This I learned from you. Now I give it back.*

Druyan opened her eyes, but for a moment all she saw

was storm, wind and rain, darkness and howling destruction. Slowly the disasters faded, as the night's dark ebbed back from the risen moon. Druyan took a breath. Her sight cleared. She was looking into Kellis' very sober gray eyes. He raised that crow-black eyebrow at her.

Had she chosen?

She had.

"Could you shift again and get back to Splaine Garth?" she asked him. It wasn't fair to ask, really, she knew he was exhausted, that he had run all night and fought most of the day. His eyes were blood-hatched, shadowed beneath. But what needed doing superceded pity.

Kellis nodded, not the least reluctant except about leaving her. He was well enough, he said offhandedly, and tired was only tired.

"Good. The marsh may hold the tide, but the wind's another matter. Someone has to warn Enna and the girls, and I'd rather it was you. Tell them a storm; they'll know what to do when they hear that. Help them do it." Kellis nodded again, and Druyan turned to Robart, raising her chin.

"The Riders have one last task ahead of them. And I'll wager you can find horses enough, if you look for them now, before this mess gets sorted out. Or Valadan could call them."

"What do you mean?" Robart stared at her, not even ready to dispute what the stallion could do. "*What* task?"

"Raising the coast—the towns, the farms. Telling them there's going to be a storm surge atop a springing tide. Telling them to make ready, to protect themselves."

"A storm?" Robart tipped his head back. The moon was unveiled overhead. Stars glittered, all across the arch of the sky. There *were* clouds—small, few as fleas on a well-tended dog, and scattered as a lost flock.

"It's a long way out," Druyan agreed. "But it will hear me."

The Riders departed at first light, on sound horses gathered by Valadan's summons, veterans of battle every one, fleet and willing. Kellis went then, also, a wolf careful not to limp while he was under her eye, Druyan suspected. At least he had slept awhile—she had seen him curled up under a wagon, nose tucked under his tail. As the day brightened, she jogged Valadan to the top of the headland opposite her uncle's mighty castle of Keverne, on the far side of the river and town. What she needed to do, she might have done from the relative safety of Keverne's battlements—but Druyan chose not to shelter behind walls. She wanted no barriers between her and the wind, not even crenelated stone.

The wind's cold fingers poked teasingly through her cloak in a dozen places as she dismounted. When she faced the sea straight on, all her hair was scooped back from her face to stream behind her like Valadan's tail. Druyan walked slowly through the heather, soaking her boots with the wind-flung spray that clung to the tough plants. Sea-pink grew in soft mounds to the cliff edge and tumbled right over—she stopped walking when she reached them, and stood at the end of the world.

There were certainly rocks in the wild waters below, near the foot of the cliff, maybe even islets, but she would not see those unless she leaned out over, and she had no need to do that. From Druyan's vantage, all was sea before her, no land in sight at all. Oh, indeed there was land on the other side of the sea—always she had heard of it, and Kellis had been born upon one of those distant shores—but it was so far off as not to truly exist. There was only the endless sea, a thousand shades of blue and green and amethyst, and the wide sky above her, full of wind.

The breeze close about her was playful as a young cat, and smelled of the coastal waters—fish and weed and salt, nothing more ancient, foreign. It was not the wind she sought. Druyan pursed her lips, breathed deep through her nostrils, feeling that she drank as deep of the wind as ever Valadan did, running.

When she held all of it that she could, she sent the air whistling out again, in a plaintive call. The summons had a long way to go—she drew a breath only normally deep, and rested a moment. For good or ill, it was begun. She might step back from the cliff now, but not from what she had done.

Valadan neighed a challenge, and Druyan turned in a windswirl of woolen cloak. There was a horseman fifty paces off—as she stared, the wind threw his hood back, and his chestnut hair caught the wind and the light as he halted and swung out of his saddle.

Yvain was visibly pleased with himself, over the matter of eluding his fellow Riders. They had departed one and all, and not a man of them—for example, Robart—was on hand to say him nay.

Plainly, he did not expect Druyan would do so, either. There was no diffidence, no hesitation in Yvain's step as he drew near, though he paused once to ease saddle cramps out of his legs. The captain made Druyan an elegant bow as he reached her, took her hand as he straightened once more and pressed his lips to it. "Lady," he said, smiling in the manner of a ginger cat well fed on stolen cream.

"What part of Esdragon is left unwarned, while you are here?" Druyan asked, dismay defeating courtesy.

Yvain's eyes widened a touch, but his smile held its brightness. "We've not such a long coast as *that*! Rank grants privilege, Lady. I chose *this* section of coast for my responsibility. And so here am I, honorably at my post."

"This wasn't Robart's idea?"

Yvain laughed outright at her suspicion. "No. I cannot imagine he'll be much distressed, though."

Druyan tried to take her hand back. She wore her glove, and Yvain knew that—and *why*—two of its fingers were empty sleeves of leather, but she did not feel easy with it in his grip. Her face went hot, despite the cool air rushing past it from the sea. She tugged gently, striving not to act as if it mattered . . .

Yvain did not relinquish his hold, gentle but nonetheless implacable. Her hand stayed his prisoner. "Lady Druyan, it may be a tedious while before all's formally done, but I would have it said between us now, so you're clear on my intentions." He smiled again, with devastating effect. "I know you are widowed, though you have found it prudent that no other should have that information."·

Now, as the long-dreaded disaster finally touched her, Druyan found to her amazement that it scarcely seemed to matter. There was windsong in her ears, roaring in her blood, and what she wanted most at that moment was for Yvain to let go of her hand so that she could issue her call once again—without having to whistle straight into his face.

"I want you to wife," Yvain declared earnestly.

"I suppose you do." With pounding heart, Druyan studied the sky. It was full of wind-tattered clouds, rushing busily along inland. "You're *far* too rich to want me just for a paltry farm like Splaine Garth."

"I am crushed! That you even jest at such a crass motive's attaching itself to me, Lady—" Yvain had got hold of her other hand, somehow, and they stood facing one another. Druyan's heart still raced, fast as the flying clouds.

"As second widow of a childless landholder, I know the laws for land passage, that's all," she said, forcing a calm she did not feel. "I have had cause to learn the legalities very thoroughly." And she discovered herself more than a little relieved not to have to bother keeping her great secret any longer. There were other matters that demanded her whole attention—if she could once get her hands free.

"I know you have tried to freehold, Druyan. I admire that. The way you have kept up your land, despite all that has befallen Esdragon, is most impressive. It does you the greatest credit. We shall even spend part of each year living at Splaine Garth, if you prefer it to Tolasta or my other properties. I have no objection. Why should we not share our homes with one another?"

Druyan closed her eyes and felt the wind pressing against her shut eyelids. Then, without warning, Yvain's lips were upon hers, and he had dropped her hands so that he could put his own one on either side of her face, sliding his long clever fingers through her hair in an amazingly pleasurable, intimate touch.

No man had touched her that way since—*since Travic?* Druyan wondered. Or was it not so long ago as that? What was she remembering? Had Travic *ever* touched her so? Ever made her feel so? But someone had—Yvain's mouth moved against her lips, and something stirred in Druyan, deep inside. Her blood sang in her ears, surged like a storm tide, matching Yvain's passion.

And at the same time she wanted to slap him, and was hard put to resist acting upon her wish, now that her hands were finally freed. For Yvain's presumption, his arrogance? Or for his waking feelings she had thought left behind with her girlhood dreams? Anger and regret twisted tight together like two threads plied together into one yarn, impossible to separate. Yvain murmured something into her hair, and her lips burned where his had touched them.

Instead of lashing out at Yvain, Druyan stepped a pace back from him, with her hands carefully behind her, just as a great blast of wind shook them both, sent a mist of salty drops between them.

"Let's see first, Yvain, whether we will *live* anywhere," she said shakily. He blinked at her, as if he had for the instant forgotten where they were, so utterly caught up by his own plans for what she would do that he forgot what she was there to do. Probably he did not believe in what she was attempting. Druyan found it hard not to hate him for that, for his so readily dismissing any part of her, but especially this part, at this critical instant. "You may not, after today, still desire to mingle your illustrious lineage with mine."

"What—" His sculptured face was blank as a sleepwalker's.

"Be still," Druyan said ungently. "Or go." She marched to Valadan and climbed into his saddle. She'd be safer from Yvain's distractions aboard the stallion. She turned Valadan's fine head into the wind. His forelock blew back between his ears toward her, like black wave spume.

I am of the wind, the stallion said. *That will aid you.*

Druyan breathed deep and sent out her whistling call once more into the restless air atop the cliffs. Higher by the height of Valadan's back, she felt even more a part of the air. It did help, as the stallion had pledged. She felt braver, surer, more herself somehow.

She whistled again.

"What are you doing?" Yvain shouted.

Druyan ignored him, sending out her call again and again. As she ran out of air, she kept her lips pursed while she drew in another breath—and that breath whistled, as well, while it was drawn into her toward her.

This is why women are reckoned to be bad luck on boats, Valadan said, tasting the wind he was kin to. *And generally forbidden whistling.*

And the wind, which had been blowing from all directions in short gusts, shifted. Now it came steadily from the sea. And its smell was different—old, wild, full of shipwrecks and thunderclaps.

Druyan sat astride Valadan's back, while the wind blew steadily inshore. Her tawny hair was twirled into elflocks, as was the stallion's mane. Her face was dry with cold, washed red by the sun's dying rays.

The sky above was yet a bottomless blue, studded with bits of cloud beautifully gilded by the sinking sun. At her back the moon was rising, very near, so full it seemed like to burst of ripeness. Once each year—only once—the moon drew so near in the night, seemed almost prepared to step down out of the sky, and its tidal pull flooded shores left dry at all other times.

Her own grandfather had sung songs of greeting to the Lady of the Moon. So, in his different way, did Kellis. Druyan only looked seaward, fretting. Where was the storm? The steady daylong wind had not increased its fury, there was no sign of the thing she was calling with all her heart.

Who can see the wind? Valadan asked. But he, too, was

concerned and restless. Druyan could feel him lift first one foot, then another.

Yvain still stood at her left hand. He looked back at the moon, following her gaze. Its pale light silvered his blue eyes till he turned them to sunfall once more.

Druyan wished he would go. She could not decide whether he distracted her—she thought she could prevent that by ignoring him, and certainly by sparing no corner of her mind for what he proposed for her. It was not that she wanted to be alone—rather that the only man she wanted to have by her side was the very one she'd sent away.

It was the only time she had ever managed to send Kellis from her side. Like a good sheepdog, he knew when 'twas utterly needful to obey, and he had done as she'd asked. But, oh, how she wished that a silver wolf paced where Yvain now nervously stood.

Where was her storm wind? Had she not summoned it? Had she not called it, all that long day?

She had called, certainly—but had she expected the wind to come? Had she *wanted* it, or was she, at the very core of her heart, still afraid of the wind and of herself? Would some coward, craven part of her accept the storm's disobedience with relief? She was exactly like Kellis, afraid of nothing so much as what lay just under her own skin . . .

"Druyan, enough of this!" Yvain shouted, tearing through her reverie. "Come with me now—"

Go with Yvain. Yes, she could certainly do that. What was it but another order, one more instruction? As youngest of a very large family, she was quite well used to doing what she was told. Obeying now would free her of responsibility for putting raiders to flight, for arranging harvests and planting crops and the hopeless task of protecting villages. And it would not be such a very bad life, as Yvain's wedded lady. He was pleasing to the eye, keen of wit, wealthy enough to know few cares—and he wanted her, without bargaining, without lands and dowry and family connections. It would be a fine life, surely, the one he offered her. Until Yvain discovered that she could not give

him a child, until he learned she was as empty within as a
hollow tree, save for an arcane power over the wild wind
that he surely could not approve of.

He doesn't care what's inside, Druyan thought, suddenly
furious with the revelation, shaking with all the pent anger
of a whole lifetime, as she began to understand her instinctive objection. *I will not be afraid of what I am—let us see
if Yvain can say the same!*

"No," she said, and turned her face back to the sea, into
the wind. She dropped the reins and lifted her hands,
stretching out her arms to embrace the wind. She whistled
once more, a piercing, demanding tone that never considered for a single instant that its quarry might mutiny or ignore it. *Come to me,* the call went out, no longer hesitant.

And like a wayward horse that has stayed near while refusing to be caught and haltered, the wind answered her.
Through its lash, Druyan looked seaward once more.

The sky above was darkening, the moon's glow not
nearly compensating for the loss of the sun's light. Ahead,
where the disc of the sun still perched on the horizon of
wavetops, the sky should yet have been bright.

It was not. In place of the expected banners of scarlet
and gold, orange and rose, there loomed a great dark mass,
like a bruise across the sky, enveloping the sun as it sank
toward the sea.

Yvain heard the startled hiss of his own breath being
drawn in, without recognizing it. Lightning flickered inside
the oncoming squall line, and white edges of cloud could
be seen to seethe and boil against the blackness. Distance
masked size and length, deceived as to speed—but blink
and the storm was closer, and that gave a true measure of
how quickly it swept upon them. Had he been aboard a
ship upon open water and seen such a bank of cloud bearing down on him, Yvain would have given himself up for
lost.

He was hardly certain that he was safe on the land. The
headland had never seemed so lofty, so at the mercy of the

air about it. The grass rolled like sea billows, and anything loose had already gone skipping and flying toward the rising white face of the moon.

The tide was roaring in. It could be heard over the wind, as the moon's irresistible pull increased its force. The storm winds would be thrusting a massive bulge of water ahead of them, and when those waters were added to the tide . . . Yvain's jaw dropped as he began to comprehend what had been only a misty plan, more hope than reality and not much attended to. He looked up at Druyan, her arms still open in welcome.

"It comes at your call," he whispered. The wind took his words, claiming the air they rode upon, and whirled them away like so many dry leaves.

The face she turned upon him was a stranger's, taut and wild and exultant. Her hair lifted around her like a living thing. Her eyes were a she-wolf's, glowing full of moonlight, and they saw his fear.

"Do you truly desire a barren witch for your wife, Yvain?" she asked.

Yvain licked his wind-cracked lips and pitched his voice to carry, but his answer died in his cold throat, just before the gust front of the storm reached them and bowled him off his feet.

Enna's eyes were twin points of cold iron. "You came back *without* her?"

"She *sent* me back," Kellis pleaded. A gust of wind plucked at the horse blanket he had draped about him in a roughly fashioned *beltran* when he reached the barn, and he shivered. He was clothed enough not to outrage Enna, but not sufficiently to keep warm if he stood still. And beyond the discomfort was the unease the wind carried. "What do you do here when there's a storm? A high storm tide?" She didn't answer. He wondered if she thought he was just making conversation. "We're supposed to do that."

"We throw shifty thieves into the marsh to appease the sea gods, so they don't flood us out." She had understood perfectly well. "With an iron spike hammered through their hearts to make sure they stay there."

Kellis stared, the wind lifting his hair out of his eyes.

"I know what you are," Enna said. "It's not only wizards can't touch cold iron. How could you leave her?"

"She *told* me to!" Kellis exploded. "Do you think I'd have left her otherwise? She's whistling up this storm to sweep away the raiders, and she doesn't want Splaine Garth swept away with it. Riders are warning the whole coast, but it's no use to warn if there's no one here to do anything! She sent me back to be sure there was. *Now what do I do?*"

She wanted to spit invective at him. But the wind's howl got Enna's attention. She'd heard its like before, but it wasn't common. "I always wondered what she could do if she had to," she whispered. "Now we'll see—think you can nail shutters closed without nailing yourself to them?"

Kellis curled his lip in a silent snarl. "I shall manage."

"There's two of my lord's men just back yesterday, they'll help. We're too high here to flood unless all Darlith washes away, but we'll need anything loose tied or nailed down so it can't blow away. And the animals need to come in; they'll drown in the marsh when the water rises."

"I'll see to that," Kellis said.

Moments later, Rook and Meddy were gathering their charges and chivvying them to safe ground. Reluctant sheep met a most persuasive silver wolf, whose nips at their woolly heels got swift results.

What have I done? Druyan wondered, not a little alarmed.

The streaky bank of clouds filled half the sky, and any lingering blue had been transmuted to a yellow gray that made her blood run cold till night fell entirely and colors could no longer be seen. The grass at Valadan's hooves flattened with every gust of wind. The air above was clogged with tumbling seabirds seeking safety inland, forsaking their normal roosting spots. Druyan's face felt like a mask to her, cold wood over her bones. Almost she could not remember a time when the gale had not been sweeping the hair back from her forehead and temples, when its ends had not been cracking behind her like whips. There were wind-trained trees a thousand yards to her right, bowing like courtiers, hardly arising from one reverence before the next blast bent them again. The wind smelled of lightning and icy hail.

"Lady, you are not intending to remain here?"

Yvain's horse was white-eyed with terror, and if he tried to restrain its flight much longer it would cast him off and make its escape, Druyan thought. She had not desired him to stay by her on the headland, both for the sake of his safety and because she could not bear to see his fear of her in his eyes. She should not think less of him for what was surely a healthy reaction. He was at least facing his terror. But she wished him elsewhere.

"*Druyan, come with me!* You cannot stay here any longer!"

Somehow Yvain wrestled his horse close enough to lay his right hand on Druyan's left arm.

The air went uncannily still for a moment, as if the heaving sea held its breath, and the wind waited for its mistress to choose.

"No," Druyan said, again, refusing far more than just a sensible retreat.

Yvain tightened his grip on her forearm as if to argue, not accepting her answer, either of her refusals.

Valadan pinned his ears, bared his teeth, and lunged at the bay horse, sending it plunging away so that its rider had other uses for his hands—and a great wave of icy air crested over them all, flattening grass and heather. As that wind passed inland, limbs were torn from trees, roofs ripped from houses. Anchored ships heeled over. Ill-made stone walls toppled. Yvain's horse seized the bit in its teeth and fled, and in an instant all trace of horse and rider had vanished behind a sheet of wind-driven rain. Lightning flashed, and its thunder came not a heartbeat upon its heels.

Valadan stood steady, unperturbed. A storm wind had

sired him, and all winds were by that his kin. He put his tail to the wind, so that his rider might breathe, but that was his sole concession to the violence.

Druyan leaned close to his ears, along his neck. The gusts beat at her. "If it comes ashore *here*, it may not be strong enough to wipe out the raiders' island! Those cliffs will break the force."

Then let us take the storm where we wish it to be.

Valadan sprang into a gallop, racing ahead of the wind. Druyan locked her eight fingers into his flying mane, tipped back her head and whistled, sharp as midwinter. The stallion swerved to follow the coastline, and the winds wheeled with him.

All was blackness as they ran. Lightning flashes showed the sand of beaches, tussocks of rank grass, and heather, mere distractions with all the color and reality leached out of them. Druyan pictured in her mind the waves lashing Esdragon's perilous coast. Sea stacks would tumble down, edges of cliffs would be bitten away, there would be new islands made of former peninsulas. All the maps would need to be redrawn. Most particularly, small islets would be wiped right away by the sea's giant hand. The waves would do the deed, but 'twas the wind that powered the waves.

Now its howl was like one of Kellis' winter songs—and suddenly the tune was hers, as well, known all her life, even when she had chosen to turn her back upon it. Druyan lifted her face into the storm and reveled in its boisterous winds. She let its rain wash over her, its lightning illuminate her, its thunder beat a dance measure into her bones. And there was not one single part of it that she harbored the least fear of.

Each time the wind shrieked, Kellis cast a wary eye at the underside of the kitchen roof, though between the nailed-closed shutters and nightfall, 'twas too dark to gauge its state. If it came off, he was sure he'd know quick enough. There'd be a great roar of wind, drowning out the lesser, varied whines and groans and whistles that the air made as it quested about the windows, the door, and the chimney. It wouldn't be something he'd be likely to overlook.

Something hit the outside wall with a thump. An overlooked pail, Kellis devoutly hoped, and not a strayed chicken left at the storm's mercy. Whatever hadn't been stowed was certain to be lost. He didn't like to think about the apple crop, which had promised to be heavy, or the barley. All the livestock was safe, crammed into the sturdy sheepfold save for the chickens, which they had with them in the kitchen. The hens had obeyed instinct and gone to roost in the darkness, headless-seeming clumps of feathers perched on high shelves and the mantelpiece, safe from the cats.

They had the dogs, too, as well as Pru and Lyn, fretting because they really wanted to be in the fold with their woolly friends—save there wasn't room enough with the pigs crowded in there, as well. And the two men, Wat and Drustan, who had been Travic's farmhands and come home into a situation they must find as puzzling as they found Kellis himself.

He'd worked alongside them, battening down the shutters. They accepted him that far. Kellis knew what Enna would have told them about him. Kellis tried not to think how many sharp iron objects lived in the kitchen.

Over the howling wind, he never heard Enna till his keen nose caught a whiff of herbal linament, a fainter scent of lavender. She shoved a soft bundle against him.

"Here. Put these on before you catch your death."

His fingers sorted out trews and a jerkin of woolen cloth, their folds emitting the dried lavender scent. A linen sark, with mended sleeves, tumbled out as he unfolded the jerkin. He tried to give the clothes back. "If I was cold, I'd shift myself into something with fur."

"Not in *my* kitchen, you won't."

The dogs notwithstanding. "These were your master's." Kellis hazarded.

"Aye. And they smell a deal better than that poxy blanket. My lord would not have begrudged you," Enna admitted. "Not my place to, either."

"Thank you."

He didn't know if she heard. The wind was blasting, as if the Wild Hunt had run right over their heads. They'd had to bank the fire and close the damper to seal off the chimney, and candles didn't stay lit, because of the drafts. The only one still burning was in the far corner—a little motion there told him that Enna had crossed the room, to settle again in her chair.

Something slid loudly down the slope of the roof. Kellis began to pull on the trews, with a wary glance or two upward and an earnest prayer that one of the two returned farmhands might be the thatcher.

"How far have we come?" Druyan shouted into Valadan's left ear, which was flat back against his neck. She got a generous mouthful of his mane.

We are beyond Penre.

Probably far beyond, if that last river had been Penre's. Druyan had no sense by then of distance, nor of time. But whatever the ground covered, 'twas far enough. She sat up, let her weight sink firmly into her saddle, and Valadan slowed obediently, finally halting.

Now what?

She had never once been able to still a wind she had raised. But she had been afraid, those other times, and had not truly expected mastery. It was different now. This storm had come to seem like a pastured horse that ran alongside Valadan. Dangerous, maybe, deserving her respect, but no foe of hers. She could send it on its way, released from service to her.

The wind still blew upon them, unabated. It was flinging drops of rain, which stung like pebbles on her face and hands. Druyan struggled to draw her cloak close about her—the wind tugged it free and made sport of it. Annoyed, she caught a fold of it in either hand and swept it about her, trapping a swirl of wild wind in the web of her weaving. *"Enough!"* she cried sternly.

Upon her command, the wind died. A steady rain began to fall. Valadan snorted in consternation.

Home?

Druyan put her hood up against the downpour. "We'd be under a roof sooner. But it must be Keverne—the Riders will all report there. We should, too."

Valadan dipped his head, assenting, and they rode back the way they had come. The rain fell for a time, then ceased. The clouds became threadbare, and by the time they reached Keverne, Druyan could see the moon once more, sinking slowly into the calm sea.

A Year and a Day

FLOODWATERS HAD SURGED over every beach, up every river, scouring banks to an extent never seen in any living person's memory. The winds had been somewhat less destructive—sea winds were a constant of Esdragon's coast, and no tall trees grew save where the lay of the land offered shelter to them. Roofs were damaged, a few walls fell because the wind had shoved them, but the great storm was felt most on the fringes of the land, in the rise of cold salt-water furlongs beyond the usual limits. The coastal folk, warned of that, had done what would best let them survive it—whether that had been to batten down and shore with sandbags and straw bales, or simply to move families and livestock inland and upland. Come dawn, the coast of Esdragon resembled an unthrifty farmyard, with trash and oddments lying everywhere, washing listlessly in receding water, but there was very little loss of life.

The air was thick with seabirds when Valadan and his mistress reached Keverne—their usual resting places disturbed, the birds wheeled through the sky in the first flush of dawn, crying like a thousand aggrieved cats as they searched for edible trash and stranded fish. Druyan rode slowly up to the castle and dismounted. She had not thought she was especially weary, but her clothing was so heavy with water that she moved as one in a dream. Her knees and ankles ached. Someone called her name, but as

317

she turned to answer, her soaked cloak tangled her rubbery legs, and she fell . . .

Kellis ventured out into the bright morning. The sky was boundlessly blue, scrubbed clean by wind and rain. Puddles stood everywhere, reflecting the sapphire sky a hundred times. Every windward wall was plastered with a green mosaic of wet leaves. The buildings beyond the kitchen were bedecked with straws from the thatch, as well. At least the kitchen still had most of a roof. Likewise the sheepfold, the unhappy bawling of its occupants notwithstanding.

The windfalls lay in the orchard thick as spring dandelions, but only a few trees had lost branches larger than twigs. All would live to bear again, and a portion of the crop still clung despite all. Kellis told a grumbling Dalkin to start gathering the fallen apples into baskets—very poor cider it would make, but better that than letting the stock munch windfalls till they colicked. He walked on alone toward the barley fields.

He was anticipating damage, and found it, but not to the extent he dreaded. Only the worst-exposed parts were flattened entirely, and the small trees at the fields' edges had offered the shelter they were meant to. A crop was possible, especially if no further rain fell for a week or so. And the lady had harvest hands to do that work now.

There was a further thing to check. Kellis put the dead Travic's clothing carefully under a hedgerow, and a silver wolf sped toward the marsh and the seacoast. From the height of the Promontory, one commanded a fine view, and needed no wings, once one knew where to look.

Every beach he passed was awash with bits of timber, torn branches, splintered planks. Kellis thought he saw a body tossing in the swells, pale limbs thrashing and beckoning. Once he began to look for them, he saw others.

He had to struggle to keep his bearings—the whole coast had been recarved by the storm, and not a few of his landmarks had ceased to exist. Waves had bitten off huge chunks of land and mined beneath other spots so that unsupported rocks fell into the hungry sea even hours later. Seeing one such stretch crumble in, he trotted hastily to safer ground, regretting that bird-form seemed to be out of the question for him.

The Promontory, too, was changed—its outflung tip had become no more than a reach of shoally water. The air was clear, not a wisp of fog veiling the distance, but Kellis saw nothing beyond large enough to be an island. The storm had seen to that. The raider's base was no more. His wolf's tongue lolled out in a contented grin.

Yet once he stood again at the edge of the barley field, in his human shape and clad in a dead man's clothes, which his people would have called unlucky and he accepted as necessity, Kellis was no longer merry. He knew that calms after storms are mere illusion, and he could not conceive of a peace that would last, for such as he was. It was, if anything, an ending.

His freedom was at hand. He had kept careful track of the passages of sun and moon through the seasons. It had been a year since he had agreed to work away those crimes he had been a tiny, but undeniably guilty, part of. The year was gone. This was the day, and his term of servitude was running out with the hours of it. Come the next dawn, he was free to go his way, to take up his interrupted quest.

He should have been rejoicing, but found himself instead profoundly unsettled, uncertain. His quest sat as uneasily on his mind as the late Travic's clothes did on his back. It was not that he doubted his ability to cross Esdragon—he had run across so much of the duchy already, Kellis knew he could reach the city somewhere past the far side of it, assuming rumor had placed it truly. Even if the tales had been imprecise, he could find what he sought. No different from hunting a deer—easier, probably, since cities did not wander, nor take it into their heads to migrate with the seasons.

If the City of Wizards existed. If the folk who had told him of it had not needed to believe in it so desperately that wishes were taken for truth.

Assume the city real, there was no harm to that, and certainly no way for him to check it anyway, at this remove. The city's reality was not the worst of his uncertainties. the wizards and sorcerors who had founded it were choos folk, would they admit to their number such as Kellis kne himself to be—more limit than power, half trained and tha half badly, thoroughly crippled when it came to matter magical? Suppose he reached the city at last, only to b turned away at its gates? Refused, he might be doomed t wander forever, a lone wolf in truth.

His left boot was leaking—he was standing in a puddl that had formed in a wheel rut. Kellis stepped back, staring down at the shining water. After a moment he went down on one knee, heedless of the damp, and scooped up a dou ble handful of rainwater. He sang the summoning over i easily, without the least apprehension. It wasn't lives at stake now, except maybe his own, and he felt no anxiety over that, at least not sufficient to overwhelm a summer's hard practice in his art. The water's surface shivered, began to throw back colors other than the sky's.

Other than the clear blue sky's. There was a gray boil of clouds, and Kellis knew for once without doubt what he saw—the past day, the storm-sky Druyan had summoned with her whistling. Towers of lightning-bladed destruction, sweeping across the sea toward the high cliffs near Keverne . . .

And atop that cliff, two people, locked in one another's embrace. One had hair the color of a red deer's summer pelt. The other's, which the wind sported with, shifted between red and gold like sunset light on water. Kellis could not have named the color, but he knew the scent of that hair, knew the feel of it, cool silk against his fingers. He had slept once with it tangled all about him . . .

The last of the water leaked away through his cupped fingers, and the image vanished with it. Kellis lifted wet hands to his face.

At last, he thought bitterly, scrubbing at his eyes, which burned with sleep-lack. *A scrying that actually makes it simple to choose an action! All it took was practice, after all.*

It didn't matter whether Kôvelir existed, or would take him in. His destination was of no importance, only his departure. What he might not have dared for himself, he owed to her.

You have no place here, Kellis reminded himself. *She took you in like a stray dog, nothing more than that. You don't need Yvain telling you to your face, to know.*

The breeze had dried his face, leaving the skin feeling tight as a mask. Kellis got stiffly to his sore feet. He would need to pack fresh wool into his boots, he thought, to make walking bearable. He must remember to see to it.

There was nothing that could make his leaving likewise bearable, save that he did it for her sake. He must hold tight to that.

Druyan awoke on a narrow cot in a curtained-off corner of the post riders' hall, with wind-snarled hair and wind-chapped skin, but otherwise undamaged by her wild night. She limped groaning to the window and saw by the sunfall light that she had slept the whole of the day away.

By the untidiness of the rest of the dormitory, at least some of the Riders had returned, but none was in the hall at that moment. Someone had left bread and cheese and sweet cider and dry clothing for her. Druyan's eyes misted as she unfolded the garments—doubtless they could have found a woman's gown for her, but instead the Riders had gifted her with a set of sea blue and gray, their own colors for one of their own. She dressed and ate the food, still alone in the quiet room, and then set off in search of her uncle.

Once she left the Riders' territory, there were folk aplenty about. Druyan could not fail to hear the whispers and note the pointed fingers, but she was not minded to duck her head and avoid them as if words and looks had been blows. Nor did she hide her hands in her clothing, as she had used to do when at Keverne. She had forgotten to

draw on her glove, but it no longer mattered—she had bee
too long learning a new grip for every action. Now he
eight fingers did as she asked of them, and she shoul
hardly be shamed by that, whatever the size or number c
the fingers. She continued serenely on her quest.

Duke Brioc was in his chapel, keeping watch beside th
bloodless body of his eldest son. Druyan had gone prepare
to beg her uncle for some sense in the matter of Esdragon'
defense, now that he had seen with his own eyes what eve
a small mounted force might do—but at the sight of hi
ravaged face her tongue clove to her mouth. The onl
speech she could shape, she had to couch in words of com
fort, which she was not certain Brioc even heard. Dima
was dead, his dream of a fleet probably dead with him. I
the storm had swept the raiders away, the Eral had swept
part of Esdragon away first, Druyan thought sadly. The nex
morning, and the next, would see changes undreamed of
bare month past.

She tarried awhile after she had paid her respects to her
uncle, with distant silent members of her family all about
her—then the chamber began to seem airless, and when she
had to fight down a desire to whistle herself a cool breeze,
Druyan knew 'twas time she took her leave.

In the stables she found Valadan most honorably housed
in a loose box deep bedded with golden straw. He had to-
paz lights in his eyes, as well, as he nickered a greeting to
her. Druyan pressed her face into his still-snarled mane, felt
the little wind of his breath riffle her hair behind her left
ear.

A greater wind and a jangle of harness announced two
men and two horses entering the stable through the tall
outer door. Druyan raised her head, and the pair of weary
post riders whooped with delight at discovering their lady
safe before them.

Druyan asked urgently for tidings of the coast, and heard
a high-hearted account of storm ravages tempered by Rider-
carried warnings, so that for all the damage wrought there
had been but slight loss of human or livestock life. The

Riders conducted Druyan—they would not hear of her leaving—back to their hall, where their fellows were now assembled, eating a hearty supper and wondering where their luck charm had got herself to, after sleeping all the day away.

Druyan thanked them for their courtesies and their tender care of her, and found she had no recourse but to let her comrades feast her and drink toasts to her and to the Warhorse Valadan with their strong cider and foamy ale, while the Battle of the Horse Fair was fought all over again with words and boasts and witty embellishments. One after another, men came forward for a personal word, a confidence or reminiscence for her ears.

As the night wore on, Druyan spared a thought—as perchance no Rider did—for Esdragon's duke, mourning his favorite son in his cold stone chapel. The man she had left there had not been a leader. Whether he could become one again was difficult to judge. Even with the Eral threat diminished, there would be hard times ahead for Esdragon—for all of them. The room exploded with laughter, and Druyan smiled sadly. None of them was thinking about that now. She wished they might never need to.

She found herself as uneasy among the Riders as she had been among her relations in the chapel. The Riders were warm where her family was cold, but home was still where she longed to be. She should go there, as soon as she could without giving offense. Druyan slipped outside during a heated debate as to the respective merits of two stallions' bloodlines, fairly sure her opinion would not be sought, since neither horse was Valadan. The torchlit dark was a surprise—sleeping by day rather than by night had disoriented her. She expected to see blue sky, and was confronted and confounded by a firmament black as Valadan's hide, spangled with stars.

The door released a burst of merriment as if opened and closed. "They all look to you," Robait said.

Druyan turned to face her brother, something in his tone making her uncomfortable.

"They would ride through the Gates of the Dead, if you went before them," Robart went on bitterly, gesturing to indicate the garb the Riders had gifted her with. All she lacked was the captain's badge.

Still she said nothing, though her heart was fluttering uneasily in her breast. He was so angry, more than he showed. She could see him holding it in, like a savage horse. She had always quivered before disapproval—his, her father's—it was hard not to do that again. It was hard not to feel guilty, even though she'd done no wrong. Her hand began to ache, as if it was a deserved punishment.

"Druyan, it isn't *right*. I'm their captain, but it's you they follow."

The unfair—yet true—accusation stung like a whiplash. "It's not as if I set out to take them from you, Robart! We were all of us only doing what we had to."

"All the same, every man of them's yours, if you only say the word," he snapped. "Waggle one finger."

"The Riders have more value than simple messengers now, Robart," Druyan told him. "Their swords and their horses and their courage saved Esdragon from the raiders. Even Brioc will have to recognize their worth, and we'll never be left so helpless again. You can make that happen. You, not me."

"I can if my command's truly *mine*." He had the grace to pause. "I'm asking you to give it back to me, sister. I don't say you haven't earned it, but you don't need it— you've got Yvain, that ought to be enough for any woman."

Druyan gazed into the dark sky. Soon, beyond the thick walls, it would be lightening with dawn, but she couldn't see it yet. She remembered, with a pang all the years between could not mute, the day Robart had demanded that she give up Valadan, the horse a mere girl had no right to. *How unfair!* she thought, seeing her life come full circle, with nothing gained at all. She felt a tiny flutter, low in her chest, as if something there longed to leap free.

How dared he ask it of her? If he wanted his command, let him take it—if he could! Robart was their Chief-captain, true, but the Riders were what *she* had made of them, in a long summer of blood and smoke and hard riding. *They* all knew it, had pledged it with every mug drained in their hall that night. Must she give them up, solely because Robart asked, because he expected her to do what a proper woman would do? Fine to lift a sword when there was no one else to do it, but once the fight was done, go obediently home and become a helpless dependent once more? Could she do that now? She had other choices. Beneath her heart, something seemed to stir. It felt familiar, yet strange. How long had she been feeling it, without noticing?

She had Yvain. She supposed she still did. He would probably learn to forget his fear of her, if she never showed him that part of herself again, if she wore a careful mask all the rest of her days. It would not be so hard to do, Druyan decided. Life with Yvain would hardly be unpleasant. He was a better catch than she could ever have hoped to make, wealthy and titled and only as vain of his looks as any proud stallion. The attitude was not unbecoming in a horse . . . she could doubtless bear it in a man. Arrogance wasn't cruelty, or anything else to make her rightly wary of the man. She could have Yvain.

Only . . . she had worked so long to be no man's possession, to be free. Every farm chore came back to her, all those endless fields of barley. And Yvain feared her as much as he loved her. There would always be that between them, a secret dagger in her heart. Could she bear that?

"It will take Yvain time to square things, of course." Robart intuited whom her thoughts rested upon. "Faster if you helped him, Druyan. Admit Travic's dead, and let Yvain ask Brioc for you."

Again that tiny fluttering under her heart, a secret even Druyan hardly dared to guess at. Warmth flooded into her face, but Robart could not see. Faint and far off in her own memory, two wolves ran together beneath the moon. In the real world, the sunward sky was paling to dove gray, even above Keverne's walls. It was nearly dawn.

"Yvain's too late, Robart," Druyan said. "It has been a

year and a day, and all the crop tithes were paid, every last one of them." She looked steadfastly at the dawn. "As of now, Splaine Garth belongs to me. And I am going home."

Valadan's swift hooves carried her to her own gate while the dew still lay upon the grass. All the jewels Yvain might have lavished upon his wife could not have looked half so fair, Druyan thought, as her own fields clothed in sun and water. The dazzle almost masked the storm damage. The flattened grass had already rebounded to hide the fallen branches.

"I wonder if the kitchen roof held?"

Valadan flicked an ear back at her question.

They reached the gate, and Druyan was just about to dismount when it was opened before her. Valadan paced sedately through, with a snort of greeting for Kellis.

"You can go into the orchard," Druyan said, sliding to the ground and giving the stallion's shoulder a pat as she pulled the saddle from his back and slipped the copper bit gently out of his mouth. "There are windfalls?" She looked at Kellis for confirmation, got a nod. "Silly question. Don't eat yourself into a bellyache." Valadan snorted again, trotted two strides, and sprang over the orchard fence between two tilted posts. Druyan spun back to Kellis with a bright smile stretching her face, uncaring for the moment of wobbly posts poorly set. "Splaine Garth is mine! A year—"

The smile slipped from her lips as she caught sight of the bundle at Kellis' feet, the closed-down expression on his crooked-nosed face. She knew what it meant, by the chill about her heart.

"A year and a day, Lady," he completed the phrase for her, formally. "My debt to you is paid, as we agreed." He didn't add that he was leaving—that was self-evident.

"I promised you a horse," Druyan said dully, in that shocked moment. It was all she could think of to say. She had never expected this . . . it was just the same as the moment when she knew her hand was cut half away—she knew that it had happened, and she knew that it hurt, but she could not *feel* it. Not till much later . . . "There's not a decent saddle horse left at Splaine Garth."

Kellis shrugged. "I'm no horseman, you'd be doing me no favor with such a gift. If I grow weary of my own two legs, a wolf can travel as swiftly as any horse."

As a wolf undeniably had, from one end of Esdragon to the other, keeping pace with the fleetest steeds in the duchy. "You're going *now*?" Druyan asked him, aghast. She flailed about for something, anything, to stop him. "What about the barley harvest?"

He had the grace to flush with the shame of deserting her, but Kellis stood his ground. "Ask me first if there'll *be* a harvest, Lady. Did you notice the fields as you rode by?"

"Yes," she said faintly, hardly able to keep her thoughts on grainfields. She remembered sun-gems, and that she had scarcely looked past their pretty dazzle. She had wanted, single-heartedly, only to reach home. To find Kellis. She'd never dreamed she'd ride into this, more dismaying than any storm damage. She'd never thought he'd be leaving . . .

"Harvest's a fortnight off, at the best," Kellis reported dutifully. "And lucky to get it, the grain's nowhere near as flattened as it could have been. Your men might have had to reap it on hands and knees."

"My men?" she asked stupidly. Nothing made sense to her, nothing. He might have been speaking in the Eral tongue, in place of hers.

"There's two of them back," Kellis explained, patient. "Wat and Drustan. They seem to think there's others headed home, too, maybe held up by the storm." He shrugged. "Either one will likely cut twice the barley I did, and not take sick from the tools after. You won't miss me, Lady." He tried to smile.

Her heart misgave her, seeing that, but all that crossed Druyan's lips by way of protest was his name, the pair of syllables sounding more angry than entreating. *"Kellis—"*

He set his mouth. "You promised me my freedom, with time to travel before winter. Didn't you?"

Panic welled up, black as a squall line, but Druyan refused to let him see it. "You still think Kôvelir is your answer?" She was amazed she could speak—something was lodged in her throat, thick as wet wool.

"I don't know, Lady," he answered gravely, wearing that open, devastatingly honest look. "I wouldn't expect any vision *I* summoned to reach that far. I will have to go there myself to find out—and best I do it soon. It's been a long journey, full of delays."

She stared at the pack as he shouldered it. He couldn't have told Enna he was going—she'd have loaded him down like a market-bound wagon, just for joy at seeing the back of him. All he seemed to be carrying was a blanket and an impossibly small bundle of provisions. *Oh, why did I think the only choice to be made was mine?*

Kellis inclined his head to her. "Be well, Lady."

Never again in this life, she wished to say, but the rising blackness had closed her throat tight. She looked mutely into his eyes, watched the colors going from silver to gold and back again as the wind shifted the dapples of sunlight on his face. Wolf's eyes. Pleading with her to do the sensible thing now and bid him the gods' speed on his journey, to thank him for a year of good service if she must, but most of all just to let him *go* . . .

He had his hand on the gate latch, and then he was closing it carefully behind him. He'd been born into an unfenced world, but Kellis knew to shut gates behind him now—she'd come that close to making a farmer out of him.

His boots made no sound in the lane—the storm-torn leaves plastering the dirt were rain-damp, wonderfully silent footing. Or she'd gone deaf from grief, Druyan thought. The breeze roved through the orchard, and a last few raindrops pattered down, like tears.

Don't look back. No, for his very soul, and for her sake, just as surely. Set one foot ahead of the other—easy, he'd been doing it much of his life. You can be a long way gone by sunfall, and no need to stop then, the moon's only starting to slide off of full. The trick to walking is, every step throws you off balance, so you have to take the next step to get it back, and then the next, on and on. Simplest thing there could ever be. You're doing fine, fool, considering you should have done this hours earlier, when you could just have *gone*, with no one ever the wiser . . .

His ears caught a soft *woof*. Kellis lifted his gaze, despite intentions not to. Rook slipped nimbly under the fence and marched stiff-legged into the lane. Meddy came bouncing behind her, tail waving high, and slid to a startled halt when she saw Kellis.

"Step aside, little sister," Kellis entreated.

Rook's brown gaze never wavered.

Do sheepdogs understand when part of their flock is sold or traded? Kellis wondered. *Do they just keep stealing them back?* He took a step and saw Rook's hackles rise, till all the hair on her back stood tall, neck to tail. Meddy whimpered.

Kellis drew in a deep breath. "We'll see who can stare longest, little sister. I am not straying now."

A year and a day. She had her freehold, and Kellis had his freedom. He was right about that. *And I have spent my life doing what others said was right,* Druyan thought as her tears joined the raindrops. *Bending to every least pressure, pliant as a grainstalk in the breeze . . . I've been what I was told to be, done what I was told I must do. Given up whatsoever I was asked to, no matter how it cost. Letting him go isn't half so hard as sending him away would be. He's doing what he wants to do, and I am letting him. Doing what anyone would agree is right, certainly.*

Warm breath on her cheek. Druyan flung her arms about Valadan's neck and pressed as close to the horse as the fence between them would allow. The contact helped, but still she could feel her heart tearing like rotten cloth, on and endlessly on, as one thread after another parted. She could see, dim and far off, a pair of wolves running beneath the moon and the windswept sky—and then there was only a

single creature, howling without the least hope of an answering voice. Only the wind, the empty wind, sobbing.

Obedience cost too dear. She could not bend again. Instead, Druyan knew, she would break, shatter, and there
would be no one there to gather the pieces save Yvain—
who would cheerfully put them back together into another
sort of woman entirely, a woman who wore her face over
a yawning emptiness where her heart used to be. A woman
who would never weep, who might summon a smile when
it was seemly, but would never know laughter. Who would
certainly never whistle the wind.

Druyan set her boot onto the second fence rail. It stayed
firm—the posts the rail ran between were neither of them
among those Kellis had replaced. Valadan sidled close, and
she climbed to the top of the fence, then slipped down onto
his bare back.

He has not gone far. The eye turned back to her sparkled
as if full of fireflies.

No. But being Kellis, and stubborn, he might not stop
walking at her bidding. Knowing himself unable to outwalk
Valadan, he would be forced to halt sooner or later, and
she'd have the advantage of easy breath for conversation
till he did. Druyan sent the stallion trotting along the fence
line, and he turned and sailed over it at the first convenient
spot, arching up like a trout after a fly.

Kellis hadn't made it away beyond the lane's end. He
stood by the lightning-blasted tree, facing the dogs. Rook
was crouched, staring her best stare, and Meddy was trying
to back her comrade up, though her whines said all too
plainly how uneasy she was about the business.

"Call them off," Kellis said, when he heard the four-beat
of walking hooves behind him.

He sounded angry, but Druyan didn't fear he'd shift to
wolf right in front of her—he never had, whether from shy-
ness or some more dire reason—and there was no other
way he'd get past Rook.

"Tell me again why you're going," she said, scarcely

able to hear her own voice over the hammering of her heart. If he'd been looking at her, she might not have been able to squeeze out a single word. Luckily, he was still trying to stare Rook down.

He pivoted to face her, a line between his brows. "You know why, Lady. Because there might be a place for me, in the Wizards' City."

"Or not," Druyan said heartlessly.

"Or not. As it always has been." Of course. He had accepted that possibility, and still sold his honor for his passage price across the sea. "No difference."

"There might be a place for you *here*," Druyan suggested. "Spare yourself a long walk. I can't imagine you aren't footsore."

The line deepened. "You have a good heart, Lady, but your kindness is misguided. M'lord Yvain won't especially want me here."

Druyan could only stare at him. What did he know about that? How . . .

Valadan snorted and pawed vigorously at a puddle that lay before his hooves. The splashing hint was plain. Druyan felt her face go hot. Whatever Kellis must have seen had been either too little or too much, depending on how one considered it, but the conclusion it had led him to was suddenly obvious. Perversely, it gave her hope, the tiniest stirring breeze of it. She lifted her chin, watching him between Valadan's black ears.

"As it happens, Yvain of Tolasta has no say about who does or does not stay on my farm, Kellis!"

His expression remained polite, but skeptical.

"You doubt me? The same year and a day that lets you walk away from here now means the time's past when I'd have been forced to wed any man my family or Travic's told me to."

His right brow gave a twitch, then settled level again. "Men of Yvain's sort don't need force, Lady, not in this world."

Kellis was trying to sound as if it didn't matter, but his

eyes gave his heart away. He looked at her the way Rook sometimes did. Meddy, now, might entreat with her blue eyes and every inch of her pied body, shamelessly, but if Rook fancied a taste of the food you had on you, the dog would never beg for it. No, she'd only *look*, with just such a wanting, a hopeless hope fit to shred the hardest heart. Such a look faced her now, whether Kellis was aware of it or thought he hid it. *I'm right!* Druyan exulted, and the breeze freshened.

"Yvain said he intended to ask Brioc for me. He never asked *me*, or I'd have told him *no* to his face, instead of letting him figure it out for himself."

That took him by surprise, very plainly. "Why would you do that, Lady?"

Druyan laughed. "I'm sure Yvain asks the same!" She scissored her right leg over Valadan's back and slid down his side, dismounting lightly as one only could from an unsaddled horse. She kept her arm over the stallion's neck for a comforting instant, then stepped toward Kellis. Meddy gave her tail a happy wag, and Rook reproved her sister, by no means sure they were relieved of their duty.

Druyan pulled the glove from her right hand and rested her shortened palm on her belly. Nothing there yet for the eye, but she could sense the gentle swelling to come, could feel a stirring through the layers of cloth. It might be her imagination, so early. It might not, given the blood she carried, given the father's. The heartbeat was surely slighter than a breeze, but she knew 'twas there—in the wind, if nowhere else. "I'm not free to wed Yvain," she said. "I owe a life deft."

He misunderstood her and denied her claim. "There's no life debt," Kellis said hastily, stepping back as if she frightened him. Rook growled, and he spared her a glare. "You're not the only one with teeth!" He snapped out, then turned back to Druyan. "Don't go on about my saving your life! You might not have died, you probably wouldn't have—"

"It wouldn't have been for lack of trying," Druyan said

soberly, letting herself remember. It seemed safe at such a distance, though it made the bright day dim in her eyes. She remembered the wolves, the courage they carried. "My head thought I should die, Kellis, and so I nearly did. But you taught me to listen to my heart, and I lived." She swallowed hard, and wished she could hold onto Valadan's mane for comfort. But she had left him behind. "So I ask you now—do you want in your *heart* to leave, Kellis? Or only with your head? You're free—but free to leave is free to stay, too."

She was cutting his heart clean out of him, to ask him that, to offer him that choice. That was what she was doing. Kellis wished desperately that he had been wise enough to slip away before ever she rode homeward. He didn't entirely believe her about Yvain—or trust that the truth of the moment would hold, once the captain began to press his suit once more.

"I said from the first, it was better if I went. And I was right. It would have been, and sick or not, I should have gone—"

"You can give me a dozen reasons why you should go," she said, eyes bright as raindrops. "Give me a thousand— none of them will make me glad of it, Kellis! And I'll never be sorry you stayed."

Kellis flinched, Rook bristled again at his movement, and while his attention was on the dog, Druyan stepped close and wrapped her three fingers about his right wrist. He could have broken her grip by taking half a step or a deep breath, but she knew he would reject that advantage.

"Have you no mercy?" he asked her, motionless and looking miserable.

"If I thought you'd be hurt by it . . . Kellis, all the times you spoke of going to Kôvelir, you never once said you wanted to *be* there. And you don't, do you?"

He shook his head, and then gave her that same look of helpless anger he'd been favoring Rook with. Druyan refused to wither. She moved her left hand over her belly, as if she gentled a restive horse.

"People want . . . so many things. When Travic died, all I dared hope was to keep this farm, somehow. How could I long for more, or other? I never knew to want it, much less expect—but the weaver can only set the warp, fate weaves in the weft, no matter what you do, or think you're doing. And warp and weft must cross, or there's no cloth. Even you can see only a little way ahead, Kellis." She looked down at the ground. Three fat dewdrops lay along a grass blade, like silver peas in a pod. Like a sign, and she took courage from their gleam. "The pattern's not the least what I thought it would be, when I began. It's all wolves, and moonlight."

"Dreams," Kellis whispered.

"Then stay and dream with me. With us."

"Lady, I cannot—don't ask this of me—" A twitch betrayed his longing to run.

"The indebtedness isn't for the life you saved—though I do thank you for it. My debt is for the new life we made between us, that night." She trailed her hand across the cloth again. "And for that child, our child, I'm asking whether you could bear to give up Kôvelir, and stay here awhile longer?"

Silver eyes went wide as twin moons, and his right brow disappeared under silver hair. The left almost managed to do likewise. *"Child?"* He shaped the word as if he had never heard it.

"About lambing time, I'm very much afraid," Druyan confessed. "I really *do* need you to stay—we'll be short-handed even if *all* the men come back, and I won't be able to do much by then. I promise you won't have to card wool all winter, or sleep in the barn—"

He wasn't saying anything, so she abandoned the jesting and faltered uncertainly on. "And then later, you could go on to Kôvelir, if you still wanted to . . . if you'd only stay here awhile . . ." She shut her eyes and felt his wrist pull free of her grasp. Her throat hurt her again, full of begging words, but she couldn't hold onto him as if she were an iron-jawed trap, not even for love of him, not even if she died of it—she couldn't make him tear free, the way trapped wolves did.

"Would a lifetime be long enough?" And of a sudden he was nuzzling into her hair, his arms going around her, his lips brushing her ear. "Wolves take mates for life. Could you bear that, Lady? I'm no wizard and I'm no farmer, and there's no one would ever tell you this was a good idea . . ."

Druyan felt her world open wide with joy, all her senses expanding as they had the night he'd sung her into the wolf form with him, to save her life. She could scent every shore the tickling breeze had touched, number the fragrant fruits in the orchard with her eyes closed, hear skylarks singing half a league off. His lips touched hers, and all at once Druyan's heart was brimful of moonlight. Her arms dared now to slide around Kellis, and she put her unequal hands into his hair. It felt as shaggy as it looked, like a wolf's pelt. "You can change your shape, but not your heart," she said, nestling her head against his shoulder. "I can hear anything, so long as that's true. Can *you* bear to take an eight-fingered witch to wife?"

"Trust me," Kellis said, and meant it. He hunted for her lips again, evidently with his eyes shut, for he roved all over her face before he ran down his quarry at last.

The wind dropped a shower of raindrops onto them from the branches overhead. Rook padded half a dozen steps and rested her nose gently against Kellis' leg. Meddy sat, sighed, and thumped her tail once with relief.

About the Author

Susan Elizabeth Dexter was born in Greenville, Pennsylvania, on July 20, 1955. She spent her whole life in western Pennsylvania except for the occasional trip to New York and a vacation in England, and is still pursuing her grand design of seeing the United States by following the World Fantasy Convention around each Halloween. She had a very basic education until high school, when she enrolled in a three-year commercial art program at the local vocational-technical school. She spent the next eighteen years slaving in the in-house ad agency of a discount department store chain, doing fashion art and layout while writing in her spare time. Her first book, *The Ring of Allaire*, appeared from Del Rey Books in 1981. In 1992 she made the leap to writing full time.

All those great cover paintings had led her to fantasy, you see. The roots of her addiction go back to her childhood, when fairy tales and horse stories were her favorite literary fare. She next dipped into historical fiction, gothics, and science fiction. At some point she crossed back over into fantasy, and knew she had come home.

Susan is fascinated by unicorns, canaries, wolves, carousel horses, pizza, birds of prey, King Arthur, silver rings, Star Wars, Fafhrd and the Gray Mouser—and of course books. She grows herbs, does watercolors and pastels, creates weavings and soft sculptures. She bought a horse and learned to ride the year she turned thirty. She was an amateur fencer (foil) and has been a member of the Richard III Society since 1983.